THE
ENGLISHMAN'S
DAUGHTER

THE ENGLISHMAN'S DAUGHTER

Peter Evans

Random House   New York

April 1983

Library of Congress Cataloging in Publication Data
Evans, Peter, 1933–
The Englishman's daughter.
I. Title.
PR6055.V218E9 1983   823′.914   82-16532
ISBN 0-394-53036-5

Manufactured in the United States of America

24689753

FIRST EDITION

For this Englishman's daughter, Lisa Jane,
and for William who has made her so happy

We fools accounted his life madness, and his end without honor:
Now is he numbered among the children of God, and
his lot is among the saints!

—*Wisdom of Solomon*

PART ONE

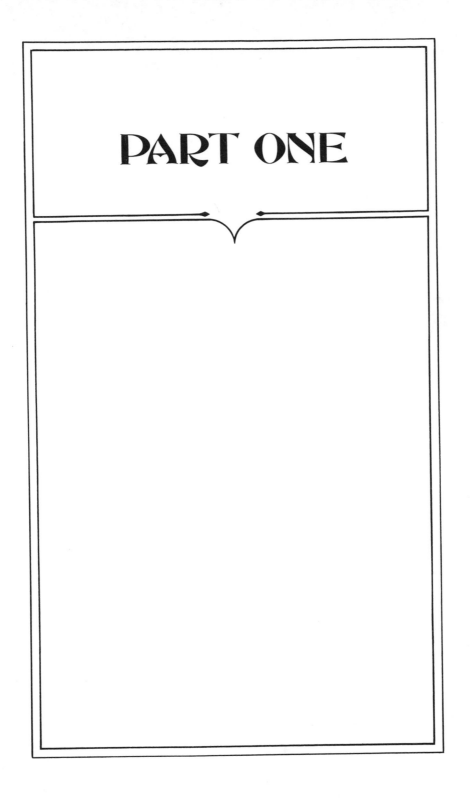

PROLOGUE

Schloss Laudon
Vienna

Thursday 10 Feb./11 p.m.

My dearest Pandora

When you read this letter—if it is permitted to reach you—I will be in Moscow, the final destination of a journey begun before you were born. How could I have known, when I started out, that one day I would have to forsake the happiness of ever seeing you again? I did not come to your room to say good-bye. You know how I loathe good-byes, even the little ones, the blowing of noses, the brave smiles avoiding the eyes. Sorry, old bean, but I simply couldn't face it—even when I knew it would be the last leave of the one person in this world I care more than a tuppenny damn about, the only one I shall miss. You were the best chum I had; after Arabella died there was only you.

You will hear many stories about me, some of them possibly true. They will tell you that I have let the side down, disgraced the family. In some eyes perhaps I have. But I want you to know that I have never knowingly caused the death of a single man, and I truly believe that I have always worked for the cause of peace.

As the years go by, perhaps I will be regarded in a kinder, more understanding light, or blessedly forgotten. If that hope approaches the impossible, I will comfort myself with the thought that you always understood so much more than I realized at the time. No daughter can have lived as close as you have lived to her father without seeing things, knowing some things and guessing at others, that must be a point of honour never to talk about. Twelve years old going on twenty, as Rufus said. (You can trust R. Always go to him when the toadies get too many for you. He is a scalawag but a loyal scalawag and infinitely nicer than his father.) I do want you to be happy, but understand that most of us live in a kind of suspense, banking on a future contentment that we keep to ourselves; we must not weep if we let it slip through our fingers in the end.

Now, this is important. You will always be taken care of. Your trust fund and covenants will continue to be administered by Hawtrey Gilbody and Co. They will receive regular instructions via Goldmex in Geneva.

Gilbody will deal with the day-to-day running of your business affairs (until you are twenty-one, when you will decide matters for yourself), but he will be carrying out specific instructions and may not always appreciate the investment strategy behind them. He will grumble, but he will also follow instructions to the letter (old as God, he is still impressed that as Treasury Under-Secretary I accompanied Maynard Keynes to the Bretton Woods conference in '44!). But remember that he is an old woman. If I should die before you are 21, don't let him panic you. "Stop thine ear against the singer," as your old Scots nanny used to say. It is amazingly good advice.

I shall not write to you again, old bean.

I've done what had to be done. Now I want seclusion like Kafka wanted seclusion: not like a hermit, that isn't enough, but like the dead. Yet I know that when all this is a matter as old as dust, in my soul will be the same absurd will, surviving to choose how next to die. I am tired and I ramble. I shall miss you with all the longing that a heart is capable of.

Adieu,

Your loving Father

The Right Hon. Lady Pandora Child/by hand

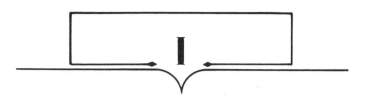

The girl on the bed had dancer's legs. The awkwardness of the pose emphasized the stretched muscles, the years of strain. Her mouth pouted with clinging childhood beneath the shiny lipstick. Twelve hours ago, Anastas Zorin thought, she must have been very desirable. Now her pale oval face had a lacquered look and hemorrhages filled her eyes with death.

"It's a rotten way to celebrate New Year's Eve," Detective Fyodor Gertsen said, offering Zorin a thin brown cigarette from a nickel case, watching the man from Moscow's face, weighing him, measuring his interest. The two men stood at the foot of the narrow bed.

"Tell me everything you know in one minute," Zorin told him quietly, ignoring the cigarettes. He seemed oblivious of the detective's scrutiny.

"There's not a lot," Gertsen said, closing the nickel case. "Her name was Lilya Kuzonev. A dancer with the Kirov. She got back from a tour in the West nine days ago—the fancy underwear's from Paris. Sixteen years old and real silk panties. How do you like that, Colonel? Black silk panties?"

"Go on, please." Zorin spoke in the same low voice. He was staring at the girl on the bed. He had never seen anything so young so dead. Rigor mortis had given her body a sort of sculptural force. The room was like a cramped film set: two floodlights, one clamped to the top of the door, another fixed to the dressing-table mirror, illuminated the dead girl with a sharp theatrical clarity.

"There's a linear grazed strangulation mark, little less than a quarter inch wide." The policeman made his voice harder, slower. He opened the nickel case and took his time selecting a cigarette. Zorin noticed for the first time that he wore gray surgical gloves. They gave his hands a dead look, like the girl's. "A cord maybe, maybe her own stocking. You see, she's got only one stocking on. The other's gone. That's probably what he used. Also"—he flipped open the front of the unbuttoned blouse, revealing her small breasts, whose nipples had been heavily rouged—"she had some weird ideas about where to put makeup."

He closed the nickel case with a snap and dropped it into the inside pocket of his jacket. There was a silence of awareness between the two big men that had nothing to do with the girl on the bed. Gertsen lit the cigarette carefully, gripping it between his teeth, as if it were a good cigar. His lips were thick and had been stitched more than once. His complexion had a faint glaucous glow; Zorin guessed a bleeding ulcer.

"So, what more can I tell you, Comrade Colonel? We found her just a couple of hours ago," Gertsen said when he was ready.

"This her apartment?" Zorin asked, looking around.

They were in a small back room in a squat three-storied building of crumbling stucco. The room was overheated and badly ventilated. The smoke from Gertsen's cigarette hung still in the air.

"She shared with a kid who works in the theater booking office on Nevsky Place." The policeman took out a notebook and flipped over a few pages. "Name of Lubov. Sonya Lubov. On vacation with her boyfriend. In . . . in . . ." Furrows of annoyance carved up his forehead and he mumbled under his breath. Zorin realized he might not be cold sober.

Zorin moved aside the lace curtain with his forefinger. An iron fire escape led to a small yard with a shed made of old doors and flattened gasoline cans stuck together with tar paper. A couple of scrawny chickens were fighting over some scraps beside the trash cans. There was a tree, but it was a lot closer to firewood than nature.

Zorin let the curtain fall back across the window. "Anybody see her come home?"

"Nobody we found yet."

"How long had she lived in Leningrad, do we know?"

Gertsen looked at his notebook. "She's been with the Kirov eight months. Before that she lived at home with her folks in Chelyabinsk."

He put his notebook away and moved closer to the girl on the bed. "Sixteen years old. What a waste," he said. Something had softened his voice. Zorin couldn't make up his mind whether it was compassion or something carnal.

"And the call was from a man?"

Gertsen removed his soft-brimmed hat and wiped his forehead with the back of his dead-looking hand. "Yeah," he said, looking at her breasts.

"What did he say?"

"He said we'd find a woman needing help."

"Nothing else."

"Just the address."

"Was there anything about the voice? Did it have an accent? Was it local? Did it sound young, old?"

"Just a voice."

"Recorded?"

"Our machine's all to hell. There was nothing on the tape."

"I suggest you get that machine working without delay," Zorin said with a look that made it more than a suggestion.

Gertsen kept quiet. He had an odd, very still expression on his face, like a caved-in smile he was trying to prop up with teeth. He seemed to be waiting for Zorin to say something else. When he didn't, Gertsen said, "Why is the KGB so interested, Comrade Colonel? May I ask? A little ballerina—"

"Is the doctor still in the building?"

Gertsen shrugged, turned and went out. His large body had a hunched hostile look.

Anastas Zorin stood in the middle of the room. His eyes moved slowly—the eyes of a man who could see freshly over and over again. It was a small room, a box, no more than eight by eight. A brown teddy bear had fallen sideways in a green wicker chair; a stack of dance magazines had spilled across the linoleum beneath an American poster for the film *West Side Story*. The yellow walls had been distempered and mottled brown with a sponge. Some dresses and a pair of blue jeans drooped on wire hangers in a curtained closet at the foot of the bed. On the dressing table a purse, hairpins, a few trinkets and a transistor radio had already acquired an abandoned look; under the glass top was a picture torn from a magazine of the Bolshoi prima ballerina Maya Plisetskaya. Zorin opened the drawers: handkerchiefs, gloves, an empty plastic billfold, woolen stockings, a bundle of letters, leg warmers . . . nothing had been disturbed. Whoever did her in wasn't after her worldly goods. He opened the purse: small change, a twenty-five-ruble note, comb, vanity mirror, tampon, pencil, mortise key, a snapshot of an elderly couple holding a small white dog up to the camera. A brand-new engagement diary for the year Lilya Kuzonev would never see.

He looked thoughtfully down at the girl on the bed. The mascara, glossy lips, those small painted breasts. It was very odd. He wondered whether Gertsen had noticed it too.

"Dr. Kamenny," the policeman said, returning with a tall, thin man with nervous delicate-looking hands and a feminine face spoiled by a slit for a mouth. "Dr. Kamenny is professor of anatomy at—"

"Doctor," Zorin nodded curtly, coming to the point at once, "what can you tell me?"

"Death due to asphyxia—you know that already, of course," Kamenny said in a dry, unhurried voice that went with his appearance. "Strangulation by a ligature. There are flagellation marks on her shoulders, back and buttocks." He took a breath and stretched his thin mouth sideways, revealing small, even white teeth. "She wasn't a virgin. She wasn't raped. No undue loss of pubic hair, no exceptional bruising. The vaginal swab shows a heavy presence of spermatozoa."

"A consenting partner?"

"She probably knew her killer. Somebody she trusted."

"Kids that age are too damn trusting," Gertsen said. He was leaning in the doorway and had been thinking about the smell of death. It was nearly always surprising. This time it was a smell of beetroot soup coming from the floor below, a homely smell that seemed to compound the sense of horror in the tiny room. "Look where it gets them."

"I'm reminded of the girl we found in the Botanical Gardens last autumn," Kamenny said quietly.

Gertsen began to look uncomfortable.

"Tell me about that," Zorin said.

"Last October," Gertsen said, straightening up, "we had a kid done in—"

"With her own pantyhose," the doctor said.

"That's right," Gertsen said.

"There were similar scourging marks," the doctor said.

"Yeah," Gertsen said. He wasn't looking happy. He moved into the room and switched off the floodlights. "There were some similarities."

"Sexual intercourse had taken place within a short time of death," Kamenny said.

"*After* death?"

"I'd say before, during and after."

"And this one?"

"I'll be able to tell you better after the internal."

Zorin turned to Gertsen. "Is that case still open?"

"I have some interesting leads," Gertsen said without conviction.

"Exactly when was this?"

"The Botanical Gardens? Exactly ... October. Second or third week sometime. I can check."

"How old was she?"

"Well, she looked a lot older when we first got to her. She had so much shit on her face—she looked like a sporting woman, you know what I mean? When we cleaned her up it was just a kid. Seventeen, maybe."

"An actress," the doctor said.

"An actress?"

"With the Summer Theater on Yelagin Island," Kamenny said.

"And she'd been whipped?"

"There were marks," Gertsen said reluctantly.

"Two actresses, both young, both sexually abused, both strangled. I would say there was a prima facie connection, wouldn't you?"

"This one's a dancer," Gertsen said stubbornly.

"Scourging marks," Zorin said. "Sexual flagellation ..."

"I don't see what a man gets out of that, whipping a kid. What sort of man—"

"Maybe a very moral sort of man," Kamenny said. "An ascetic."

"*Moral*, you say?"

"A moral man who has overstepped the mark."

"We're looking for a moral killer? A moral man did this?" Gertsen said to nobody in particular.

Kamenny said, "When morality gets to a certain pitch, it becomes an obsession. From there it's only a short step—"

"Perversion, Dr. Kamenny. We're talking about a very sick pervert," Gertsen said. He flicked the floodlights on again. It was like a sudden flare, lighting up the girl on the bed. The three men stared at the girl, her rouged nipples, the wide bloody eyes. Gertsen put the lights out.

"Take the old religious penitence of scourging," Kamenny went on in the same practical tone. "It starts out as a penitential exercise, a genuine atonement. It ends up a sexual need. A perversion, if that's what you want to call it. An algolagnic desire."

"Algolagnic? What is that?" Zorin asked.

"To seek pain, to inflict it. Sadomasochism, more or less."

"We're looking for a whipping boy," Gertsen said in the small silence that followed.

Nobody smiled.

"You're looking for motives, and I—" Kamenny started to say.

"I'd like to see the file on the first girl," Zorin interrupted. "Have it sent to my hotel, please. Room"—he took the key from his pocket and looked at the tag—"one seventy-one."

"The Botanical Gardens case has been a bitch," Gertsen said quickly, starting to remove the surgical gloves, pulling at the fingertips like a man tearing off his own skin. "But I've got some ideas. Cases like this—"

"One seventy-one," Zorin said. "Hotel Astoria."

"Keep on like that, comrade," Gertsen said when Zorin had gone, "and you'll be eating your dinner through a glass tube."

"I only mentioned—"

"Too much. Just shut it."

"Come on," Kamenny said, taking the policeman's arm. "I prescribe a drink."

"I don't like Moscow poking their noses in, having to play ball with those people. I'd rather play leapfrog with a unicorn."

"Next time I won't say a word."

"You think there'll be a next time?"

"Probably," said Kamenny with misanthropic amiability.

VIPs are divided into forty-two categories by the public relations people at London airport. The girl in the mink trench coat did not know into which category she now fitted; all she was certain of was that the reporters would be there to meet her. They always knew when she was due. They always knew when she would be flying out. She never understood how they knew, but that was how it had been for a long time. There was almost a kind of harmony to it now, although they always acted as if her arrival were the most unexpected event of their day. It was a game, and she participated in it with a sort of superior apathy, an incuriosity which the unwary mistook for something they called her insouciance. It made her laugh, but the reporters did not know that. There were many things they did not know about her. What they did not know they sometimes made up. But the girl, they all agreed, had style. It was the word they always used when they wrote about her. They also mentioned that she was one of the most beautiful women in England. She had long blond hair and was tall with the kind of face that somebody had once written, in some golden prose, looked as if it had been made with bones of contention and the petals of Iceland poppies. She was nineteen years old and her name was Lady Pandora Child.

In the early days she had seen reporters and photographers fighting each other to get their pictures and ask their questions, and she had often found pleasure in the memory of these people hurting each other. It is still the same game, she thought as once more they closed around her with their excessive cordiality, their quick professional assumptions of friendship, taking her picture, taping her words, as if to confirm her existence. It was the game they had been playing since she was twelve years old. "Give them just enough to make a caption," Rufus Gunn had told her in the beginning, "and keep moving." She never gave them more, and kept moving.

She lost them at immigration control. In the ladies' room she ran cold water over her wrists, patted her temples with wet fingers, and used the courtesy telephone to call the parking lot. Within twenty minutes she had collected her luggage and her little black Fiat XI/9 and was touching seventy on the M4 to London.

"I do *hate* you sometimes, Daddy," she said angrily under her breath.

3

It was a few minutes after first light on the first day of the New Year, and the only sound was the crunch of the limousine's tires on the frozen winding-sheet of snow that covered the city. A cold glow filled the scentless streets. Trolleybus lines, stiff with ice, stretched into the distance like high wires in a forsaken pleasure park. The city's coldest night in forty-seven years: minus forty degrees in the inner city and five degrees colder than that in the Lenin Hills.

Major General Valentin Buikov was thinking of the warm bed he had left behind, and of Anna, who was in it.

The Zil slid to a stop at a signal on Mokhovaya Street. He glanced at his new black Porsche watch. Four minutes past six. He reached into the folds of his fur coat and took out the small brown card that had come with the watch. "Each passing year," Anna had written, "robs us of some possession." He turned the card over and read, "Happy birthday, darling." Slowly he tore the card into small pieces.

"Lights," the driver mumbled, sensing Buikov's eyes on his back and the critical presence of a higher authority calling him to account for every thought and dream he'd ever had. "I know what it's like having the Cheka breathing down my neck every day," he often said to his wife, using, as most people of his generation did, the old name.

Buikov said nothing.

This was his favorite hour in Moscow. The immense cold precipitating the moisture in the air made the buildings and monuments seem almost translucent beneath the heavy zinc sky.

Across the street a gang of women was already at work breaking up the ice with crowbars: sullen faces, quilted greatcoats, wadded caps and felt boots. Twenty-four years ago, when he first came to Moscow, he had passed an identical gang. Were these the daughters of the women he had seen then? Perhaps some of them were even the same women. It was a depressing thought.

What had those years done to him? he wondered. He now employed a better tailor, bought his shirts and shoes in London and Zurich. His hair was now trimmed once a week, his fingernails manicured and finished with pale varnish. On this, his forty-second, birthday he still had the build and slim good looks of a Nordic athlete. His blond hair had receded an inch or

is narrow face. His chin still thrust forward in
go he had given up liquor; now he drank only
enbad with his meals. He occasionally smoked
a taste acquired in Phnom Penh more than a

d the limousine moved forward, slipped side-
gathered speed. He lowered the window, no
e nostrils seemed almost to collapse with the
through clenched teeth, he lifted his gloved
and released small pieces of brown card into the wind.

But its message stayed in his mind; it had touched a nerve he did not know was there—*Each passing year robs us of some possession.* He closed the window and settled back.

His wariness was still more a matter of intuition than anything else: he possessed that stimulus which causes animals and agents to behave instinctively when self-preservation is at stake. It's strange, he thought, how the best examples of instinct are found in the lowest species; the garden spider cannot learn from its mother to make its web because its mother perished in the first frost of winter, yet every garden spider must spin its own mystifying plexus of silk to survive.

"How convenient of Zorin to be in Leningrad for your birthday," Anna Zorin had said when he arrived at the apartment in the Lenin Hills.

"It wasn't easy," he told her, dropping his coat across the back of a chair in the hallway.

"You didn't!"

He followed her into the living room, smiling at the back of her head. "No, I didn't."

"But you could have?" she persisted almost coquettishly. She was never really herself in the early moments. "You could have done that?"

"Possibly."

She turned and held up her face to be kissed. He took her head between his hands and kissed her mouth with a satisfying knowingness. He felt the tenseness go out of her body.

"I suppose it's no good offering you a drink?" She stood back a step to look at him, taking hold of his hands. "To celebrate?"

"No."

"I haven't anything else."

"I have," he told her, "but later."

She helped herself to a whisky and soda and sat down on a large ottoman covered with a peasant shawl fragrant with lavender. Lithographs of early Russian modern art covered one wall: Brodsky's *Red Funeral,* Gregoriev's *Peasants,* a Tatlin, a Rodchenko and a Malevich. A television was hidden behind a fan-shaped screen on which were fixed several family photographs: her mother with Anna's smile and eyes but without the humor; a younger brother, now dead, looking as innocent and irredeemable as small boys always do in sepia prints; her father in his long white coat, a stethoscope around his neck, posing stiffly, as if by habit, outside the Sklifasousky Institute; Zorin, about ten years younger and fifteen pounds lighter, waving from a chairlift.

"I hope you're hungry," Anna said. Her breasts showed subtly through the beige silk blouse. It was the one she had worn when they first met at a reception at the Pushkin Museum seven months before.

"I think I'm ready," he said.

She lifted her hand, palm upward like a maître d', and led the way to the dining room. "Caviar, smoked sturgeon, pickled mushrooms," she said, pointing to each dish in turn. "And to follow the zakuski—"

"There's more?"

"Sterlets. Boiled in red Crimean wine."

"No wonder your husband puts on weight."

"With him it is the drink."

"No."

"You think not?"

"No."

"Why do you always contradict the first thing you say?"

"Do I?"

"Twice tonight."

"Answers are not oaths."

" 'Agricultural forecasts are not harvests'—one of my father's favorite sayings."

Buikov smiled. "Fortunately, that is not my problem."

"What is your problem, Comrade General?" she asked solemnly.

"You."

"Me?"

"And Anastas."

"*Anastas!*"

"Because of you. Strictly personal."

"Do you want me to get out of your life?" she asked in a cheerful voice that did not disguise a sense of misgiving.

"No," he said. Professional habit impelled him to anticipate the end of every event, but the end of his affair with Anna was something he did not want to think about.

"It would make life simpler for you," she said in the same almost baiting tone, with the same underlying apprehension.

"People who try to simplify their lives are usually well along the road of self-deception."

"Then what's the answer?"

"I'd like Anastas Zorin to be out of my life."

He watched her closely. She was not conventionally beautiful. Two front teeth were set slightly crooked in a wide gamy mouth; a scar cleaved the bow of her lips like a crystal arrowhead. A nascent silver streak ran through her dark hair. She had green eyes with yellow irises that reminded Buikov of tiny-petaled flowers.

"Poor Zorin," she said thoughtfully. She spread some caviar on a slice of brown bread and gave it to Buikov. "It's been a difficult year for him."

"For a lot of people." Interest softened Buikov's voice. "Does he talk about it?"

Anna hesitated. After thirteen years of marriage to Anastas Zorin she knew all about the minds of men who trade in secrets. "Not very much." She dipped a piece of tartine into the caviar. "Caviar and whisky is not a good idea," she said, making a face at the taste.

He continued to watch her closely, wondering whether anybody told the truth anymore. "He never brings his work home?"

"Are we going to talk about Zorin all evening?"

"Do you know what his problem is?" he persisted, ignoring her cautionary look.

She knew she would have to give him something. Be careful, Anna, she thought, be careful. Betrayal is always a process, never an event.

"Nilus Dollsky," she said after a pause.

"Nilus Dollsky! Department Twelve's sweating Nilus Dollsky?"

"Mulder Khor's latest bête noir. He put Zorin onto him a couple of months ago."

"A deputy head of department hand-running a film producer!"

"Director. He's a director, not a producer."

"I don't believe it!"

"Zorin puts it down to Khor's cussedness."

"Or Khor's law."

"Khor's law?"

"Create a villain, then invent a crime for him."

Anna smiled.

"What do you really think, Anna?"

"I think only what it is safe to think."

"Why is Dollsky a problem? He isn't a dissident, there's nothing subversive in his—"

"He's a genius. Geniuses get up Comrade Khor's nostrils. He distrusts geniuses. He says they're all crazy bastards and have to be watched."

Buikov was amused. "That's all there is to it, you think?"

"It wouldn't do for Russia's most famous film-maker to be found out."

"Found out?"

He seemed to miss the almost imperceptible pause, the anxious glance. "Some indiscretions," she said as casually as she could. "Zorin says he's a little imprudent sometimes."

"Genius must always be forgiven before it's recognized," Buikov said easily, but a vein moved in the hollow of his temple.

"You're the best lover I ever had," she told him later, in bed. Semen and hashish and burning candles gave the room a scent that was part cathouse, part holy. "Why didn't I meet you sooner?"

"Speaking of which." He turned his wrist to get the candlelight on his watch. "It is now three-forty."

"I don't want to know."

Anna often felt depressed after making love and a little too much wine. The first night they had spent together, at the Central Committee Hotel, the most discreet hotel in the most discreet district of Moscow, she had cried so hard and so long that her eyes and nose were swollen for days. Zorin had decided she was allergic to the kitten he had given her for her birthday and had it destroyed. So she had cried some more. Now they laughed about it, Valentin and Anna, conspiratorially, in the dark, but they never went back to that hotel again.

He moved a finger across her lips, tracing the tiny scar with his nail. "Such a wicked woman."

"Only *you* know how wicked."

They were quiet for a long while. One of the candles began to gutter, throwing shadows about the room like drunken ghosts. Anna turned away from him, but stayed curled and nestled in the crook of his arm. She pressed her back and thighs into his body.

"Spoons," she said.

"Long spoons."

He pressed his lips onto the back of her head. Her hair was damp, clinging to her skull. She smells of vanilla, he thought.

"It's a good marriage," she said. "Zorin is a good man."

"Don't you know about the great universal law of nature—evolving evil out of good?"

"Is our affair evil?"

"I don't know. Evil is something contrary to nature. I read that once. Evil is evil only because it's unnatural. I don't think that applies to us, do you?"

"I hate doctrines. Dogmas and doctrines. Nothing important should ever be dogmatized. Nothing important is ever that simple."

"What do you believe in?"

"I don't know."

"In Zorin?"

"I love Zorin, but I don't necessarily believe in him."

"That's very cynical."

"Or very wise."

"Perhaps."

"Everybody wants to believe in happiness."

"What would happiness be for you?"

She thought for a long moment. "Being able to sleep without guilt."

"That doesn't seem so much."

"You wouldn't understand."

"Why do you say that?"

"It's the least forgiving territory in the world—the marital bed."

"Don't I make you happy?"

"You please me."

"That's something."

"Doesn't it ever worry you?"

"What?"

"Us."

"Making love here?"

"Yes, that too."

"It has a certain piquancy."

"That isn't very nice."

"It's what I think."

"I'm still learning things about you. In many ways you are not a nice man."

She watched him dress, then went with him to the door and kissed him good-bye. She was naked. She said, "Things we think are important when we don't have them—they're usually not so important in the end."

It was nine minutes past six o'clock in the morning. The big Zil drew up at the unmarked building in Dzerzhinsky Square. Before the Revolution it had been the head office of the All-Russia Insurance Company; now it was the headquarters of the KGB. Insurance and espionage. They weren't such different kettles of fish, Buikov had often thought. Both trades demanded premiums, both were in the high-risk business, the business of expediency and speculation, jeopardy and gain. But Major General Buikov was not thinking about that now; he was thinking about Nilus Dollsky and the indiscretions that Anna Zorin did not want to talk about.

Anna was still sleeping when Zorin telephoned to tell her that he was delayed in Leningrad. She was disappointed, of course; she would try to change the Bolshoi tickets for a later date. She did not complain or ask questions. She was a good KGB wife.

His next call was to Lieutenant Vano Stashinsky at Moscow Center. He wanted the answer to one question: Had Nilus Dollsky visited Leningrad last October?

4

"And how are we this morning?" Pandora Child came into the room, her head to one side, towel-drying her long blond hair. "How's my hero today?"

"Terrific," said Rufus Gunn. The stitches in his left hand were beginning to hurt now that the anesthetic was wearing off.

"Terrific? Really?"

"No, but I'm getting there."

"You look like death warmed over."

"Try not to think about it."

"Just the teeniest drop too much of the falling-down water last night, I think."

"That's very perceptive of you, Pandora."

"How many of those have you had this morning?"

He held up the large bullshot in his good hand as if surprised to discover it there.

"My first," he said in an unconvincing voice.

"That should fire up the breathless clay."

He closed his eyes. His head, cocked at an upward angle, moved slowly from side to side like a man trying to catch the last rays of an elusive sun. He was a tall man with slender, hard-muscled legs; his hair was long and straight and somewhere between red and yellow, according to the season. The lid of his left eye, like his father's, drooped heavily, giving him a lazy insolent look. He still held the record for the Gaisleger-to-Langden downhill powder run, and he had once ridden in the Grand National, falling at Beecher's. But he could not pronounce his *r*'s, and had a drawing-room aplomb that was almost effeminate. Some men made the mistake of trusting him with their wives.

Pandora continued drying her hair, watching him with amused violet-gray eyes. They had been friends since childhood and lovers since her thirteenth birthday.

"Penny," she said.

"A good screw always makes me sad."

"Sad?"

"That there's no such thing as love."

"That's very inspirational, Rufus," she said. "You rotten sod." She tied the towel on her head in a turban knot and pushed her face close to the tall gilt mirror behind his chair.

"The hideous upshot of pleasure," she said solemnly to her reflection. "Mirror, mirror on the wall . . . dear God!"

"Try not to think about it," he said again.

"Moderation," she said in a determined voice, turning from the glass. "My New Year's resolution."

"A terrible mistake. One should discover one thing that one can do really well and do it at least three times a day."

"You'd screw a snake if they held its head. How's your paw?"

"Hurts, thank you," he said, examining the bandage.

"I've never seen anyone actually break a bottle like that before. Not in real life."

"One thing actors hate, my pretty, is the sound of breaking glass. They're all terrified of getting their profiles damaged."

"He didn't seem terrified."

"He's not much of an actor, is he?"

"What made you sock him in the first place, anyway?"

"A gesture."

"What did he do to deserve this gesture?"

"I can't remember."

"How many stitches was it?"

"I wasn't exactly counting."

"It looked awful. All that blood *and* the red plonk."

"That red plonk was thirty-five quids' worth of Margaux '63 down the drain."

"Mostly," she said, "it was down my new Zandra Rhodes."

"Don't start in on me again about that. I told you I was sorry."

The truth was, he felt quite indifferent toward the fracas, the spilled wine, the spoiled gown. He regretted that he did not live in a more chivalrous age, when ladies knew how to appreciate a romantic spirit. Gestures that once were celebrated in legends and folk songs now ended up in gossip columns or night court.

"I suppose Annabel's is off the visiting list from now on?"

"They won't be pleased to see my jib in Berkeley Square for a while."

"Running out of watering holes, Ru."

"Is it my fault that I exemplify everything about the aristocracy that the aristocracy cannot forgive?"

"You're getting repetitive."

"Consistent. I prefer consistent."

"Very soon, Ru, you're going to be socially quite dead, your funeral pyre stinking to high heaven of burnt boats."

"Haven't you noticed how the chat stops dead when I walk into a room? Perhaps they're planning a surprise party for me." He changed his voice.

"Rufus Gunn—Playboy, Photographer, Cuckolder and Lush—*This Is Your Life!*"

"Have you booked a table?"

"One-thirty," he said. "The Ritz. Time we pushed off."

"You drink too much, but you're not a lush."

They got a table by a window overlooking the park, ordered omelettes with smoked salmon and a bottle of Krug.

"How's the noble Lord Gunn?" she asked after the waiter had poured the second glass of champagne.

Rufus made a face at his father's name.

"As bad as that?"

"Know what he called me last week?"

"What did he call you last week?"

"A society *middleman*." He remembered his father's look, enshrined by political cartoonists, of absentminded distaste as he had said it. "A bloody *middleman!*"

"Not bad," she said with amused approval.

He gave up the pretense of being hurt. "The bastard," he said with a rueful grin.

Rufus Gunn's readiness to introduce the show-business elite to the English aristocracy was well known. Pandora knew it amused him the way famous actors wanted to mix with the upper crust, and the way the upper crust craved to have a few stars around to amuse them. "It's a two-way traffic jam," he had once told her, absolving his role in the trade-off.

"Society's just another commodity," he reflected. "Safer than cocoa, a whole lot simpler than cotton."

"I wouldn't know. I have a little man who takes care of that sort of thing for me."

"How is old Gilbody?"

"Still following orders. Pissing and moaning."

"But making you rich."

"All the time." She smiled.

"Cocoa or cotton?"

"Gold, mostly."

"You can sink the ship with that."

"The Midas touch all the way," she said. "Want some tips?"

He shook his head. "Horses for courses."

"If only your sense of business was not always—" She stopped, suddenly feeling sad.

"Go on—not always what?"

"—scuppered by your jazzing around all the time," she finished lamely. But the remark went home. His grandmother's legacy had gone within three years. His father had made him sign away his inheritance in return for squaring his last load of gambling debts. He would still get the title, of course, and carefully handled, that was worth twenty thousand a year in boardroom fees. But the serious money would go to his younger brother Hamo in South Africa. "I'm sorry," she said. "It's none of my business."

"I'll surprise you yet."

"When?" She managed to smile again.

"Just as soon as I've finished this champagne—and perhaps the smallest glass of Taylor's."

She made a gesture of disbelief, but her eyes had a tender expression. "You'll never change," she said.

"You'll see."

"Never in a million years."

The waiter poured coffee and went away. Pandora dipped a sugar lump into her cup and sucked it reflectively. "Ru, do you remember that letter Daddy wrote? The one from Vienna?"

"Yes."

"I read it again the other day. There was that article in *The Times* about him and Philby, and I remembered that odd thing he wrote."

"About your old Scots nanny?"

"Why do you think he wrote that? He knew I never had a Scots nanny in my life. I'd never heard that expression ever."

"I told you. I think he was having a nervous breakdown. He was under tremendous pressure, darling."

"I think he was trying to tell me something."

"Like what?"

"I don't know."

"What was the line again?"

" 'Stop thine ear against the singer.' "

"Obviously a quote. Sounds nineteenth-century. A piece of poetry?"

"Suppose he was trying to tell me something important?"

"Why didn't he just come out with it? Why the mystery?"

"It had to go through other hands. 'When you read this letter—*if it is permitted to reach you.*' Remember?"

"I think you're reading much too much into it, P."

"The trouble is," she said, "if it *is* important, I don't want to go around asking every Tom, Dick and Harry about it."

"If it doesn't mean a bloody sausage to you, how can it mean anything to anybody else?"

"It just nags me, that's all."

Rufus took out a notepad. "What is it again. 'Stop . . .'?"

" 'Stop thine ear against the singer.' "

He wrote it down. "You never heard it before? You're quite sure?"

She shook her head. "And I never had a Scots nanny either."

"I'll see if I can track it down."

After lunch he put Pandora into a cab and walked back to his flat on Elizabeth Street. The rain had stopped, and he cut across the park. The Krug had lifted his spirits, and his hand had stopped throbbing. There was hardly any traffic at Hyde Park Corner. He remembered that New Year's Day was now a public holiday. He was pleased about that. The more public holidays the better if they kept the proles out of the city. He hated crowds, unless they were his crowd. Only three times a year was the Hon. Rufus Gunn happy in a crowd: Ascot, Henley and Cowes.

The phone was ringing as he put his key in the lock. It was still ringing when he ran up two flights of stairs and answered it.

"Felix here," a voice said after the pips of a public call box had finished. "Felix Crick."

"Felix Hartley Crick," Buikov read the paragraph again, "is one of the finest spinners of a leg-break in the long history of English cricket." No doubt that still meant a lot to the Englishman who wrote it. It was strange how a man could betray his country and still be passionate about its games. It was mawkish sentimentality, of course, a nostalgia that some traitors never lose no matter how long they've been away, no matter how shabbily they've behaved toward their country or how badly they've let down their friends.

The photograph on the cover of the file showed a large, heavyset slouching man with a straight nose and well-made mouth. For several years in his twenties, Crick had lived in a monastery and had been in the habit of shaving his eyebrows as well as his head. The eyebrows now grew thick and spiky, and time had given him a natural tonsure. (It was rumored that alone in his rooms at Cambridge he still dressed in a monk's cowl.) His eyes were pale and age-softened, with a look in them that might have been humor or evil or just a trick of the light.

Buikov turned the pages slowly, scrutinizing facts, searching for their remotest cause; the most telling truths, he knew, were often hidden between the lines. Although now he had largely to trust to what case agents and analysts told him, he still made a point of reading Registry profiles and updates on key operatives under the control of Special Services.

". . . perhaps the most popular classical don of his generation . . . in establishing early contacts, Crick has shown a consistently accurate eye. Driven by political convictions, content with philosophical rewards . . ."

Buikov closed the file. The photograph on the cover interested him as much as the summary inside. The look in those pale eyes, he thought, was the look that creates trust between officers and their men. He liked the irony of that. He hoped it wasn't a trick of the light.

He stood up and paced slowly around the office. A picture of Lenin, in an overcoat with an astrakhan collar, reading *Pravda*, hung on the wall behind his desk; next to it a faint shadow, like the outline of an unmarked grave, showed where Stalin's picture had once been. The suite was on the third floor of Moscow Center, in the new building, but the furniture had come from an older room and evoked a curious antiquated atmosphere. The velvet chairs and sofa were full of camphoric smells; a rosewood pedestal library table had that almost radiant fragility which imbues things that are very old. Perhaps once cherished—they reminded Buikov of hereditary pieces in a Chekhov play—they now had a desolate look. He had requisitioned new furniture several times. Men came and measured, men came with equipment brochures and fabric books, but nothing happened. It was remarkable how a man controlling fortunes in unvouchered funds could not defeat the bureaucracy of fixtures and fittings.

His adjutant came in with a pot of coffee and two cups and saucers on a tray.

"Company, Vlakus?"

"Ten o'clock, Comrade General." Lieutenant Vlakus was a tall young man, an honors graduate of the Frunze Military Academy. "General Khor, sir."

Buikov had almost forgotten the monthly meeting with Mulder Khor. The head of Department Twelve would be punctual, even on New Year's Day.

They got through the official business briskly. Khor gave Buikov the list of ranking citizens under surveillance inside the Soviet Union. The names would be forwarded to Buikov's people in the embassies and trade missions to check for any external connections. The feedback was perfunctory, seldom useful, but the arrangement continued, sustained by men who had a military regard for routines and protocols, for the chapter and verse of their trade.

Nilus Dollsky's name did not appear on the January list.

"I trust you celebrated well?"

"Quietly," Buikov said with a smile of reminiscence.

Khor lifted his cup. "To the New Year," he said and tossed the coffee back in a gulp.

A square-cut man, he had arms that were thick and short with a look of great strength. His hair was gray and needed trimming. His face, razored and cologned to a pink shine, had the amiable menace of an uncle who would cheat you at checkers. It was easy to underestimate Mulder Khor. He was perhaps the most dangerous man to cross in all of Moscow Center; the inhabitant of the next valley was his natural enemy. There was no man in the entire Soviet Union better equipped to run the office of internal repression and surveillance.

"Still no sign of the new furniture?" He looked around the room with bright dark eyes, making no effort to leave.

"As you see."

"You like too much the good things of life, Comrade General. So much sybaritism!" He spoke lightly, but there was real disapproval in his eyes. "Be like me, I am inured to the infection of luxury."

"Is it such an infection?"

"The luxuries of Capua annihilated one of the bravest armies the world has ever seen."

"You go back a long way."

"The best lessons go back a long way."

"But we never learn?"

"Some people don't." Khor leaned forward and pushed his empty cup toward the head of Special Services. "Tell me what is happening in your world that I ought to know about."

Buikov refilled their cups. "We lost a couple of people in West Berlin a week ago," he said matter-of-factly. If Khor did not know already, he would soon find out. Buikov gave the details and possible ramifications. He spoke with a curious kind of underemphasis, like a grocer checking an inventory of dry goods. He did not falter or elaborate.

"And the Mig-25 in Hokkaido? The Englishman reckons the Yanks are already crawling over it like flies."

"Defecting aircraft are not exactly my—"

"Your people in Tokyo should have blown the fucking thing off the runway before the Yanks could even think about it."

"It's not the first Mig they've got their hands on. The 21 they got in Israel—what did they learn from that? That the pilot had limited rear vision, that—"

"We don't know what damage it caused down the line, the technological repercussions, the psychological effect," Khor interrupted, stirring his sugarless coffee thoughtfully, his breathing slow and harsh. Suddenly he smiled. "Anyway, all is not lost, we may yet be of use to each other."

Buikov was more perturbed by the idea of their indivisibility than he showed. It was a moment before he realized that it was the second time that morning that his calm had been disturbed.

6

"A charming girl, a child, a lovely child. Very shy, you know. At that age, mixing with so many older, more sophisticated people, traveling . . . it was most affecting, her shyness."

Ludwika Grigoriev did not sound particularly upset. Perhaps Lilya Kuzonev's death was not yet real to her.

"On tour she was well behaved?" Zorin asked. He was picking over the dead girl's belongings that the Kirov *régisseur* had collected from the theater in a cardboard box and brought to the hotel.

"No, no, no—no trouble. Ask your people. Ask them. They were with us all the way in the West," she said matter-of-factly. "She gave them no trouble. Speak to them, they will tell you."

"She bought some expensive underthings in Paris. Where do you suppose she found the money?"

"She didn't *buy* them, Colonel. A lingerie company gave all the girls a gift of pretty things." She smiled. "Even me. Slips, stockings, panties. Very nice."

"What about boyfriends?"

"Lilya? She liked the boys well enough, but she liked dancing more. She had such discipline, such control. She had this spark, this impression of spontaneity . . . She might have distinguished herself one day. She was an ambitious little rat."

"Rat?"

"*Les petits rats* . . . the name we use for beginners."

"No particular boyfriend in the company?"

Ludwika Grigoriev thought for a moment. "No, I don't think so. She was a friendly kid. She mixed with everybody."

"Did she have much mail?"

"Once a week a letter from her parents in Chelyabinsk. It came to the theater. Most of the new kids have their letters sent to the theater until they get settled." She sat in a vinyl armchair by the window, back straight, her legs crossed. She wore black stockings, probably from Paris. She was a hard-looking woman of forty or so. But it was the alabaster hardness that comes from years of exercise, diet and self-denial. A chiseled hardness a lot of men like to see in a woman. She had been a dancer. But at five-six, hers was a dangerous height for ballerinas. She probably had never made it very far. That also helped to make a woman hard.

Zorin lifted a scarf to his nose and sniffed. If it smelled at all, it smelled of jasmine. Zorin liked jasmine; it went well with furs.

"Did she always wear so much makeup?" he asked casually. He dropped the scented scarf back into the cardboard box.

"Makeup? Lilya? She had beautiful skin, Colonel. A lovely complexion. At sixteen, a girl with beautiful skin has no need—"

"Madame Grigoriev, when she was found her breasts were rouged."

"Little Lilya? No, I can't believe that!"

"She was heavily made up. Her breasts were covered with an expensive rouge."

Ludwika Grigoriev shook her head from side to side slowly in disbelief. "Lilya . . . Colonel, she *loathed* makeup."

Zorin crossed the room and picked up a bottle of vodka from the sideboard by its neck and gestured toward Madame Grigoriev. She nodded. He went into the bathroom and returned in a moment with another glass and poured two large shots. She watched him carefully. He was an attractive man.

"The thing is," he said, handing her the drink, "we didn't find any makeup in her room. No rouge, no lipstick. No powder or mascara." He went back to the cardboard box and waved his glass over the meager contents. "And there is nothing here."

"I told you," she said. Her voice was patient, low.

"Not even stage cosmetics. I find that odd," he said.

The *régisseur* shrugged. She held the glass close to her side, her elbow resting on her knee. "Perhaps the other girls . . ." Her voice trailed away. She swirled the vodka slowly in her glass and took it to her mouth and sipped slowly. She was on show, enjoying it.

"What? Helped themselves?"

She jerked her head upward. It was an angry sort of movement. "All her personal things are here. Everything. Even her points," she said defensively.

"But no makeup."

"It was of no use to anyone except—"

"Yes, of course," he said abstractedly. "*Les petits rats.*"

The air was that luminous blue with the cold of a thin January sunset; statues were crated against the frost, giving the city a strange packed-up-ready-to-go sort of feeling. Zorin walked briskly, keeping to the crowded Nevsky Prospekt.

The foreign-language bookshop was on the corner of Herzen Street. The assistant was young and efficient. There were two books on Nilus Dollsky, he said, consulting a worn catalog: a French publication, *La Vérité sur Nilus Dollsky,* and an illustrated English paperback called *The Nature and Art of Dollsky.* There was also a chapter in *Directors of the Soviet*

Cinema, published by the Moscow Workers' Press. Zorin bought the French and English books.

In the Aurora Café he got a table by the window with ruched curtains. A pot of plastic flowers wrapped in a paper frill like a shabby tutu decorated the table. It reminded him of Lilya. He ordered vodka and a plate of zakuski.

The Nature and Art of Dollsky was a collection of photographs from his films and early stage plays, the captions culled from Ministry of Information handouts padded with quotes from Soviet and foreign critics. He turned to the preface. The author seemed to be in love with Dollsky: "No longer faceless, directors are the prima donnas of our time. With his leonine head, pale skin and sensual aura, Dollsky is the supreme apotheosis: a demanding, complex egoist, a dark poet with a kind of savage charm."

The elderly waitress brought the vodka and asked him to repeat the rest of his order. "Bring me another one of these." He held up his glass. "And a pot of coffee."

"Didn't you order zakuski?"

"I lost my appetite."

"There are people waiting to eat," she said, but there was something in his silence that warned her not to push it. He returned his attention to the book: "A small figure, five feet eight, almost boyish, he will stalk you with a smile, or the scowl of a man sniffing for a deeper truth."

The French book was better produced, more expensive, but written along similar lines. "There is a subtle horror—a stone-hewing eye for grotesque detail—in his treatment of mundane and familiar themes . . . so much mystery behind so much brilliance, one can only compare him with the artist Gauguin."

Zorin read slowly, interpreting the florid text with a mixture of amusement and exasperation. He turned to the last paragraph on the last page.

"But Nilus Dollsky must surely know that to stay too long in one land is to capitulate to comfortable deceptions and to settle for illiberal truths."

He closed the book with a small thoughtful smile.

Obviously, the censor had not read *La Vérité sur Nilus Dollsky* with as much attention as he might have. He made a note of the quotation and page number. One day he might want a favor from the Ministry of Culture.

"Comrade Dollsky arrived in Leningrad October twelve and stayed five days. He spent two days at the Europe Hotel, then moved to number twenty-seven Stavropol Street, a private accommodation registered to the director of the Lenin Komsomol Theater. He twice visited the Lenfilm studios. He returned to Moscow on the Red Arrow Express on October seventeen, three days earlier than scheduled. He canceled two lecture appointments arranged by the Ministry of Culture." Lieutenant Vano

Stashinsky gave the facts over the phone slowly and concisely. Zorin knew that he must have written them down in his large schoolboyish writing, checked them, edited them down to the barest necessary detail. People never change, he thought. Before the Revolution, Stashinsky would have performed with the same air of incurious obedience, opening doors for the rich, taking shit from them all his life.

"Thank you, Stashinsky," Zorin said.

"When will you be returning, sir?"

"I'll let you know."

"Yes, Comrade Colonel."

"Shred that note, Lieutenant."

"Yes, Comrade Colonel."

"Good night to you."

There was no moon. He sat in the dark, smoking. It was curious how the dark of hotel rooms in unfamiliar cities evoked memories. The mechanism of memory—stirred by a smell, a sound, a shape in the dark—fascinated him. That night he had dreamed he was a child again, lost in a dark forest with his mother. Her face was faint, like a faded pencil sketch. He never dreamed of his father. His father had died on the Don, near the village of Zymlianskaya built on a hillside surrounded by vineyards. His mother had framed the page of *Pravda* announcing that he had been made a Hero of the Soviet Union. Nine weeks later she too was dead, shot in the Bryansk Forest, fighting with Mikhail Romashkin's guerrillas. That was in the famous Orphans' Winter of '43—the mild winter sent to protect the waifs and strays of war, they said. It was the year his childhood ended. He was eight years old.

He lit another cigarette and tried hard to think of other things—of recent important matters. Was Dollsky a killer? It was an incredible idea. Was it too incredible? He wondered again just how much Mulder Khor really knew.

He slept.

Telephones always sound louder in the dark.

It was Fyodor Gertsen. "That kid in the Botanical Gardens died the night—" The policeman started to cough; Zorin waited, holding the phone away from his ear. "—the night of October sixteen."

"And the report I asked for?"

Gertsen said it was at the desk downstairs. Zorin thanked him and said he would read it with great interest.

He heard the policeman draw on his cigarette like a man taking a deep breath before starting something difficult. "Will you be staying much longer, Comrade Colonel? In our city?"

The line deadened as Gertsen covered the mouthpiece to muzzle a new fit of coughing.

Zorin said he did not know his plans yet.

It was six-fifteen. He took a shower, ordered coffee, and asked the porter to send up the report. Then he telephoned Pulkovo Airport and booked a seat on the 9:00 A.M. flight to Moscow.

Rufus Gunn watched her coming through the restaurant with that long-legged libidinal prowl of hers that very few women can sustain away from a catwalk. "Her walk has an eternal defensiveness that reminds me of Garbo a long time ago," Cecil Beaton had written in his memoirs. He stood up and kissed her cheek.

She ordered spinach and bacon salad. The waiter suggested melon. "*Fa venire l'acquolina in bocca,*" he said, kissing the tips of his fingers slowly.

"*Questo non mi calza,*" she said politely.

"*Vino?*" Rufus held out his hand for the list.

"Mineral water for me, Ru. I'm working at four."

"I'll have another of these." He tapped the rim of his glass. "And the *pollo sorpresa* with a little zucchini."

"How have you been?" she asked when the waiter had gone.

"Frantic."

"Making pots of money?"

"Tons," he said without conviction.

"Would you like to? Make a bit?"

"Is it legal?"

"Gilbody's going to market again next week."

"The yellow brick road?"

She nodded.

"I told you. Too rich for my blood."

"He hasn't put a foot wrong yet."

"Ingot we trust."

"Very amusing. I saw some really nice pictures of yours in one of the glossies last week. Who was the girl? She was stunning."

"Some Swedish bimbo. Tell me what's happening about *Daisy Jordan.*"

"Heflin definitely wants me."

"And?"

She hesitated. "And I don't know."

"You'd better make up your mind soon. He's not going to hang about. A guy like Lyall Heflin can take his pick."

"He has to find a director first. One minute he's talking to Louis Malle, the next minute he wants Bertolucci. I don't think he knows what he wants."

"But he does want you?"

"Passionately," she said gravely. "Is this why we're having lunch?"

"I want to get you sorted out. Do you *want* to be an actress?"

"I suppose so."

"*Suppose so!* For Christ's sake, Pandora, what sort of answer is that? You can't be so *offhand* about something like this. It's not a *game*, acting."

"I know. It's just that actresses seem to have so little control over what happens to them."

"All actresses have to be a little bit Faustian."

"That sounds a bit hazardous to me."

"Crossing the street is hazardous."

She lit a cigarette. "What do you think I should do?"

"I'm not making your decisions for you. You're not a kid anymore."

"Let's talk about something else, shall we?"

"I want to talk about you and this movie."

"Stop bullying me."

"I'm not bullying you."

"Yes, you are."

When the food arrived they called a truce while they ate and gossiped. Rufus was amusing, but there was a look in his eyes that she could not work out, and when the coffee came he returned to the subject. "It's up to you. What do you say?"

"I vant to be a movie qveen," she said in a Swedish accent.

"It's like being a hooker who knows she's pulled a vice cop, but still wants to turn the trick. If you don't have that kind of determination, that kind of obsession—it's a sort of madness, I suppose—you might as well forget it."

"*Madness!*"

"The nut who thinks he's Napoleon. Actresses have to have that same unshakable belief in their own greatness."

"Not tonight, Josephine."

"I was an agent, remember."

"For five minutes."

"A minute more than the notice we'll get at the end of the world," he said. She made the sign of the cross. "It's a good script, P. It still needs a little more work on it, but it's all there."

She took hold of his wrist across the table. "You know it scares the hell out of me," she said quietly.

"I know."

"You know me better than anyone in the world."

"It's the best role since they were cutting each other's throats over Scarlett O'Hara," he said. "You'll knock the socks off them, P." He signed the check.

"Had any luck with that quote you were trying to find for me?" she asked on the way out. He shook his head. She was disappointed; she suspected he'd forgotten all about it.

They got the only taxi on the rank in Sloane Square. He kissed her lightly on both cheeks, careful not to smudge her makeup, and gave the driver the address of Donovan's studio. "Who's going to be the next big movie star?" He smiled at her expectantly. She closed the door without answering, but as the taxi moved slowly into the traffic she slowly opened her mouth to shape one unmistakable word: *me*.

Reaching the bar ahead of the intermission crowd and choosing a corner table in the far part of the long red-and-gold room Zorin ordered a bottle of champagne. "You were lucky with the seats," he said after the waitress had opened the wine, half filled their glasses and left the bottle on the table between them.

"Luck," Anna said, "and a small stick."

"What do you mean?" His tone had a glint of admonishment in it.

"I got the lovely Lieutenant Stashinsky to arrange them. One call from Dzerzhinsky Square."

"Don't ever do that again, Anna."

"Why not? Whose fault was it that we canceled in the first place? I would much rather have seen *Petrouchka*."

"Stashinsky isn't an errand boy." Zorin's hard-muscled face had no expression except perhaps an expression of repressed force.

"He doesn't mind. There are always tickets for the Center. Don't be angry. Anyway, how *was* Leningrad?"

"Cold."

"And lonely?"

"And lonely."

"I missed you," she said.

The bar was now filled with the unleashed sound of people who have been attentive and silent for a long time. Zorin answered Anna's questions about his trip, the hotel, the food. Were the women as smart as Moscow women these days? She is still jealous, he thought, pleased that their marriage had not become a habit. "I never want to possess you," she had told him in the early days. "And you must never try to possess me." A threat? A challenge? He had never been sure. The uncertainty sometimes excited him. He looked at her closely. There were small wrinkles by her eyes now. But her neck—a perfect *Giselle* neck, he had once told her—was still white and unlined, her hair still soft. She has not changed so very much in thirteen years, he thought.

"What?" she said defensively, becoming conscious of his scrutiny, remembering Buikov and the things they had done together. "What is it?"

"Just thoughts."

"What sort of thoughts?" The question came out like a protest this time.

"You are a beautiful woman, Anna Zorin." Compliments were never easy for him.

The sense of reprieve went through her body like laudanum. "It takes a little longer now, it's more of an art than it used to be."

Waving his hand in a gesture of disagreement, he recognized the truth in what she said: the audit of time is always stricter on women, he thought.

"*Who* is that amazing-looking man over there?"

"The Englishman," he told her quietly, following her eyes.

"Really! I didn't think he'd look anything quite like that." Tall and lean, his face the color of the unlit yellow of mustard flowers, obviously tinted with a sunlamp, he reminded her of a fading romantic film actor. "And the people with him?"

"Don't stare. The heavy little man with the thick glasses is Jozef Dabrowski, a Pole, chairman of the Comecon trading organization secretariat. The one next to him, the one who looks like a white rat, is Sarkis. Robert Sarkis, director general of the Reserve Bank of Pretoria," Zorin told her without appearing even to glance in their direction once.

"South Africa! What's *he* doing in Moscow?"

"Enjoying the ballet."

"He doesn't look much like a ballet lover to me," she smiled. "I've never seen such a strange collection of men. What on earth do they find to talk about together?"

"Business?"

"*Business!*"

"Why not? Poland's at the bottom of the barrel, the cupboard's bare. South Africa's so rich it doesn't know what to do with its money. They could be made for each other."

"And the Englishman? Who is he made for?"

"He's got his fingers into everything. Cock-of-the-walk Comecon consultant, the Politburo's special adviser on the board of the Narodny Bank, philosopher and friend to the Foreign Trade Bank, ringmaster of our gold sales to the West."

"I didn't realize he was such a catch."

"Bigger than Philby in his way. The Chervonetz was his idea."

Anna looked blank. Zorin explained it was the Soviet answer to the Krugerrand; there were now over a million of them in American investment portfolios alone; it had been a great success.

"That must help the grain imports," she said.

"Dabrowski wishes he had a few. It's probably why he always looks so glum."

"When did he join us, the Englishman?"

"It must have been eight or nine years ago now."

"I wonder what makes a man like that want to change sides?"

"Enlightened self-interest?"

"Don't you think it odd, though?"

"He must have had his reasons."

"Obviously."

"Nothing is ever clear-cut. The traitor's trade is a very odd trade," he said.

"It took him nine years to come up with the gold-coin idea?"

"I imagine he's had his moments. Some results can't always be seen."

"For someone who's supposed to know so much, I don't call that much of a summary of a man and his work," she complained.

"It's useful having a man on our team with his knowledge of the webs of capitalism, someone who can anticipate their moves, knows how they think, how they will react."

"Perhaps that's why," she said.

"Why what?"

"Why he came over. It's a game, an intellectual challenge, he was bored."

"It's unprincipled enough to be possible," he said, smiling.

They fell into a comfortable silence, sipping their drinks, glancing knowingly at each other as pieces of conversation, fragments torn from the hubbub, drifted by.

". . . gaping wounds in his soul, only when he danced was he whole . . ."

". . . beautiful arms, beautiful elevation . . ."

"Dollsky owns a key to every Beryozka shop in the Soviet . . ."

"True?" Anna whispered to Zorin, leaning forward.

"That business is getting interesting," he said. "If you think murder's interesting."

"*Whose?*"

"A little ballerina with the Kirov. He knew her, but I'm not sure how well. They had lunch together two days before she died. She was strangled." A waitress brought them a small dish of olives; he poured more champagne into their glasses. "Last October, not far from where this kid was found, an actress, about the same age, was also done in. The circumstances were very similar. They never found the killer."

"Where was . . ."

"Close."

"Leningrad?"

He nodded thoughtfully. "The estimated time of death was nine P.M. He left on the Red Arrow at midnight the same evening, although he had planned to stay three days longer. I can't find any reason why he took off so suddenly."

A bell rang. *Three minutes*, a woman announced over the speakers. He poured more champagne. Anna stroked the back of his hand, tracing a finger lightly across the smooth gold of his wedding ring, the only jewelry he ever wore. "What are you going to do?"

He had committed an uncustomary indiscretion and hesitated about going on. "I don't know," he said. "I could have the wrong sow by the ear. It's very circumstantial."

"But you have an instinct?"

He shook his head slowly, and after some silence Anna asked how much the police knew. "They're still bouncing on the top board," he said.

The bar was almost empty. A small desiccated woman in a green apron began collecting empty glasses. After a while she too was gone, and the chandeliers began to dim until the room was enclosed by darkly luminous shadows. Anna sat very still, very straight, as if she were on a stage, in a tableau, at a funeral, waiting. "What does Khor say?" she asked, ending the silence, her voice sounding like somebody at prayer in an empty church.

"I haven't told him."

Somewhere in the dark recesses, as a heavy door opened before closing again with a sighing sound, Anna heard the distant chords of Minkus's score and tried to imagine the dancers fitting movements to them. Zorin picked up an olive between his thumb and forefinger and studied it thoughtfully, the half-light intensifying the pallor of his lean, hard face.

"If I do go on with this, if I do make a connection, a man like that . . . it could be messy, politically. Is that what Khor wants? Is that what he's waiting for?"

"I don't understand."

He put the olive back in the dish carefully, as if it had its own special place in a complex organism. "He's fifty-six years old, Anna. Maybe he feels I'm breathing down his neck."

"Are you?"

"One day."

A large ormolu clock on a table behind Zorin had stopped at three minutes to twelve: Anna dully wondered what day, what year, what century that was. Or had it stopped at all? The closer you get to a black hole, she had read somewhere, the slower time moves: every tick an eternity.

"But if he is setting you up, using Dollsky as bait?" she finally asked, the thought panicking her.

"All right, let's assume that he knows something—something he's keeping to himself," he said calmly, setting out his stall, pricing nothing. "Is he waiting for me to open the can of worms?"

"And the alternative?"

"The alternative—he's got no idea at all. He just wanted me out of the way. Dollsky was a blind, a dummy, a chaw of tobacco."

"And if he's not so harmless after all—what do you do then?"

"Dump him back in Khor's lap?"

"Won't that look bad for you? Like you're admitting you can't handle—"

"Now you've got it. Without knowing what game Comrade Khor is playing, it calls for the most delicate skills."

"Drop it, darling. Leave it alone, you've got no proof, let it go."

"All the same, it would be nice if I could use it somehow—swing it to my own advantage," he said, suddenly smiling like a man being carried forward by the momentum of chance.

"Were they very young?" she asked that night in bed.

"In their teens. Sixteen, the one I saw."

"Could you ever fancy a girl that age?"

"I don't think so."

"A lot of men prefer young girls."

"So I'm told."

"Not you?"

"I prefer—"

She put her fingers across his lips. "I once read that there comes a moment in every woman's life when a man will tell her that he prefers older women. And whenever that moment comes, it's always too soon."

"I was going to say that I prefer married women," he said, kissing her fingers. "One particular married woman."

"I think despairingly of the future sometimes."

"You have no reason to." Holding her gently, his hands caressing her hips beneath the thin satin of her nightgown, he slid his knee between her thighs. After a little while, as her breathing became uneven, he eased her closer, kissing her throat where the jugular betrayed the cadence of her longing. "I do love you, Anna," he told her, taking her slowly, deeply.

In the dark, the noises she made were very young, very vulnerable.

Mulder Khor turned off the Kremlevskaya Embankment and crossed the Moskva River, using one of the smaller bridges down beyond Gorky Park. He drove east at a steady thirty-five on the inside lane. At almost eight o'clock in the evening, there was little traffic on the riverside highway. Lights glimmered in the windows in the tall apartment blocks on the other side of the river. He switched on the radio and listened to the news; he heard nothing he did not already know. He found Radio Warsaw, the best station for music in Eastern Europe; it was broadcasting Tchaikovsky's last symphony, the sixth, in B minor. The Poles play too much tragic stuff these days, he thought.

He traveled at the same cautious speed for forty-five minutes before turning off the highway. He switched off the radio and began softly humming to himself. Reducing speed, he continued for another fifteen minutes, bumping over ruts in a road that was sometimes barely more than a track.

After a while he stopped humming, and his eyes began to search for something in the shadows. Twice he stopped the car and opened the window to listen. The cold wind from the east, a sibilant wind, creased his smooth pink face.

After what seemed a long time, he saw what he was searching for. It was half concealed beneath a clump of pine trees about twenty yards back from the road: an old Volga sedan, its lights out. There was no sign of life. The whole area had a sense of recent desolation, like a place that had been evacuated in a hurry.

Khor stopped about fifty yards along the road and walked back, his hands pushed deep into his pockets, as puffs of snow climbed like tiny pillars of smoke from the ground winds around him.

"Khor." His name was uttered with the sound of sharp-drawn breath. "*Khor.*"

He stood very still. A figure emerged from the shadows and led the way to the Volga. The two men got into the front seats. The man's voice was soft. "You come late, but you come."

"I teach you patience," Khor said.

"I'm as patient as the grave."

"There is hope in patience," Khor said.

In the darkness, his coat collar turned up, the man smiled. "Which is more than can be said for the grave," he said.

"I hate the country," Khor said with an air of surly resentment, a faint mist drifting from his mouth. "It's too aimless, unplanned."

"I think nature has got it worked out all right."

"It's too *exposed.*"

The man said, "It's safe enough here."

Khor said nothing. The man reached for him. "How are you, my dear?"

Khor gripped the wrist and removed the hand contemptuously. For a time they sat in silence, as if partitioned by the dark, while outside the branches of the trees creaked with age and ice.

The man took a flat leather-bound flask from the glove compartment. Unscrewing the silver cap, he handed the flask to the Russian, who took a long swig and wiped his mouth with the back of his hand before returning it without a word.

"Malt. Twelve years old. A present from the West."

"You have nice friends," Khor muttered. "I hope you know what you're doing."

The man filled the silver cap and sipped the whisky with an air of fastidious judgment. He took a handkerchief from his sleeve and patted his lips. "I leave the risks to others," he said.

"You people usually do," Khor answered with the kind of cutting civility people learn in politics.

They were rum partners; there would always be irreconcilable discords. Khor resented their alliance, that abstract devious thing this man called friendship. Friendship was not in Khor's nature. But the needs of his trade overwhelmed his nature. This man knew things, was close to people who knew things, things that Khor could never even guess at. He had other men inside the Kremlin, but he could learn more from the mockery of this man's asides than from all the others put together. This one had judgment as well as information. Khor could live with the prurient abnormality of the man's terms, the second-rate excitement of his passions.

"I have learned to live with culpability," the man said gently. He spoke Russian with a marked accent. "I have an indefatigable lack of shame. What matters is—"

"The Zorin situation," Khor said, as if starting in the middle of a sentence he did not know how to begin.

The man made a soft clucking sound with his tongue. "Khor, dear Khor." He suddenly spoke in English, with an Oxford accent that would not be hurried. "You know what I want first. There is time to talk about other matters . . . later."

"You're a bastard, Englishman." Curbing an impulse to strike him, Khor reached for the flask and took another long swig.

"Not just a lick and a promise," the Englishman said in the same languishing voice. "Afterwards we shall talk all you want. Afterwards."

He reached out with strong bony fingers, and this time the Russian did not object. He moved as if half awake from some dissolute dream, pulling open Khor's clothes, stroking his face. His fingers were cold and smelled of coal-tar soap. It's such an English smell, Khor thought. Their caresses had a clumsy restraint, a kind of deepwater slowness in the small dark space. Khor jackknifed his bulky body, forcing his face downward until he was breathing in the scent of expensive linen and talcumed flesh. The man held Khor's head, rocking it to the rhythm he wanted. The slow creak of their heavy coats had the lazy sound of a swing moving in a summer breeze; it was pleasantly disorienting.

Khor began to move more quickly.

A small cry shriveled in the Englishman's throat. The whisky on Khor's mouth was like a flame on the nerve fibers of his engorged flesh. He closed his eyes in a grimacing paroxysm that was terrifyingly aging. As always his lust went as quickly as it came. When he opened his eyes again, he felt nothing but emptiness. It was not the emptiness of relief, but of loneliness. There was no satisfaction in it at all. He could never understand those people who made such a ritual of sex.

Khor's head felt heavy in his lap.

"It's uncomfortable," the Englishman said irritably. He hinged his head back so that his face was close to the roof of the car. "I'm getting frightful cramp in my side."

Khor straightened up and reached for the whisky to wash the ammonia taste from his mouth. The Englishman started the engine; the heater came on with a smell of burning rubber and oil.

They talked in fragmented sentences encompassed by stretches of silence: a conversation between men skirting one subject and not sure how to start the one that mattered. Yet it was noticeable that the sense of power had moved away from Mulder Khor. He had lost his air of contempt. Khor was the lover who loved less; that was his strength. Now he was the man who needed most. Both men knew that the whiphand had shifted, as it always did, as it always would.

"You make the mistake of all specialists, Khor," the Englishman said. He switched on the overhead light and studied the Russian in the dim glow. "Your little parish is not the center of everything."

Khor swallowed some more whisky.

"You hit out too quickly. Your angle is too narrow. The specialist never looks at the whole picture. That can be a fatal flaw."

Khor resented the disdain in the Englishman's voice. The way he flaunted his Englishness: he still wore his old school tie, Winchester, and took tea, with imported shortcake biscuits, at four o'clock every afternoon in his office in the Kremlin. It seemed to be part of a private penance, the final purgatorial torment of a man who had betrayed a country he loved for a cause he no longer quite believed in.

"Zorin," Khor said.

"Ah yes, Comrade Zorin." The Englishman flicked the wiper blade across the windshield in a single back-and-forth movement, wiping it clear. "Meteorologists can tell us a great deal about the weather, but did you know that the tiny snowflake is still a total mystery to them?"

"You're not making sense, Englishman."

"Each flake is an exquisite crystal of frozen cloud, a unique miniature gem as finely fashioned as if the greatest craftsmen of Byzantium had worked on it for a lifetime. Not even Fabergé gave us anything so beautiful."

"What the fuck has this got to do with Zorin?" Khor hated the Englishman's gift for complication; even his truths were complicated.

"Meteorologists discovered a long time ago," the Englishman went on in the same unhurried way, "that the snowflake is fascinating but unimportant."

"I haven't come out here for a nature talk."

"Zorin. He is a single flake, don't you see? Quite different from all the others—fascinating but irrelevant. What you should be asking now is: Why is it snowing?"

"Kiss my ass."

He didn't expect to be told the whole truth, even if he asked, even if the Englishman knew it. Power is not letting the right hand know that there even *is* a left hand.

"Zorin has found himself an admirer," the Englishman said quietly. "Very soon he will have the full weight of a direct personal interest."

Khor picked up the flask and shook it thoughtfully by the side of his head; he tipped it to his lips until all the whisky had gone.

"This interest is inside the Politburo?"

The Englishman nodded. "Sooner or later somebody was going to take him up. Right age, fine record. It's hard to duck the Darwinian purging process once it starts."

"I have never made the mistake of assuming otherwise."

"When I see you in your uniform, I sometimes forget that you are also a politician," the Englishman said.

"Don't make sport of me."

"I'm perfectly serious, I assure you."

"Zorin's admirer, how good is he?"

"How powerful, do you mean?"

"Does he have it?"

"I'd say he was pretty virile."

"Virile enough to—"

"Strong as old socks, my dear. Mark my words."

"Does Zorin know his good fortune yet?"

"I shouldn't imagine so."

"How much time do I have?"

The Englishman shrugged.

Khor bared his teeth in a thoughtful grimace. The Englishman understood his dilemma. The Russian did not want to ask questions. Every question exposed his vulnerability and his need. Every question was a kind of indiscretion, a kind of confession. He held the steering wheel with both hands and stared impassively ahead into the darkness.

"You won't give me a name?" The single reluctant question came after a long silence.

"It wouldn't help," the Englishman told him. "It might even frighten you."

Khor gave a short laugh like a snort, and was silent again for a long moment. Then, in an almost cheerful voice, he said, "Well, friend, the tallest trees are most in the power of the winds."

"But think of the view, Khor. You can't hate a man for—"

"In my trade," Khor interrupted, "it is hard not to hate."

"Just so," the Englishman answered amiably.

"And Dollsky? Is he just another snowflake?"

The Englishman chuckled good-humoredly. "What has Zorin turned up, by the by?"

"On Dollsky? Not a lot. He smokes marijuana and uses cocaine—when he can get it."

"That's enough to keep the surveillance active."

"Dollsky has admirers too."

"How much has Zorin put in his reports?"

"He doesn't commit much to paper."

The Englishman looked thoughtful. "That's good. Let him have his secrets."

"I don't understand," Khor said. He had the look of a man who is shaving himself closely with a new blade, waiting for the first nick and smell of blood. "I don't understand a lot of things. I don't understand why you wanted Dollsky watched . . ."

"It keeps Zorin out of your hair, doesn't it?"

"There are less risky ways of doing that," Khor said, remembering that he was at the mercy of the Englishman's whims as well as his favors.

"We have a saying in England about killing two birds with one stone."

"It still leaves me—"

"With everything still to play for." The Englishman's smile was slow. He gave Khor's knee a reassuring squeeze. "It's time to be going," he said.

"My weaknesses . . . very well, vices, call them what you will," Rufus Gunn went on mellowly when the port came. "They must upset a few applecarts—all those people who put their faith in the old hereditary credo. There can't be many serious students of the gossip columns prepared to deny my place among the scoundrels of our time."

"Rufus, Rufus," Felix Crick said, a sort of silent laugh lifting his shoulders in a series of small shrugs, "you are incorrigible."

"Do you know, Felix, my father had only one affair in his entire life? She lived in Chelsea. Worked for him in his F.O. days. A homely little thing, by all accounts, who kept knitting him Fair Isle pullovers. He had to hide the bloody things in a suitcase he kept locked in the boot of the Rolls. I prised it open one day and they leaped out at me like a bloody woolen rainbow."

Crick shook his head, smiling.

"We always knew when he'd been visiting the Royal Borough. He'd come home with Ovaltine on his breath." Rufus could never resist embellishing a story with jagged fragments of fiction that often revealed deep and genuine sentiments. "Ovaltine and Bath Olivers. I swear. Now I can't even smell Ovaltine without getting horribly horny. Talk about the sins of our fathers."

"What happened to the lady in Chelsea?"

"Old Church Street. God knows. The usual, I suppose. It's a pastime of progressive disillusionment."

"Adultery?"

"Women."

"Yet you persevere with them?" There was a look in Crick's pale eyes that was often mistaken for humor, but it was a look men acquire from the habit of observation.

"It takes a particular kind of libido or madness to do what I do."

"Don't you ever get hurt?"

"I heal quickly," Rufus answered, touching the ash of his cigarette against the saucer.

"And your father?"

"I've no idea how he feels about anything."

"You never talk?"

"About women? Never!"

"I mean *talk*—about anything."

"He'd rather I read his speeches in the *Daily Telegraph.* Can you imagine that twit on that paper calling him the shrewdest man in politics today?"

"I thought he said the most *practiced,*" Crick corrected him mildly.

"All that Grand Old Man guff. He's not only ten years younger than he tells everybody, but now he's hinting that he's actually dying."

"I should think he's still a far cry from that."

"Pegging out's one thing, but watching him lapse closer and closer to death duties is quite unbearable."

"You don't mean that." Crick's voice was gently reprimanding.

"He worries himself sick that he might only get a ceremonial funeral. He wants a full-blown state send-off like Winston. He *hated* Winston, you know."

"Good Lord! It's always replenishing talking to you, Rufus."

"Not that I stand to collect a brass button. The black sheep has been well and truly shortchanged."

"You'll get the title."

"Not if he can find a way of taking it with him."

"Families can be cruel sometimes," Crick murmured, remembering the story: Lord Gunn and his lawyers stomping into Rufus's bedroom at six o'clock in the morning, making him sign away his inheritance in return for wiping the slate clean with his bookmakers. A clean slate, eight thousand pounds a year, and a covenant to cover his medical bills for life. The contract said just about all there was to say about Lord Toby Gunn, Crick thought. Decline from greatness always brings with it sanctions and pettiness. Toby Gunn could not see that it was not simply his son going to the dogs but a whole class going down the drain.

The restaurant was emptying.

"My best hope now is to seek refuge in matrimony, a decent dowry— and pretty damn soon. I've got restaurant bills as long as your arm."

"You're a terrible scamp," Crick said affectionately. He admired his cheerful, reckless cynicism: it gave him his charm and his license. Rufus had led a fairly calamitous life but belonged to a class that forbids one to be moved by it.

"I'd be quite a catch for a girl with the root of all evil and social ambitions."

"I always thought that you and Lady Pandora—"

"She knows me far too well."

"How old is she now?"

"Pandora? Nineteen."

"She's come out of it all very well, hasn't she?"

"She's amazing."

"A sad business."

"She wants to be an actress."

"She has the looks. Does she have any talent?"

"I think she might."

"I've often thought that the aspirations of a nation are reflected far more honestly in its choice of film stars than in its election of politicians," Crick said. "A mannequin, isn't she?"

"They don't call them mannequins anymore. She's what the papers call a top model."

"I always thought that meant a clever adventuress."

"Not in her case."

"Does well out of it, does she?"

"Immensely."

"Good for her."

"Did you see that *Times* piece on her father? The idea that he might be a double agent?"

"I think *The Times* was being a little bit mischievous. He is definitely one of theirs, I'm afraid."

"He behaved like a shit."

"Treason . . . a transfer of allegiance . . . you musn't hate a man for that. A change of heart, a change of mind. It could happen to any of us."

The restaurant was empty. Nobody came with the bill or made those finishing noises that waiters can be so good at when they want to go home. Rufus was a good customer at La Famiglia.

Crick sat back from the table, his arms folded across his chest, his hands beneath his elbows; it was a stance familiar to his students, his recollection stance. "It is fearfully *old*-making to think of Pandora so grown-up. I went to her tenth birthday party, you know. Luncheon at Claridge's. Her mother had been dead—oh, four or five years at least. The thing that struck me even then was her complete savoir faire—and her beauty, of course. She had Arabella's looks, and then some."

"You must know, Felix. How *did* Arabella die?"

"In a motoring accident."

"Yes, but the circumstances have always been a bit vague, haven't they? I've heard so many stories."

"She was traveling with two of her lovers. The car came off the road just outside Madrid. They all died. They were coming back from the fiesta of San Isidro."

"It was an extraordinary marriage, wasn't it?"

"They had what I believe today would be called an *open* marriage."

"He was a homosexual, wasn't he?"

Crick nodded. "But they were very much in love, you know. It was very sad."

"What kept them together?"

"I'm not sure. In their separate ways I suppose they both possessed a sort of daring. They both went to extremes. It was a sort of bond, I suppose."

Rufus smiled. "Not many kids get taken to Claridge's for their tenth wingding."

"He spoiled her terribly."

"Presumably he knew what was ahead, the heartache he was storing up for her."

"Hard to say. What he did, a decision like that, sometimes it happens suddenly, like an illness, like love."

"But it was proved, Felix. He'd been working for them for years."

"So the newspapers had us believe."

"What about that shindy he had with my father at the Athenæum? Everybody knew about that. Our people should have tumbled to him then."

Felix Crick's mind fled back eleven years.

"Equality," Lord Gunn was declaiming in that famous voice of his, "is tosh. The blether of Bolsheviks and pinko intellectuals."

The old boy's mind was not what it had been, but the party was still able to wheel him out to good effect for the big occasion. He could still look as strong as the Sutherland portrait, as vital as he looked in all those Karsh photographs. But at the club he was on his own: anachronistic, preposterous and slightly sad.

He had reached the middle of a familiar piece of saber rattling when Henry Child broke in: "You know what your trouble is, Toby dear? You want to see the Lord in napalm. Well, you're not going to. You're not Moses. Moses is dead, and the burning bush is out, finished. There are no more miracles. Not for us, not for our lot."

"You, sir, are blasphemous and drunk, sir."

"Tiddly, perhaps."

"Drunk, sir. You are a disgrace to our class."

"Our class? Let me tell you about our class. Extremely dubious zoological folklore is what guarantees rank and status to most of our class, my dear. Bred-in-the-bone bloody nincompoops. My God, Toby, the F.O. is full of 'em. Talk about the bloody teddy bears' picnic. We are all—"

"Continuity, sir, scholarship, culture, courage. Continuity is the soul of the empire, sir. Our heritage, our—"

"Gunboat claptrap, old man."

"How dare you say that to *me*, sir!"

It was a silly conversation—Child repudiating his own class and upbringing; Gunn revering an England as dead as Queen Victoria—and it went on far too long before Toby Gunn climbed to his feet in a ponderous movement of departure. It was beautifully timed and had the somber compelling grandeur of a great statesman's last exit; after all, he had rehearsed it many times.

"One day you may learn, sir, that there is none so incorrupt and none so innocent in this world as not to be criminously spoken of," he said, pausing at the door.

Henry Child had been tight, of course, far more so than anyone that night had realized; his languid clubman drawl disguised the true extent of his inebriation.

Crick had reported the incident to Moscow. Had that been the start of it? You could never tell with Center. For all he knew, Henry Child had been working for them forever.

Eleven years ago, he thought, dear God.

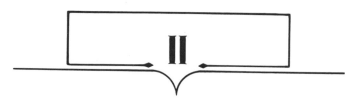

It was a large Armenian place behind the metro on Revolution Square. The manager, a small dark-skinned man with a black patriarchal beard, promised to find him a table in ten minutes. The Englishman ordered a vodka in the regretful murmur he always used with waiters; the idea of the servant class dedicated to making his life more comfortable now only seemed to make it less so.

The bartender was watching a football game on a television set with no sound. The room had wooden beams and the floor was uneven. The windows were made of cheap glass flawed with bubbles. A sepia photograph of chefs and waiters standing in front of the restaurant in the days before the Revolution hung on the wall.

The football game ended; the bartender became engrossed in a marionette show, watching the dolls with the self-absorbed fascination of a child. The manager returned. A table would be ready in five minutes.

"Just for the one person?"

"Alas."

"It is better alone than in bad company."

The Englishman ordered another vodka. He knew that the table would not be ready for at least forty minutes. He invited the bartender to have a drink.

"*Der Weg des Verderbens*," he said as he impassively poured himself a stiff vodka from a separate half-liter bottle he kept under the bar. He downed the drink with one quick gulp and a backward jerk of his head. "*Der Weg des Verderbens,*" he said again.

"The road to ruin," the Englishman repeated it in Russian, lifting his glass. "I'm English, by the way, not German."

"Ah, *England.*" The bartender grinned broadly, showing a row of black teeth. "I think you are German. I have no stomach for Germans." He held up three fingers and pushed them forward like an insult. "Three years prisoner. Very bad."

He poured a drink from his own private bottle. "You drink with me," he said, his voice moldered with strong cigarettes and cheap liquor. He refilled his own glass, finished it off in another quick gulp and tore a piece of black bread from a loaf for a chaser. "You don't come here before?"

The Englishman was not listening. His attention was riveted on the face that had replaced the marionettes on the soundless screen. It was handsome in a strangely mischievous way. Both impish and demoniacal, it could have been the face of a forty-year-old man or a fourteen-year-old child. The look in the eyes was almost animal. Women probably found him sexy; the Englishman had never found sexiness likable.

"Do you think we could have the sound up, old chap? I'd like to hear what he's saying."

The bartender looked at the picture. The idea that anyone should want to *listen* to television seemed to puzzle him. "Okay," he said finally, turning up the sound.

"Method is unimportant to a director compared with his obligation to get at the truth," the face was saying in a soft, almost caressive voice. "The viewfinder is like a keyhole. Through a keyhole you will always see the truth, whether you like it or not."

The camera pulled back, revealing the androgynous vulnerability of the body that went with the face.

"Who is this person?" the bartender asked.

"His name is Dollsky." The Englishman had known at once, although he had never seen him before. It was the damnedest feeling. "He makes films."

"He should make haircut." The bartender stroked the back of his own shaven neck. "He looks like girl with hair like that."

Dollsky was still talking: "Ilyich Lenin said that the mainspring of a revolution was fantasy. To make revolution you must visualize its success. That is how it is with films. I start every film as if it were a revolution. You don't start a revolution to establish a democracy."

The voice had a faraway sound, the voice of a mesmerist. Its quietness seemed to give him a freedom to say unquiet things.

"A camera affects the way people behave, behind it as well as in front of it. That is why I must be in control, totally and absolutely. Politeness won't do on a film set. The director has to be the boss, he must apply the heat from the first day."

"You are beginning to sound like a Hollywood czar," the interviewer said.

"No Russian wants to be a czar. History hardly encourages such ambition."

"A slave driver, then."

"Aristotle said that slavery was human nature. Plato said it was a political necessity. But I'm not convinced that you can frighten *everybody* into line."

The camera cut to the interviewer. He had an apprehensive look; he was getting rapid instructions through his earpiece.

"Critics admired your last picture," he said in a different tone, groping for the words as he worked his way toward new ground, "but many felt—beside the work of the imagination, the Dollsky style—you were toying with the false values, ignoring the schizophrenia of Western capitalist societies."

It was easy for Dollsky to parry the clumsy rebuke. "There will always be some failure of detail in a picture. That is not important. What is important is that I should reveal people's feelings, their fantasies, their dreams."

"A moment. I quote *Izvestia.*" The interviewer read from his clipboard: "Our culture stands on an immeasurably higher level than bourgeois culture. Is it not obvious that our culture has the right not to act as pupil and imitator but, on the contrary, to teach others the general human morals?"

"People still want a good plot."

There was a clip from one of his films, followed by more conversation, which the Englishman found difficult to follow. Dollsky said something about the escape velocity of most people's lives never going faster than twenty-four frames a second. The Englishman ordered another vodka.

"Look at Ulanova," Dollsky said straight into the camera, revealing his early training as an actor. "She stopped when she still had much dancing inside her. When they asked her why, she said, 'I went to class one morning and it hurt.' When it hurts, that is when a director must go on. Making pictures *is* painful. For me, for my actors—even for my critics sometimes." He smiled with unsettling innocence. "At the end of every picture I make I feel at risk. I have made many enemies, bruised many egos."

The credits began to roll up on the screen.

"Shit from a rocking horse," the bartender said as the image faded from the screen.

A dry husk of a smile appeared on the Englishman's face. "Do you have a telephone I could use, comrade?"

He answered on the fifth ring. "Yes?"

"Can we meet?"

"When?"

"Tomorrow?"

"You know the place. Seven o'clock." Mulder Khor put down the receiver without waiting for agreement.

Sir William Bunbury read the letter three times, each time with a different expression in his pale-blue eyes. There was not the least doubt in his mind that it was genuine. The handwriting could have been a clever forgery, of course, but it was not the handwriting that convinced him. He recognized her touches, her baleful sense of humor. She had written it, all right. It displayed fully her fondness for tittle-tattle, her aptitude for rather vulgar slang.

He looked at James Anselm for a long moment before speaking. "The interception was fortuitous, you say?"

"Fortuitous, Sir William."

"You can't tell me more than that?"

"I think 'fortuitous' is the wisest explanation. I think I cannot go any further, sir."

"Then I shall assume that it was the purest accident. That is my official position. Do you understand that?"

"Yes, I do, sir."

Bunbury gave him a hard look, which turned slowly into a solemn sort of smile. He said, "You do appreciate the delicacy of the matter? The position this places me in?"

"I might say the same to you, Sir William."

"I daresay," Bunbury said dryly. He began to read the letter again, running the palm of his small, pudgy hand across the top of his pink, freckled bald head. His hand moved slowly and continually from his forehead to the thin red fringe of hair at the back of his neck. Perhaps a long time ago he'd had unruly hair, Anselm thought.

It was eleven o'clock in the morning. The two men stood at the French window facing west. Outside was a wide marble terrace; beyond the terrace a fine extensive lawn stretched down to a lake. He could see flamingos moving solemnly across the water. We could be in the heart of Berkshire,

Anselm thought. A white marble-and-gold Vulliamy clock—Father Time clipping the wings of Cupid—made the only sound in the room. Anselm's eyes appeared barely to move at all, but they were eyes that never missed a thing. Later he would be able to tell his wife the shade of the crimson silk curtains, describe their rose, thistle and shamrock borders worked in gold thread, about the crowns and lions carved on the backs of the rosewood-and-gilt chairs and the ormolu mounts on the doors and describe the sets of Sèvres, Dresden and Chelsea china in the glass cabinets. From the inlaid satinwood floor to the painted ceiling, James Anselm's eyes missed nothing.

Bunbury finished the letter, and this time he folded it slowly and returned it to its envelope. He held the envelope between his thumb and forefinger, and tapped it thoughtfully in the palm of his left hand.

"A glass of refreshment?" he asked, arching his reddish eyebrows.

Anselm looked at his watch and considered for a moment before saying, "Perhaps a small whisky, Sir William."

Bunbury walked over to a drinks table with quick short steps, poured a large Scotch, and mixed a pink gin for himself.

"A princess makes her impact on the public imagination, on public affairs, in many ways, Mr. Anselm—but, dash it all, I do think that her private affairs should not be one of them," he said, handing him the Scotch. "The monarchy is moving into difficult times. And this young woman—not so young now, of course—her stock especially can hardly fall any lower than it is at this moment."

James Anselm said nothing. A big-boned lean man in his early forties, he had light-brown hair of the kind usually described as frizzy. He spoke slowly, quietly, with a pleasant northern burr, and the way he pronounced some words—Bunbury had noticed it particularly in *fortuitous* and *whisky*—suggested Scottish connections. He wore a gray flannel suit that looked expensive enough (what would the number two man in MI5 be getting these days? Bunbury wondered), yet there was a certain lack of finesse about his appearance. It showed in the way he stood and moved his hands. But Buckingham Palace could do that to the most sophisticated men. Sir William Bunbury had seen it overwhelm kings.

"So many people appear to enjoy her misfortunes. Although she often provokes unnecessary irritation, I've always felt that she stands in particular need of protection," Bunbury said. "You say that the Secretary to the Cabinet has not been told? Nobody in the Cabinet Office at all?"

"No, Sir William."

"It is unorthodox, to say the least."

"There was no other viable strategy on offer, if you think about it, sir."

"Oh, I've thought about it, Mr. Anselm." He had an expression on his face that was hard to fathom, but Anselm suspected there was humor in it somewhere.

"Let me see if I've got this perfectly clear. This is the only letter you have—come across?" Anselm nodded. "And you have no idea whether others exist or do not?"

"Their friendship extends over several years, so we must work on the assumption that it is one of several, perhaps one of many."

"And, naturally, you would like to know how many."

"It would be a start, sir."

"And this one was on its way to a West German magazine, you say. You don't think that Rufus Gunn is personally in any way—"

"We're certain that he doesn't even realize it's missing. He has been careless, extremely careless, and that sort of carelessness is reprehensible, Sir William, but it is not criminal."

"Considered going directly to Gunn, have you?" Bunbury said. "Go to him, put it to him absolutely. He will appreciate that politically they are priceless. He is a scalawag, but he knows the difference between good and bad form."

"We did consider that approach, Sir William," Anselm answered hesitantly. "But he does have some very close contacts with the newspaper world. We know he sometimes supplies them with stories—tips. Under the present circumstances . . ."

Bunbury shook his head thoughtfully. He looked at Anselm, at the letter he had propped against a bottle on the drinks table, then at Anselm again. "But you think he would return them—if she were to ask for them personally? Is that it?"

"I think it might be our best shot, sir."

"And you would like me to—to act unilaterally in the matter?"

"As few people as possible who know . . ." Anselm said carefully, annoyed by such a direct question. He did not like being pinned down in these matters. Experience had taught him that explicitness often made for trouble.

"You do realize that there is a serious question of protocol—" Bunbury began.

"Informing the sovereign," Anselm interrupted. If Bunbury wanted it spelled out he would spell it out. "It could place her in a very difficult position, a position of considerable embarrassment."

"Doubtless so."

"May I put it to you, Sir William, that the sovereign may prefer *not* to know? If anything should go amiss—"

"She could say in all conscience that she did not know?" Bunbury finished the thought for him.

"As our American cousins say: she wouldn't be caught holding the smoking gun."

Bunbury's smile was almost boyish. His face was ruddy in color, and barely lined at all. He did not look like a man of wily skills, whose life was spent amid the intrigues of high politics. For twenty years, with a cunning mixture of apparent impartiality and expediency, he had devoted himself to protecting the interests of the royal family. Anselm knew that behind that genial English charm Bunbury was tough as old Harry. He had been on Ruttledge's Everest expedition in 1933, and before joining the palace he had been the best director of security the intelligence service had ever had.

"You make it sound almost incontrovertible," Bunbury said to Anselm finally. "But what I must ask myself is whether it is sound navigation to enter these uncharted waters at all."

"If she were to be reminded that scandal works cumulatively, that this one letter—"

"I understand that," Bunbury cut him short, but not unpleasantly. He pulled the thin feminine lobe of his ear. "Dealing with this particular lady is always a ticklish business. One is treading on eggshells."

Anselm was disturbed by Bunbury's apparent uncertainty. He had not expected it from him. When the MI5 man spoke next, he had the look of a man who has wound himself up to a difficult decision. "There is a point I haven't touched on, Sir William. Rufus Gunn. She could hardly have picked a *worse* penpal, Sir William."

"He is a scoundrel, I should say, but at least he isn't dull. Most of the chaps she surrounds herself with are as dreary as semolina pudding."

"He has remained *very* close to Lady Pandora Child."

"Lovers, are they?" Bunbury asked with a new sharpness in his tone.

"They have been, sir. Their liaison is still a loving one. It would look very bad, Rufus running between the two of them. A traitor's daughter and—"

"Oh, Lord!"

"You do see."

"Her choice of lovers is exceedingly careless," Bunbury said almost petulantly.

"The press would make a most terrible meal of it."

Bunbury went to the window and stared out, not speaking for a long moment. When he turned, his face was expressionless. "Very well, leave it with me," he said, holding out his hand.

A servant appeared to lead Anselm away. Bunbury turned back to the window as if something fateful was going on in the distance, in the trees beyond the lake, something he could not quite make out.

13

He climbed the grand staircase, thinking about the fate and vicissitudes of buildings: how a palace built by a czar becomes a Moscow bathhouse. The decline itself did not trouble him; he had disciplined himself to accept such levelings. But the high ceilings and Corinthian columns reminded him of the Athenæum. It was the closest he ever felt to being homesick. It did not seem strange to him that his club, that life in a lost world, should be the last thread to break.

He gave the banschik twenty-five kopecks for the sheet and pillowcase. It included a good tip; sometimes the old man would press his suit in gratitude. But it was never spoken of; it was as if instinctively he understood the Englishman's dislike of privileges.

He stripped and weighed himself. His thin body had a whiteness "like the wood of olive trees," Arabella had once described it with unconscious cruelty. He never looked at his body now without recalling her remark. He slipped the fresh pillowcase over the hard bolster. Wrapping the sheet around himself, he stretched out on a marble slab in the smallest of the rest rooms on the second floor. The bathhouse, in the eastern suburbs, was as ornate but less fashionable than the Sandunovsky. Here there was less chance of running into somebody from Dzerzhinsky Square, or from the bank.

He closed his eyes, and his thoughts began to drift.

He dreamed he was back in London, in Saint James's Park. Pandora was a child again, waving to him from the top of the slide. She was calling to him, "Watch me, watch me," and he answered, "I'm here. I can see you. I won't go away." She started to move down the slide, nervously at first, holding on to the side to slow her descent. "Let go," he called to her, "you must learn to let go." She threw her hands into the air and began to move swiftly, then started to scream. Her screams embarrassed him and he hurried away. "Daddy, don't leave me," she called over and over. . . . Then he was on the plane. "Austrian Airlines welcome you aboard." The stewardess was smiling down at him, checking his seat belt. She had Pandora's grown-up face. "Let go," he said to her angrily. "You must learn to let go." The stewardess looked puzzled; "Please?" she said. Only it wasn't Pandora's face anymore. The noise of the jet engines became a roar. The ground raced beneath him and fell away. Below, an ambulance and yellow emergency trucks moved alongside the runway, growing smaller as the plane lifted steeply into the sky. "I love you, Daddy." Pandora's childhood voice came from a long way off. He wanted to tell her that he loved her too—only, she was beyond his reach. The plane started to shake violently, like a thing with the ague.

"You have bad dream, Englishman?" Mulder Khor was standing over him, shaking his shoulder, grinning.

"I must have dozed off. I was dreaming about my daughter," he said, sitting up. "Disobliging dreams."

"You miss her, your daughter?"

"Miss her?" He thought for a moment. "Children are much like one's childhood. Something that has to be left behind, although it'll always be part of you—absolute, irrevocable."

Khor grunted as if he understood. Wrapped in his sheet, with his large head and thick short arms, he looked like a Roman emperor.

"Let's get some heat," the Englishman said. "My shoulder aches like the devil. I must have been pressing on a nerve."

An intestinal maze of pipes covered the walls and zigzagged across the ceiling of the hot room. The Englishman took one of the cooler lower steps; Khor sat behind him, several steps up. The heat never bothered the Russian. The only other occupant, a soft-fleshed man with alopecia, got up and padded out without a word.

"Speak."

"I was watching television last night," the Englishman began. The heat scorched his nostrils. His mouth and throat filled with the dry hot air. "The genius was on."

"Dollsky?"

"Is the surveillance still operative?"

"Yes."

"Anything new?"

"Zorin is basket-weaving. What do you expect?"

"I'm not sure."

"Last week," Khor said slowly, "Zorin asked for a list of Beryozka stores in Moscow and Leningrad."

"You think that had something to do with Dollsky?"

"Dollsky is all he's got."

"Dollsky has Beryozka privileges?"

"What do you think?"

They talked in quiet expiring voices, with long gaps between sentences, sometimes between words. The almost doleful drawn-out intonations reminded the Englishman of hot summer afternoons long ago. He closed his eyes and pictured shadows moving slowly across a lawn.

"His attitude on the television," he said after a long silence, "was interesting. I kept thinking . . . it was a possibility."

"Possibility?"

"Defection," the Englishman said softly.

"Dollsky? Are you off your head?"

"Watching him last night—he struck me as a man who might wish to put a more commercial value on his talent."

"The reality of the situation isn't that—"

"*You* must invent the reality, Khor."

"He won't jump."

"It would astonish me if the thought had not crossed his mind."

"That sugar-ass has it too good here."

"He *breathes* expediency, Khor." His voice was gentle. "And if I'm wrong, why don't we try a little push?"

"What are you talking about?"

"Let's see what happens."

"Sure. We'll let him out on sale or return."

"You want to fix Zorin, don't you?" the Englishman asked. "Dollsky is—"

"What does Dollsky have to do with it? Why involve that little bastard? Zorin is my problem."

"Why separate Zorin from Dollsky, Dollsky from your present problem? Sooner or later he's going to spell trouble—a lot of trouble. The West is already calling his pictures masterpieces. They write books about him. The clock is wound and running. Before you know it, he's going to think he's the conscience of Russia, Solzhenitsyn's heir, a bloody great thorn in your backside, Khor."

There was a sly movement of understanding in Khor's eyes, but he stayed silent. His eyes glinted like freshly broken glass. Clothed he looked fat, but he wasn't at all: he had the solid body of a man who has spent his life in training. The body, full of primal energy, of a circus strong man.

The Englishman reached out and felt the inside of Khor's hard thigh. "Two for the price of one," he said. "It's worth thinking about."

"I distrust complication, clever plots."

"But it's so simple. Dollsky is Zorin's pigeon. Your hands are clean. If Dollsky runs, it's on him entirely Colonel Zorin will never worry you again as long as you live."

"Is that what you call psychological politics?"

"Psychological politics is getting the other fellow before he gets you."

"I can think of easier ways."

"We've got a kite by the tail. Let's see where it takes us."

"Dream of escape—it's a sickness," Khor spoke carefully, picking his words. "Only the innocent or the insane confuse escape with freedom."

The Englishman smiled. It was a smile of polite formality. He sat with his bony arms crossed over his chest, his fingers opening and closing on each shoulder. A puddle of sweat grew at his feet.

The corner of Khor's mouth suddenly twitched. "I want the bastard dead," he said angrily. "Dead is the best way."

"Achilles absent was Achilles still."

"I hate your fucking riddles."

"Wind him up, Khor. Make him run. You want Zorin? His goose is cooked if Dollsky runs."

Suddenly Khor grinned. "You've heard of Hunters' Row?"

"Hunters' Row?" The Englishman was surprised by the question.

"The old game market. It got its name back in czarist times. Sportsmen dropped in there to collect a brace or two after a day with their fancy women. Something to convince their wives."

"Life is like that," the Englishman said with an abstracted smile, aware of the smell of Khor's sweat and maleness permeating the heat. "People buying their own halos."

Khor moved his head. "This bird you offer me on a plate, is it a gift from Hunters' Row?"

"You are a suspicious fellow."

"The human condition is one of suspicion."

"I'm a rogue, but not completely a rogue."

"I wonder about your motives."

"I just want to help a friend. The pure motive of one to whom life can offer no more bribes."

"I have no intention of being made into a cat's paw."

"You deeply offend my Western sensibilities," the Englishman answered mockingly."

"I just want the truth."

"You want a lot."

"Just the truth."

"The truth is always more than the sum of the facts," the Englishman said in the same lightly mocking tone. "The truth is always negotiable."

Khor stared at the door, as if he felt imprisoned. "Just don't fuck with me," he said.

"I think it's worth a try."

"Let him go over the wall? That's your solution, is it?"

"It's something to think about." He was becoming bored with the Russian's problem, with his ungratefulness and moody fluctuations.

"There are enough pricks going over the wall without us encouraging—"

"What about that Mig business in Japan?" The Englishman changed track in a tone of casual curiosity, although the affair had been exercising his imagination since the day it happened. He had even caught himself half-consciously making up repentant scenarios. "What do you hear? I've rather lost touch on that one."

"An emergency landing. They're holding our pilot against his will."

"That's our line, is it? The Pentagon must be having a field day."

"The latest, the fastest, the best thing we've put in the sky since Sputnik—a fucking gift to the Yanks."

"What are we doing about it?" He did not know why he went on with this conversation, or why he had started it. Khor could tell him nothing he did not already know. One day I will fool nobody, he thought, except myself. He knew that he was beginning to be afraid, and that it was a sensible fear. He felt very tired.

" 'What are we doing?' " Khor seemed angered by the question, but not surprised. "Making the usual threats, a lot of noise. Our bunch of piss-artists in the UN are foaming on cue, the usual crap."

"I suppose it impresses some people."

"Somebody's going to lose his balls in the grinder over this one. Someone should be shitting in his pants right now."

The smallest look of distaste moved across the Englishman's face, hiding the disquiet beneath. In his mind's eye, and not for the first time, he imagined the scene inside the hangar in Hokkaido as the Mig was stripped of all its secrets, and perhaps the greatest secret of all. The thought became unbearable. "I feel very tired now," he said, slowly getting to his feet. "I have an early start tomorrow, a long day."

Khor knew that the Englishman was going to the Muruntau mine in Uzbekistan with the director of the Moscow Institute of High Pressure Physics. Muruntau had the highest restricted classification in the USSR; there were areas there where even Khor himself could not go, and yet the Englishman had a Collegium Code 7 clearance. Whatever else he did, his part in the Muruntau project was important. The Muruntau clearance, more than all the Englishman's connections inside the Kremlin, impressed and troubled Khor the most. A CC7 clearance was Yuri Andropov's personal stamp of approval, and not even Mulder Khor was going to question the man who had run the state security machine for more than fifteen years.

"Checking whether the yellow stuff's still there?" he said to let the Englishman know that at least he always knew his movements.

" 'Only the innocent or the insane confuse escape with freedom,' " the Englishman answered going to the door. "That's very good, Khor, very good."

The Russian closed his eyes. After a while he began to smile. It was the smile of a man dreaming.

Galya Mikhailovna had been found dead at eight-ten on Tuesday morning. It was now five o'clock Friday evening. The medical examiner's report and pictures were on Fyodor Gertsen's desk; the lab report would be ready in an hour—another hour in which to think, to try to figure out what to do. His ulcer had not troubled him for almost a month, but he knew that the pain would soon be back, and waiting for it to return was almost worse than the pain itself: sometimes pain could be almost a relief.

The station house on Soyuza Svyazi Street had been built in 1850, an annex to the Smolny Hospital, and Gertsen's windowless office on the top floor at the back of the building had been part of the mortuary. The original white enameled bricks remained on three walls; the fourth had been covered with hardboard and painted green. He lit a thin brown cigarette and stared thoughtfully at the overhung brickwork that had always offended his sense of craftsmanship. Probably too lazy to go and find a club hammer, the bricklayer had tried to work it back with a trowel handle. Gertsen's father had been a bricklayer, and from the age of thirteen to his seventeenth birthday, when he joined the army, Gertsen had worked alongside the old man on the high-rise housing estates in the northern suburbs. Those years still showed in the telltale deformity of the index finger on his trowel hand.

Kamenny arrived, carrying two large books and his familiar music case. When he spoke, his voice had a tone of excitement. "I have something to show you, something quite fascinating," he said. "It's very stuffy in here, Fyodor."

"It doesn't bother me," Gertsen said, stubbing out his cigarette, waiting while the doctor selected several large prints from his music case and spread them across the desk.

"Here we have the scanning electron micrographs of the hairs we found on the pillow, in Mikhailovna's left hand, and on the spread," Kamenny began, fussily arranging the prints in two lines. "We've established that these are from the head of a male person," he went on, tapping four of the prints with the tip of a silver pencil. "These are in the anagen phase, this one was at the catagen phase, the last two had reached the telogen state. And these two here are from the sexual parts of a male, almost certainly the same male—but, as you know, the hair from the head cannot be matched up with pubic hair with much hope of positive verification of identical subject."

"But they're definitely not the girl's?"

Kamenny shook his head. "The pubic hair of a young girl of Mikhailovna's age has very fine tips. These are claviform, and the cellular structure and pigmentation—"

Gertsen lifted his hands. "I believe you," he said. "What does this *tell* us?"

Kamenny smiled, stretching his thin ascetic mouth sideways like a rubber band. "We know that Galya Mikhailovna's killer is about thirty-four years old, blood group B. We know—"

"That's a positive reading? Thirty-four, the blood group?"

Kamenny ran his little finger along the blue Y-shaped vein on his forehead. "We recovered one strand with its root. The root of human hair tells us a lot. Let me give you one example: a child's root will dissolve in a solution of caustic potash almost at once; a septuagenarian's will resist the solution for many hours."

"You're saying there's a time scale? A clock?"

"An approximate scale, yes, within a few years, good enough certainly for medical-legal inquiry. What was the other thing? His blood group? Blood-group antigens of the ABC system are present in hair—he's definitely group B." He handed Gertsen a large envelope. "You'll find it all in here."

"Just tell me what's important."

"Well, we know that this hair had been recently washed with an expensive shampoo. Even so, apart from the *odor di femina*, probably picked up from the victim, it contained strong traces of tobacco dust."

"You going to give me the brand?" Gertsen grinned. "Make my day?"

"Possibly French," Kamenny said seriously. "We'll know a little more when we get the final results of the neutron-activation analysis from Cosmonaut Street. We should have several more trace elements then. But there's something more interesting than that."

"Go on." Gertsen's smile had faded and his voice contained a hint of resentment, as if the doctor's expertise rebuffed his own professionalism.

"The strands we recovered were dark. Examining the medullary substance and the cortex, we discovered that the pigment had extremely high levels of cortical fusi, air spaces of vacuoles that—"

"I don't understand a word of this."

"Our man has almost certainly dyed his hair. My guess is he's blond, certainly very fair. The final NAA printout will probably confirm it."

Gertsen slowly removed his jacket and hung it on a wire hanger behind the door. Patches of sweat darkened the armpits of his blue polyester shirt.

"Fyodor, there is something I have to tell you, " Kamenny said, speaking quickly as if impelled by an abrupt panic. "I never ordered tests on

Lilya Kuzonev's hair, not at the time. I wasn't as careful as I should have been. The hair we found was dark, it was long, I just assumed ... On Wednesday, after I started getting the Mikhailovna results and the picture started coming together, I decided to take another look at the Kuzonev stuff. I went over all her things—combs, hairbrush, collars, hats, scarves." He extracted two more prints from his music case. "I found these under the sweatband of the hat she was wearing the day she died. They match the strands we found on Galya Mikhailovna's pillow. The high levels of cortical—"

"Are you telling me this stuff ties Kuzonev—" He broke off and picked up the microprint of the hair found in Mikhailovna's hand. "It's the same bastard?"

Kamenny met the policeman's look of hostile surprise with silence. "*Shit*," Gertsen said quietly after a silence that reproached the doctor. "Where did you say you found these?"

"Under the sweatband of her *papakha*, between the band and the lining."

"How do you suppose they got *there?*"

"He must have tried it on, took a fancy to it, wanted to see if it suited him," Kamenny said.

"We know he's a twisted bastard—dressing up in her clothes?"

"I thought about that. We tested her underwear. Tights, knickers, stockings—nothing, negative. Just those strands inside the hat."

Gertsen closed his eyes as if suddenly exhausted. Kamenny began leafing through one of the large books he had brought with him. Reaching a page marked with a pipe cleaner, he pushed the book across the desk. Gertsen opened his eyes, turned to the cover and read aloud: "*Enlarged Photographs of Hair of Various Human Races. Gustav Fritsch, 1912.*"

Kamenny turned his attention to the second book. "*The Atlas of Friedenthal*," he said, "a few years older than the Fritsch, drawings, transverse sections, Europeans, Asiatics—a few primates."

Gertsen stared at the top of Kamenny's narrow, feminine head as the doctor turned the large pages, talking under his breath. "Here," he said finally, sliding the book across the desk. "Look at this plate and compare it with the photograph. Look carefully—the morphology, the structure." He walked around the desk and stood by Gertsen's shoulder. "You see how the hair shaft, the cuticle, is made up of a layer of flat overlapping cells, cuticular scales—and beneath that the cortex, keratin fibrils of pseudo-crystalline protein, sort of hollow cylinders. Now, see how this complex, tangled ammonite conformation creates patterns. They're not as good as a fingerprint—nowhere near as good as that—but both Fritsch and Friedenthal believed it was entirely possible to identify a man's race by a single strand of hair. The—"

Gertsen started to laugh. "You're going to narrow the killer down to a *race?* You're going to tell me he's European? Asian? You're telling me you can help me eliminate about a third of the world's population from my inquiries? That's very good!"

"Nobody bought the Fritsch and Friedenthal theories," Kamenny said quietly.

Gertsen made a noise in his throat like the sound of retching; perhaps it was a laugh. "All that—that *bullshit,* and now you're not even giving me a race!"

"Be patient, Fyodor. Listen to me. In the thirties, about '33, I think, an Italian named Gamba, Dr. Carlo Gamba, looked at the discredited Fritsch and Friedenthal theories again. He wondered what would happen if he *did* accept their basic premise. What if the Germans had been on the right track? Was it possible to classify hairs of one race, one zoological group, into subgroups, suborders, or families? Nationalities, Fyodor."

Gertsen stiffened with interest. Kamenny told his story slowly, simplifying and skipping wherever he could, avoiding the prodigious complications arising from some of the experiments and ignoring the clinical minutiae which fascinated him most and in which he had been immersed all afternoon. He talked slowly and evenly for about ten minutes before, quite suddenly, he came to the end of the story—or more accurately, to the end of Dr. Gamba. Somebody in Rome had heard about what he was up to. What if the results conflicted with Hitler's master-race theories? Nobody wanted to risk upsetting *Il Duce*'s favorite Nazi, and so Gamba was found floating in the Tiber. They said it was suicide; some experiments had gone badly wrong and the balance of his mind had been disturbed. But his daughter saved his papers, and when she died in 1949 she bequeathed them to the Italian Communist Party. Eventually Togliatti presented them to the Soviet Academy of Sciences.

"But Stalin was still with us," Kamenny went on, watching Gertsen's face carefully for a sign of scorn, but none came. "You know what lunatic prejudices *he* had," he continued, reassured. "Einstein's relativity, Linus Pauling's resonance theory of chemical structure, Wiener's cybernetics— God, the stuff that man anathematized. Nobody knew what he would take against next. When I stop to think! The genetics of Mendel, the classic biology of Virchow—it was an impossible time, wasn't it?"

The Gamba business, Gertsen reminded him irritably. What happened *after* Stalin? He's hooked, Kamenny thought with satisfaction. "After Stalin nothing happened," he said, stringing it out. "The papers got lost until a friend of mine at the Academy came across them, muddled up in a file on textile and cordage fibers and rope, and thought I might be interested. Did I mention—I don't think I did—that Gamba had concentrated his research on just two European subgroups?" He found an illustration among the papers he had taken from his case, covered the caption with his hand and said, "Look at this and compare it with the micrographs of the hairs we recovered from Kuzonev's hat." Gertsen stared at the pictures, then slowly shook his head. "I don't even know what I'm looking for," he said.

"Compare the pattern, man, the structure—the running twist, like a figure-eight knot . . . Here the same pattern, and once more here almost exactly the same conformation." In his excitement Kamenny's thin voice had climbed to near falsetto. "An almost perfect example of the Gamba concept in action—the detail of style which betrays the artist!"

Gertsen lifted the doctor's hand from the page and read the caption: *Lithuanian*. Kamenny patted his shoulder and returned to his chair. "A thirtyish Lithuanian with dyed hair," he said, his voice under control again. "Does that help?"

Gertsen sat back in his chair, looked at the ceiling and sat very still, like a man waiting for a familiar pain to return, anxious to avoid provocation. "*Seventy-year-old* drawings," he spoke in a low voice, "*a fifty-year-old* theory that apparently has never been tested. Why? Because it's all baked wind, Doctor, a bunch of bullshit. Your internal environments, your refractive indexes and density counts—it's all hen piss. From 1912! A fascist barber who ended up as fish bait!"

"Listen to me, Fyodor. Scientific theories are not instant coffee; sometimes you must be patient. The theories of Edward Jenner, who discovered vaccination, were heresy for *a hundred years*. Semmelweis, who discovered the importance of antisepsis—disinfection, antiseptic surgical techniques—was physically assaulted by his colleagues and dismissed from his hospital for his pains. Scientists themselves don't always understand what they have achieved. Niels Bohr, who was practically the *father* of nuclear physics, practically up to the moment they exploded the first atomic bomb was saying that the power of the nucleus would never be tapped. Do you understand what I'm saying, Fyodor? Even now, nobody knows how an aspirin gets rid of a headache."

A telephone ringing in a distant office was the only sound in the silence that followed. Gertsen opened the drawer, took out a bottle of vodka and a couple of glasses, filled them and pushed one toward Kamenny. He stood up and walked to the end of the room and back again with the curious restlessness that Kamenny knew often comes with extreme mental fatigue. "I apologize, Stepan." He rarely used the doctor's first name. "It's just that I'm in the woods with this one. The Botanical Gardens, the dancer, now this sad cow." He flicked a picture of Galya Mikhailovna across the desk.

Kamenny glanced at the colored picture. The ligature mark ran horizontally around her long, pale neck like a tight crimson ribbon and her dilated nostrils were wet with the edematous fluid which gave a bizarre glow to her cyanosed lips. Her distorted mouth reminded him of a boxer's rubber mouthpiece grin. He looked away; it was strange how the pictures always disturbed him. He could cut a body to pieces on the slab, probe and measure the ugliest wounds (the groove in Galya Mikhailovna's neck was 1.3 centimeters wide, 0.4 centimeters deep; the right lamina of the thyroid cartilage had been crushed) without a qualm, but the pictures always disturbed him.

"No flagellation marks this time," Gertsen said. "But sodomy. He hasn't done that before."

"A man who wants to experience all things?"

"I'm sorry," Gertsen said again. "I know you're trying to help. I'm an ungrateful bastard. I won't blow up like that again."

"You probably will, but I'll chance it anyway."

"Chance what?" Gertsen said, but Kamenny didn't seem to hear him. The doctor stretched his mouth, took a sip of vodka to moisten his thin, pale lips and looked past Gertsen as if he were reading something puzzling on the wall behind his head. It was several moments before he began to speak. "There are more ways of classifying racial stocks than you can shake a stick at," he said. "The most reliable guide is probably the cephalic index. Very simply that's the ratio of the breadth of the skull to its length. The length is taken at one hundred. When the ratio drops below seventy-five the skull is called dolichocephalic—narrow-headed. Between seventy-five and eighty is medium-headed, what is called mesocephalic. Anything over eighty is brachycephalic, broad-headed." He stopped and looked at the policeman.

"I'm still with you," Gertsen said. "Only just."

"We know that our man tried on Lilya Kuzonev's hat and that it fitted him well enough for several strands of his hair to be caught behind the sweatband. It didn't just sit on top of his head, and it wasn't too large: it *fitted*. Which almost certainly places him in the upper limits of mesocephaly."

"Lithuanian?"

Kamenny nodded, but admitted that it wasn't the sort of evidence he would want to have to offer in Kalanchovskaia Street, alluding to the old law courts in Moscow. "But Gamba *and* the cephalic index—It's circumstantial, but it's not to be sneezed at, Fyodor."

Again they went over what they had: a man who dyed his hair, grew it long, was in his thirties, with access to beautiful young girls.

"What did Mikhailovna do?" Kamenny asked.

"She was taking some sort of art course at the Lenfilm studios."

"Interesting," Kamenny mused. "Dressing up, trying on the girl's hat, the autoerotic praxis, the narcissism—they all make an interesting pattern. An exhibitionist, a man who washes his hair with expensive shampoo, smokes foreign cigarettes, women find him attractive . . ."

Gertsen had stopped listening. He broke in moodily: "What do I tell Zorin?"

Kamenny clicked his tongue against his teeth. "What does all this have to do with the KGB?"

"What did Kuzonev have to do with the KGB? And the kid in the Gardens?"

"Fyodor, listen to me, take my advice: if this isn't local stuff, don't stir anything up—you know what it's like with those people. Stay out of it. Let them get on with their business and you get on with yours."

Long after Kamenny left, Gertsen sat staring at the unlevel brickwork. The most important thing about brickwork is the way you build the corners, because one bad corner means four bad walls. If you want safe walls, his father used to say, never make a mistake in a corner.

He picked up the telephone and asked for Moscow Center.

The two men stood in the quadrangle of the Royal Academy.

"It's most awfully kind of you to make it at such short notice," Sir William Bunbury said. "Two years, is it? Must be at least two."

"More like three," Felix Crick said. "As nearly as I can remember."

"Too long, much too long. Do you get up to town often?"

"Less so these days," Crick told him, thinking how nobody pronounced "often" quite like Bunbury, who made it sound like "orphan."

"Can't say I blame you. Traffic's getting more wretched every day. Infernal charabancs, tourists everywhere. Still got your little place over the river, have you? Southwark, is it?"

"Lambeth," Crick said shortly. He did not want to talk about his domestic arrangements.

"They tell me South London is getting quite fashionable."

"I do hope not."

"You got in on the ground floor."

"It's convenient."

"Very clever of you to have so much foresight."

They made their way into Burlington House. Bunbury acknowledged the commissionaire's salute with a slight upward tilt of his furled umbrella, so perfectly English. Likable on sight, he was a shortish rotund figure with a large round bald head and blue eyes that really did twinkle. It was said that he had curious interests, but nobody was quite sure what they were.

Bunbury led the way through a series of rooms opening into one another until they reached a small boardroom behind the Diploma Gallery. "The Holy of Holies," he said. "We won't be disturbed in here."

They sat opposite each other across a polished expanse of table. "I have a request to make of you, Felix. I speak in the knowledge that our conversation—whatever decision you may come to regarding this request—will never be repeated outside this room."

Crick nodded his understanding. Bunbury took a thin gold case from his waistcoat pocket and offered him a cigarette.

"I don't anymore."

Bunbury selected one for himself, tapped it against the case and fixed it into a small ebony holder. "The Queen is a remarkable woman," he said at last. "Seven prime ministers from Winston down have come and gone during her reign. Thirty years, difficult years, most difficult times: Korea, Northern Ireland, Vietnam. People have become far more sophisticated in thirty years, a great deal more aware, a great deal more suspicious, alas. We now live in prying times, the age of audit and information. Even the palace is no longer out of bounds. The Queen personally has few critics, but the monarchy itself . . ." He smiled with a tangible air of regret, then continued: "The fact is, Felix, the royal family is losing its aura, its *charisma*, as the Americans call it. It is more human perhaps—I'm certain that is a good thing—but it has also become more vulnerable."

There was a longish silence. Crick was still unable to guess from this guarded preamble what Bunbury was leading up to. He waited patiently. Marble busts of Reynolds, Gainsborough and Stubbs stared down at him. Bunbury fixed a fresh cigarette into his holder.

"You said you had a request, Sir William," Crick reminded him equably.

"Rufus Gunn's one of your boys, isn't he?" Bunbury asked in a tone of casual reminiscence, pausing to light his cigarette.

"We dined a few weeks ago, as a matter of fact," Crick said, surprised by the sudden change of direction.

"I want to be frank, Felix. He has enjoyed a close liaison with a certain royal lady. The name of the lady—you must know it perfectly well, I'm sure."

"I think I can guess."

"She has written letters of a somewhat unguarded nature."

"To Rufus?"

"Exactly so."

"Love letters, Sir William?"

Bunbury nodded. "Some men appear to be born to be lovers."

"He *is* an attractive chap."

"We have repossessed one of these letters," he said in an almost apologetic tone. "It was on its way to a West German magazine."

"One of how many, Sir William?"

"We are given to understand that there might be as many as fifteen."

"Oh dear."

"Names are mentioned. Embarrassing names." There was more humor in Bunbury's tone now. "Some of them aren't even mentioned in Debrett," he said.

Crick smiled.

"But more to the point, the letters contain some private views in areas that, to say the least, Felix, are politically delicate. Asides about our Irish friends and their sectarian idiosyncrasies. One or two of our cousins in Washington are picked out for special mention. She is gifted with a waspish tongue, alas. If this correspondence were to come to light—I tremble to think of the consequences."

"Women do excel in the art of confession."

"I wish it were otherwise."

"It is a way of exorcising demons."

"You can imagine our disquiet."

"Indeed," Crick said.

"It's a horrid nuisance."

"So you would like the letters returned?"

"Are you peckish?" Bunbury asked, suddenly standing up. "Some luncheon?"

They walked to Bunbury's club in St. James's. His table was some distance from the rest. They ordered from a carbon-copied menu card inside a plastic cover.

"The club claret is rather good," Bunbury said, returning his menu to the waiter.

It wasn't until the waiter had poured the second glass and creaked away that Bunbury returned to the question of the letters. "We would not be uninterested in learning what monetary value Rufus attaches to these *billets doux*," he said softly.

"Aren't you rather rushing your fences, Sir William?"

"What is one to do?"

"You've intercepted one letter, probably stolen, possibly strayed. There's no evidence at all to suggest that he has even remotely considered selling—"

"We must act to see that it never comes to that. We must move to avoid a scandal of inadvertence."

"I understand what you say. At the same time, theoretically there are—"

"Stolen or strayed, Felix, somebody has been *very* careless."

"Aren't you in danger of precipitating something close to blackmail? As far as I can see, no such threat exists. To raise the question of payment is an option that must be considered very seriously."

"I simply want to precipitate a quick conclusion, Felix. We don't want it hanging around, however faint the smell may be. Let's nip it in the bud."

The gravy on Crick's roast beef had gone cold; a fine layer of fat was gathering on the surface.

"Rufus is a gambling man, isn't he?"

"I believe he likes a flutter," Crick said.

"Rather more than a flutter, I think." Bunbury took a memo pad from his pocket and glanced at what was written on it in pale-green ink. "At the moment, he owes three bookmakers a total of twenty-three thousand seven hundred pounds. He owes a further four thousand two hundred and fifty pounds to the Clermont. A total of twenty-seven thousand nine hundred and fifty pounds. A daunting sum."

"Extremely," Crick murmured. Knowing Bunbury's past associations, he was not surprised by the efficiency of the palace's present intelligence service.

"A man short of funds— You do see?" Bunbury said. "One day he may find himself in a situation even more awkward than anything he has experienced before. A sudden convergence of crises could put the most honorable of men in the most desperate bind. There is no telling what a chap might be obliged to do one day simply to shake off the wolves."

Bunbury dabbed at his mouth with his napkin; a smell of breakfast kedgeree still hung in the air. "A quiet word in his ear?"

"You want me to be your go-between?"

"An intermediary. I seem to remember it's what they call a 'cut-out' in the jargon."

"No mention at all of—"

"I think not."

"Is the Privy Council aware of this—proposal?"

"Best they stay unsighted, I think," Bunbury said pleasantly. "How is your claret? You didn't eat your beef!"

16

The short-haul Yak-72 Aeroflot trijet from Moscow landed on runway zero-five at Pulkovo Airport at six o'clock Sunday evening. Fifty minutes later Anastas Zorin was in his room at the Hotel Astoria reading the medical examiner's and lab reports that had been waiting for him in a sealed steel box at the desk. At seven-forty-five, Detective Fyodor Gertsen arrived, sweating slightly; by eight-thirty he had told the KGB man everything.

Zorin sat in a chair by the window, the evidence spread out on the carpet: photographs of Galya Mikhailovna alive and dead *in situ*, Kamenny's antique books, the Gamba synopsis, statements typed on yellow flimsy.

"If we buy this Lithuanian theory," Zorin asked, "could it be that we're being taken in by a lack of alternatives?"

"That's possible," Gertsen said. He blew his nose and wiped his forehead and the back of his neck with a large blue handkerchief. "Theories, Colonel—all you can do is put them on the slipway and hope."

Zorin was beginning to like the policeman. The cynicism Gertsen had showed the first time they met was gone. He was more efficient than Zorin had reckoned, and he had integrity. Integrity and efficiency seldom went hand in hand.

He stood up and went over to his case, which lay unpacked on the bed, unzipped a side pocket and took out a sheet of paper, which he handed to Gertsen. "I want to fit in some shopping tomorrow. Would you mark the stores within walking distance of"— he hesitated as if making up his mind— "the Lenfilm studios, the Europe Hotel and Stavropol Street."

Gertsen studied the list of Beryozka stores without comment. Hidden behind locked doors marked BUREAU OF STATE TRADING or DEPARTMENT OF NON-STANDARD PASSES, the stores dealt in luxury foreign goods and scarce domestic items at concessional prices. They were repugnant to Russians who knew of their existence but did not have the permits and the special certificate rubles to use them.

Gertsen marked four and handed the list back. Zorin sensed the deep resentment in the policeman's silence; his status did not entitle him to Beryozka privileges. Zorin suppressed the instinct to apologize; he went into the bathroom and washed his hands.

"Colonel, is there anything you can tell *me?*" Gertsen asked when Zorin returned.

"My interest is of a peripheral nature," Zorin said, drying his hands. "You were right to alert me to the situation here. I'm sorry that for the moment the traffic appears to be one way."

Gertsen gathered up the papers and photographs strewn across the floor, and inserted them in his bloated briefcase. He rewrapped the old books in plastic. "I'll send for the security box later," he said, "if you'll leave it at the desk."

"Did you have a coat?"

"Downstairs," Gertsen told him, stuffing the briefcase and books under his arm.

Zorin opened the door. "If I do discover anything that will be of use to you, you will hear from me." He put his arm briefly around the policeman's shoulder, as if he were genuinely sorry for having caused him to work so late on a Sunday evening.

Zorin rang for a bottle of vodka and began to unpack. At the bottom of his case, beneath the Velcro lining, was a folder he had code-named Trout. His eyes moved swiftly over the pages. It took several minutes to find what he was looking for:

> Mother b. 1919, Ujekpils, Lith., SW.
> relig: Eastern Orthodox Church
> trade: schoolteacher   d. April 1976
> Father: b. 1915, Vilnius, Lith.
> relig: Jew   trade: musician
> killed Smolensk 1943 (soldier, private)

"So," he said half aloud, closing the file thoughtfully. "Our little Lithuanian trout."

A girl came with a bottle of vodka and one glass on a wooden tray.

Smolensk, 1943, he thought as he poured his drink. It was the year his mother had died in the Bryansk Forest, also as a private soldier. Strangely, it brought him closer to Dollsky.

It was almost eight o'clock when he woke with a hangover. A remnant of a dream guttered on the edge of his consciousness and died out. A sharp wedge of daylight had driven itself between a gap in the red velvet curtains and spread a thin gauzy glow around the room, softening the lines of the furniture, the Volgograd copies of the worst of Scandinavian modern. It saddened him the way hotels threw out their best pieces the moment they got their hands on something modern. The pain shifted behind his eyes as he got out of bed.

He took a shower and shaved. Over coffee he studied the list Gertsen had marked: the stores closest to Dollsky's known points of contact in Leningrad. Consulting a street map, he wrote down the addresses in the most convenient order.

He left the hotel at nine-thirty and walked briskly ("You always walk as if you're under doctor's orders," Anna had once told him) toward Nevsky Prospekt, where the largest stores and crowds were. It was the best place to find a taxi, and to lose anyone who might have decided to keep an eye on him.

The first store, on Rossi Street, was behind a shiny black door with a spyhole and a small brass nameplate: BUREAU OF STATE TRADING. He rang and showed his red plastic permit. A woman in a black dress and knee-length boots entered his permit number in a ledger.

"Perfume?" he said, slipping the permit back into his wallet.

"Cosmetics, second floor, top of stairs, turn left, last door straight ahead," she said curtly, continuing to write in the large book with a concentration that was very close to unpleasantness.

The assistant was younger, friendlier. "I'm looking for a scent my wife likes," he said. "I think it's called Calèche."

She consulted a stock list, reading aloud: "Cabochard, Caline, Coeur Joie, Diorama, Le Dix . . . No, no Calèche. Plaisir's nice." She took a small atomizer, sprayed the inside of her wrist and held it up to his nose.

"A little too young for my wife," he said, letting go of her hand. "It suits you."

She blushed. She had the sort of pretty face that probably would not last long. She wore a tunic blouse with a collarband buttoned at the side of her neck. Her nipples pressed against the white silk like hard little berries.

"I'm not good at this sort of thing."

"Not many men are," she said.

"I have a friend who always knows what women want. Always knows the exact shade of lipstick."

"There are not many such men."

"You'd remember such a man."

He gave her a few moments to think about it, then said, "Perhaps you've seen my friend on television. He is quite well known. He makes films."

She wasn't impressed. "We had Yevgeny Yevtushenko in once," she said. "He writes poetry."

He went through similar routines at the store on Moyka Street and the one close to the Lenfilm studios.

The last store on the list was on Voinov Street, close to Stavropol Street, where Dollsky had stayed in October and again a week ago, two days before the third girl was murdered. It was the smallest, most discreet Beryozka store he had ever seen. A beautiful old gas chandelier tinkled softly in the drift of wind that came though the door when he entered.

One more time he told the receptionist the Calèche story as she led the way up a Palladian staircase.

"The perfume department," she said, smiling, going to a mahogany cabinet with carvings of ivory and satinwood veneers. "It was once Catherine the Great's jewel cabinet." She unlocked it. "I like the irony of that, don't you?"

"Irony?"

"You don't know the story? How she saw a filthy Gypsy boy in the street and ordered that he be brought to her apartments?"

Zorin shook his head.

"That night he was presented to her—cleaned up, bathed and scented. '*Fools, I wanted him the way he was,*' she screamed. '*You've ruined him!*' You don't know that story?"

Zorin smiled. "A nice story."

"And now her lovely cabinet is used to sell scent. Calèche, you said,

Calèche . . ." Her fingers danced along the shelves. "You are in luck: the last one!"

He made a sound of appreciation.

She wrapped the scent in brown paper and tied it with kitchen string; Beryozka stores don't advertise.

As she made out a bill in a carbon account book, Zorin said, "Usually I go to Moyka Street. A friend told me about this place."

"It's nice to be recommended."

"I always listen to him when I need something for a woman. He knows about women."

"He wouldn't be Nilus Dollsky, would he?"

"How did you know that?" He feigned astonishment, but he felt no surprise or satisfaction.

"Last week, in here, he spent nearly a whole morning discussing lipstick for a girlfriend."

"He likes to make them over," Zorin said.

He noticed for the first time the teardrop curve of her breasts; they were the sort he liked best. They swayed gently as she moved. It was easy to imagine such a woman in a sexual frenzy. She had the almost neurotic thinness, maybe five pounds more than gaunt, that turned to madness in bed. The thought stirred him. He thought of Anna's body in the early days. But it wasn't like that with Anna now. She could still exhaust him sometimes with her passion, but the surprise, the unbargained for, had gone. When you know a woman too well, when you love her almost too much, something goes out of the relationship too. When you know her conversations, thoughts and tastes, when you know the animal smell of her, the feel of her naked, asleep and aroused, it is hard to be surprised by her anymore. It takes a lot of imagination, a lot of courage, to invent something new after thirteen years, he thought. He had never been unfaithful to Anna. Perhaps that had been a mistake. But if ever he did decide to go off the rails, he knew that this was the sort of woman he would take a run at.

"Dollsky," she said in a different sort of voice, not her shop voice. "He's a lightning rod for women. It's a pity he likes them young."

Zorin put her at forty. He said, "Young girls bore me." He almost added that he preferred older women but remembered Anna's rebuke just in time.

"Young girls," she said, "have nothing to talk about afterwards. I'm sure you've discovered that"—she looked at his permit—"Colonel Zorin?"

"You think so?"

"It is not unusual. An attractive older man, he needs to test his—whatever it is that makes him attractive."

Zorin grinned. "What makes Dollsky attractive?"

"Ahh," she said, drawing the sound out, "I think because he actually *likes* women. He sometimes stays with a friend of mine when he comes to Leningrad. His house is close to here, on Stavropol Street."

"He just *likes* women?" Zorin said, shaking his head, prompting her to go on. "That's his secret?"

"It's more than *like*. He's interested, he cares. But it's subtle. Women hate a man who dances attendance and expects you to applaud the choreography."

Zorin paid for the scent, and they walked back toward the staircase. He moved with a deliberate slowness, the speed of a man deep in thought. Then he stopped. "You wouldn't happen to remember what he bought the last time he was in?" He grinned sheepishly. "The girl he's with now—she's about my wife's coloring. If I could . . ."

She turned and went back to her desk, opened a drawer, took out a receipt book and turned the pages. "The twelfth. He bought just one item. A lipstick. Lancôme rouge rose."

There was one left.

At the station house on Soyuza Svyazi Street, Fyodor Gertsen was typing a memo to himself when the telephone rang.

"There is something I want you to do for me." Zorin came straight to the point, the friendliness with which they had parted on Sunday evening gone from his voice. It was once more the voice Gertsen had first heard in that small back room on New Year's Eve. A picture of Lilya Kuzonev dead on the bed, her nipples rouged, went through his mind. "I want you to do one more test," Zorin was saying.

"On Galya Mikhailovna?"

"The medical report mentions substantial makeup. I want—"

"Colonel," Gertsen broke in quietly, "I don't know how much you know about homicide cadavers, the procedures— There are certain things that happen. When disposal is delayed for any length of time, once the external examinations are completed, it's usual to sponge and cover the body with a film of cream."

"*Cream?*"

"To prevent mold."

"Her body's covered in *cream?*"

"It's standard procedure."

Zorin was silent for a long moment, then said slowly, "Get hold of Kamenny. Tell him I want him to make every test he can think of—biochemical, toxicological, environmental, microbiological—on what's left of her makeup."

"Makeup?"

"Especially lipstick."

"I'll call him now," Gertsen said, winding the memo out of the typewriter.

"I want to know the moment the report is ready. It's to come straight to me."

Gertsen crushed the memo into a ball.

"The lipstick," Zorin went on as if it were a minor detail. "I want a complete breakdown. Solvents, resins, emollients, moisturizing components—whatever's in there I want to know about it."

Gertsen hurled the ball across the room.

"Didn't you explain?" Kamenny said when Gertsen gave him the message. "Didn't you tell him that her face was soaked in edematous fluid, that the body's already creamed and—"

"He said 'Do your best,' " Gertsen said and laughed.

Kamenny swore.

Fyodor Gertsen replaced the receiver and retrieved the crumpled memo from the floor beneath the clock. He walked back to his desk and, lifting his hand high above his head, dropped the ball into the wastebin. He wondered why he had laughed. Perhaps it was relief. It was Kamenny's problem now. But what the hell did the KGB want with a lipstick analysis?

17.

"Major General Khor, sir." Vlakus came into the room ahead of the small officer who, despite his untidiness, possessed the demeanor of power: it was something in the bone and muscle of his face, in the look in his bright dark eyes with their hint of a Mongolian droop at the outer edges.

Buikov glanced at his watch; it was ten o'clock exactly. The two men shook hands formally as Vlakus left the room, closing the door with that aura of reverence for superior officers that is drilled into subalterns at the Frunze Military Academy. Buikov claimed he could always recognize a Frunze man by the way he left a room.

Khor made himself comfortable on the yellow sofa. The barrel of an M61 Skorpion automatic poked out from among the papers in his briefcase: a small pistol, deadly at close range. He handed over the lists with the current crop of ranking Soviet citizens under special surveillance and the names of those who were marked for intensive forty-eight-hour spot checks—"vigils," as they were called inside the department.

Buikov casually turned over the pages; Dollsky's name was not there. It had been four months since Anna had told him about Khor's odd obsession with Dollsky. He knew that Zorin was still glued to him, yet the name did not appear on the lists. It puzzled him, but it was always pleasant to know what others think they are keeping from you.

When they came to the end of the official business, Khor asked, "That West Berlin business blow over?"

Buikov said it had.

"You should trim the fat off that operation. Too many dabchiks peddling too many moldy apples."

"Information from the past is important. We're all influenced by what happened yesterday."

"That's shit. Tomorrow's what matters."

"You have to step back once in a while to see the picture."

"Any news about that Mig?"

Buikov shrugged indifferently; military intelligence had taken over that operation. "The pilot's in the States. We'll get the plane back in due course."

"When they've put it together again?"

"It's the game we both play, General."

Vlakus brought in a tall pot of coffee with cups and saucers set out on a tray. When he had left, Khor said, "I have a proposition to put to you, Comrade General. A requirement."

"Requirement?"

"You heard of Nilus Dollsky?"

"Yes," Buikov said, showing no surprise.

"I want him to defect. I want you to approve his application for an external passport."

"To enable him to defect?"

Khor smiled. "To help him on his way."

Buikov stood up, left the room, and returned with a folder. Opening it, he started to recite a list of names, dates and places: "Rudolf Nureyev, Le Bourget Airport, Paris, 1961. Natalia Makarova, London, 1970. Mikhail Baryshnikov, Canada, 1974. Alexander Godunov, New York, 1979. Leonid and Valentina Koslov, also New York, 1979."

He stopped and looked at Khor, who was still smiling.

"This is the ballet list. I have other lists. Do you want—"

"One external passport."

"Do you mind explaining why Dollsky wants to defect?"

"He doesn't. Not yet. I am going to persuade him."

"Persuade him?"

"That it is in his own best interest."

Buikov refilled Khor's cup. He hesitated deliberately, as if gathering up all the threads of some complex thought. "I have always believed that Special Services and Department Twelve should not merely coexist but actively cooperate, Comrade General, but it is difficult to cooperate in the dark."

"Ask me no questions and I'll tell you no lies," Khor said in a childish singsong that was chilling from such a man.

"His defection would reflect rather more disagreeably on my sphere of interest than on yours," Buikov pressed gently.

"Take my word. I am proposing a mutually advantageous arrangement."

"It is our convictions that determine our decisions."

Khor closed his eyes.

"You're a mysterious fellow, Khor," Buikov said as if the idea amused him.

Khor's eyes stayed closed, moving slowly beneath the wrinkled lids, like something breathing, listening, menacing.

"I have to have answers, General."

Khor opened one eye, then the other, and said with sudden candor, "There is a man I want to get rid of. Dollsky's defection is necessary to my plan."

It was pointless pressing him harder. For a man who smelled of the barracks, Mulder Khor handled himself very well in the boardroom. Self-interest has become a kind of narcissism with him, Buikov thought. It was the narcissism that distrust and misanthropy finally breed.

Khor lifted the barrel of his pistol and took out a sheet of paper from his bricfcase. "This is a list of film festivals: Berlin, Edinburgh, Budapest, Venice, Cannes—he has standing invitations from most of them." He slid the paper across the desk.

"I can't help you, Khor. Special Services cannot involve itself in—"

"Cannes," Khor said, adopting a languid air. "The South of France should appeal to him. This is what we do—"

"We do nothing."

"First, external clearance."

It was something more than firmness in Khor's voice that made Buikov hesitate. He sounded like a man whose capacity had by no means been reached. Buikov knew it was better than even money that he still was holding his high cards.

"Didn't you hear me, Khor?"

"Have you noticed, Comrade General, how there is always a margin between what things seem and what they really arc between a man's image, let us say, and the reality?"

He took a file from his briefcase. "Look at your own situation," he said, removing a yellow index card covered with small neat handwriting. He studied the card for several moments with an exaggerated look of amusement. "It has always interested me. Why do they do it, these women? Is it a kind of reprisal? Repayment, some sort of retaliation? Or is it simply the thrill of it, the sense of hazard? I'm told that danger can enhance the—"

"Get to the point, General."

"Betraying a husband in his own home, in his own bed. Surely there is no greater fanaticism than a woman's prurience once aroused?"

Buikov's face was perfectly still, expressionless.

"The Pushkin Museum, May ninth last," Khor was reading from the yellow card. "Central Committee Hotel, June seventeenth. July twenty-one, twenty-nine, and August five at your apartment. Moscow Hippodrome racetrack . . . August, August, September, nothing October, twice in November. You like horses? Or is it the gamble that attracts you?" Khor's voice dwindled to a mumble as he skipped through similar dates and places. He turned the card over. "Then we come to an occasion on New Year's Eve in an apartment in the Lenin Hills. This is pure conjecture, of course, but it's my guess that at that rendezvous in the Lenin Hills you were given a present—"

Buikov's hand instinctively went to his wrist.

"It was your birthday? A Porsche watch made in Switzerland. I will not embarrass the lady by telling you how many of her certificate rubles she parted with on Granovsky Street."

"Anything else you'd like to tell me?" Buikov asked contemptuously.

"There are pictures."

"I don't doubt it."

"Nothing of an intimate nature, but interesting, I think." He produced a print of Buikov and Anna coming out of the Central Committee Hotel. "And tapes."

Buikov said nothing.

"There is nothing quite as vital in an affair of this kind as preventing it from getting out."

Buikov smiled.

"I'm pleased that we have been able to appreciate each other's position so quickly," Khor said.

Buikov's smile was like a wound that wouldn't heal. "I'm curious about one thing."

"What is that, Comrade General?"

"Why the vigil?"

"Routine, nothing personal, you have my word."

"You really are an extraordinary man, Khor." His voice was calm, pitched somewhere between the affronted and the amused. "You really expect me to submit to a cheap trick like this? Because I'm having an affair with a married woman—"

"Not just any married woman."

"Another officer's wife."

"You miss the point."

"The point is—"

"Anna Zorin is a Jew."

This time Buikov could not keep the surprise out of his face.

"You didn't know? You didn't know that her father was Dr. Lazar Slepak? Slepak? The chairman of the Presidium of the All-World Anti-Hitlerite Committee?"

Buikov looked puzzled. "As I recall, that committee was set up by one of your own predecessors."

"To rope in the Jews in America, get them to cough up support for our brave troops fighting the Nazis. Correct. Unfortunately, some members of that committee betrayed a bit too much Zionist zeal." Khor grinned. "Some people with wicked minds reckon that was Beria's whole idea—to flush out the prophets over here."

"Slepak was a Zionist?"

"He got buried for seven years in Vorkuta."

Buikov was silent.

"You see the danger you are putting her in, Anna Zorin, Anna Slepak, the Jew. Married to one *komitet* officer, playing games with another." He made a clucking sound. "It is a serious business. She's made some clever connections: married to a deputy head of one department, sleeping with the chief of another. Her deceit is plain."

Buikov stood up behind his desk.

"It's a good offer," Khor said. "If you have any feelings for the girl."

"What guarantees do I get?"

"The negatives and tapes will be burned. I used a single controller. He reported directly and only to me. He can also be burned if that is what you want. If that's what you want I'll fry his ass. Do we have a deal, Comrade General?"

"Do I have a choice?"

"You understand the arrangement?"

"You've made it perfectly clear."

Khor nodded. "That is a most attractive watch. She must love you very much."

"Call off your dog, Khor," Valentin Buikov said quietly.

She signed her full name: Pandora Cristabel Child.

Walter Greenspan smiled at the signature as if it were a clever aphorism before pushing the document across the desk to Lyall Heflin.

"Perhaps you should call yourself Cristabel," he said as Heflin put his name to the contract. "Cristabel Child. It has a nice ring to it."

"Just look after the small print, Walter," Heflin told him. "Leave the billing to me."

The lawyer grinned. "They're both pretty names," he said as his secretary came in with a bottle of champagne and three long-stemmed glasses on a tray. "I thought a toast would be in order," Greenspan said. "To Lady Pandora," he intoned when their glasses were filled.

"May the road rise to meet you," Heflin said. His voice had a resonant Boston sound. Nobody told a Lyall Heflin story without trying to impersonate his voice. "How d'you feel, kid?"

"I don't know." Her smile was bemused.

"You must feel *something*," Greenspan said.

"The loneliness of engulfing fame?" Heflin said. He picked up the contract by the corner and shook it gently. "*One—million—dollars,*" he said with gravity. "Don't tell me your toes aren't tingling!"

"She's overwhelmed." Greenspan spoke as if he were talking about a shy child stranded among grownups. "The cat's got her tongue."

Their voices babbled around her, skimming the surface of her consciousness. It was true she had expected to feel *something*— a sense of beginning, of commitment—but she just felt numb. A million-dollar deal that was just part of the come-on for the media. A million dollars, a million ifs: *if* Heflin picked up the options, *if* the writers delivered the right scripts, *if* all three pictures were made. She knew from the beginning what most actresses only discover by degrees: stardom is a game of chance, and the winner is always the one with the most luck. Even so, she had expected to feel *something*.

She heard Heflin saying, "This will be the most memorable day of your life, Pandora."

No it won't, she thought, remembering the day her father went away. She wondered how many girls could give you the exact date they started to menstruate. She remembered the headlines denouncing her father, the blood on her sheets. It was strange how she could never think of one without the other.

"Stardom's a mysterious process," Heflin was saying. "Like a force of nature, a star will rise to the surface, overcoming every difficulty, forcing a way through granite. Nothing can stop a true star."

"And when does Lady Pandora actually metamorphose into Daisy Jordan?" Greenspan asked, refilling their glasses.

"A matter of finding the right director," Heflin answered. "I've been thinking of the Russian Nilus Dollsky. What's the position there, Walter?"

"He speak English?"

"That never stopped Preminger."

The lawyer missed the joke. "Russian," he said. His thin graying hair was arranged carefully across a balding pale skull. His eyes moved rapidly, almost imperceptibly, from side to side behind gold pince-nez, the look newscasters have when reading from an autocue. "We'd need Home Office clearance. We'd have to convince them that there's a valid reason for wanting to bring in a Russian."

"Dollsky's got talent coming out his ears," Heflin said.

"I'm sure we could make a credible case at this end." He spoke as if he were delivering a judicial opinion. "What happens in Moscow is something else. I know that Dmitri de Grunwald went through this a year or so back. He'd know the ropes. Would you like me to talk to him?"

"Fix a lunch, the three of us."

Pandora had heard this sort of conversation many times before; only the names changed. Malle, Bertolucci, Truffaut, now Dollsky.

She said, "Gentlemen, I'll leave you to sort out the intricacies of international diplomacy." She put on a soft tweed Gillie hat matching her English tweed suit. "I have a lunch date."

Heflin followed her to the door and kissed her cheek. "You look stunning. Like a Modigliani madonna." It sounded like something he had said before.

"Goodness me!" Pandora smiled.

It was eleven o'clock, a Sunday morning. Gorky Park, or the Gorky Park of Culture and Rest, to give it its proper name, was filled with noisy infants and family groups moving across the grass. Girls with small-town pretty looks strolled in pairs; elderly couples kept to the footpaths, arm in arm. The snow had almost melted in the Lenin Hills; only a few patches remained here and there like discarded Styrofoam.

Nobody paid attention to the two men in good clothes, carefully groomed, who walked along a path close to the river where it began its wide loop beside the foc. of the Hills.

"I love park on Sunday mornings. Saint James's was a favorite of mine. Do you know it?"

Buikov said he didn't. He did not look like a man torn with anxiety. He let the Englishman ramble on about the parks he had known in London and Paris, New York and Berlin.

"Forget the flags. A country's true colors are in its parks. A park says more than all the anthems. If you want to understand a country, stroll through its parks on a Sunday. You wanted to talk?" He had suddenly stopped and was facing Buikov. It was an old trick, but always effective.

"A few days ago the head of Department Twelve came to me with a plan," Buikov answered. His tone was gentle and cautious.

They resumed walking in slow lockstep as Buikov continued: "The plan is not to my liking. But for various reasons I find myself fated to go along with it."

"Why do you tell me this?"

"It occurs to me that you might have—discussed it with General Khor."

"Why should you think that?"

"It has a certain style."

"Am I to be flattered or insulted?"

Buikov took hold of the Englishman's arm to guide him around a small hole in the graveled path. "It is meant as a compliment, I assure you."

"What exactly is this proposal? Can you tell me?"

Buikov told him the story, leaving nothing out. He spelled out his own indiscretion, gave Anna's name, her relationship to Zorin, and Zorin's position in Department Twelve. From time to time he glanced around. He did it casually enough, sometimes with a smiling interest in a distant child, sometimes with a concerned look at the clouds, but the Englishman recognized the signs. A pro to his fingertips, Buikov missed nothing: not an intonation in the voice, not a dark place in a smile. He was a man to be handled with the greatest care.

"Did you know she was a Jew?" the Englishman asked when Buikov had finished.

"No."

"Would it have mattered?"

"I would have been more careful."

"Yes," the Englishman said in a noncommittal voice. "Yes, of course." He was surprised that Khor had pursued his idea with such imagination, but was disappointed that Khor had not consulted him. He felt a sense of hurt at being excluded.

"Am I right?" Buikov asked.

"About?"

"You."

The Englishman shrugged. "Sometimes I am used as an instrument is used. I always try to operate impartially—a gyroscope keeping people on an even keel."

"You must have your favorites."

"You are all my favorites."

"That's very judicious."

"What exactly is it you want from me?"

"I'm not sure," admitted Buikov. "Some advice?"

The Englishman had moved a step ahead. He had an air of loneliness, the look you see in out-of-season hotel dwellers. He did not appear like a man who has secured a place in the traitors' pantheon. He turned his head to look at the Russian, his hand limply gesturing to the park around them: "People look at their leaders and believe that some truly cosmic process is at work, some natural destiny. How shocked they would be to discover the truth." He liked to talk, and seemed to do so unguardedly, but Buikov guessed the words hid the sound of wheels going around.

They had been walking for more than an hour. "Khor is a deeply nasty man, but shrewd." The Englishman came to the point suddenly. "He has a peasant cunning."

"Cunning like that is sometimes a sort of genius," Buikov answered.

"You must not assume too apocalyptic an attitude, General Buikov. Do not imagine you are reduced only to defensive tactics."

Buikov knew that he had finally scratched the man's ego, had challenged his sense of machination. "I don't know what else I can do," he said.

"Did he tell you the name of the man he wants to get rid of?"

"No."

"Then I have something to tell you which I think will surprise you. The man Khor wants is Anastas Zorin. He never mentioned that?"

"It must have slipped his mind," Buikov said calmly.

The Englishman chuckled.

"Will you answer me something else?" Buikov said.

"If I can."

"Why Zorin?"

"Too much promise, perhaps?"

"Promise can undo a man, all right, " Buikov said.

They had now turned back, retracing their steps.

"You have heard of the Astors," the Englishman said.

"I know they are rich."

"John Jacob Astor was a German butcher's son. Now the family owns half of Manhattan. In England they are aristocrats."

"The Astors," Buikov said as if it were a name he had been told to remember.

"They had one simple secret. They bought land and sat tight. They let others develop it."

A breeze started to blow, and a couple of kites had gone up across the park. Buikov had made his own kites as a boy. One began to swoop and dive like an eagle. He envied the boy at the end of the line.

"You've got the land, dear boy. Let Khor improve it for you."

"What?" Buikov's thoughts had drifted. "I'm sorry, what did you say?"

"Do nothing. Patience is a kind of strategy too, you know."

"Let Dollsky go?"

"As free as that kite up there is free."

Buikov stared at the kite bobbing and soaring; they were too far away to see the string.

"Doing nothing requires resolution," the Englishman said. "It is a trifle monotonous, but it is not always an activity for meek souls."

"And what exactly am I waiting for?"

The Englishman fixed his amused pale eyes on him. "Why does it have to be a happy ending in the West?"

"Liquidate him?" Buikov grinned incredulously. "A wet job?"

The Englishman shook his head. "Russians cannot cope with freedom. They hold themselves up like the cabman's horse between the shafts. You know the saying."

"Not Dollsky."

"I understand he has certain weaknesses."

"Dope, yes."

"His social impulses—cut loose in the West?" the Englishman said, glancing sideways at the Russian. "With some encouragement from your friends?"

"Debauch him? We let him go and then debauch him?"

"Debauch. What an old-fashioned word that is." The Englishman pronounced it again slowly.

Buikov shook his head. "It wouldn't work."

"Khor wants him out of Russia. You tell me that you're stuck with that. Very well, find a use for him in the West. Make him *your* pawn."

"You really believe—"

"The consuming separation from his roots. My dear fellow, properly handled—the reverberations, the indignation, the sheer fascination of it. A talent like that being corrupted by the West, the permissive society, the whole world looking on."

Buikov thought about it for a long moment.

"It's an awfully neat twist, you know."

"You don't get marks for neatness where I live," Buikov answered.

"Get him into the thick of things. The jet-set people, the beautiful people, whatever damn thing they call themselves these days—they take to people like Dollsky like ducks to water."

Buikov pushed his fists deep into his overcoat pocket.

The Englishman said, "How long did it take Nureyev to get caught up in that world? Hostesses were lining up to give parties for him. They were fighting each other over him."

"He learned to live with it."

"See that Dollsky doesn't."

They had returned to their meeting point in the park. The Englishman lifted his head and sniffed the air appreciatively. "Now I must cut along," he said. "But do think about it, General Buikov."

20

"Ash nineteen hundred." The voice had sounded faraway, as if vitiated by bad ventriloquism. But it was Khor's voice, all right. He used five trysts, as he called their meeting places, each with a single-syllable code name. Ash was Nikolo-Archangelskoe, the municipal crematorium.

Lieutenant Stashinsky, in dark civilian clothes, had given himself plenty of time. The crematorium was on the edge of a small village five miles beyond the city's outer limits. He drove slowly because he thought slowly, and he had a lot of thinking to do. Also, he hated hanging around the crematorium any longer than he had to.

He had been working for Khor for fifteen months. His duplicity did not disturb him; he felt no guilt. Only pity for Zorin—Zorin who knew so much about so many things, who knew how to lay open other people's innermost secrets, yet did not know what was going on right under his own nose.

He wanted to savor the journey. Involuntarily his hand reached out and patted the attaché case on the seat beside him. My future is in that case, he thought.

He had good reason to feel satisfied. First he had found out about Zorin's wife and the head of Special Services. Now this. He remembered how pleased Khor had been when he told him about Anna Zorin and Buikov. But this was the whole case of turnips. There would be more than compliments this time. Perhaps I will even get my own section, he thought. He thought about that for a while.

Only one question bothered him, and it wouldn't go away: Why was Zorin protecting Dollsky? Why should he want to cover up for a maniac? Khor was going to ask, and he had no answer. But if he waited any longer for all the pieces to fall into place, it might be too late. No, he had to report his findings now. Let Khor puzzle out the whys and wherefores. There is much to be said for handing over a case that requires only Khor's final nail, he told himself.

Stashinsky left the highway for a smaller road running through a sprawling petrified forest of wooden crosses of the Russian Orthodox Church. After a few kilometers he turned off the smaller road onto a dirt track winding through a wilderness of blackened undergrowth. Ten minutes down this track he came to the burial walls, standing in the twilight like the remains of some jungle civilization.

He swung off the track and stopped the car beside one of the big walls. Even after driving leisurely he was early, so he smoked a cigarette. At twenty-seven, he had never seen a corpse. His parents and all his grandparents were living. As a child, brought up in the Orthodox Church, he had felt personally responsible for keeping them alive, unfailingly blessing them all by name and address at the end of his prayers. He had never killed a man, although he was trained and prepared for the eventuality. Khor's code name for him was Virgin.

Stashinsky finished his cigarette, opened the window and flicked the butt into an empty niche in the wall. He took his attaché case, locked the car doors, and made his way toward the crematorium.

A low-wattage bulb over an iron door threw a yellow glow down six stone steps. He pushed the bell.

"Lieutenant!" A woman in a white coat stood aside to let him enter. "You are early."

"A few minutes."

She closed the door, slipped a bolt, and led the way down a narrow corridor, her high heels clicking on the stone floor. The building was extraordinarily cool. Stashinsky commented on it.

"The best air conditioning in Moscow. It comes from the same eductors that put the fresh air into the flue to force the gases out of the cremators."

"Oh, really," he said as casually as he could, nervous that his observation might be mistaken for a genuine interest. He didn't want to think about the dead, furnaces, the finitude of life.

She escorted him to a bare, brightly lit office with frosted-glass walls that looked and felt like the inside of an icebox. She sat behind a wooden desk and invited him to sit on a bench that ran along one wall. A long time ago the bench and the desk had been painted a bright shade of blue. An electric toaster and a record player were plugged into a double socket near a stack of records. A television set sat on top of a steel filing cabinet.

"I'm a whisky man myself," she said, opening a cupboard by the side of her desk and taking out a bottle of Johnnie Walker. "You?"

He shook his head.

"Vodka?" She produced a bottle of Monopolowa and stood it on the table like a trophy to be won.

He said he didn't drink at all.

"This is the Comrade General's favorite," she said, looking at the label as if it were the photograph of a much loved child before slipping it back into the cabinet. She splashed some water from a tap into her glass, added about five fingers of whisky and took a deep gulp.

Lifting his eyes, Stashinsky noticed that the office had no ceiling. The lights hung on long electric cords suspended from the crematorium's high vaults. It was as if they were in a bright trap, bound by the darkness around them.

"So all men are liars," she said for no reason.

He looked at her curiously and said nothing. She was small, about fifty, with a lined friendly face. Her hair, a sort of singed color, was cut short in a style that had been fashionable a long time ago. She wore a wedding ring. Her teeth were very white and unmistakably false. Beneath the spotless white coat she wore a cornflower-blue frock the color of her eyes. She reduced the primal horror of the place.

"My name's Vera Volk, by the way."

"Comrade Volk," Stashinsky murmured politely.

"You never?" she asked, holding up her glass.

"I never started."

"You must be in good shape."

"I smoke an occasional cigarette," he admitted.

"I like a man who knows how to look after himself."

"I think it's important," he said stiffly, not sure whether she was mocking him.

"What is it they say—every cigarette takes five minutes off your life?"

"I smoke very little," he said. "Not enough to worry about."

"Five minutes here or there, we all end up the same. All men are cremated equal. Five pounds of ash in the refining chamber."

"Is that all that's left?"

"If I get the burners right. Five pounds of inorganic ash. The soft stuff—the carbon, fat, water—they're no problem. Water evaporates; the rest burns."

A quietness came between them.

Vera Volk helped herself to more whisky and said with regret in her voice, "It would be better if they went in standing up. A vertical committal would cut down the cremator's horizontal dimensions. As the body breaks up, the remains would collect in a smaller space. It would be a great saving."

She picked up her handbag from the floor, took out a small bottle of perfume and dabbed the scent behind her ears and on her wrists. "You're sweating," she said. She took a man's handkerchief from her pocket and wiped his forehead with motherly concern. "You're not getting sick?"

"I don't think so."

"It's easy to catch cold this time of year." She checked her watch. "Anyway, it's time to meet the Comrade General."

She led the way to the committal chamber, where they always talked. "I will come and let you out when you have finished your business."

It was a bare, windowless room lit by a single bulb that hung over a short conveyor belt. The belt ended abruptly at two big furnace doors.

Stashinsky gripped his attaché case that was so full of evidence and promise. The air was heavy with her scent. The last thing he noticed was the small automatic security camera high in the ceiling as it slowly swiveled toward him.

The bullet smashed through the light strong bones of his skull, severing the lowest part of the brainstem from the spinal cord, collapsing his blood pressure and cutting off control of his heartbeat. Deflected upward, the bullet spun through the capillaries, veins and arteries of that part of the brain which held all his memories and most of his hopes. Spinning around his head at a thousand feet a second, it tore apart the frontal vein, the muscles and optic-nerve fibers before leaving his body through the left eyeball.

It was impossible to tell what Mulder Khor was thinking as he watched the killing on the monitor screen in Vera Volk's office. It was not that there was no expression on his face; there was. Something happened to his mouth and eyes, but they were fragments of emotion, too small to make sense of.

Vera Volk dragged Stashinsky's body onto the conveyor belt, and the sound of distant machinery started up.

The furnace door opened. She picked up the attaché case, looked at it for a moment, then placed it like a wreath on Stashinsky's chest as he slowly rolled into the flames.

Khor poured a large glass of Monopolowa, switched off the monitor screen and waited.

Sometimes he wanted to make love; sometimes he just wanted to drink and listen to her records. But he never left the building until the job was finished and the last remains had fallen into the combustion chamber. Suspicious beyond the normal pressures of power, his skepticism was like some baleful vanity.

Tonight he wanted to make love. Writhing and heaving with crude energy, they fucked with loud inarticulate sounds, feeling the distant vibrations of the furnaces through the floor beneath them. When it was over, they lay still beneath the bright electric lights like things waiting to be recharged or reborn.

Khor spoke first. "My first virgin," he said.

Vera Volk laughed a small animal laugh. He could always make her laugh, even when she didn't understand.

They had lunch at Mimmo's across the street from Rufus Gunn's flat, and sat at a table by the window. Pandora unclipped her hair and gently shook it down to her shoulders.

"How's the great Heflin?"

"A true star is like a force of nature," she said, imitating the producer's voice. "Nothing and nobody can stop it."

Rufus smiled. "Still, he's good. He still after Dollsky?"

She nodded. "It's just that he has such a high opinion of himself."

"Some women find him attractive."

"Attraction's a dangerous word. Gravitation is a kind of attraction. It pulls things down."

"Don't be a smart-arse." He grinned and changed the subject. "Who did that picture?"

She looked at the large photograph of herself on the wall. "Bailey."

"I prefer your hair the way you've got it now."

"My boobs were bigger then." She leaned across the table and whispered in his ear. He stared at her. The waiter arrived with their drinks. When he had gone, Rufus said in a quiet, stricken voice, "If I'd had any idea—"

"You'd have let me keep it?"

"Why didn't you tell me?"

"You'd have run a mile. God, you'd have *died*."

He touched the back of her hand, his fingers tracing a pale vein. "Why—"

"I never felt loved enough, I suppose."

"How can you say that?" he asked in a hurt voice.

"I'd have been a hopeless mother and you'd have been a bloody awful father, old bean." She smiled. She was over it now. "Anyway, it was nearly two years ago."

"Life would be so much simpler if people didn't take to loving one another," he said in a gentle voice.

"There's no more bloodiness than the bloodiness of devotion, is there?"

He knew that she didn't want to discuss it. He said, "A little lust is the answer, my pretty. It's by far the most sensible passion. Yield to it with good grace and it's often mistaken for love."

"So it was lust!"

"Never with you."

"Ha!"

"My finger's wet, my finger's dry, cut my throat if I tell a lie," he said, licking his finger, wiping it under his armpit and drawing it across his throat.

"I'm looking forward to the weekend," she said.

Two hours later they left the M4 at the Newbury turnoff. Like most old country houses that people of Rufus Gunn's class call cottages, Little Claymorrow had been built, pulled down, rebuilt, restored and added to, till it was impossible to put a date to it or to see where one period ended and another began. Full of passages and crooked, strangely shaped rooms, it was Pandora's favorite house. She had played there as a child "in the days when I was me." She had lost her virginity there and gone to ground there when her father had defected. The place was seldom discovered even by travelers lost in the narrow lanes that ran like flint veins between the tiny Berkshire villages and landmarks with their incantatory names: Cold Ash, Coombe Gibbet, Inkpen Hill. From some upstairs windows in winter it was possible to see the tower of the Norman church in Blewbury, and faint lavender smoke betrayed Boxford village amid the woodlands. The flagstone hall was cold and homely: gumboots of different sizes were lined up against one wall together with a bicycle, a garden fork, a couple of umbrellas, a pair of shears. A schoolboy's cap had been stuck on the head of a marble bust of the first Lord Gunn.

"I'll get a fire going," Rufus said.

"We should have brought some muffins."

"Chokky bikkies!"

"Bad news for fatties," Pandora said, then, changing her tone, said temptingly, "Strawberry tarts!"

"Doubtless God could have made a better berry," Rufus rejoined in a governessy voice, "but doubtless God never did."

"I'll put the kettle on. Do you like coffee, do you like tea, do you like sitting on a blackman's knee?"

"Two teas for two fleas."

It was strange how quickly they fell into the language and habits, the ritualized responses and giggles of their childhood, when they were alone together. It made their conversations sound silly, but it was a kind of bond, an idiosyncrasy of class, a mannerism of breeding. *We're not at home to Mr. Rude; "I want" never gets; good people must remember that dressing badly does not help the poor.* Nanny's nuggets, Rufus called them. The nursery clichés were an idiom of affinity that joined them together closer than the marital bed ever could.

Pandora sat on the floor, her back against the sofa. The only light came from the fire and the candles on the old refectory table.

"You're not a bad cook for a Lady." He picked up a poker and pushed at a log, sending sparks spluttering high into the chimney. "You'll make somebody a good unfaithful wife one day."

"Don't change the subject."

"I've forgotten. What were we talking about?"

"*You.*"

"Me. Yes, well, I think I'm a fairly uncomplicated sort of chap. My character basically boils down to two things: the desire to make money and a deeper desire to spend it."

"Why do you always want people to believe that you're such a bloody brainless playboy—"

"Being a playboy is a hazardous business, my lovely. Nobody should mess with it if they don't want to get hurt." He looked at the wine in the bottom of his glass. "Open another bottle?"

Pandora's glass was empty. "Oh I'm so easily led."

He opened the second bottle and filled their glasses.

"How's the divine Miranda Jane, by the way?"

"She called Monday evening to announce that she had just taken an inordinate number of pills."

"I don't believe it! What did you do?"

"I sent her a get-well card."

"Rufus, you're such a shit."

"I know. My manners want mending."

"Have you ever really been in love, Ru? Really, really."

"With you."

"It was good with us, wasn't it?"

"Very."

"Aren't you secretly pleased it's over?"

"It's safely in the past now," he said, "but it will never be over for me."

"You'll turn my head."

He brushed the hair off her forehead. "Love is just a trick we play on ourselves."

They sat in silence for a long time, watching the flames, as though lost in thought. It was past midnight when they finished the wine, and the logs had burned down to white ash.

"Up the wooden hill to bed?"

"It's been a lovely evening," Pandora said.

"Will you sleep with me tonight, P.?"

"Let's not and say we did." She smiled.

They slept in separate rooms.

Buikov turned over the pages of the summary prepared for him by the Ministry of Culture. It was Saturday. He was dressed casually in gray flannel trousers with a dark-blue cashmere sweater worn over a blue silk shirt. His blond hair was longer than men in Moscow Center usually wore their hair. Closed in on himself, like a man meditating, it was impossible to guess at the substance of his thoughts; nothing showed on his pale narrow face. He removed his glasses and rubbed his eyes. The glasses, which he never wore in the presence of others, had made a groove in either side of his nose. For ten hours he had worked alone, undisturbed, with claustral calm and concentration.

The Venice film festival had recently been revived after a seven-year break. "It has always been considered the most influential festival: 'the undisputed doyen of festivals,' says the London *Times.*" He read the line in the MOC rundown for the third time. It would seem perfectly reasonable for Nilus Dollsky to choose the major autumn event in the cinema calendar for his first appearance in the West. That was important: everything had to appear natural; nothing should seem out of the ordinary or look contrived. The festival committee had already extended an invitation to Dollsky.

He closed the file. The oddly lingering camphoric smell of old furniture mixed strangely and not unpleasantly with the smell of the hashish he had smoked earlier. He poured a glass of mineral water.

It was all falling into place. When the time was right, he would approve an external passport for Dollsky which the Ministry of Culture would be told to apply for. The timing was important. Valentin Buikov was wise about men. He didn't want Dollsky sitting and brooding, wondering why he was being allowed to leave the country at a time when Mulder Khor was making life uncomfortable for him at home.

Now that he had put his mind to it, Buikov found it an interesting operation. His talk with the Englishman had been productive. It was good to have his suspicions about the gray eminence behind Khor confirmed.

He sipped the mineral water. Since he had given up alcohol two years ago he had lost nine pounds. It added to his fastidious air, and to his aura of quiet, lethal fanaticism.

His hand wasn't as bad as he had first reckoned. He went over in his

mind the different ways he might play it, then set down all the arrangements that had to be made; all the facts that had to be checked; all the
people who had to be bought and briefed and placed. It was past seven
o'clock in the evening when he finally finished.

On his notepad, amid all the scrawls and squiggles, he had doodled over
and over again just four words: *Dollsky, defect, debauch, destroy.* In script,
in block letters, in minuscule and shadow writing: *Dollsky, defect, debauch, destroy.* He tore off the page and several sheets beneath it and
slowly fed them through the shredder in Lieutenant Vlakus's empty office.

Now that his strategy was complete, he had become as relentlessly an
enemy of Nilus Dollsky as was Mulder Khor himself. Yet he was conscious
of the imperfection of his motives, and while programming Dollsky's defection, making it possible for Khor to lay the blame at Anastas Zorin's
door, he knew this was not the end of it.

There remained the problem of Anna. Her name coming into his consciousness now produced an almost palpable sensation of sexual excitement and longing, followed at once by a pang of sadness. Whatever happened to Anastas Zorin after Dollsky defected, his affair with Anna was
finished. Khor had seen to that.

He remembered the message that came with the watch she had bought
him for his last birthday: "Each passing year robs us of some possession."

Zorin was in Leningrad this weekend. Buikov picked up the telephone
and dialed Anna's number, but when it started to ring he changed his
mind and replaced the receiver. Sipping a little of the water from Marien-
bad, he remembered the first time they had made love: that little room on
the second floor of the Central Committee Hotel. A picture of Anna, the
bed, her nakedness, the dark walls of that room, went through his mind.
Her telling him that a woman always remembered the first time she made
love with a man but seldom the last. When he asked her why, she had told
him that most love affairs simply run their course and fade away in a series
of diminishing orgasms. "Will that happen to us?" he had asked. "That's
up to you," she had said. "In the end, the man is always painted the villain," he had said. He didn't know why he had said that, but she seemed
to understand because she had replied, "No, in the end love makes villains
of us all."

It was strange how clearly that conversation, their first intimate one,
came into his thoughts now. He knew then what it was that he wanted.

"Sleep well?" Rufus asked when Pandora brought him a cup of coffee.

"Like a babe," she said. "I've been for a nice long walk."

"What time is it, for Christ's sake?"

"Time you were up."

"Is that an invitation?"

She smiled. "I think I saw the first pair of house martins return. They circled the house a few times, then made for their old corner. Do you remember, Ru? Under the eaves, bits of last year's nest are still there."

"I still don't believe they fly all the way from Bongoland."

"Tough little sods," Pandora said. "I remember Daddy saying that in the autumn when it's time to push off, if a baby's unfledged—too bad, good-bye, baby."

"That's not very nice."

"Question of survival." She sat on the end of the bed and lit a cigarette. "Filthy habit," she said, blowing smoke away from Rufus.

"The best habits usually are."

"I wake up every morning determined to stop."

"I'll have a soak, scrape my whiskers and we'll stroll into Boxford for a little heart-starter."

Holding his hand, Pandora walked for long stretches with her eyes closed, trying to guess where they were. They got to the pub at one-thirty. Rufus ordered a bottle of Chablis, and they drank it with French bread and a flaky Wensleydale cheese that had a taste of honey in it. Rufus bought a cigar and smoked it as they walked back home.

"You all right, Ru? You seem very quiet."

"I'm fine."

"You don't have something you want to talk about?"

"Don't think so."

"How's the cash flow?"

"I'm ahead of the game."

"That makes a change, old bean."

"It happens."

A vapory mist was lifting off the road after a heavy shower that had fallen during lunch. They heard the sound of an ax, then a tree crashing in the woods.

"Poor tree," Pandora said in the silence that followed.

"What would be the last words of a tree?" Rufus said.

"Who was it said they liked trees because they're resigned to the way they have to live?"

"That's nice. I like that."

"I don't want to go back to London."

"Then stay."

"We start fittings Monday."

"That can wait. Christ, you don't even have a director yet."

"I've been trying not to think about it," she said.

"It's going to be fine. You're going to be terrific, Pandora."

"I want you to hold me."

"Feel my heart." She took his hand and put it below her breast.

"You really do get carried away, don't you?"

"If you don't know it now, you don't know it."

"Tell me something."

"*Anything.* Name, rank, number of my Swiss bank account."

"Good old Gilbody, right?"

"You should listen to me, you'd be a damn sight richer."

"I do love you, you know."

"Not enough to listen to my advice. Speaking of Gilbody, did you trace that quote?"

" 'Stop thine ear against the singer'? No, but I haven't forgotten."

She stretched out on the bed. In the dusk her body had a radiance. He licked the front of her throat.

"We didn't eat," she said.

"Are you hungry?"

"Are you?"

"There's a vein in your neck." He licked it. "I'm going to nibble that."

She felt the tension come into his mouth, and she made a little movement in his arms which brought a fresh intimacy to their embrace. After a little while her breathing became a kind of whimper. He moved quickly. Her eyes opened wide in surprise and pleasure. "Christ's blood!" Her voice was shaky. "That's beautiful, that's so beautiful."

After lunch on Sunday Rufus said casually, "What you were asking yesterday, coming back from the pub? Felix Crick came to see me Thursday evening. On a sort of errand."

"Somehow I can't see old Felix as an errand boy."

He lit a cigarette. "Some time ago you know I had a bit of a thing with a certain royal lady."

Pandora smiled faintly. "How's Felix involved in *that?*"

"He was sent to save the lady's rump."

"It isn't over?"

"Oh, it's over."

"Good friends, are you?"

"The melody—the missives linger on."

Pandora began to laugh.

"Leave it out."

"Hell's bells," she said, trying not to laugh.

"I didn't write the bloody letters."

"But they would like them back? Please, sir, can we have our ball back?"

"That was the general drift."

"Frightfully indiscreet, are they, these belles lettres?"

"Some of them."

"What did she say? I won't be shocked."

"Yes, you would."

"So they sent Felix to do the dirty work? Poor darling, he must have been *mortified.* What did he say?"

"That's it, you see. I got the impression that he thought I should hold on to them."

"Hold on to them! Felix told you to keep them?"

"Not exactly. Not in so many words."

"Tell me what he *said.*"

"We talked a long time." He told her the whole story. "At the end he said that since I had all the apparatus for blackmail except the intent, my first duty was to secure the safety of the rest of the letters."

"Was money mentioned?"

"Obliquely," Rufus said after reflection.

"How obliquely?"

"He said that in a situation like this the palace will preach statesmanship but they'll always practice expediency in the end."

This made her smile.

"But once they had the letters under lock and key, would it end there? Would it?"

She looked at him oddly. "What do you mean?"

"In their eyes I've already committed the cardinal sin."

"It takes two to have an affair."

He didn't answer. She went into the kitchen and started some coffee. Rufus followed her. "Now, yes, fine, I have a certain notoriety—lock up your daughters, count your spoons—but they'd see I was exposed to real obloquy. They play hardball, these gentlemen. How do you think the monarchy has lasted so long? They've got it all wired, P."

"And that's why you think Felix was hinting you shouldn't make a deal? As long as you've got the letters—"

"It makes sense, doesn't it? Anyway, one has to be practical. They're not a bad hedge against inflation, are they?"

"You know what I think? I think you should call Felix and sit down and talk to him again. Ask him straight out what you should do. All this oblique nonsense, this court intrigue, is crazy. Just cut the crap and—"

"It would put poor Felix on the spot."

"That's what he's paid for, Rufus—poor Felix nothing."

"Let me think about it," he said, suddenly wanting to end the conversation. "That coffee smells good."

"You *will* think about it?"

"Like billy-o, old thing."

"You're not such a bad egg," Pandora said.

They made love for a very long time. He took her with such a force, with such a sense of desperation, in so many ways—with tenderness, with lust, with a sort of forlorn brutality and a sort of beauty too—that she knew it was going to be the last time. It was as though the old tricks and habits and pleasures would not be remembered.

She felt his hands exploring her, exciting her, familiar hands doing unfamiliar things to her. I'm making love with a stranger, she thought; I don't know this man who is doing these things to me. She shook with excitement.

"Am I hurting you?"

"I want you to," she told him, driving herself backward, her face twisted sideways, wanting to watch, wanting everything. "Yes, oh yes." Her voice was strange and unrecognizable, her throat constricted with the passion that shook her body.

He lifted himself higher on his haunches. She felt the new rhythm moving into her. Slower, longer, deeper and slower.

"*Yes*," she urged him, rolling her buttocks, her ankles kicking in the air behind his back, squirming, frantically trying to force the tempo. "*For me.*"

She's like a wild thing caught and thrashing for its freedom, Buikov thought. His hands moved to her hips and gripped her tight until she was almost still again, then turned her on her back. "Tell me what you feel," he said. "Tell me how it is for you," as he entered her gently this time.

She felt as if an orgasm hung in the balance. She spread her arms. Her breasts felt heavy. She felt juices flowing like warm honey out of her. "I'm so wet," she said, afraid to move, afraid to spoil the sensations, afraid to tell him more. "Did you come into me?"

"I thought I'd never stop."

"You're still so hard."

He kissed her mouth, joining them together completely.

She felt calm again.

She was pleased that they had come back to this first place. Like the first time, she had brought a scented Rigot candle. It flickered on the dressing table, closing the room in deep shadows like a painting half hidden under layers of old varnish. She lay very still, enclosed by the past of that room. She could hear the traffic moving slowly in the rainy night. She loved the hardness of Buikov inside her, pressing hard against her—like a statue pausing in an erotic dance, she thought.

A quiver, like the first tentative jolt of a train about to move, ran through his body.

"Oh, yes, my darling," she whispered, their mouths together.

She used her muscles. He felt it at once. "So strong," he said, shifting his weight on her, pressing deeper into her. "You're so clever, so strong."

He held her with both hands around the back of her neck.

She had never screamed before, not like that. She screamed as if she were being murdered. He smothered her mouth with his hands, but still she screamed. He reached out and found her panties and put them in her mouth but it only excited her more. She bit him like an animal through the silk, and still she screamed.

Afterwards she said, "You were so funny. Do you know what you said?"

"What did I say?"

"You said, 'Be quiet. People will come.' "

"Two people did come," he said.

"Oh we did, didn't we?"

He offered her the joint he was smoking and she took a puff, but she wasn't used to smoking and it was wasted. She handed it back to him.

"Why did you stop drinking?"

"Because it was no longer fun."

"Did you drink a lot?"

"I was beginning to."

"Zorin drinks too much," she said, using her husband's last name as she nearly always did with Buikov.

"When I was forty," he said. "I realized time was running out, so I stopped."

"Our lives are such a little while," she said. "We are all things of a day."

He pinched out the joint and took her in his arms.

"It's over, isn't it?" she said after a long silence.

"How did you know?" he asked softly without surprise.

"I'm glad we came back here," she said. At no time in her life had she felt as sad as she did now. Perhaps it was a kind of loneliness, as if Buikov had already gone away.

"I'm sorry," he said.

"So am I."

"It is not always possible to let matters go on as they will."

"Coming back here to this hotel," she said, "proves that life is cyclic. There's hope in that. Maybe next time around . . ."

"I think not."

"Never never?"

"We've been found out," he said. He spoke carefully, trying to decide how much to tell her, how much she needed to know. "It was a routine check. It was unfortunate; we were unlucky."

"Department Twelve?"

Buikov nodded his head.

"Zorin—"

"No, no," he said quickly. "He isn't involved. He has no idea."

"Just bad luck? You believe that?"

"I'm sure of it. A routine vigil. We were caught."

He could feel the uncertainty in her body.

"It's a mistake to assume that design, plots, clandestinity always motivate the Center," he said in an amused voice. "More often than not it's pure chance. Accident and chance motivate the Center most of the time."

"That's not true," she said, angry at being treated like a child.

"It's true this time."

"Who was it—"

"Mulder Khor."

"What did he say?"

"That it had to end."

"Just that? That's all?"

"He made a meal of it, but that's what it came down to in the end. He didn't want one of his officers being cuckolded by the head of another department. Nothing personal, he was acting in the interest of his own department, et cetera, et cetera."

"You believe that?"

She was not a fool. He said carefully, "I don't know, Anna. He might want to use it sometime. It's something he won't forget."

She moved out of his arms and sat up. "I don't think you're telling me everything."

"Why do you say that?"

"I don't know why. Instinct. Intuition. Like I knew that tonight—that tonight was going to be our . . ."

"What can I say to you? I've told you what happened. What choice did I have? What choice do *we* have?"

"He said nothing else?" she persisted.

He hesitated. "He mentioned you were a Jew."

"You didn't know that?"

"It never crossed my mind."

"And he could make it bad for me, I suppose?"

"It was something I had to reckon with," he said noncommittally. "It was a factor I couldn't ignore."

"He told you about my father too?"

"Yes."

He got up and went into the bathroom. The floor was wet from the shower they had taken after making love, and he slipped and fell. Anna heard the crash and called out.

"It's all right," he said coming back into the bedroom. He was bent sideways, rubbing his shin.

Wound up by the slow mechanism of misgiving and shock, the sight of Buikov naked and doubled up released the tension. She laughed. "If you knew how funny you looked," she said.

He sat beside her on the bed. He had caught his shinbone on the edge of the bathtub, and it began to swell.

"We're a hopeless pair," she said. When she kissed his wound she felt him stir, and her mouth moved upward, slowly, lovingly.

Afterward they slept.

"Do we truly have no choice?" she said in the early moments of waking. They were her first words; she knew he was awake. She could sense his sadness. "There's nothing we can do?"

He held her close. "Once upon a time there was a philosophical hedgehog." He sounded like a parent telling a very young child a bedtime story. "One day this fellow thought, Why do I carry all these needles on my back which bristle at the slightest thing? I will get rid of them. So he did. But a weasel came along and, finding him unprotected, gobbled him up like an egg."

"We don't want that, do we?" she said, rubbing his bristly chin.

"You do see?"

He felt her head nod almost imperceptibly on his chest.

"I shall miss you," he said.

There was the same small movement of her head against his chest.

As she lay in the bath the tears rolled down her cheeks. She wiped them with a face cloth, ran cold water into her cupped hands and splashed her face. There were no more tears after that.

While Buikov shaved she did her face in the bedroom. She could see him reflected in the dressing-table mirror. He looked up and caught her watching him. "Are you going to be all right?" he asked.

"Of course," she said to his reflection. Her voice was calm.

She dressed slowly. She wore dark stockings and a garter belt because they were what he liked best. She pretended to have mislaid her tissues so that she could let him look at her once more as she walked about the room hunting for them. He came out of the bathroom with shaving cream still on the side of his face. He kissed her, smelled her hair and ran his hands over her, stroking the flesh between her stockings and her black panties. She could feel his fingers faintly touching her groin, feeling her warmth.

"I may have to ask you to stop that in an hour or so," she told him, gently buckling her knees and falling into him. He kissed her again, pushed her upright and went back to the bathroom to finish shaving.

Everything she did, everything he did, she thought, is for the last time. The last time I'll see him shave, the last time I'll see him smile and smell his skin and feel his hands between my legs. Stop this, Anna, she said to herself.

"You leave first," he said, coming out of the bathroom with his black leather sponge bag.

She finished dressing. "We'll say good-bye now, then," she said in a steady voice she had rehearsed under her breath.

"Good-bye, little bird," he said. He touched her cheek as she passed and spoke her name.

She didn't look back and didn't hear the door close behind her. She didn't hear what the concierge said to her in the lobby. She didn't hear the traffic. All she could hear was Buikov saying her name as she left him for the last time that Sunday morning in Moscow, in the Central Committee Hotel, in the place where it had begun.

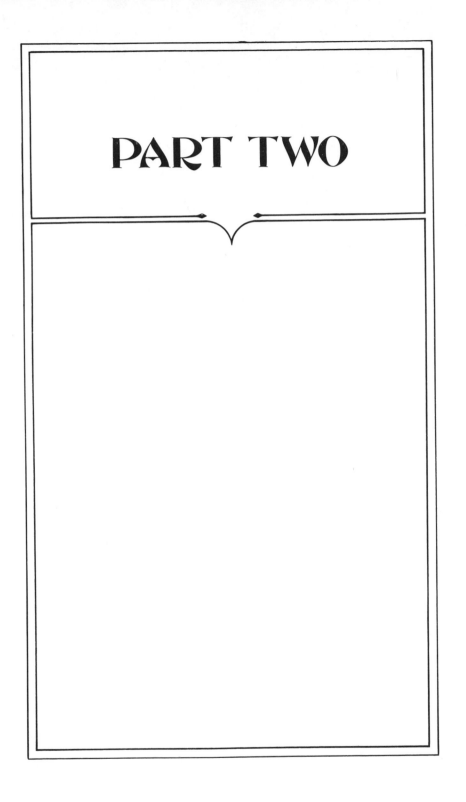

PART TWO

25

"Memories are like old movies. You can rerun them in your mind, recut them, recast them in your imagination, but in the end they are always the same—inviolable," Nilus Dollsky said. "So I never watch my old movies, and I don't have memories. It saves a lot of regret and aggravation."

The restaurant car of the Red Arrow night express from Leningrad to Moscow smelled of solyanka soup mixed with a faint smell of disinfectant.

"How can you not have memories?" the girl from the Ministry of Culture asked. "Everybody has memories."

"Nilus Dollsky is not everybody," he said solemnly. He looked so young that even when he smiled and lines appeared around his eyes and crescents showed in his smooth cheeks, he still looked boyish. It was easy to forget that he was an artist of world acclaim. "People exhaust themselves going over old ground."

"People like to leave tracks," Sonya Petrovich said. "It reassures them."

"I have never set much store by other people's weaknesses. All my energies go into my future. Tomorrow and tomorrow, never yesterday. The next script, the next movie, the next woman. People are shackled by memories—like those strings they used to tie down Gulliver."

"Gulliver?"

"A giant of a man held down by pygmies. You never read Swift?"

She shook her head.

"*Gulliver's Travels.* I will get you a copy. It will help you to understand giants."

"Nilus Dollsky is a giant?"

"Genius was my cradle gift."

"It is a pity you had no gift of modesty to go with it," she said tartly.

There was a long silence, which Dollsky ended with an eruption of laughter. "Yes, yes, good answer," he said throatily between bursts of fresh laughter. "I'm pretty good at showing off, so I show off. Why not? Why not show off a little bit?"

"Why not?" She smiled. "When you're Nilus Dollsky, you're entitled to a few enfant-terriblisms."

"We are going to get on well together. I can't bullshit you."

"I expect you can," she said, "but not all the time."

"You are smart. You know how to wound a man. I like that in a woman."

"Did I wound you?"

"No matter. Like the wounded oyster, the genius mends his shell with pearl," he said, watching her closely. It was the first time he had looked at her properly, or thought of her as a woman at all.

She was an inch or two taller in her heels than Dollsky; her face was small and a little too serious, but that might have been a self-protectiveness that had hardened into habit. He had met a lot of Sonya Petroviches. Listed as liaison officers, they were there to smooth his path, deal with local officials, arrange transport, brief journalists, see that schedules were kept to on the lecture tours periodically arranged by the Ministry of Culture. It was also the ministry's way of keeping tabs on him.

Dollsky had a reputation for behaving badly. One girl had had a nervous breakdown after ten days with him; some of the younger ones he used like whores. Every so often one of them would put in a report to the Ideological Section denouncing his "uncomradely spirit" or his "lack of respect for the collective." He always knew when a bad report had been filed; there were delays in renewing his Beryozka privileges. It was a game that would lose its point if either side admitted it was going on.

Sonya Petrovich held a tall glass of tea in a metal holder between her palms. Twenty-eight or so, she had an intelligent charm that some men found more dangerous than beauty. She wore baggy beige linen trousers and a dark-brown sweater over a man's shirt; a green silk scarf wound around her head pirate-fashion covered her short curly auburn hair. It had been her favorite daytime outfit on the trip; on most evenings she wore a black wool jacket with matching trousers. I've never seen her legs, Dollsky thought.

"Have you enjoyed the trip?" he asked.

"It's been an experience."

"Would you do it again?"

"With you? Why not?"

"That's brave of you."

"You once said that your strength as a director was that you gave actors the confidence to take risks in their performance."

"But you're not an actor."

"All women are actors."

She sipped her tea as she was gently rocked side to side by the sensual motion of the train.

"Where did you hear that—what I'm supposed to have said?"

"Didn't you say it? It's in your file."

"You're the first one to admit that files exist."

"I don't think I can bullshit you either."

He laughed again. "Tomorrow night I will take you to dinner." It was not a request; he took a small diary from his pocket and studied it. "Wednesday we'll have lunch. Afterwards we'll get you some good makeup. You must do more with your eyes. You have beautiful eyes, but they have to be helped a little bit."

Sonya Petrovich felt herself blush. She was pleased that the lights were not bright on the Red Arrow express as it moved through the night across the flat terrain to Moscow.

The black Zil drew up outside her apartment building at exactly 10:00 A.M. "Welcome back to Moscow," Valentin Buikov greeted her as she stepped into the car. The glass partition between them and the driver closed as he touched a button by his side. "You must have much to tell me."

Sonya Petrovich knew he didn't want small talk. Her report was precise and so thorough that she might have been reading from a script: details of conversations, the names of friends and professional colleagues Dollsky had seen, his asides and some of his jokes, anything that might reflect a viewpoint or reveal a private opinion, anything that indicated how his mind worked. She talked for fifteen minutes without a break as the Zil moved swiftly through the city in the lane reserved for VIPs; it was impossible for anyone to follow them without being seen.

"How is his health? He looks pale," Buikov said in an almost commiserating tone when she had finished.

"He showed no sign of fatigue, and it was a hard tour. He's probably tougher than he looks. He darkens his hair, and I think his eyebrows too, which accentuates the look of pallor."

"How do you evaluate the state of his mind?"

She answered with care and a professional sense of orderliness. Not by as much as a nod did Buikov disclose his own thoughts, but he knew that he had found the right woman for the job. He had first noticed her possibilities when she was a clinical lecturer in psychiatry at Vilnius University, and had arranged for her transfer to the Clinic of Nervous Diseases in East Berlin, his domain. He had brought her back for the Dollsky job; not that he doubted the efficiency of Khor's gorillas—their crude, heavy-handed methods usually did the trick—but Dollsky was his pawn now, a special case, and he didn't want any slip-ups. Besides, the flagrancy of Khor's behavior demanded a reply of some kind, and trespassing on Department Twelve's territory, a small transgression, was for the moment enough to satisfy the latent wish for tit for tat, as well as giving him an opportunity to see how Sonya Petrovich performed under operational status. "Does it interest you, this kind of work, Doctor?" he asked when she had completed her analysis.

"It's different."

"The next stage I think you will find more interesting."

"The next stage?"

"I want you to cultivate this private relationship, win his confidence. I want you to put an idea into his head."

"What sort of idea?" She could not help smiling.

"I want him to defect."

She was quiet for a long time, staring out the window. He did not hurry her. "He's very shrewd," she said eventually with no surprise in her voice. "He knows how Ministry of Culture people are used. He'd be on his guard."

"But the initiative is his. Isn't that—psychologically disarming?"

"Plant a thought in his head?" she asked. "Something he must act on?"

"Yes."

"How much time do we have?"

"Weeks rather than months."

She shook her head. "In a year, with that type of man, yes. In six months, possibly. In weeks—it is asking the impossible."

"Let us talk about the impossible."

A small vertical frown gathered the skin across the bridge of her nose. She became aware that the car was moving around the city in circles.

"Planting the idea is only the beginning of a complex activity directed to its realization," she said. "It's a question of creating a climate so that the required idea or belief finally appears to come from within. It must seem to take possession from inside his own skull." She looked at Buikov with a small hopeless smile.

"Please go on," he told her.

"It isn't an easy subject to put into words."

"Take your time." He abhorred halfway answers. "I know it must be difficult trying to explain it to somebody outside your profession."

She was encouraged by his tone. "There is voluntary action and impulsive action," she went on carefully. "The difference is important. Impulsive action follows the isolated conative tendency—the faculty of desire, in simple language. In voluntary action, conations are weighed in their relation to the total system of tendencies that make up the conception of—"

"I'm afraid you've lost me," Buikov interrupted with a small self-deprecating smile.

"Is there a deadline?"

"August twenty-five," he said, surprised by the sudden simple question.

"Well, let us assume that we wish to plant in Dollsky's head the idea of marriage. And, for the sake of argument, let us say that celibacy has been a habit, a principle of a lifetime. Now, we might succeed in planting the idea. We might succeed in getting him all the way to the wedding-palace door. But the conflict between impulse and the normal self—at the last minute, that one false note could prevent the final step."

After a long pause, Buikov spoke slowly: "Tell me about the other way."

"Voluntary action. The transition from the state of suspense to the state of resolution. It has all the outward appearance of free will: counteractive conative tendencies have either ceased to function or they will appear only as minor bottlenecks in the way of realizing the planted ambition."

"But it takes longer? Is that what you're saying?"

"Under controlled conditions—six months."

"We don't have six months."

"There are no shortcuts."

"The dark ways of the mind. I had no idea it would be so tricky," he said, looking first at the backs of his hands and then at his upturned palms.

"Civilians never do," she said, also staring at his palms; they looked very soft. She had never met a man like him before. She knew little about him except that he had the power to manipulate her life. It was hard to believe that this quiet elegant man with soft hands had so much power.

"You don't give me much optimism," he said.

"I'm a psychiatrist, not an optimist."

"The impulsive action," he said reflectively. "That's the only shot we have?"

"But you must risk losing your groom at the—"

"Would you like to try it, Doctor?"

"Do I have a choice?"

"Neither of us does," he said. They were traveling along Aleksey Tolstoy Street for the third time.

26

The brown Cardin bathrobe was a size too large, emphasizing his smallness. He had slept badly despite the sedatives, and now he felt exhausted. But it was not the exhaustion of a sleepless night. The nightmares were back. The nightmares *and* the KGB. Too damn much, he said to himself.

He must have fallen asleep in the bath before he became aware of the telephone ringing. It had that neglected sound, as if it had been ringing for a long time. He waited for it to stop. It was several minutes before the caller gave up. He climbed out of the bath and dried himself slowly.

He dressed in American blue jeans and a white cotton polo-neck sweater, then pulled back the curtains and looked out. The quiet tree-lined street behind Kutuzov Prospekt was empty except for a small plump man in a dark overcoat. A black Chaika was parked a few yards down the street. The driver was reading a newspaper and smoking a black cheroot. They had made no attempt to disguise their presence. They might as well have painted *KGB* on the doors of the car, he thought.

The telephone started to ring again.

It was Sonya Petrovich. "I phoned you earlier." Her voice reverberated a little more than usual as somebody adjusted the recording control; she had a quiet voice. "Were you out?"

"I went for a walk," Nilus Dollsky lied. He often lied to confuse the tappers. He liked to think of the cross-checking that went on between the watchers and listeners: the discrepancies in their reports, the arguments he caused. He carried the phone to the window. The man in the overcoat was talking to his companion in the car. "So," he said looking down at them with bored languor, "are we on this evening?"

They fixed a time.

He made a pot of coffee, took it to his study and read over the pages of the script he had started before the tour. It did not begin well; it was obvious that he did not have a clear picture of his heroine. He had needed a model, and Sonya Petrovich had been it. They had been to the Bolshoi, to the circus, had seen a couple of movies together. She was almost thirty, well educated, independent and not a bit bedazzled by the cinema world or his fame. Her intellect was infused with an irony that still surprised him. She was not his type at all. He wondered whether he would lose interest in her when the script was finished.

He worked well today. When he worked he forgot about the men in long overcoats waiting in the street, about the listeners on the line, about the nightmares. This was the time he loved best. When the small alarm clock on the desk went off, he was startled; it was six-thirty. He read over the new pages. The best dialogue had been lifted straight from conversations with Sonya. He wondered whether she ever noticed it. She had never commented on it when he gave her pages to read. Perhaps she is too embarrassed, he thought. Or perhaps she doesn't recognize herself, the way some people don't recognize their own voices when they hear themselves recorded for the first time.

He began to hum a tune.

"I'm being followed," he told her when the waiter had poured the coffee and gone away. He wasn't drunk, but his speech had slowed down. He'd had two vodka martinis before the wine.

"Who is following you?" Sonya was smiling but there was something in her voice that didn't go with the smile.

"KGB."

"What have you been up to?" It was all she could think of to say.

"What have *you* been up to?" he said quickly.

She was appalled by the possibility of his discovery. She kept her face very still. Her mind raced over possible explanations.

"I think you've told the Ideological Committee bad things about me," he went on in the same accusing tone.

"Dollsky, you're crazy if you think—"

"It was a joke! It's all right. I don't blame you. It happens." He spoke carelessly now, almost as if it didn't matter. "From time to time it happens."

She glanced around the room. "Are they following you now?"

"The man by the window, our left, eating alone. You can look. He knows I know. It's a game."

She turned and deliberately stared at the man Dollsky had indicated. He was eating trifle with a spoon. His face was red and creased with an expression of complacent gloom. The spoon traveled between the trifle and his mouth like the slow-moving part of some machine.

"I don't think it's a very nice game," she said, turning back to Dollsky. "Why do they play it?"

"Our games strip us bare, disclose our secrets. If you want to find out about a man, Sonya Petrovich, play a game with him. Any game—chess, poker, night games. Would you like cognac with your coffee?"

She shook her head. "Do you have secrets, Dollsky?" She was twisting the small coffee cup round and round in the saucer. The realization that he suspected nothing gave her no comfort. For the first time since she'd been caught up in Buikov's world she felt ashamed and a little afraid. The red-faced man was horrible. The whole business seemed almost too incredible to be real. She dismissed the disquieting thoughts with mild coquetry. "Perhaps I should play games with you, Dollsky, and discover your guilty secrets."

"I don't know what guilt is. Steal fifty kopecks from widow, you are swine. Steal diamond tiara from Hermitage, you folk hero," he said, lapsing into his showing-off voice, the clipped solecistic sentences he often used with strangers. "Bigger crime gets, more guilt shrinks."

"You're playing with words. Be careful I don't find you out." She smiled.

"I like to live dangerously."

"Is that why they follow you?"

He shrugged and slouched deeper in his chair. It never seemed to bother him to appear smaller than he was or than the woman he was with. She was still not used to his ways of dealing with situations.

"It's happened before?" She nodded toward the red-faced man.

"Once when I praised Solzhenitsyn for *Gulag*. Once when they arrested him—Yevtushenko and I sent telegrams to Brezhnev saying it would hurt Soviet prestige abroad. Just a *respectful* reminder. I have my own kind of morality, a very *prudent* morality. I distrust glorious causes."

"But why do they do it so blatantly?"

"Intimidatory surveillance," he said, "to concentrate my mind. Empty threats, a triumph of style over substance. An exercise in sinister futility, that is all."

"It must be very unpleasant."

He shrugged. "There are worse fates. What can they do to me? I'm not a dissenter or troublemaker. I don't give a damn about politics. Sometimes I'm a little bit impertinent, but what is that? Changing society is not my worry."

"Still, you should be careful."

"I was never prone to causes except my own." He grinned. "I'm too self-centered."

"Can we go soon?" she asked.

"We can go now," he said, "I hate long dissolves."

The red-faced man stubbed out his cigarette.

The Englishman closed the report prepared by the Military Intelligence Directorate. It told him little beyond the fact that the Mig-25 which had defected to Japan was now back at the Sokolovka air base a hundred miles east-northeast of Vladivostok, and that the pilot was being debriefed in a farmhouse in Virginia that the CIA still believed was safe.

He dialed the Scientific and Technical Directorate, identified himself with a number code and asked to be put through to the controller. "I've got the GRU statement," he said when he had been further checked through a voice print auscultator and transferred to a scrambler line. "What do your people say?" He listened for several minutes while the technical controller expressed his views: it was a debacle, it should never have been allowed to happen, how could the counterintelligence people have given such a high-priority clearance to a *defector*, how could they have cleared such a man to pilot a plane as important as the 25? And where were the Special Services people when we knew the plane was just sitting there on Hokkaido?

The Englishman said that it was an unfortunate business. His tone was patient; he had learned that patience was always the best way to deal with Russians. "I share your concern, Comrade Controller, but may I remind you that there is a great deal more at stake here than engines and missile systems? The secrets of your aeronautical technology are by their nature temporary: *we* have the lead, *they* have the lead, five-minute rides. But if they even suspected what else was in that aircraft—you do take my point?"

Of course he did, the controller replied in a much calmer voice. He was one of the handful of men in the Soviet Union entrusted to keep the biggest secret of all. "It's just that I'm a simple physicist. This other business . . ." He let it go. Even on the scrambler he did not feel comfortable discussing this matter. The Englishman agreed to go to the Russian's office a few minutes' walk away in a beautiful town house on Tverskoy Boulevard.

"How close do you think they might have got?" he asked the controller fifteen minutes later, as he settled himself in an old leather armchair by the tall window on the third floor.

"The canopy had been removed, but that was probably only to get freer access to the cockpit. We've found no evidence to suggest that they attempted any extensive examination of the screen itself," the controller told him, polishing his half-lens spectacles with the end of his tie. "They were probably far more interested in finding out if we'd corrected the 21's vision squeeze. That probably blinded them to anything else in that area. We were putting up a tremendous squawk, don't forget, and they knew their time was limited. It wasn't as if they had all the time in the world."

The Englishman nodded thoughtfully.

"And as you know, we finally didn't trust any of the early-run metal in the computer conductors," the Russian went on in a more optimistic voice. "So even if they did run metallurgical tests, we used only 0.995 fine in all the technology, in the microelectronics, even on the heat shields."

"Is there anything they could have done that might have given them any sort of clue?" the Englishman asked.

"They could have checked the atomic weight of the screen—the specific gravity, say—without our being any the wiser. They could have done so if it had occurred to them. But why should it have occurred to them? After all, they were the first to use liquidization techniques—they used them on the Gemini and Apollo missions, as a heat shield, against thermal radiation glare. They used liquidization on their life-links when they walked in space—it's old hat to them. Unless somebody happened to notice . . ." He stopped to light his pipe and did not finish the thought. He was a tall man, in his late fifties, with short, thick dust-colored hair. He could be a little distant sometimes, and there was an unconscious growl in his tone that deflected from his natural shyness, but he was a kind, honorable man, respected by his staff and liked by almost everyone who knew him.

"You were saying?" the Englishman prompted in the mildly curious tone of someone being polite. "Unless somebody happened to?"

"Oh, a very small chance, really. It was just that the windscreen had a slightly deeper virescent tint than is normal with 0.995. It was probably due more to the new laminating process than to the compound itself. Still, there *was* a very slight visuality regression in the glass. Several of our pilots commented on it."

The Englishman bit the side of his lip worriedly and stared out the window. On the strip of railed grass running down the center of the boulevard a woman was walking a white poodle. It could have been Paris, he thought.

"I still don't think it's a problem," the controller went on. Sympathy had entered his tone. "I'm sure the Americans were far more interested in establishing our range, service ceiling, full-thrust duration—the technological ins and outs—don't you? They would hardly be looking for the stuff of fable? Would you like some coffee? Tea? Something stronger?"

"Coffee would be nice, thank you."

The controller lifted the telephone. I wouldn't like to be in your shoes, he thought with feeling. The Englishman was the chairman of the Joint Coordinating Control Committee that had approved the use of the early-run metal in the Mig-25 windscreen. If anything went wrong, it would be the Englishman who would be holding the bag. It was unfair, of course. Others on the JCCC had pushed much harder for its use than he had—scientists as well as defense policy strategists from Kalinin Prospekt—and bore a much greater responsibility. But it would be the Englishman's head on the block. That's what chairmen are there for, he thought: someone to punish when things go wrong. Since fear is nearly always at the root of committees, it never surprised him when the end result was collective funk.

A uniformed girl brought in the coffee in a silver pot with two slices of Napoleon cake.

"If they *did* find out," the controller asked when she had left, "what would happen exactly? The consequences?"

"The whole world would be in the most fearful mess, my dear chap. The worst kind."

"The whole world? Including us?"

"Including us. Very much so. The Soviet Union backs gold as the basis for international trade. Since we don't belong to the International Monetary Fund and don't have access to IMF credits, gold is as important to us as it is to the West. The West uses it as a standard for the parities of currencies, the guarantee of value for the Special Drawing Rights, for the creditors and debtor positions—"

"It makes," the controller interrupted with a genuinely baffled smile, "physics sound like child's play."

"I'm sorry. I make it sound much more complicated than it is. It's really very simple. The great danger—if anyone found out what we're up to—would be instant demonetization. Gold would have to be withdrawn as a monetary metal, and that, apart from creating God knows what kind of chaos in the West, would most certainly destroy us."

"Perhaps I'm just not very bright," the controller said. He was helping himself to the Napoleon cake, which seemed to take all his attention. "How would the collapse of capitalism destroy us?"

"We've got pressing cash problems; we're very short of hard cash. Bad harvests, a big drop in energy exports, the pipeline sanctions, the constant drain of Poland and Romania—a lot of problems. We're constantly having to press Japan and West Germany for more and more time to settle our bills. More and more we are depending on our gold sales to the West to bail us out."

The controller looked up and smiled. "*Ah*," he said slowly. "Of course. Now I understand."

It was extraordinary, the Englishman thought, how a man so brilliant in one field could be so impercipient in another. "But we have to be careful. The West is already uneasy about the amount we're selling. Nearly three hundred tons this year—three times the amount we sold last year. It's supposed to be a state secret, but Consolidated Gold Fields, a mining finance house in London that keeps an eye on these things, has estimated our output almost to the bar. It's a delicate business; there are so many factors to consider, and one whiff of what's really going on in Uzbekistan—"

"It was only one-sixth of a millionth of an inch thick!"

"One-sixth of a millionth of an inch sounds like an abyss to me," the Englishman said with an apologetic smile.

28

Time was running out, and it was still impossible to tell which way Dollsky would jump. In the last few weeks he had been tense and complained of headaches. He said he had been sleeping badly and had nightmares, but he could never remember what they were about. Sonya Petrovich had put it down to the strain of finishing the script. The surveillance continued: he seemed surprised that it was lasting so long this time. But it was hard to imagine his getting rattled enough to want to defect. He had position, privileges, acclaim, and he knew the game; he took pride in that.

Dollsky lived on the third floor of a beautifully preserved nineteenth-century yellow-brick house on a small residential street running south from Kutuzov Prospekt toward the north side of Red Square. The taxi driver made a mild but unmistakable pass when he counted out Sonya Petrovich's change. He liked boldness on a woman's mouth, he said. It reminded her how much she had changed since meeting Dollsky.

"I had no idea it was so late," Dollsky said. kissing her cheeks.

She saw that he had stopped typing in the middle of a page. "If you want to go on working—"

"That is enough today. Let me fix you a drink."

"Do I smell coffee?"

"Fresh twenty minutes ago." He made his own, a blend of mocha, Martinique and bourbon beans—a secret blend invented by Tolstoy, he said. She never knew when he was being serious.

He disappeared into the kitchen and she sat in the easy chair opposite his desk. It was a high-ceilinged room, painted white, spacious and uncluttered. It contained no paintings, no plants, no ornaments, no photographs or mementos; a sofa, two easy chairs and his desk were the only pieces of furniture. It was the room of a man who drew all his resources from within himself. A box of copy paper, an enamel mug filled with pencils, a Sony digital alarm clock, a dictionary and a thesaurus were neatly placed on the desk alongside the finished pages of the script. If it were true that neatness was the test of character, Nilus Dollsky would be perfect. Sonya Petrovich found the tidiness merely touching. The ascetic orderliness, the signs of so many solitary habits and routines, his unadjustable ways of doing things, all the evidence of an inward lonely man was there on that desk. It was the room of a man who disowned even his own memories.

He returned with the coffee and a vodka martini for himself.

Sonya held up her cup. "To the new picture," she said.

"To the new Sonya Petrovich," he replied, touching the cup with the glass.

"The old Sonya Petrovich with a new coat of paint." She told him what the taxi driver had said.

It was as if the compliment had been paid directly to him. "You see, I was right. And the shadow in your cheeks makes the bones here more striking."

"If you like bones, Dollsky, I'll send you an x-ray of my foot."

"I have made you beautiful," he said solemnly.

"You're a genius." She was embarrassed. "Is there anything I can read?"

"You're not just being polite?"

"I want to."

He rolled the page out of the typewriter, put it beneath a dozen or so other sheets and handed them to her.

"All this today?"

"A rewrite of the circus scene."

He watched her closely, wondering whether she would connect it with their own visit to the circus. He had used her reactions. The girl's short monologue recalling her first visit to Moscow as a child came almost straight from her. The script was his vision of Sonya Petrovich and of her vision of the world. It was a strange feeling watching her read those pages now.

She read slowly. Sometimes her lips moved as she almost spoke the dialogue aloud; sometimes she smiled; sometimes she made little noises of approval and nodded her head. When she came to the end, she straightened the pages, tapping them down on the desk with a grave look. "It gets better and better," she said after a long pause.

"You've been a good influence, Sonya Petrovich."

It was the closest he had come to acknowledging her immanent collaboration. It was nice to be the model for his heroine, even though she had decided not to recognize herself. She was afraid that to talk about it openly, to risk an analytical discussion about expectations and convictions invented out of her own personality might reveal too much. It was like hiding the fact that you understood a language well when people were using it around you. This constant deception was one of the things that made her so self-conscious with him. She knew that little escaped his notice, even when he had been drinking or was high on one of his drugs.

"I'm writing faultlessly—like a computer," he said, suddenly morose.

"Is that bad?"

"It's not good. The temptation is to *become* a computer. The temptation is to base everything on technique and tricks."

"We should all be accessible to temptation sometime," she said, thrown by his sudden change of mood. She still had no idea how his mind worked. The outburst appeared disconnected; it didn't seem any part of what had gone before. Was he playing games with her? Was he getting pleasure out of her confusion?

"That sort of temptation," he said, "is the temptation to become merely accomplished. My compulsion to be good needs to be exacerbated. Nilus Dollsky has to be *driven*."

"Then I must try to drive you. You must teach me to excite you." She surprised herself by the salacity of the remark. Even as a joke—and they had only joked about sex together—it surprised her.

"Let me read you something." He left the room and returned quickly, turning over the pages of a book.

"What's that?"

He turned it over and read the title with a small grin. "*La Vérité sur Nilus Dollsky.*"

She repeated it in an impressed voice.

"They love me in France."

"You speak French?"

"I speak English better." For nearly a minute they remained silent while he searched for what he wanted to show her. He stopped turning the pages, and there was a different kind of silence between them while he read through a passage, silently at first. Then: "This critic says that I should leave Russia. He says that I should work in another country. He says I need that to develop, to grow as an artist. He says—and this is his conclusion—" He found the beginning of the passage with his finger and started reading in his actor's voice: " 'To stay too long in one land is to capitulate to comfortable deceptions and to settle for illiberal truths.' "

Sonya Petrovich felt her heart begin to pound. Had the weeks of subtle pressure, the slow careful drip of ideas finally paid off?

"What do you think?"

"It's an interesting thought," she said noncommittally. "I'm not sure I care for the way it's expressed."

"Of course, that's just capitalist bullshit. But the *idea?* The premise? Isn't that valid? I'm getting a little bit stale, perhaps. Same actors, same technicians, same studio—"

"But isn't it good that people can recognize a Dollsky movie?"

"But not because it is just like the last one and the one before that."

"I didn't realize you were so unhappy."

"Neither did I."

They looked at each other.

She said, "You feel you've somehow capitulated—*settled,* is that it?"

"To whatever, for whatever," he said. "It's death. Don't you see?"

"Yes, I do," she said purposely as if she didn't. "But we must all live with some self-deceptions, some reassuring lies."

"That's death," he said again.

"What are we going to see this evening?" She changed the subject at the psychological moment.

"The new Krzysztof Zanussi picture."

That night she wrote her final report to Valentin Buikov announcing Dollsky's critical state of resolution. It was a long report, and it was after three o'clock when she finished and had read it though. She frowned and squeezed her eyes tightly together. When she opened them again, she began to tear the pages slowly into small pieces. She went to the bathroom and dropped the pieces into the lavatory and flushed the bowl several times until the last fragment had disappeared. She went to the kitchen and boiled some milk. Her back ached; she felt very tired. The milk almost boiled over. She caught it just in time and poured it into a mug and took it into the bedroom. Sitting on the edge of the bed, she sipped the milk and thought about Nilus Dollsky. What would it have been like with him? Why had nothing happened between them? She was pleased now—no, not pleased: thankful, and a little sad in a way that she couldn't define. After a while, she took a postcard and several envelopes from her bedside table. She wrote three words on the card, sealed it in one of the envelopes, which she then put into a larger, thicker envelope. She went back to the kitchen and sealed the outer envelope as instructed with the white of an egg to prevent it from being steamed open. In this day and age, she thought. She wrote Buikov's name in block capital letters and the address of a small hotel in the east end of Moscow. It was her ninth report.

29

He was a small saturnine man with a thick nose and bulging watery eyes who smelled of shag tobacco. The lack of eyebrows gave his face a naked unfinished look. He unlocked a small safe and removed an envelope with both hands as if it were something precious but puzzling. "It came this morning early," he said with a heavy Georgian accent.

Buikov took the envelope like a parent removing something harmful from the hands of a retarded child. He stood by a window that overlooked a stone courtyard that had been partly roofed over with red tiles, trapping the summer heat. Inspecting the seal, he slit open the two envelopes with a gold penknife, removed the postcard and read:

HE WILL GO

The smile came onto his face slowly.

"I got you coffee." The Georgian appeared through a door behind a bench that had once been the backseat of a bus.

"So the wine is poured," Buikov said, taking the cup. "Now we drink it."

The Georgian looked confused.

It was August 8. There was no time to follow his usual procedure, outlining the overall strategic purpose, inviting senior officers and section heads to make suggestions, meeting with them one by one to explore their ideas and listen to their views. He had seventeen days.

He sent for the file on Felix Crick, going back to the beginning, and went through everything. He had Registry rummaging for records, texts and photographs—material not looked at since the thirties. His own people knew, and the communications people knew, that something was on, but nobody knew what it was. In Registry the clerks made bets on what he would ask for next. At 1:00 P.M. he enciphered a short zemstvo message to the embassy in London, and took it to the communications room himself. Only ambassadors and first secretaries were authorized to deal with zemstvo traffic. At five o'clock a one-word open cable came back from London. It read *Affirmative*, and was signed by the first secretary. Shortly afterwards he ordered up the current RI/HW/10 file.

Nobody in Registry had money on that one. It was the file on the British royal family.

It was almost eleven o'clock before Buikov sent for Vlakus. "I'm going to London for a few days." He waved the lieutenant to sit down. "Let's look at some of our in-play pieces that might need attention in my absence."

Vlakus was efficient, his instincts were good, and traffic was always at a minimum on weekends; the West liked its weekends in the country. After the briefing, Buikov handed him a copy of the "talking paper" he had prepared—the oral demarche, as it was more properly known. "Go through it carefully, Lieutenant. If it differs in any way from your own notes or your understanding of anything I have said, tell me in the morning. Is there anything you want to ask me?"

"Venice, sir?" Vlakus was surprised that it had not been mentioned.

"Ah, Venice." Buikov said it as if it were a small matter that had slipped his mind. "I don't expect any developments on that front—not yet." It was still too soon to let Vlakus know the reason for all the Italian activity in the past weeks. If all went well in London, he could dispense with the Italians completely.

"Speaking of Venice, I spoke to Tarkovsky at the Ministry of Culture this morning," Buikov said casually. "He wants Nilus Dollsky to go to the festival this year. The Italians have invited him. Tarkovsky will submit an application for an external passport. We shall approve."

It was past midnight. Buikov did not move, but sat looking into the young officer's face. He noticed how old Vlakus's eyes looked. They were cold gray craters. He had never noticed this before.

"It's been a long day," he said. His voice was friendly, not the same voice he had used for the briefing. "You've done well, Vlakus."

"There were some calls, sir, but you asked not to be disturbed."

"I'm on the nine o'clock Aeroflot. You can drive me to the airport. We'll go through them in the car."

Vlakus arrived at the apartment at seven o'clock looking as if he had just returned to duty after a month in the country. Buikov's housekeeper gave him scrambled eggs, bacon and black coffee. He ate alone in the kitchen while Buikov finished dressing. It was extraordinary how different Vlakus looked out of uniform, more like a professional sportsman than an honors graduate of the Frunze Military Academy and an officer of the KGB. He wore a brown herringbone jacket, a green striped necktie and brown corduroy trousers. Out of uniform, he seemed to smile a lot more.

There was little traffic on the road. Vlakus had no queries. He found Buikov's text of the briefing in accord with his own understanding. He took a folded sheet of notepaper from inside his jacket. "A list of the calls yesterday, sir. The ones I've marked have been dealt with."

There were five names. Alongside each one Vlakus had noted the exact time of the call. Buikov read one name aloud. "The fixtures-and-fittings man," he said. "Perhaps at last we're going to get our new furniture, Lieutenant."

"There was one other call, sir. A woman, sir. She called three times. She wouldn't leave her name, sir."

"Through the switchboard?"

Vlakus thought for a moment. "Our own line, sir, I think."

"So all is well, then," Buikov said pleasantly. "Just remember Talleyrand's advice to young politicians: And above all, not too much zeal!"

The Lieutenant grinned. "Yes, sir."

"So tell me, Vlakus. What is happening at the Center that I should know about?"

"There's little you don't know, sir."

"I wish that were true," Buikov said. "No scandals, no goings on?"

"You heard, sir, that they found Stashinsky's car yesterday? Lieutenant Stashinsky, sir."

"He lost his car?" Buikov seemed mildly bemused by the information.

"The car, sir, and Lieutenant Stashinsky, sir, both went missing a little while back. He joined Department Twelve not long after I came to you, sir. We were at the academy together, sir." Vlakus cleared his throat nervously. He had never talked so much with Buikov before. "He was Colonel Zorin's adjutant, sir."

Buikov continued to gaze out the window. Some of the streetlamps were still on, like fluorescent oranges at the top of long sticks. They seemed to give a loneliness to the streets, like lights left burning in an abandoned house. "And now your friend's car has turned up?" he asked offhandedly.

"He wasn't a friend, sir. I just knew him a long time."

"And where did they discover the car, Lieutenant?"

"Out at the Nikolo-Archangelskoe Crematorium, sir. What was left of it. The local villains, sir, obviously found it first. The wheels had gone, they'd smashed open the doors. Apparently, sir, it was an empty shell inside. Stripped bare."

Sheremetyevo had the intense atmosphere of a busy hospital rather than an international airport. No Muzak, no tanoys spilling out gate numbers, boarding calls, arrival times, apologies for the interminable delays. Travelers gathered in front of the electronic information boards, silent, solemn, expectant, like crowds waiting for a bulletin on a dying and beloved leader.

"There's no point in your waiting, Lieutenant."

Vlakus started to salute, remembered he wasn't in uniform and grinned sheepishly.

Buikov held out his hand. "Anything I can get you in London?"

Vlakus looked flustered by the offer.

"Shirts? Soap?" Buikov suggested helpfully. "Would your young lady like something?"

"Perhaps a record, sir? A Rolling Stones record, sir?"

Buikov nodded. "One final thing. Are you familiar with the word-left procedure?"

"Yes, sir."

"Beginning twelve hundred hours in-zone time Sunday, place a word-left call every three hours. Use the Novosti Press Agency. Our old friend, Mr. Principal."

The TU-154 left Moscow ninety minutes late, lifting steeply, the nose twenty degrees up, on full power. Buikov took the negotiating scenario from his briefcase, but did not open it. Something else was on his mind: "They had smashed open the doors," Vlakus had said. But why had Stashinsky locked the doors of a car, hidden in the middle of nowhere, if he had not intended to return? Nobody bothers to lock up a car, or anything else, that they plan to abandon. Buikov went over it again and again in his mind. Zorin's adjutant disappears. The day his car is found a woman telephones three times on the restricted line. Anna Zorin knew that number. She was the only woman Buikov could think of who would repeatedly refuse to say who she was, who could not *possibly* say who she was. Had something happened that was so serious, so disturbing, that she was forced to break her promise, the promise they had both made, never to contact each other again? Three calls. Anna was a level-headed woman. Three calls told him a lot about the state of her mind and the depth of her anxiety.

With an effort he turned his attention to the London brief.

He went through immigration using a diplomatic passport. His bag was mislaid long enough for MI5 to arrange a tail. There it was, five or six cars down from the embassy Zil. A Ford Cortina, dark blue, three occupants.

"We've got company, sir," the chauffeur told him.

"You've made the necessary arrangements?" Buikov asked, looking straight ahead.

"Yes, sir."

As the Zil moved off slowly the Cortina tucked itself in behind a couple of cars back.

"Just the one, you think?"

"They vary it, sir."

The Zil picked up speed.

At a red signal before the exit underpass a heavy hydraulic commissary truck eased out of a service sliproad and sat behind the Zil.

The Cortina pulled out and sat behind that.

The signals changed.

The Zil moved slowly into the underpass: *Welcome to London*. The truck followed, the Cortina close behind it.

What happened next happened quickly. The truck's headlights flashed once. The Zil picked up speed. The truck jerked forward as if pulled on a towline, veered to the right, overcorrected, shifted down a gear, and hurtled into the wall. The impact jammed the horn. The hydraulic body started rearing slowly into the air on its scissor-legs like a wounded howling beast, and toppled over exactly in the middle of the underpass.

The man who did that was a professional; he had picked the angle, the speed, the spot. It took skill as well as nerve to block a road so completely.

Seconds after the Cortina had slammed into the underbelly of the truck and glass was still breaking, almost before the screams, the smell of blood and gasoline and fumes set off the panic as more cars and an airport bus piled into the wreckage, Valentin Buikov was changing cars. With a new passenger, the Zil continued to London.

The red Japanese Datsun Sunny turned west away from London on the M4. "We'll double back through Windsor, sir," the driver said. "Have you ever been to Windsor, sir? The Queen of England lives at Windsor, sir."

30

Buikov took a taxi to the Imperial War Museum. "Used to be a bloody loony bin. Bethlehem 'ospital it was when my old man was a nipper. Bedlam, they called it rand 'ere. Now it's the bleedin' War Museum. Somebody mustuvada soddin' great sense of 'umor." The taxi driver kept talking as he counted out the change so that there was plenty of large silver for the tip. Buikov gave him fifty pence on top of the fare from the Strand. A generous tip for a short run across the river, he reckoned.

The museum didn't open until two on a Sunday, the taxi driver told him. "You got the Three Stags on the corner." He nodded toward Kennington Road. "*Bierkeller, ja?*" He prided himself on always being able to spot a German; they were good tippers as a rule, especially if you threw in a bit of kraut like *Guten morgen* or *Bahnhof* or *Das ist recht.* "*Bierkeller, ja?*" he said again. "*Bierhaus?*"

"*Ja, ja,*" Buikov said solemnly. "*Danke schön.*"

He had miscalculated the journey and was more than thirty minutes early. He bought a paper at a small newsagent's shop and strolled back to the pub. Crowded with the Sunday prelunch crowd, the smoky atmosphere was as friendly as an impromptu party. It took him ten minutes to be served at the bar and find a corner to stand in. He did not want to be drawn into conversation and used the newspaper as a screen. He did no more than glance at the headlines as he sipped his shandy: he was thinking about the meet. But one inside-page headline caught his eye: SOVIET DEBTS RISE. It was a short item, and he read it through:

> The Bank of International Settlements in Basle has revealed that the Soviet Union's net debt to Western banks has risen by more than $9,000 million in the past 6 months. International bankers are viewing with growing alarm the increasing amounts of Soviet gold, oil and timber being offered for sale in recent months. Gold sales last year more than trebled to over 300 tons compared with the year before.

Buikov thought about the Englishman and smiled behind the newspaper. He must be working his tail off, he thought: advising Khor and me *and* struggling to solve the Soviet cash crisis. He looked at his watch; it was time to move.

He crossed the road and walked slowly past the house opposite the museum. It was a narrow, well-kept building rented as flats. In the forties and fifties it had been a Soviet safe house; never blown, it had been discarded in the sixties in line with the KGB's "prevision insulation" policy. He walked to the end of the block, crossed the road again and strolled back. There were five bells on a polished brass plate screwed to the wall, with names in small plastic slots by each bell: R. Shepherd; Bill Edwards; W. Pratt; Misses Tasker and Scofield. He pressed the one bell alongside a piece of plastic without a name.

Crick stared for a moment at the Russian. His face might have been Scandinavian, he thought, or pure Saxon: blue eyes, soft blond hair and oval head.

"Do please come in." Crick carried a book in his hand and had the faintly bemused air of someone interrupted in the middle of an engrossing read. It was a device he used when he was especially on his guard. He closed the door quietly, like a man aware of people sleeping, and slowly led the way along a narrow, dim passage and up the stairs to the second floor. He helped Buikov off with his raincoat, slipped it on a wooden hanger and put it in a closet in the tiny hallway. "The secret about living in a small flat is absolute tidiness. A place for everything and everything its place. Sherry?"

Buikov shook his head.

Crick poured himself one, moved over to the window and looked down. Lambeth Road was deserted in one of those August drizzles that Londoners hope presages a fine September.

"It's all right. I'm clean."

"My dear fellow," Crick said as if he had never doubted the efficiency of Buikov's precautions.

Buikov sat in an old, low brocade armchair. An Oriental rug covered most of the floor. The curtains were blue velvet, rather worn, and showed the dust. The room was stuffy. But it was not the stuffiness of a room left unused for long periods; rather, it was that strange smell created by the very old, by people who won't break with the past. There was no radio or television in the room, and Buikov could not see a telephone. His mind raced over Crick's file. There is no London number, he remembered. There were books on the dining table, volumes in old leather, a bottle of Croft's, three sherry glasses. A white azalea plant partly obscured a framed photograph of a group of young men in white flannels and shirts. Even from across the room it was easy to spot Crick cross-legged in the front row holding a cricket bat like a banjo. He had more hair then, thick and wavy, but the wide humorous mouth and that beak of a nose were unmistakable. Buikov moved his eyes back to Crick. He was a much larger man than he had imagined him. Photographs gave no hint of his size.

Crick sat at the table, his hands held loosely together in a perfunctory praying gesture, waiting for Buikov to begin. But the Russian was in no hurry to get to the point of his visit. The small talk was preparing him for an important discussion in a foreign language.

Buikov was younger than Crick had expected; that was the only real surprise. Down the years, with the antennae of a blind man, Crick had compiled a picture of the Russian that was as accurate as any dossier in Moscow Center. Crick knew he'd be fastidious from the questions he had asked, the points he picked on. And the Italian shoes and Paris suit and well-kept hands did not hide the fact that he was also the sort of man from whom one day you might wish to flee for your life.

So there they were: two men who had communicated in their strange and perilous ways for so long, yet had never met before, had never shared a meal, never had a conversation or laughed at a joke together, had never looked into each other's eyes. Two contemplative men who worked best secretly and alone.

Buikov had been talking for nearly twenty minutes when he suddenly said, "Your last communication interested me."

So it began. It was not an interrogation, but it was no longer a conversation either.

"These letters. Genuine, you say?"

"Judging by the tizz the palace is in."

"Please?"

"Yes, genuine."

"He has them still?"

"I advised him to sit on them."

"Sit on them?"

"Keep them. Do nothing for the moment."

"Good. That is good. Sir William Bunbury, you have told him what?"

"That I'm looking into it, doing what I can."

"And he is satisfied?"

"He understands that you can't rush these things."

"Love letters? Not political letters?"

"Not overtly. Some embarrassing asides."

"What does this mean, please? Overtly?"

"In that area there is no point where privacy ends and politics begin."

"In ordinary circumstances I would not be interested in this woman's affairs."

"But these are not ordinary circumstances?"

"He is still—what is English expression?" Buikov asked, without answering Crick's question. "Tied up to roofbeams?"

"Rufus? Strapped to the ceiling?"

"Strapped to the ceiling," Buikov repeated slowly with an appreciative nod. "It means he has no money, yes?"

"No serious money."

"Serious money?"

"He gets by."

"But he has many debts. To bookmakers, to his gambling club. Twenty-seven thousand pounds."

"Englishmen of his class always owe their bookmakers, bootmakers and tailors. They don't believe in frittering away their money on tradesmen's bills."

Buikov did not smile. "It is a lot of money, twenty-seven thousand pounds."

"A tidy sum," Crick agreed. He was impressed with Buikov's performance: the names, the details, the sums of money, all in his head.

"A year ago you sent profile. You brought him to our notice, Rufus Gunn. Why you do this?"

"Because of his connection. He was deeply disenchanted with his father and—"

"*Lord* Gunn," Buikov interrupted, wanting to keep it straight in his mind as they went along: the complications of English nobility, the tangled genealogy, the intermarriages and mixed bloodlines always confused him. "That is Lord *Toby* Gunn, father?"

Crick nodded. "Rufus had just been disinherited. I thought it was a situation worth recording." Crick smiled bleakly. "If only as a piece of English social history."

"Lord Gunn called his son society middleman?"

"A sore point with Rufus. It came too close to the wicket."

"But you say *true?*" Buikov asked.

"Oh, perfectly."

"Because he takes money to introduce the show people, people in theater, to his friends in the society?"

"Yes." Crick thought it best to stick to simple answers.

"Yes," Buikov repeated, looking strangely at him, expecting him to continue.

"He is a photographer," Crick said after a silence. "He meets a lot of people. He used to be a theatrical agent. He's been many things in his time."

"Tell me how it work—middleman."

"I suppose exactly the way it sounds. Actors want to hobnob with princesses. Princesses like to meet their favorite actors."

"And he get money for this?"

"I don't believe there's an actual exchange. I assume it's more subtle than that."

"Under the counter?" Buikov said, pulling out the dated phrase. It reminded Crick of those Indians who had learned their English before the war, at the peak of the empire, and still talked as if Elgar were playing quietly in the next room.

"A question of give-and-take," Crick said. "Man is a reciprocating animal, the only reciprocating animal. Undoubtedly, he gets a rewarding amount of work out of his introductions."

"Answer me this, please. He still is in good position in the society?"

"He knows *everybody*. He is drenchingly well connected."

"These dealings—it is common knowledge? He has not been—what is word—made unwelcome by his friends? Forsaken? There is other word?"

"Abandoned?" Crick offered. "Blackballed?"

"*Blackballed!*" Buikov said, delighted with the find. "He has not been blackballed?"

"When he puts his mind to it, he can charm the birds out of the trees. It makes him a hard man to moralize about. It's impossible to be angry with him for long."

Buikov stood up, went to the window and examined the sash. Crick sipped his sherry and finally Buikov returned to his chair.

"Let us move on. We come to recent events." He rubbed his eyelids with the tips of his fingers in small circles. "He introduced Englishman's daughter"—he stopped rubbing his eyes and smiled at Crick—"Pandora Child, the Lady Pandora Child he introduce to film man Lyall Heflin. Have you heard of lawyer Walter Greenspan? He has offices in Bedford Square?"

"I don't think so." Crick feared he was losing the thread.

"He is lawyer for Heflin. Walter Greenspan?"

"The name isn't familiar to me."

"He make inquiries about Soviet subject, Nilus Dollsky. You heard of Nilus Dollsky, I think?"

Crick nodded. "What sort of inquiries, may I ask?"

"Heflin want Dollsky to make film in London, and in France also. Greenspan talk to our cultural attaché. Cultural attaché talk to Moscow, Ministry of Culture. Ministry talk to us. Backward, forward, many papers, many desks."

"Bureaucracy is bureaucracy the world over."

"I could make possible for Rufus Gunn to acquire Dollsky."

"*Acquire* him?"

"Make contract, make deal, become agent."

"That is a sort of acquisition, I suppose."

"That would be worth plenty money, I think."

"If Dollsky were in the West, I imagine it would."

"I fix. I fix for Rufus Gunn to deliver Dollsky here in West."

"It sounds all terribly obliging." Crick smiled, blinking with an expression of cynical patience.

"But first I buy letters."

"*Ah.*" Crick pulled his ear reflectively. "That mayn't be so easy, you see."

"He does not like money?"

"It isn't necessarily a question of money. Some people—"

"Let me tell you about some people, Professor Crick. You don't teach some people greed. Like you train animal. You let animal tell you what he can do. The monkey in circus that goes to bicycle, that is monkey you teach to ride bicycle. Rufus Gunn, already he has gone to bicycle."

"The difference between—"

"No difference. Us or newspapers, no difference. Only maybe we never publish letters."

"I don't understand, Mr. Buikov."

"I define my position. I control very big budget. Very large. But my organization is bureaucracy. As you say, bureaucracy is bureaucracy, whether is in Whitehall or Washington or Moscow. It want receipts. Bureaucracy cannot work without receipts. Without receipts it cannot function. This makes life sometimes difficult for me personally."

"I can imagine."

"I want Rufus Gunn perform service for me. It must be paid for, this service. I want my people not to know where money exactly goes."

"You wish to hide for the moment your involvement?"

"It possible I won't *ever* want them to know."

"If it doesn't turn out the way you hope?"

"The tree is known by its fruits."

"And your business being the inexact horticultural science it is—"

"You understand."

"And the letters are—"

"Something to pin to expenses."

Crick smiled. It was the first consciously amusing thing Buikov had said, the first indication that he had any sense of humor at all. "And the service, Mr. Buikov?"

"I want him go to film festival in Venice. We know Dollsky is maybe thinking already that he will leave our country."

"Jump ship? *Defect*, Mr. Buikov?"

"I want Rufus Gunn to oblige these thoughts Dollsky have."

"Good Lord!"

"But afterwards, in West, middleman must lean little bit more our way. He must not be so much in middle."

"A middleman by definition—"

"There is also middle state between being and not being: becoming. There is saying in my country: I am becoming what I am not."

Crick looked puzzled.

"I want middleman to give Dollsky everything. He want women, plenty women. Boys if he want boys, plenty boys. He has appetites, much curiosity. Drink, drugs, *paradise*— if that is what he want I want him get it. The cost will be very much for these things, but no matter. You understand what I say, Professor?"

Crick said nothing. He could see Buikov measuring his silence, gauging his comprehension.

"Good," Buikov said eventually, satisfied that Crick had grasped the situation. "Now, the money. How much these letters you think they worth?"

"I haven't given it a thought."

"In dollars I think two hundred and fifty thousand." He took out a thin gold ballpoint and made a rapid calculation on an Asprey notepad. "At rate now is almost one hundred and fourteen thousand pounds. Take away twenty-seven thousand he owe—eighty-seven thousand pounds."

Crick watched him make another rapid calculation.

"One hundred and ninety-two thousand American dollars after he settle debt."

"To launch Dollsky in society?" Crick asked incredulously.

"I think we should pay not all in one piece." Buikov nodded as if the matter had been settled. "I think first payment, then—"

"A slush fund, Mr. Buikov? You want me to operate *a slush fund?*"

"For middleman's expenses."

"Hold your horses, Mr. Buikov, hold your horses. Are you actually suggesting that we *tell* Rufus? Spell it out?"

"How else—"

"Won't work," Crick said flatly. "My dear fellow, he's bound to want to know *why*. What do I tell him when he asks awkward questions?"

"Tell him nothing. Let him draw own conclusions. He know you Bunbury's emissary, palace go-between. What he think if you tell him nothing?"

"You think he will ascribe his good fortune to Miss Havisham, do you?"

"Why should he suspect Magwitch?" said Buikov, who knew his Dickens.

Crick grinned. "Are you sure you won't have a glass of sherry?"

"I don't."

Crick refilled his own glass, sauntered across to the window and gazed out. "Let's think about this," he said turning toward Buikov.

"What is to think? I tell you already he has gone to bicycle."

"I do believe we can persuade him to hand over the letters. You are perfectly right—my involvement would seem to sanction that transaction. That takes care of your—outgoings. But why not separate the two issues and proceed as if they were entirely separate matters? The letters. Dollsky."

Buikov waited for him to continue.

"Do you have contacts in Venice? People who can get Rufus invited to the festival?"

Buikov nodded. "How you explain invite to such person?"

"I believe these sort of occasions positively *vie* for the presence of the Rufus Gunns of this world. Who knows who he might turn up with? A princess? A famous heiress? A President's widow? People like Rufus are considered practically the condition of success in these things, I believe."

"Would accept?"

"Invitations are quite his weakness."

Crick sat down at the table and began moving the stem of the glass between his long supple fingers. Buikov recalled the line in the file at Moscow Center: *Felix Hartley Crick is regarded as one of the all-time finest spinners of a leg-break in English cricket.* Are they typical bowler's fingers? he wondered.

"The arrangement more or less as before," Crick said. "The same chance encounter and so on."

Buikov did not look convinced.

"Dollsky will be accompanied, I presume?" Crick asked. "You will have one of your own people with him?"

"Yes."

"Somebody who could talk to Rufus? Somebody capable of throwing out the right sort of hints without arousing his suspicion?"

"I have person," Buikov said slowly, thinking of Sonya Petrovich. "There is person."

"I think this would be infinitely the wiser course."

"And afterwards?" Buikov asked, carefully watching Crick's face. "Afterwards, tell me how we get—"

"Rufus is a generous, hospitable fellow. With money in his pocket, let nature take its course."

There was a sudden stillness in the small room. The sound of one man breathing and another man holding his breath. A door opened and closed on the floor above, there were footsteps on the stairs, the street door slammed. Buikov let his breath out slowly and said in a quiet voice, "This way will work, what I want?"

Crick shrugged. "They're the best terms on offer. In my opinion."

"I *hate* the unplanned," Buikov said vehemently.

Crick said nothing. His fingers stopped playing with the stem of his glass. He sat very still.

"I like *control*," Buikov said. He had a look around his mouth as if he were resisting some physical pressure. He knew he had reached the point of no return: the concept was on the verge of becoming a reality, of having its own ungovernable future.

"May I ask one question?" Crick said.

Buikov shrugged permission.

"Why?"

"I have slate that must be wiped."

"I often wonder whether men become spies because life is not serious enough," Crick said as if he understood perfectly.

Buikov smiled.

"This business," Crick said. "Its success will depend as much on your man as on Rufus, you do see that?"

"Dollsky has correct psychological profile."

They both smiled at the awful jargon.

"Has many weaknesses," Buikov said in simpler language.

At the hotel Buikov used a pay phone in the lobby to call the Novosti Press Agency in South Kensington. "Mr. Principal," he said in English when a woman answered on the seventh ring. "You have message?"

She told him there had been several calls and that he was to ring International on 104 and ask for Operator 5. He replaced the receiver, waited a moment, then dialed the number.

"International. Which country, please?"

"Russia. My name is Principal. I have message to contact Operator Five."

It took about eight minutes before he heard a Russian operator on the line speaking English. "Mr. Principal?"

"Speaking."

"I have a call for you. I will connect you. Stay on the line, please."

A few moments later Vlakus came on.

"You have a pen, Vlakus?" he spoke quickly in Russian.

"Yes, sir."

"That woman, the caller, you know the one?"

"Yes, sir," Vlakus said after a pause.

"If she calls again, tell her this: *The eighty-kopeck finish.* You have that?"

"The eighty-kopeck finish."

"Tell her just that."

"She will understand, sir?"

"I hope so, Vlakus."

Buikov dined quickly in the hotel's Carriage Room. In his room he smoked a stick of black hashish and watched the BBC television news. Troubles in Poland and El Salvador, a strike at a cheese factory in France, an English ice skater's success in some European competition, a financial expert explaining the Soviet "cash flow crisis" and why the Russians had to play their "gold card." His mind drifted. It was strange how physically dissimiliar Crick was from the Englishman, he thought, yet how alike their minds worked. He finished the stick and in two minutes was sound asleep.

On Wednesday evening Buikov drove out to the Moscow Hippodrome and parked the dark-gray Zaz two blocks from the track. Long lines waited at the twenty- and forty-kopeck gates. He joined the short line at the eighty-kopeck entrance, bought a race card and made his way to their favorite place down by the rail.

She wasn't there.

He waited by a column about halfway up the stand, pretending to study the card. The horses were under starter's orders for the first race.

She still hadn't showed. He had almost given up hope when she appeared on the edge of the crowd. He saw how pale she was. He moved quickly to his left and worked his way down the aisle as a roar went up at the start of the third race.

"Anna." He was directly behind her, his voice low. She didn't turn. He saw her body tense and reached for her hand. "Hello, Anna," he said quietly.

"I was beginning to panic," she said, not turning her head. "I was afraid I'd got it wrong."

"You did very well." The crowd was surging and shouting around them. He squeezed her hand and let go. "Make your way to the bar."

The brightly neon-lit bar at the back of the stand was almost empty. Anna sat at a small red metal table close to the door. After a few minutes, Buikov joined her. He had never seen her looking so pale or thin. She had lost five or six pounds. It suited her.

"I'm sorry," she said quickly. Her heart was pounding. "I know we promised never to—"

"It's all right, Anna."

A small hard-looking woman behind the counter clattered some plates, and when Buikov looked across she called out, "Counter service only."

Buikov smiled and looked at Anna. Her eyes seemed overlarge, perhaps because her face was thinner. She wore a blue silk dress beneath a long dark cardigan. "Can I get you something?"

"A beer, perhaps. My mouth is so dry."

He bought a beer and a coffee for himself.

"How have you been, little bird?"

She nodded. They stared at each other. "You look wonderful," he said.

"This isn't exactly the best light for a lady."

They fell silent.

"I don't know where to begin," she said. He recognized the edge of panic in her voice. It was not her customary nervousness in the early moments. It was more than that.

"At the beginning," he said in a low calm voice. "Take your time."

She sipped at her beer.

"Remember Trout?"

"*Trout?*"

She lowered her voice: "Khor's genius?"

Buikov nodded his head, but not immediately. "Yes, go on."

"At first, Zorin thought that Trout was a fish to keep him—you know, fishing."

"At first?"

"Something happened."

"With Trout?"

Anna frowned. "At first he thought it might just be a coincidence. The dates, Trout's visits to Leningrad—the killings."

"Killings?"

"Three girls murdered."

"How were they murdered, Anna?" Buikov asked softly. There was no surprise in his tone.

"Strangled." Very carefully, with as much detail as she could remember, Anna told him about the deaths of Lilya Kuzonev, Galya Mikhailovna and the girl in the Botanical Gardens whose name she could never remember. She told him as much as she could understand about Detective Fyodor Gertsen's ideas and the theories in the old German textbooks. She told him about the makeup, the way the girls had all been found painted with rouge and lipstick and mascara.

Buikov did not interrupt, didn't prompt her in the long silences. When she had finished, Anna said, "May I have another drink, please, Valentin? A vodka, perhaps?"

He came back with the vodka and another black coffee for himself. The bar was now crowded and noisy; they sat with their heads close together across the table.

"These girls—the fish can definitely be placed in the—pond at the time?"

"At the deep end," Anna said.

"You say he knew the second girl? The dancer?"

"He had lunch with her a few days before she died."

"But the police don't know that? This Gertsen—"

"No. Zorin's told him nothing."

Buikov didn't look impressed. "That's a bizarre theory, Anna," he said. "About the hair."

"Zorin ran tests on the lipstick on the last girl's mouth. They did these tests and discovered the make of lipstick. It was expensive, foreign— French or English, I don't remember."

"And?"

"The fish bought it, the same lipstick, the same brand, the same shade, in a Beryozka store in Leningrad a week before."

"What does Khor say to all this, Anna?"

There was a long pause. Buikov watched her face. He knew how to be patient; he had the patience of an expert.

"He doesn't know," she said finally.

"Zorin's told him nothing at all?"

"It started out—he thought Khor was using Trout—to keep him busy, to keep him out of the way."

"Why should Khor—"

"Valentin, a lot of things are going on in that department. A lot of rumors. They say somebody very important wants Khor out. When these things started to happen, started to add up—Zorin didn't know how to play it. I mean, did Khor know about Trout? Did he know that Trout was going around . . . Just think about it for a moment; put yourself in Zorin's shoes. Putting the finger on somebody like the Trout—it could go very badly wrong, you know."

Buikov said: "In these things calculation is more important than duty. I still think he should go to Khor."

"He can't. Not now."

"Why not?"

"Strange things," she said. She was beginning to sound nervous again. Buikov spoke to her calmly: "What kind of things, Anna?"

She finished off her vodka and looked around the bar. "Can we go somewhere else, Valentin?"

He led her through the crowd, pushing through lines of people at the betting windows, which ran along the back of the stand. In the street they walked quickly, without speaking, like two people hurrying home before a storm. Buikov was thinking hard as they got into the car. Would he now have to pay the price for ignoring the fundamental rule that improvisation makes bad politics? But what was the alternative? Call the whole thing off? Abandon Venice? The situation was dangerously more volatile than it had seemed a few hours ago. Simply by passing, time had altered everything.

Buikov kept to the side streets for a couple of miles and made two U-turns, doubling back over the same route before he stopped watching his rearview mirror and relaxed. He didn't speak until he was back on the highway. "Tell me about these strange things, Anna."

"Zorin's adjutant, Lieutenant Stashinsky, a nice young man, very bright, very loyal to Zorin. I was very fond of him. About a month ago he disappeared. Last week his car turned up at the Nikolo-Archangelskoe crematorium."

"Just his car?" Buikov asked abruptly. "No Stashinsky?"

Anna shook her head. "Zorin went out there to look around. When he came back he was— I've never seen him so shaken."

"Crematoriums do that to some people."

"Stashinsky's car," she said, half turning toward him, "was parked by one of those walls with little recesses for the urns. You know the walls I mean? Burial walls."

He could feel her left breast against his arm. After all the things they had done together, all the intimacies they had shared, his total awareness of her breast brushing against his arm came as a surprise.

"In one of the recesses, Zorin found the butt of a cigarette. A Polish Carmen, the brand Stashinsky smoked. They're mild and—"

"Anna, I don't see anything remarkable in that. The man's car was found there. Why shouldn't he have smoked a cigarette and thrown—"

"He smoked hardly at all. Only when he was nervous. He had been with Zorin for three years. Zorin knew his habits well—"

"So he smoked a cigarette. He was nervous."

"Valentin, he had smoked it all the way down. He must have been passing time. Zorin thinks he had a meet."

"Anna—"

"That butt, a Carmen cigarette butt, proves that Lieutenant Stashinsky was there and that he had gone there of his own free will," she said with a new stubbornness, without emotion. "Yes, he was nervous, but he had driven there himself. He was sitting in the driver's seat when he smoked that cigarette. He opened the driver's window to flick the butt into the niche. Don't you see, Valentin? It means that the car wasn't dumped there. Vano Stashinsky drove it there."

"Go on, Anna," Buikov said gently.

"Zorin is convinced that Stashinsky was murdered out there. And far from being some lunatic, unpremeditated attack, it was all worked out . . ."

Buikov pulled off the road and parked the little Zaz by a clump of trees. In the summer twilight it was almost black beneath the trees. When he rolled down the window, the smell of pine scented the air. Anna turned and sat staring ahead. The silence exposed the tension between them.

"Finish the story."

She started nodding her head. Her lips moved but no sound came out. She reminded Buikov of a child silently hurrying through an interrupted poem looking for the next line.

"Zorin talked to the woman who runs the place," she said, the sound suddenly returning to her lips.

"The woman who runs the crematorium?"

"A woman called Volk. She had never heard of Stashinsky. She had no idea what his car was doing out there, had no idea who had looted it, how long it had been there . . ." Anna smiled. "Zorin said she must have been made by the same people who built those walls."

"Go on, Anna."

"He ordered a P184 on the woman."

"Volk?"

She nodded. "How well do you know Mulder Khor?"

"I know what I see. A hard, professional officer."

"Mulder Khor was five years old when his mother died. She died shortly after giving birth to her second child. That child, a girl, was Vera Volk— née Khor."

Valentin Buikov said nothing for a long time.

"Do you remember you once told me that accident and chance motivated the Center most of the time?" Anna asked.

"Yes."

"Do you think this is chance?"

"No," he said quietly.

"No," she said with satisfaction.

"Zorin's told no one?"

"Who can he tell? Apart from me, who can he trust? That department— Everybody is telling everybody so many lies. Nobody wants to know the truth. The truth is too dangerous."

"Tell me what you think," he said. "You think *Khor* killed Stashinsky?"

"Why did he assign Zorin to watch Dollsky? Why did he have *us* watched?" she said. "He is so venomous, so—wicked. He broke us up— What was it he said? He didn't want one of his officers hurt? He didn't want his department upset. The niceties of conscience . . . Maybe he killed Stashinsky for the same reason," she said bitterly. "The same niceties of conscience. Was Lieutenant Stashinsky two-timing Zorin too, do you think?"

He touched her thigh. He could feel her cool nakedness beneath the thin silk dress.

"Anna," he said in the gentle voice he used when they made love. "Try to understand— In Department Twelve, in my department, in any department in any directorate there will always be mistrust. Khor's behavior can be reduced to very primitive human instincts. Let us assume that for a mixture of motives he wanted to isolate Zorin. A simple strategy of containment. And if, as you seem to think, Khor is under some pressure, if he feels threatened . . . You can appreciate those sort of pressures, Anna? Zorin is obviously marked as a possible successor. A deputy head of department at—what is he now, Zorin, forty? Khor's an old fox. He isn't going to go for him out in the open. He doesn't want blood on the walls; he just wants his department to look secure. Stability is sometimes more important than a display of strength. Khor is an expert in the politics of survival."

"You think he killed Stashinsky?" she asked evenly after a long silence. "Tell me what you think."

"I don't know. And neither do you, Anna. But it's possible. It's possible that somewhere along the line Khor's strategy went wrong and he found himself in difficulties." His voice had changed; it had a sharper narrative tone. "He realized perhaps that he couldn't shuffle off responsibility for Dollsky. I don't know. I don't know how Stashinsky got involved. But I do know that it comes down to a game as old as ambition . . . Zorin has to go into the arena alone, Anna."

"Is that all you can tell me? Zorin's on his own?"

"It isn't my fight. It isn't my cause."

"Stick to your own potatoes, right?"

"If you want to talk it through, I'll talk it through. But in the end it isn't anyone's fight but Zorin's."

They stared at each other, their faces close together.

"I wish I could help you, Anna, but I can't."

"I just thought . . . Oh, shit, these pathetic entreaties."

"Where are you supposed to be this evening?"

"The cinema."

"And Zorin?"

"What?"

"Is Zorin out too?"

"Oh, yes," she answered as if finally understanding a difficult question. "A girl from the Ministry of Culture. A *mystery?* Is that what you call them, the MOC girls?"

Buikov moved his hand beneath the silk and stroked the inside of her knee.

"Zorin thinks maybe she's working for Khor."

"Why should he think that?"

"She turned up a month or so ago holding Dollsky's hand on a ministry tour. After the tour, she stayed around." She parted her knees. "No stockings," she said.

"Maybe she's just a girlfriend?"

"Maybe," she said. "But he seems to like them younger, judging by the ones he's left by the wayside."

It was completely dark now. The cars on the highway drove with their headlights blazing. Coaches and minibuses mostly, the race crowd going home, too far away for the sound to reach the car beneath the trees.

"I wish you'd brought something a little more comfortable," Anna said, lifting herself off the seat and pulling up her skirt.

She came acquiescently, emitting little moans, in a succession of long gentle tremors beneath his fingers.

"I will always love you, Valentin," she told him afterwards. "Even when you no longer love me."

"You said it was important, I hope it's important," Khor's disembodied voice came out of the wall grille as he released the electronic lock. Buikov smiled into the security camera above the door and entered the office on the top floor of the Lubyanka. The concrete room was too bright, like an operating theater, and chilled by an overactive air conditioner. The room seemed to complete Khor, as if reflecting some implacable self-image. "Can we make it quick? I've got a full day."

"I'll make it as quick as I can," Buikov said, crossing the large, almost bare room as the door locked behind him. He took the chair opposite Khor's desk. The desk contained nothing but two red telephones and the electronic door control. The closed-circuit monitor sat on a small instrument trolley next to his chair. He got straight to the point. "When you first put the Dollsky idea to me, you said that his defection was a small but necessary part of a larger plan to pigstick a person you declined to name."

"Still do," Khor said.

"I admire adventurism, Khor. It's fine to take risks—"

"It's as risky as shaking the drops off your prick."

"—if you win," Buikov finished. He took a yellow sheet of folded paper from his pocket. "I have completed the arrangements for Dollsky to attend the Venice Film Festival, which starts August twenty-fifth. He will leave Moscow on the twenty-fourth. A person from the Ministry of Culture will accompany him."

"I hope there's more to this call than discussing that little bastard's travel arrangements," Khor said impatiently, looking at his watch as Buikov slid the yellow paper across the desk. Khor picked it up, unfolded it curiously and stared at the name written on it as if he were checking a shopping list or adding up a difficult sum. Then he looked at Buikov and smiled. "So what? It was inevitable you'd put two and two together sooner or later. I knew you'd figure it out," he said imperturbably, raising his forefinger in a sort of owning-up gesture. "I'm a wicked old sinner, you know that, Buikov."

"You may be in deeper than you know," Buikov said softly. "I hope you've left room for some flexibility in your plans."

No longer smiling, Khor stood up and walked around to lean against the edge of his desk. He folded his arms and crossed his legs. The nonchalant pose did not carry through to his eyes, which had begun to glint anxiously, but he said casually, "Talk to me about flexibility."

"He might know more than you bargained for."

"Zorin doesn't know where his ass hangs."

"This time your instinct for revenge—"

"Why are my activities always interpreted so unkindly?"

"—has led you into a perilous miscalculation. Far from rendering Zorin harmless, you may have created a most dangerous situation for yourself."

Khor went back to his chair and sat down. "Tell me about it."

Buikov told him about the murdered girls and about the dossier Zorin had built up on Dollsky. He talked quietly, concentratedly, with an air of impartiality. He did not mention Stashinsky, or the Nikolo-Archangelskoe crematorium, or Vera Volk, née Khor. He didn't have to; Khor's face had hardened terribly. "If he should reveal any of this," Buikov concluded with a shrug. "You see the problem?"

"Dollsky's defection is still the key," Khor said staring at a guard on the monitor screen picking his teeth in the corridor outside.

"I'm sure it is, but can you afford to wait? Zorin could blow this business wide open at any moment."

Khor got up and paced around the room behind Buikov. "Why's he holding back?" he said to the back of his head. "Tell me that?"

"Perhaps he knows too much," Buikov said over his shoulder. "Too much knowledge—it takes time to figure out how to use it best. Once he figures that out— Self-interest is the criterion for all of us."

The exposure of Buikov's two best people in West Germany had been a blow, and his failure to destroy the Mig-25 on Hokkaido had caused some harsh criticism inside the Kremlin. He needed a success in his territory soon, and Dollsky was the best chance he had. Dollsky had become as much his device as he was Khor's. It's strange how one small idea can dictate the shape of your whole future and precipitate every move you make, he thought, remembering that morning in Gorky Park when the Englishman had calmly suggested how he might turn Dollsky's defection to his own advantage. He still found siding with Khor abhorrent, but what alternative did he have? Go directly to Andropov? Tell *him* about Dollsky? Certainly that would fix Khor's little game, but would Andropov regard Anna any more kindly than Khor had? Himself married to a Jewess, might not Andropov find the matter personally distasteful as well as politically embarrassing at a time when there was so much rumor about his nearing advancement to perhaps the pinnacle of the party? Not only had Anna betrayed her husband in bed with another officer, but she had leaked a KGB investigation, which certainly wouldn't do anything to save Zorin's skin— or his own. And what about his own complicity? Sleeping with a Jew, Lazar Slepak's daughter, a lady doing a little double time who couldn't be trusted to keep her mouth shut? No, if he went to Yuri Andropov, *nobody* would win. He didn't like the idea of throwing Zorin to the wolves, but if he didn't, they'd *all* go through the grinder.

"Self-interest," Khor repeated to himself in a dull voice. He reminded Buikov of a man who knows he has been stabbed and is waiting for the blood to flow and the pain to begin.

"The spirit of self-interest's in every ambitious officer. Sometimes it turns against the system, sometimes against superiors," Buikov said gently. "Zorin's secrecy must ultimately be hostile to you, Khor."

Khor went to a military chest in the corner of the big room and took out a bottle of Starka. "You don't, do you?" he said, pouring one for himself and returning to his chair with the bottle. He asked Buikov to go over the details again; he wanted to know about each girl, each killing, and kept interrupting and asking questions. He laughed when Buikov told him about Lilya Kuzonev's rouged nipples, a brief dirty humorless laugh that ended the cross-examination. "What you think? Is he mad, this fucking genius?"

"I suppose all geniuses have a streak of madness in them. An insane temperament— I'm not sure that necessarily means he's certifiable. And you?"

"I think it's a very delicate situation," Khor answered slowly, his Mongolian lids falling even lower over his bright dark eyes. "Any suggestions?"

"Khor, surely you don't expect me to debate method and detail with you?" He was not going to be drawn into any kind of conspiracy against a fellow KGB officer. "I told you the situation. What you do about it is up to you."

Khor eyed him bleakly, finished his drink and, thoughtfully pouring another, asked Buikov where he thought Zorin might take his evidence, if not to Department Twelve. Buikov seemed to think about it for all of ten seconds before suggesting Andropov.

Zorin's admirer, if you knew his name, it would frighten even you. The Englishman's warning came back like a heatflash. Could it be the chairman of the KGB himself?

"Battles never turn out quite the way they are planned," Buikov said as he walked to the door.

"It doesn't matter how they turn out. The important thing is to make sure the retribution always outweighs the provocation," Khor said, releasing the electronic door. "Rouged titties. That runty little bastard. Rouged titties."

The British Airways Super Trident lifted off runway five at the London airport to the music of Mantovani.

"So, Man of Mystery," Pandora said, "all would be revealed when we got off the ground, you said. We're off the ground."

"It's a long story," Rufus said.

"We've got three hours and five minutes."

"May I have a drink first?"

"*Di posta!* I want to know. Who provided the Rolls, who's forking out the eight hundred and forty-six quid, *first class*, who's picking up the tab at the Gritti Palace, who's—"

"You're not complaining? I don't believe it! Are you *complaining*?"

"I'm simply curious."

"Very well. I am an official guest of the Venice Film Festival for one week. All expenses paid for two."

"*Ad ogni santo ha la sua festa!*"

"Again, slowly."

"Every saint has his own festival."

"Exactly."

"But why are they springing—"

"Never look a gift horse in the smiler, my pretty. Take the lira and—"

"The Rolls?"

He grinned. "That was my treat. A fellow stamps his style by his departure."

"*You* hired the Rolls?"

"Modesty, restraint, all the virtues which behoove the English gentleman are quite lacking in me—you know that."

"You're winding me up. You can't afford a bloody Rolls!"

"Just one of the little hidden costs in life a chap saves for."

"*How*, Rufus?"

"I've come into a small inheritance."

"Phooey."

"It's true. *Felix.*"

"Felix? What do you mean, *Felix*? Felix Crick?"

"Sort of."

"Sort of?"

"Sort of."

"You can go off people, you know."

The steward came with the champagne.

"Okay," Rufus said, after sipping his drink. "I'll tell you."

"The truth."

"I always tell you the truth. Remember the letters?"

She gave him an innocent look and recited in a whispery voice: " '*Lives of famous people / All remind us / As their pages o'er we turn / That we're apt to leave behind us / Letters that we ought to burn'*— Those letters?"

"Those letters."

"They settled?"

"Out of court, so to speak."

"Are you serious?"

"Are you shocked?"

"I don't know," she said, sounding bemused.

"The establishment usually works in ways nice people would disapprove of."

The steward refilled their glasses. "They got a good deal," Rufus said defensively.

"I'm sure," she said pleasantly.

"I could have held on to them. I mean, everything is worth something today except money. Everybody is scared of his own currency today."

"Why didn't you hold on to them? Wasn't that Felix's advice?"

"He changed his tune. A long rigmarole about how ill used she is by the press, how—"

"The little sister?"

He nodded. "How another scandal could be most awfully embarrassing, et cetera, et cetera."

"Et cetera what? Et cetera simply won't do, Rufus."

"The Queen can pardon murderers, declare war, dissolve Parliament— you know, little things like that"—he sipped his drink—"so they can't have it look as if she's got no control over her own loved ones."

The steward topped up his glass. "Don't get drunk," Pandora said quietly.

A smile came and went on his face like something operated by a spring. "You see, my dear fellow," he mimicked Felix Crick, "the good conduct or misbehavior, the moderation or excesses, the popularity or otherwise of all those around her Majesty reflect the nature of her Majesty herself."

"What else did he say?"

"That all women should be sisters is the aspiration of women who have no sisters."

"You made that up!"

"It's what he said."

She smiled. "So you agreed to hand them back?"

"I'm as patriotic as the next man."

"You're as opportunistic as a cat."

He smiled at her.

"And a scoundrelly lover," she added.

"They came to me, my pretty. It wasn't my idea."

"That's true," she agreed affably. "I'm never sure about Felix."

"How do you mean?"

"Is he straight, do you think?"

"Is he an iron?"

"Iron?"

"Iron hoof—poof."

She smiled. "Is he?"

"I don't think so."

After a silence, Pandora said, "The iron in the man mask."

Rufus laughed. "It's a sort of mask, I suppose. He knows everything, but he never shows how much he knows."

"So now you're filthy rich, you filthy beast."

"It's very agreeable."

"Don't abuse it. A taxi would have been fine this morning."

"Windfalls must be indulged."

"Rufus . . . " She sighed.

"We all have our own little ways of keeping the panic at bay."

"What are you going to be when you grow up?"

"I'd like to be a foreign correspondent, but I have absolutely no sense of direction."

She laughed.

"I've never really found a proper profession. I'm not even sure that I've found an identity. I'm just another working stiff who hangs out with the famous. Dentists, hairdressers, abortionists—we're a special sort of breed, mechanics servicing the jet set."

"Don't belittle yourself. You're a very good photographer."

"I'm not bad. I wasn't a bad agent, actually. I simply can't take anything that seriously."

By the end of lunch they were both nicely tipsy, their heads close together, their voices conspiratorially low.

"Did you tell your producer that you were coming to Venice with me?"

"I like him to know where I am. He has this ungovernable habit of sending flowers."

The plane banked, the engines dropping to a deeper, more judicious note, as the captain prepared for the final descent.

"I was asked to describe you the other day."

"What did you say?" Pandora felt the pleasurable stirring of narcissism and became embarrassed. "No, don't tell me," she said quickly.

"I said that you were like a child going into woman—a woman who has not yet outlived her innocence."

Sunshine glinted on the wing. He shaded his eyes with his hand and looked at her intently. "I think I was drunk."

"Of that I am persuaded."

"You are beautiful," he said more simply.

"I thought you preferred American ladies. The divine Miranda Jane. How is she, by the way? Last I heard she'd OD'd. You'd gallantly sent her a get-well card."

"She's fine."

"The card did the trick, then?"

"Had her up on her feet in no time."

"She write you any interesting letters?"

He grinned and spread his hand over her face.

34

"Guess who I saw having breakfast on the terrace." Pandora came into the suite with a pleased expression on her face.

"Give up," Rufus said, standing by the window overlooking the Piazza

Santa Maria del Giglio, sipping his coffee. "Who did you see having breakfast on the terrace?"

"Nilus Dollsky. I'd love to meet him."

"He'll probably be at the reception this evening." He checked the schedule. " 'Six-thirty, Hotel Cipriani,' " he read. " 'Delegates and invited guests.' Was he alone?"

"He had a woman with him. Quite pretty. Attractive more than pretty," she said, wrinkling her nose thoughtfully. "What's our itinerary for today, chaps?"

"The day's our own till the reception, followed by a movie at eight. You still want to go to Saint Marks?"

"Please." She wore her hair full and loose. She had washed it herself that morning, and now it was curving out at the ends the way Rufus liked it best. "What's the movie?"

"French. Starring"—he sorted through the invitations—"Isabelle Adjani."

"Good. When do we eat?"

"After the movie."

"I'll starve! It'll be midnight!"

"Can't you think of anything but your belly?"

As she grinned and nodded her head eagerly the telephone rang.

"*Pronto,*" he said. "Who wants her?" he asked after a moment. Then, "*Momento, piacere.*" He held out the phone to Pandora.

She took it with a puzzled look, listened for a moment and said, "Yes, that would be lovely."

"Who the hell was that?"

"Sonya Petrovich."

"Oh, Sonya Petrovich. Who the hell is Sonya Petrovich?"

"*Comrade* Sonya Petrovich from the Soviet Ministry of Culture."

"The more-attractive-than-pretty one?"

"I guess so. Dollsky noticed *me* in the lobby. He'd like to meet me."

"He's not slow on the uptake, is he? When?"

"Twelve, in the bar."

"Am I invited?"

"No, but since when did that ever stop you?"

"I'd hate to cramp your style."

"What shall I wear?"

"Something that would look good on a tractor, I suppose."

"Very droll."

The phone rang again. It was Signor Ettore Barrelet of the Festival Committee; would Signor Gunn and Lady Pandora be his guests at luncheon today? Excellent. One-thirty at the Lido Excelsior? He would send his launch at one-fifteen.

"They step lively round here, don't they?" Rufus said. It was not quite nine-fifteen.

"You'd better stir your stumps if we're going to make Saint Mark's."

"Wouldn't you rather worship at"—he opened his bathrobe slowly, like a stripper—"Saint Peter's?"

"We don't like smutty talk," she told him in a governessy voice.

"Think about it." He stood before her, opening and closing his robe, one side after the other, never quite exposing himself.

"Stop that filthy nonsense at once," she said in the same voice, only smiling.

He swayed in front of her.

"Stop it!"

He opened his robe completely.

"Let's go and look at the Tintorettos," she said firmly.

"We can look at Tintorettos in London. I think I'm falling in love," he said, looking down at himself.

"I'm jolly glad I grew up as fast as I did."

"I'm definitely in love. I'm passionate about you."

"Love and passion are mutually exclusive words."

"Who told you that?"

"You did."

"Hoist with his own petard."

"I've never understood what that means."

"Beaten with his own weapon."

She smiled wickedly at his nakedness, and he covered himself with an air of affronted dignity. "The spirit of adoration grows weak very quickly, you know."

"*Behave.* Have your bath. Then we'll go and find a glass of something cold and Venetian before meeting Mr. Dollsky."

"You shouldn't have said yes," he said with sudden irritation. "Not to his *first* invitation."

"Oh, piffle, Rufus. Don't be so stuffy."

"You must learn to be more careful."

"I don't want to spend my life being careful."

She heard him running a bath. He is a good man, she thought. What was it that woman in *Tatler* had written about him? "A man who beckons and breaks you with his charm." She obviously fancied him like mad, she thought.

She strolled around the suite. It did not seem like a room for transients. The lamps, paintings and knicknacks seemed genuinely to be part of some old house. Heflin's flowers were arranged in vases. Movie companies had sent bowls of fruit and bottles of Scotch. The room was filled with the gauzy tones and glittery reflections that gave a look of gentle movement to everything in Venice.

"That girl who did the piece in the *Tatler*," she called through the bathroom door. "Did you go to bed with her?"

"Certainly," he answered, turning off the taps.

"Was she good?"

"When she was bad she was better."

"Why was she so mean about you?"

"I thought it was rather good. Don't you think she caught the real me?"

" 'A man who beckons and breaks you with his charm'? You liked that, did you?"

"I thought it gave me a certain *je ne sais quoi*. What's this soap?"

"You're not using my Crabtree and Evelyn, you dirty dog!"

"Smells interesting. What is it?"

"Avocado oil," she said, entering the bathroom.

"I like it."

"I'll treat you to some for your birthday."

He was stretched out beneath a drift of Badedas, his lean muscular arms running along the sides of the huge tub. It was a large bathroom, brightly lit, with a marble floor and lots of mirrors. He made a deliberate hole in the lather.

"I see you've overcome your lifelong problem of shyness," she said, gazing at him with an amused look.

"I love the curve of your throat," he told her, looking up.

"I must say she described your body very well."

"I can't remember."

"Yes, you can."

" 'Phidias,' " he recited, closing his eyes, " 'who made statues only of the gods, would have grabbed the Honorable Rufus Gunn for a model before you could say Zeus.' "

"Word for word."

"Vanity, vanity, all is vanity."

"I had to look Phidias up."

"Stick with me, kid, and you'll be well laid as well as well read."

She sat on the edge of the bath and ran her fingers over his shoulders. "You're very forward," he told her.

"You prefer ladies of howling propriety, do you?"

"Not exactly, no."

"What do you like?"

"Elegant tramps."

"Was the lady from the *Tatler* an elegant tramp?"

"Piss elegant."

"It *is* a very large bath."

"I thought you wanted to see the Tintorettos," he said, opening one eye curiously.

"I was simply thinking, a chap good enough to inspire Priapus—"

"Phidias. Priapus was the god of hanky-panky."

"I know what I'm talking about." She dropped her hand into the water and found the slit with her long thumbnail. "I think the Tintorettos can wait."

"They've waited three hundred years."

She stood up, undid the belt of her skirt and let it fall to the floor, took off her blouse and stood alongside the bath, naked above the waist, her legs parted expectantly.

"What are you?"

"A brazen hussy."

Her body was warm and familiar to him.

"You know me much too well," she said as she felt his mouth through the thin silk of her panties. "You know my predilections, young sir, you do, you do, you do so know my predilections . . . Oh, you do, don't you?"

He had an air of votary absorption. She made small acknowledging sounds of fulfillment. He toweled her breasts and her belly, working his way downwards without haste. Between her thighs, in the soft white creases of the groin, wiping from the bow to the buttocks (how strange that it was Nanny's language that still went through his mind). He flexed her elbows, steepled her legs, drying all the hollows and niches of her. He had first dried her when she was two years old, instructed and encouraged by Nanny Francis. After a short while, the tickling and giggling had given way to a sort of solemn habit, and the habit became a ritual. He had seen her pubic hair come, her breasts swell, her curves appear and still she submitted to the pressures of his hands and fingers, turning, lifting, arching her body, silently accommodating and guiding his ministrations. Sometimes as his hands moved over her body, intimate and paternal, detached yet loving, she had a kind of orgasm, through the sensation was not in her genitals. She felt it in the palms of her hands, in her calves, in the soles of her feet, and sometimes in her head. She had once told him that it was like being pushed too high on a swing as a child, or leaping down a flight of stairs in the dark, her whole body floating as if it had no weight at all. But it was not quick; this sensation lasted, traveling slowly through her bones and being. Sometimes she thought it was better than coming itself.

"How about a negroni?" he said, "before we go downstairs?"

"I haven't had a negroni since the last time I was in Italy," she said. "One never thinks of asking for a negroni in London."

"I only drink martinis in New York."

They dressed and he phoned room service. When the drinks came, Pandora lit a cigarette and said, "You never bore me, you know."

"Thank you."

"I wanted you to know."

"That I'm not a bore?"

"That you're very special."

"I bet you say that to all the rich boys."

She combed her hair and pulled it back in a chignon like a ballerina's. "I want you to promise me that you'll be nice to Nilus Dollsky. It costs nothing to be polite."

"I'm coming, am I?"

"I'd like you to be there."

"You got it," he said in what Englishmen of his class take to be a terrific American accent.

"And be nice, promise?"

"I'm always nice."

"No, you're not, but when you are, you can be very nice, and that's what I want you to be this morning."

"You got it," he said, again in the same accent. It made Pandora uneasy, but she knew that it was best not to push him.

Dollsky was dressed in a pink mandarin-collared shirt and khaki pants, and was talking to a woman sitting on a barstool with her back to the door. At a distance in the cool gloom of the bar he looked about sixteen years old.

"Hell's teeth," Rufus said out of the side of his mouth. "He's overdone the *rive gauche* a bit, hasn't he?"

"Nice, remember," Pandora said, smiling.

"I suppose it makes it easier to forget the Revolution."

"*Nice.*"

Dollsky saw them approaching and said something quickly to the woman, who turned around and smiled at them.

"Good morning. Lady Pandora Child?" she said in excellent English, slipping off the barstool. She was noticeably taller than Dollsky. "My name is Sonya Petrovich. We talked on the telephone. May I introduce you to Nilus Dollsky?"

Pandora held out her hand and Dollsky lifted it to his lips.

"Mr. Dollsky—Rufus Gunn," Pandora said, turning to Rufus as Dollsky released her hand and straightened up. The two men shook hands, watching each other's eyes the way men do when they are introduced by a beautiful woman.

"We're drinking something called Bellini," Dollsky said, also in good English, but with more of an accent. "A mixture of champagne and peach juice. Will you have glass? I can recommend it."

"Without the champagne," Pandora said.

"A negroni," Rufus said.

After Dollsky had ordered the drinks, Sonya Petrovich said, "Dollsky was asking why all the gondolas are painted black. I don't know. Do you know, Lady Pandora?"

"A long time ago some of the grandees felt that the gondolas were getting too festive-looking for Republican sensibilities—"

"So they passed a law that boatmen could paint their gondolas any color they liked so long as it was black," Rufus concluded the story.

"You know Venice well?" Dollsky addressed the question to Pandora.

"Not as well as I'd like." Standing next to him, like Sonya Petrovich she was several inches taller. "I came here often as a child. I was too young to appreciate it."

"It is city for grown-ups," Dollsky said. "A beautiful playground for grown-ups."

"Have you been here before?" Rufus asked.

"My friend, I have never been in West before."

The drinks came and they all touched glasses.

"How long will you be staying?" Pandora politely directed the question to Sonya Petrovich.

"Until the end of the festival."

"I start new picture in Leningrad November," Dollsky said.

"I love your pictures," Pandora said, knowing that she was young enough to be ingenuous.

"You are an actress, I know. I am sorry I have not seen—"

"Just a few commercials and a *tiny* part in one movie so far." She held up her thumb and forefinger, almost touching, when she said the word *tiny*.

Sonya Petrovich turned her attention to Rufus. "What is it you do, Mr. Gunn? Are you in the cinema world also?"

"I'm a playboy," he said seriously.

"A playboy! Is that *legal?*"

"The limits of what is legal are pretty vague in England. So much illegality is sanctioned by money—even by a person's charm sometimes."

"Then I am sure that is how you get away with it." She smiled at him. "It is your charm."

"It's not necessarily the kind of charm you cotton to at once."

"Are you a very wild playboy?"

"Recklessly."

"You certainly don't look it now."

"You must take my word for it. You work for the Ministry of Culture, Pandora says. What does that mean, exactly?"

"At this moment it means keeping an eye on Dollsky."

"I imagine a chap like him needs a lot of watching?"

"He is an artist," she said as if that explained everything.

They both glanced at Dollsky, who was now deep in conversation with Pandora. "They seem to have hit it off," Rufus said. He looked at his watch. It was one o'clock. "We have a motorboat picking us up at one-fifteen."

"So have we."

"We're lunching on the Lido with Signor Ettore Barrelet."

"We too."

"A stroke of fate."

"Things are what they are, or what they are made to be."

"You don't believe in fate?"

"Fate is usually an excuse when things go wrong."

"I must remember that." He looked at her with photographer's eyes. She had good bones, a delicate nose, a wide but thin mouth. She was dressed extremely well for a Russian woman: a simple white linen shirtdress, a narrow red leather belt, white stockings and red leather pumps. A toughie with style, he thought. She would have no trouble getting Dollsky out of the sort of pickles men like Dollsky get themselves into, whether they come from Malibu or Minsk. He wondered whether she was having an affair with him.

"Have you seen any of Dollsky's films, Mr. Gunn?"

"I expect so."

"Don't you know?"

"Hitchcock, Huston and Howard Hawks are about the only directors I can ever remember."

"That's terrible."

"I know. Pandora constantly scolds me for my ignorance. I really must try to mend my ways."

"They are showing one of Dollsky's films on Friday. Will you come?"

"Is that an official invitation?"

"I would like you to come," she said. It was the invitation of a confident woman who was not afraid to like someone spontaneously and show it.

"Thank you." The formality he instinctively used with strangers hid his surprise and pleasure at what was almost certainly a pass. "I should like it very much."

It was a long, unhurried lunch. Ettore Barrelet, who looked and spoke like an aristocrat and owned vineyards in Piedmont and a movie distribution company in Milan, had organized a table for about twenty people. They sat on the cool east side of the terrace of the Excelsior looking out over the gardens toward the sea. Pandora loved the way the Adriatic slowly shifted beneath the bright sky, sometimes mauve, sometimes the color of jade. She loved the way its breezes mixed with the smells of fresh fruit and acacia trees and the expensive scents on the expensive women around the table. Groups of strangers fascinated her. She sipped her wine and listened to the conversations going on about her in English, French and Italian.

"Where does one put one's money today? I personally know two people in Houston who think they own the original 'Les Poseuses.' One of them has to have been taken to the cleaners, and if you ask me they both have."

"Gold, my dear, is the only answer. In the long term you know where you are with gold."

"She had her breasts lifted when she was sixty. It's her ambition to live till she's ninety and be buried topless."

Pandora began to play her private game: remember something about each person in turn. The princess: once married to a racing driver, she had made the memorable exit line, "Jean-Michel has fantastic cool and no imagination at all. On the track that's genius; in bed it's boredom." She married her aging Italian prince four weeks after the divorce, had a well-publicized miscarriage and wore a black veil for six months, including in a cover photo for Italian *Vogue*. The English designer had once drained his dope-polluted blood and received a complete refill in order to pass a blood test to enter the United States. The lady novelist liked a touch of pain with her fun and games, according to Rufus, who had appeared thinly disguised in one of her books.

It was, Pandora thought, an average gathering of Beautiful People. She wondered what Dollsky was making of it all. Did he disapprove of these people? Was he out of his depth with their preoccupations and social jibber-jabber? He was several places away to her right. She did not mind not sitting next to him; there was a kind of relief in being separated from him for a while. The hour they had spent together before lunch had been extraordinary. She had been very attracted to him.

"What did you think, Ru?" she asked when they were back in their suite. "What did you make of Dollsky?"

"The rich live very well."

"A sexy little sod."

"Stay away from that one, P."

36

Even now, driving out to Zorin's apartment in the Lenin Hills, Khor could not believe that his plan had come so badly unstuck. He kept thinking of the look of pleasure on Buikov's face when he had said that battles never turn out the way they are planned. That remark was lodged in a part of his brain where he filed old scores. It was eight-thirty on a beautiful morning.

Zorin's telephone had been tapped since February, and Khor knew that Anna Zorin would already have left for a nine-fifteen hair appointment on Granovskovo Street. He parked his small unmarked car in a tree-lined side street, entered the apartment building through the rear entrance and walked up the emergency stairs to the fourth floor.

Zorin was astonished when he saw him through the spyhole.

"I was passing," Khor told him, entering the apartment. He was breathing hard. Zorin guessed that he had avoided the elevator. Khor wore civilian clothes and carried his familiar briefcase. "I thought I smelt coffee."

"You're not mistaken," Zorin said calmly. He went to the kitchen and returned with black coffees on a tray.

Khor was standing in front of the Brodsky lithograph. "You like this stuff, Colonel?" he asked, taking a coffee from the tray. "Modern art?"

"'Red Funeral,'" Zorin said, not answering the question directly. "That's my wife's favorite. I prefer the Malevich over there."

Khor went across the room and stared at the white-on-white design and read the caption aloud: "'White Square on a White Background.'"

"The essence of simplicity," Zorin said. "I like its delicacy, I suppose."

"You find comfort in art. Art has always seemed to me to be a limited satisfaction."

"Milk, Comrade General?"

"Black. I've never been to your home before." He went to the window and looked down, then turned and looked slowly around the room. His eyes rested on the family photographs that Anna had fixed on the fan-shaped screen. "Who is this?" He pointed to one of the snapshots.

"My wife's younger brother. He died very young. I never knew him."

"And this?"

"Her mother."

"And this man in the white coat is her father? Dr. Lazar Slepak?"

"Yes." Zorin stood very straight, his hands behind his back. When Khor said that name, he felt a chill of apprehension in his spine. It was not surprising that Khor knew Anna's history; he would have seen her file. But knowing her father's name off the cuff like that was a bad sign.

"Nice apartment," Khor said, taking his coffee and sitting on the ottoman where he had dropped his briefcase. "You have been here two years, is it?"

"Three in October."

"You have done well, Colonel." He began to stir his coffee slowly. He was courteous and soft-voiced. "This interest in art—you have a sensitive streak in you, Colonel. That is why I first assigned you to Dollsky. Did you know that?"

"No, sir."

Khor nodded his large head. "I thought you would understand a man like that. They say he is a genius. You think he is?"

"He is talented. Not a genius, I think."

"I've never met a genius," Khor said with a sense of satisfaction. "Why are people so impressed with *creativity?* It puzzles me. *Information* is the only way to achieve anything worthwhile. These artists—did any of them have power? Genius is nothing without information. Without that you're screwed."

He waited for Zorin to answer; when he didn't, he said quietly, "I'm telling you something important, Colonel. Do you understand what I'm saying?"

"I think so, sir."

Khor's animosity toward geniuses seemed suddenly to evaporate in a burst of laughter that took Zorin by surprise.

"You did not expect Dollsky to take off like that? The Venice trip? You did not expect we'd let him go?"

Zorin shrugged. "I appreciated the break."

"Ten months," Khor said. "In ten months what have we turned up? He smokes cannabis. He sniffs cocaine."

"You expected something else, General?"

"I'm disappointed. I won't hide it from you. I'm disappointed."

"I don't understand, sir."

"I think you understand, Colonel." Khor still spoke softly, like a man with dangerous secrets in him. "I think you understand."

Something almost imperceptible happened to a muscle beneath Zorin's left eye, like a blip on a seismograph. He said nothing.

"I understand your dilemma." Khor had the sad air of a man doing his best to save an unworthy friend: it was a fine performance for someone so inept at ordinary human contacts. "It is absurd to distrust each other. Why tear off each other's heads? Why play into the hands of others?"

There was a long pause. Just when Zorin was beginning to think that Khor was merely working on instinct and had no real idea of the enormity of Dollsky's guilt, his superior said calmly: "Nilus Dollsky is a madman.

He is a fucking maniac, Colonel. We both know that. Those girls in Leningrad—they didn't choke to death on fishbones." He grinned viciously. "This cat-and-mouse game with me is stupid, my friend. Stupid and dangerous."

"General—"

Khor held up his hand. "Let me tell you something. When I gave you Dollsky, it was for a different reason. I never expected a haul like this. But a man making the kind of decisions I must make every day would be an idiot if he did not build into his plans the possibility of such twists."

Khor talked for a long time, smiled a lot, made small jokes, chuckled amiably, asked for more coffee. He went around in circles. But the longer he talked, the more Zorin realized how ill at ease he really was. It became clear that Khor knew the broad outline of the story, but did not have the facts. "I'm sure that we can polish this business off between us," he was saying now. "Keep it in the family. Keep it simple."

"Direct action?" Zorin made his voice sound incredulous. He wanted to draw Khor out as far as he would go.

"Executive initiative, Colonel."

"But Dollsky—"

"Executive initiative is more reliable than the law, less troublesome than a trial." There was no reason to doubt the truth of that. "I have never cared for this man," Khor said, as if that was enough to invoke the final initiative. He finished his coffee and put the cup and saucer on the floor by his feet. "Shall we start?"

"General?"

"I want to see everything you have."

Zorin did not answer because he did not know what to say. He knew that it was not as simple as Khor tried to make it sound. He thought about Stashinsky and Vera Volk. Why was it that despite Khor's offer he had the feeling of being trapped? Yet he was sure that somehow Khor also felt threatened.

Breaking the silence, Khor said, "Let me remind you that you are not well placed to make deals with me."

"My inquiries are not complete, Comrade General."

"You're sitting on an olive branch, Colonel Zorin. You've been blowing smoke up my ass for ten months and I'm offering you an olive branch. Don't saw it out from under you. It's a long drop, believe me."

Zorin stared at him.

"Colonel, you do understand the position you are in?"

It was not a question that Zorin felt required an answer.

Khor rummaged in his briefcase and took out a thin mauve file. He said, "Ten months, and all you've turned up is this shit." He tossed the file on the floor between them. "It doesn't amount to a belch in a gale of wind, Zorin."

Zorin stood at the window, not speaking.

"What is it to be, Colonel? One way or another I have to have answers."

Zorin could see the short barrel of Khor's Skorpion automatic poking through the papers in the briefcase. He remembered Khor's care not to be seen entering the building. *Not even Khor would go that far*, he told himself. *Not in my own apartment at nine o'clock in the morning.* But he knew that the point of maximum danger had come; how he handled himself in the next minutes would be crucial.

"Very well, Comrade General," he said at last in a relenting tone.

Khor smiled amiably—the smile of a simian seraph, Zorin had once described it to Anna. "I am pleased you've seen the sense of it," he said, nodding for Zorin to continue.

"He is an important man. When I first began to suspect what was happening in Leningrad—"

"You have evidence?"

"Some facts."

"What sort of facts?"

"I think they are conclusive, sir," Zorin said with the care of a man whose life depended on keeping his answers evasive.

"I've gone over your reports. There is no hint in any of them that—"

"It's in my head, General."

"The milk is in the coconut," Khor said in an approving tone. "You've talked to nobody?"

Zorin seemed to hesitate. "My adjutant, Lieutenant Stashinsky, knows a certain amount. But as you know, Comrade General," he said without inflection, "he disappeared some weeks ago."

Khor saw Stashinsky rolling into the furnace, the brown attaché case on his chest. He said, "Nobody else? You never discussed it with your wife, for instance?"

"No. I never discuss Center business at home. Never."

Khor seemed to accept this. "So," he said, nodding slowly. He sounded relaxed, almost dreamy, like somebody lulled by the rhythm of the sea. He picked up the file and put it back into the briefcase. Zorin watched him carefully as his hands moved toward the automatic. "This business is between the two of us?"

"Now it is."

"That is how it must stay."

"Yes, sir."

"You will prepare a report for my eyes only." He closed the briefcase.

"Yes, sir," Zorin said, relaxing. He had bought the time he needed: thinking time, time to talk it over with Anna.

"When he returns from Venice, we shall make an end of it. A road accident, a heart attack, perhaps. These drugs he is so fond of can be dangerous pleasures."

"Yes, sir."

"You should have turned to me sooner, Colonel. You should have trusted me." He stood up. "I will say good-bye to you now."

They shook hands.

Zorin's second caller that morning was a woman. He studied her through the spyhole for a moment before realizing who she was. What the hell did *she* want?

"Comrade Colonel," she said nervously when he opened the door. "May I come in?" She carried a shopping bag full of groceries, as if she had called in on her way home from the shops. Zorin was puzzled; she was the last person he'd expected to see. "I have an important story to tell you," she said, sounding still more nervous as he escorted her into the living room.

"I want you to look at this," she said, rummaging inside the heavy bag.

The bullet went through Anastas Zorin's right temple. A small fleck of blood spurted from the neat wound onto the Brodsky print.

It was a casual, an almost gentle death. Murder is not a spectacular sport, she thought. Often it is simply a challenge to beat one's own best performance. The hole in Zorin's head was small and almost exactly where she'd meant it to be.

She wiped the gun with a cloth she carried in the bag and pressed the weapon into his right hand before dropping it next to his body. She took the cups and saucers to the kitchen, rinsed them in cold water, dried them, and placed them with other crockery on a shelf. She had a sort of intensity, a sense of purpose, a woman whose job is a constant sorrow that must be subdued or quickly forgotten.

It was ten-thirty.

She went out the way she came in. She saw nobody. She drove slowly home. Vera Volk never let her brother down.

37

"I think you're with the KGB," Rufus said. "I think you're a KGB agent."

Sonya Petrovich made a dismissive, angry sound. "You should not make jokes about such things."

"Here we can make jokes about such things," he said. He was looking pale. She knew he'd had quite a lot to drink. She poured more Chianti into his glass.

"You trying to get me drunk, madam?"

"Why would I want to do that?" She refilled her own glass.

"I must warn you I'm no good when I'm sauced."

"I thought playboys were always drunk."

"Squiffy, mellow, listing to starboard sometimes, but never drunk—never, never blotto."

"Perhaps that's why there are no playboys in my country."

"I'm told that Russian men are great goat drunks."

"Goat drunks? What is that?"

"They get amorous with booze."

She smiled.

"You smile, but you do not answer me."

"How can I answer such a question?"

"Is Dollsky a goat drunk?"

"Are you worried?"

"Worried?"

"Because he is out with your lady friend?"

"Pandora is a lady, yes, and is a friend most certainly, but she is not my lady friend."

"I'm sorry. My English is not always so good."

"Your English *iz vonderful.* I just wanted to make the distinction."

"You smile, but you do not answer me."

"Pandora can look after herself."

"Have you ever been wrong?"

"A man who has never been wrong has never been right."

They were in the walled garden of a trattoria next to the Palazzo Vendramin-Calergi. He looked at her closely. She was one of those fairly attractive women who become lovely at night. The candlelight, softened by tumbling wisteria and the purplish-rose Judas tree behind them, gave a glow to her complexion. It was Sonya who had suggested that they slip away after the screening of Dollsky's picture. Pandora had gone on to the official dinner as Dollsky's guest.

"Doesn't he mind you playing truant?"

"He is delighted."

"You checked with him first?"

"Naturally. He is very much taken with your—with Lady Pandora. A professional interest."

"I don't believe in professional interest between a man and a woman. It's almost always something else."

"It is natural that they should be drawn to each other. She is an actress, he is Dollsky. And . . . "

"And?"

"And you are stuck with me."

He smiled. She was not exactly hilly going. "Do you share a room with him?"

"No."

"Connecting rooms?"

"No connecting rooms."

"Well, I should mention that—"

"I know. Suite 115–116. Signore and signora."

"They call it the Hemingway suite. He wrote one of his books there. I thought you and Dollsky were lovers."

"No."

"You fancy him?"

"He is a very attractive man."

"You don't want to sleep with him?"

"Yes, but it would be a mistake."

"Are you always so strong-willed?"

"Fortunately, no."

"I'm pleased to hear it."

"Do you want to sleep with me?"

"Yes."

"I'm pleased to hear it," she said. It was not the way one repeats a phrase in a language one knows but which is not one's own.

"Are you in love with anyone at the moment?"

"No."

"You should be. Beautiful women should always be in love."

"I am not one of those women who cannot live without involvement."

"I have never made love to a Russian woman before."

"Why should a Russian woman be any different from any other sort of woman?"

"I heard they were very cold," he said straight-faced.

"Have you read *Anna Karenina?*"

"Not lately."

"I chose you. Have you thought about that? Does that sound cold?"

She never seemed to answer him the way he expected; she was a surprising woman. He ordered a second bottle of wine. They talked about many things, and she laughed in nearly all the right places. She told him about her childhood in Tbilisi and described her favorite village, a two-hour bicycle ride from the city. "People say I have dancer's legs but they are really cyclist's legs." Her father had worked for Amtorg, the Soviet trading company in America; her mother had been a buyer for the state store GUM. He told her about his boyhood in Scotland and the grand parties his parents gave at Castle Claymorrow.

"A real castle? Are you a lord?"

"When my father goes, but there's plenty of snap left in him yet."

"What does that mean in England now, being a lord?"

"Not much. Accidents of accidents, somebody once called us."

"Then why bother?"

"It's no bother."

"Tell me about your mother," she said.

"She moved on her wedding night."

"*Moved?*"

"Several times," he said gravely. "My father never quite trusted her again. He was convinced he'd saddled the wrong horse. *Always remember, boy, ladies don't move*, he warned me." Sonya said she thought that was poor advice, and Rufus said that his father had a genius for passing on poor advice.

They talked in this vein for a long time, telling their own special stories, admitting their lesser, more amusing weaknesses, revealing nothing too personal and little of value. It was the conversation between a man and a woman who have not yet slept together but who both know that they will and that the time is not far off. But for Sonya Petrovich the game was not completely frivolous; she was trying to reach his mind. Would he take the bait?

"What do you want to do with your life?" she asked after a short lull in the conversation.

"Why do people always ask me that?"

"Do they?"

"Constantly. All the time."

"What do you constantly answer all the time?"

"To lead a long and happy life. To pass muster."

"That sounds not so much to want."

He thought again. "I'd like a yacht as well."

She laughed. "You take pictures. Do they pay much money for that in your country?"

"Photography is a pretty amusing way to stay broke," he said. "Who taught you about makeup?"

"You don't act broke."

"I told you: I'm susceptible to bouts of prodigal good times." It was a great deal truer than he liked to think. "Who taught you about makeup?" he repeated.

"Dollsky."

"You like him very much, don't you?"

"I care about him very much," she said after turning the question over in her mind.

"You say that as if you're worried about him."

"This is not a thing for me to talk about."

"We've talked about almost everything else." He caught a waiter by the arm and ordered two Stregas. "Why is this so hard?" he asked, turning back to her.

She looked at him for a long moment without answering.

"What's wrong? Don't you trust me?"

She said, "Human nature being what it is, it is unfair to expect from it trust."

"That's a pretty heavy remark."

"It is what I think."

"I thought we were starting to groove together."

"What is that?"

"Understand each other."

"What has that to do with trust?" Her face was suddenly blank. "You in the West don't understand the meaning of that word. Where I come from, when you trust somebody it means everything."

"How can you judge me by what I don't know?"

"You use words like 'trust' too easily. It rolls out of your mouth. It is like prayer you know by heart; you never think about what you're really saying. Do you still say your prayers, Rufus?"

"Only as a backup system."

"My mother used to say that praying took the place of serious thought."

"Didn't you pray for her when she was dying?"

"What was the use?"

A waiter put a fresh candle on the table. The patron himself brought the Stregas.

"What is this?" she asked, holding up the glass.

"You'll like it. It's made by monks."

She sipped it and nodded approval. "Now at least I know what monks think about when *they're* praying." She smiled.

Rufus said again, "How can you judge me by what I don't know? You can judge a person only by the things he knows."

She said nothing.

"Wagner died in that palazzo," he said in a bored small-talk voice after the silence had stretched for almost a minute. "The Palazzo Vendramin-Calergi. Do you like Wagner? Personally, I hate Wagner." As he said this all the lights in the palazzo went out. "You see, God agrees with me. He *trusts* my judgment."

She smiled. "Very well. I trust you."

He clapped his hands together once. "*Lights!*" The palazzo stayed dark. "Drat!"

"He isn't always the greatest help," she said.

"He made you trust me. But I've forgotten the point."

"Whether I was worried about Dollsky."

"Oh, yes. Well?"

She pretended to have to think. "It is only when you are prepared to risk everything that— I think he should get out of the Soviet Union for a while." She said it quickly.

"But he *is* out of the Soviet Union."

"That is not what I mean."

"If you mean what I think you mean . . . " He looked around the almost empty walled garden.

She said, "Now you know what I meant about trust."

"Is it in the cards?"

"No," she said, shaking her head. "There is no plan."

"What does he say?"

"We have never discussed it. It is not a subject. But he has gone as far as he can go in the Soviet Union. In my country he is not being stretched, that is all. I am not saying anti-Soviet things."

"You just think it would be a good career move, is that it?"

"You make it sound very trite," she said in a hurt voice.

"I didn't mean to. I'm sorry. But people would see it as a political—"

"Dollsky is not political. He is simply a great artist."

"But if you've never discussed this with him?"

"I feel it." The candle flickered in the warm night air.

Rufus did not know what to say.

"Have you heard of Sergei Paradjanov? Next to Dollsky he is probably the finest director in Russia today."

"I told you: Huston, Hitchcock and Hawks."

"In 1975," Sonya said, "he refused to dub a Ukrainian picture into Russian. He hated the idea of dubbing. It was a question of taste, his motives were purely aesthetic, but he was accused of supporting Ukrainian nationalists. It was all silly. Paradjanov could have just swallowed his principles and dubbed the film. Who would have blamed him? Who would have *cared*? But he dug his heels in, so they got him on a charge of homosexuality. He went to a labor camp for five years."

She lifted her glass and saw that it was empty. "Do you think I could have another drink?"

He ordered two more.

She said, "I'm told that people scrawled *Free Paradjanov* on the walls of the Paris Métro, but what a terrible waste of five years of a man's life!"

"It's a sad story."

"Dollsky has the same spirit. He answers back. Sooner or later he is going to do something they really don't like."

A waiter put the Stregas and fresh coffee on the table. When he had gone, Rufus said, "What you're talking about takes a special kind of courage."

"Yes, I know."

"It can be a lonely sort of freedom," he said, watching her face. "Do you think he has that kind of courage?"

"I don't know."

"It's important to know."

"He has always said what he believes. He does not mind if people attack him—he is too conceited to worry about critics." She spoke slowly, as if working it out as she talked. "He likes shocking people a little bit, you know? Making scandal, making showmanship."

"We're talking about someting a little more important than showmanship."

He became aware of the silence in the garden; they were the last customers. He lowered his voice: "Let me ask you this. What's to stop him getting on the next plane out of here to London or Paris? Or just asking for asylum right here in Italy?"

"He has no money, no place to go to."

"Don't say anything else. It's late. We've both drunk a lot of wine. It's not the time to discuss something like this."

"It never is."

"I want you to think about it. Tomorrow it may seem quite different. But sleep on it." He felt quite sober. "If you still feel the same way tomorrow, talk to him. If he really wants it, I might be able to help."

"*You!*" There was just the right tone of surprise and disbelief in her voice.

"It's possible," he said. "We'll see."

Sonya Petrovich felt a sense of triumph. But more than that, she felt amazed at the unexpected part of herself that was capable of such perfect cunning.

38

Rufus took Sonya to her room and kissed her good night. He did not invite himself in; they had talked beyond the moment, and they both knew it.

Returning to the suite, he crossed the drawing room slowly in the dark, pushed open the bedroom door and listened.

"You dirty stopout," Pandora said softly.

"I wake you?"

"Yes," she lied.

"Have a nice evening?"

"Lovely. You?"

"Not bad."

"*Not bad*, he says coming in at three o'clock in the morning!"

"I'm awfully tired."

"The least convincing remark in the lexicon of explanations is the remark that a chap has had a *not* bad evening," she said. "I suppose truly original explanations are almost unheard of these days."

"At three o'clock in the morning they are."

"Be a chap, pour me a glass of water."

He gave it to her, sat on the edge of the bed and took off his shoes.

"I'm really bushed," he said. It was not true. He was preoccupied. He did not want to talk. Ideas were going around his head that he had to sort out.

"How was Ninotchka?"

He seemed not to hear the question.

"Bomps vill fall, civilizations vill cromble—but not yet, my dahlink, not yet—give us our moment!" Pandora intoned the Garbo line.

"I'm too tired to smile." He emptied his pockets, put his wallet and loose change on the bedside table, took off his jacket and draped it over the back of a chair.

"When you wake me up in the middle of the night," she said, "at least *talk* to me."

"The Russians are coming."

"*Quel monstre!*"

"But not tonight."

"No?"

"Absolutely no."

"You must be slipping."

"Getting old."

"I want you to excite my jealousy."

"She put the make on me, all right."

"And you *declined?*"

"We got onto other things."

A tone in his voice puzzled her. She switched on the bedside light and looked at him intently as he began to remove his trousers; fcet apart, perfectly balanced, he lifted first one leg, then the other.

"You're not even a little bit pissed," she said accusingly.

"We killed a bottle or two." He folded his trousers under his chin and dropped them over the arm of a chair.

"Why aren't you tiddly?"

"I sobered up. We had a very sobering conversation." He went into the bathroom and stayed there a long time. When he came out he was naked and his breath smelled of peppermint. He opened a window; a cool night breeze came into the room.

"Are you asleep?"

"Yes."

"Want to talk?"

"I thought you were exhausted."

He got into bed and kissed her on the forehead.

"You're forgiven," she said. "Besides, I hate being the aggrieved party. I can never keep it up."

Lying side by side, not touching, they talked like roommates about their separate evenings. After a while, Pandora sat up and reached for her cigarettes. Her lighter flickered in the darkness, lighting up her face. She looked pensive as she blew smoke gently into the air. "Why is it that I cannot shake this feeling that there's something you're not telling me?" she said.

"No," he said in a thoughtful voice. He had it almost worked out. "Tell me about Nilus Dollsky."

"Tell you what?"

"He's not quite your cup of tea, is he?" he said, feeling his way.

"I like his boyish hips."

"Did he say anything interesting?"

She shrugged. "Had I known that you were so fascinated I would have taken notes."

"You have a very good memory."

"He did say one thing, actually," she said. "I asked him whether he enjoyed his fame, all the fuss they make of him, and he said that fame was dehumanizing. He said that being famous was a wearying business and that he hated it—but that he dreaded its absence. He said that the worst kind of loneliness must be the loneliness that follows a lost fame. I thought that interesting."

"Once you're on the escalator, it's hard to get off. What else did he say?"

"Chitchat—you know."

"Did he say anything about the future?"

"He starts a picture in November."

Rufus slipped out of bed, walked to the window and pushed it open. He liked the old-church smell of the canals at night. He sat down in an armchair next to the window. Pandora watched him closely. He had thrown a bathrobe over his shoulders.

"Did you happen to mention *Daisy Jordan* to him?" he asked. He played with the French window with his bare foot, pushing it to and fro.

"I did, actually. I told him how Lyall Heflin had been in touch with the Russian embassy about him."

"What did he say?"

"They would never allow it. He said he was surprised that they had let him come to Venice."

"Why was he surprised?"

"He didn't say. It's just the way they work, I suppose."

"Pandora, this is important. Can you recall anything else he said? Anything at all?" He did not try to disguise his deep interest now. "It's important, darling."

"He said that nothing's worth counting on," she said quickly as the line came into her mind and triggered a whole other conversation earlier that evening on the Lido. "He was talking to Ettore Barrelet about that politician they kidnapped and shot here—"

"Aldo Moro."

"Right. And Dollsky said this thing—" Pandora hesitated as she tried to remember the phrase exactly. "He said that movies and politics both dealt primarily in images—in images and deception."

Rufus sat nodding his head, slowly opening and closing the window with his foot, staring into the darkness. Suddenly Pandora laughed. "You look like a man who's just read one of those books."

"What books?"

"That are going to change your whole life."

"You could be right," he said.

"Fuckaduck!"

Rufus stood up, put on the bathrobe and began to walk around the room. They talked for a long time, mostly about Dollsky. Rufus wouldn't get off the subject; he couldn't seem to leave it alone. Neither felt tired. It began to get light; the domes and towers of the church of Santa Maria della Salute took shape in the early-morning mist, its stone walls rising from the water. Quickly, in the space of minutes, the sun had risen. Pandora got out of bed, slipped on a white silk wrap and went to the window. A dawn wind made small ripples on the water. She was pleased that she was awake at this hour to see the color seeping into the city.

"Rufus, tell me what this is all about," she said evenly. "I want to know."

"There's nothing to worry about."

"I *do* worry."

He knew too well the limits of his own powers to deceive her to attempt to keep her completely in the dark. The question was how much should he tell her. Where should he begin?

He told her haltingly about his conversation with Sonya Petrovich. He told her the whole story impassively, with no asides, without once giving way to his propensity for cynicism and elaboration.

When he had finished, Pandora felt a mixture of fascination and apprehension. She said quietly, "Let me see if I've got this absolutely right. You want to help Dollsky come over to the West?"

"That's it."

"What about Ninotchka?" she asked, her eyes fixed upon him, her mind racing. She thought she knew Rufus Gunn inside out, but this had really jarred her compass.

"What about her?" he said amiably.

"Wouldn't it be a bit awkward for her if he hops it?"

"I guess she knows what she's doing."

"I hope so, for her sake."

"She said it's not a political thing. The need is purely artistic, the motive is just—"

"*Everything's* political with those people—sport, art, *juggling's* political with those people. They don't fool around."

He picked up the telephone, asked for room service, and asked Pandora what she wanted for breakfast. After giving the order, he said, "He'll need looking after, organizing, proper handling. An agent, a manager, somebody—"

"You?"

"Why not me?"

"I thought you hated all that? On the plane you were telling me exactly how *much* you hated it all."

"It would be a bloody miserable life if we were bound by what we said yesterday, don't you think?"

"I think this is very big," she said after a long pause.

"I know."

"I'd hate you to get scorched."

"I won't."

The idea began to excite Pandora too, but at the same time she was reluctant to give it her approval. She could not help feeling uneasy. She stared at the church across the water.

"I have no real career, no real achievements—what have I got to lose?" he said. "For God's sake, P., it's a heaven-sent opportunity. It couldn't have come along at a better moment. With the money I collected from you-know-*where*—"

"You might need that for your wheelchair."

"No riches without risk."

"You've really got to watch those Reds in the rough," she said.

"Don't think I haven't thought about it."

Pandora smiled wanly. "I suppose you're getting rather used to risks by now, talking of you-know-*what!*"

"On the whole," he said, grinning, "I think I'd rather face the wrath of the Cossacks. Never did care for the Windsor knot, my dear."

"Horsing around with the Russians is something else, Ru."

"I know," he said, more serious this time.

She turned away from the window, walked to the middle of the room and faced him. "Very well. Where do you go from here?"

"A quiet chat with Boy Wonder."

A small waiter with a friendly mouth arrived with breakfast and a long-stemmed red rose in a tall vase for Pandora. She took the rose and arranged it with Lyall Heflin's flowers massed on a table in the middle of the room. A single flower made her sad. When the waiter had gone, she said, "Do you think Dollsky will do it?" She poured coffee and handed it to him.

"Pandora, some people will put up with a lot, with almost anything just to survive. For some people, survival means solitude, withdrawal, don't get involved, look the other way. For others it's compromise, accommodations, turn the other cheek. But for a man like Dollsky—in the end his hope is to cut and run. He must know that sooner or later, with his ideas and his mouth, he's going to get into an awful lot of trouble where he comes from."

"Do you trust her?"

"Petrovich? Why not? She's the one who has to face the '1812 Overture.' "

"If he agrees, then what?"

"We get the hell out of here. We leg it, P.D.Q."

"England?"

"I'd feel a lot safer there."

"England," she said reflectively.

"Lyall Heflin."

"*Daisy Jordan.*"

"What's today?"

"Tuesday, I think. I've lost track."

"I've got four days," he said.

It was eight o'clock in the morning and they'd had no sleep. The telephone started to ring in the drawing room.

39

Khor took the news of Zorin's death with a convincing show of surprise and irritation. "Who found the body?"

"His wife, sir. At about two o'clock this afternoon, sir."

It was almost five; Khor had just returned from the crematorium. "Who is at the apartment now?"

"Malik and Nekrasov, Comrade General."

"And the wife, where is she?"

"At the apartment also."

"One shot through the right temple at close range. Malik is sure that it was self-inflicted, is he?"

"Yes, sir."

"And Nekrasov agrees?"

"Yes, sir, Comrade General."

"And nobody else—"

"I checked with you the moment—before informing *anybody*, Comrade General," the young adjutant interrupted quickly.

"You mean to tell me you haven't alerted the chief medical examiner's office?" Khor asked sharply, as if this breach of procedure displeased him. "Nobody's been in touch with—"

"We felt you should know the situation first, sir," the adjutant said nervously.

Khor appeared to think deeply. "You've done the right thing, Lieutenant. It is always a delicate matter when one of our own . . . Yes, yes, let's keep it in the family. Have the body removed. The CME's office can do whatever has to be done at the morgue, the report to come directly to me. Start a PM evidentiary. For our own eyes only. Let's get it out of the way quickly. Bring me Zorin's F20—and his wife's too. Do you know anything about her, Lieutenant? Any trouble at home, do you know?"

"I haven't heard anything, sir. Her name is Anna, sir."

Khor looked thoughtful. He said, "I will go and see the widow Anna myself. Have my car downstairs in fifteen minutes. Call Malik and tell him to release the body to the CME people. He and Nekrasov should wait at the apartment until I get there."

"She's in the bedroom, sir." Captain Nekrasov spoke in a soft respectful voice. Zorin's body had been removed, but the aura of death in the apartment was palpable. "She's quiet, sir; she seems to have taken it well."

"You get a statement?"

"Yes, sir."

"Where was she when it happened?"

"The hairdresser's, sir. We checked. A place on Granovskovo Street. She has a regular appointment there."

"You've finished there?"

"There's nothing more we can do, sir. We were waiting for you."

"Is there anything you want to tell me?"

Nekrasov shrugged. "A self-inflicted wound, a—"

Khor lifted his hand for him to stop. "Put it all in the evidentiary. Write it up with Malik. I don't want any contradictions or loose ends. We're keeping this inside the deparment, but should anyone ask I expect it to stick. Keep it short and simple."

When the officers had gone, Khor sat down in a chair and waited. He sat for a long time. The calm of the summer night fell around him. He sat very still, like a man inwardly praying in an empty church, yielding himself to God. There was a look of blankness on his face that could have been piety. It was almost dark when he heard the bedroom door open. Anna crossed the room and stood looking at the place where Zorin had fallen, as if scrutinizing the lifeless body itself. She wore a long black gown and looked very thin.

"My commiserations," Khor said gently.

She jumped. The voice, so quiet, coming out of the dusk, could almost have been Zorin's. She switched on a table lamp.

"General Khor," she said as the light fell across his face. She sounded composed enough, but she could feel her heart thumping against her chest; she felt as if she were being squeezed inside a straitjacket. "I didn't realize anybody was still here. I heard the officers leave. I thought I was alone."

Khor stood up slowly. He seemed smaller and heavier than she remembered from their one previous meeting. She went around the room switching on lamps. She knew she looked awful, but she did not want to sit in shadows with this man.

"Can I get you a drink, Comrade General?"

"No," he said. "But, please, if you—"

"No," she said. She was aware of the odor of men mixed with the familiar smells of the room.

"The department will miss him. Center will miss him."

It was a voice unused to showing sympathy. Anna said nothing. Why had this cruel and terrible man come to her home? The answers that went through her head frightened her. She felt sick. The feeling of tightness around her chest grew. She folded her arms to stop them from shaking and tried not to think about Khor and all the things he knew about her.

"You're shivering," he said, taking her arm and guiding her toward the ottoman. "Can I get you a jacket or something?" He picked up the peasant shawl that covered the ottoman and offered it to her.

She shook her head. "I'm just exhausted," she said, sitting down. She knew it would be a mistake to draw hope from his display of concern. He was the source of her agony; all her pain and sorrow came from his malign power. She would have no happiness and no peace so long as he existed.

"The shock," he said. She felt herself flinch as he reached out and almost touched her hair. "It must have been terrible for you to come home and find him like that." It was the tone he used to elicit an incriminating response from a suspect.

She did not answer.

"It was quick," he said. "To go out like a light. For a man to want death so much . . . You know that he was not afraid to die. At least you know that. That must be a comfort."

"He shot his brains out, General," she said expressionlessly.

"Death is always an unpleasant business, however it visits us. Although it sometimes seems to me that it's a lot more unpleasant to anticipate than to accomplish."

"I can't think of many things more unpleasant than putting a gun to your head and pulling the trigger."

"It is a soldier's way."

"I never thought . . . "

She did not finish the sentence. Khor said, "What didn't you think?"

"That he would ever do such a terrible thing."

"There are many terrible things in this world, but nothing more terrible than the unexpectedness of the human mind."

"I will never understand why he did it." A sort of numbness settled over her. She felt drained, dead to every emotion. The trembling gradually subsided in her limbs. "I will never understand why he did it," she heard herself say again like an echo coming from a long way off.

"Then, I suspect you are like me," Khor said. "You have a greater predilection for life than for death."

"I did once," she answered.

"But not now?"

After a long silence she shrugged.

Khor walked to the fan-shaped screen and studied the snapshots Anna had fixed to it. He pointed to the picture of her brother. He said, "When your little brother died, do you remember how you felt? Feelings, emotions—they pass. You must accept that you are alive and Valentin is dead."

"His name was Anastas."

"Yes, how stupid of me. I'm sorry. Anastas," he said.

Somewhere in a small, still-alive place in her deadened mind she recognized the warning signal: Khor was reminding her of his power and knowledge. He knew everything that was going on. She tried to concentrate, but her mind felt numb.

"You walk a thin line," Khor told her. He saw her torpor as indifference, her passivity as a kind of defiance.

"I don't understand you, General."

"Adultery is a secret poison," he said without raising his voice.

Unconsciously her hand touched her breast. "He never knew," she said.

"Can you be so sure?"

"He never found out. Unless . . . "

"No," he told her. "There was no reason."

"Why have you come here, General?"

"Death makes amends for most defects, but it does not undo them all."

She tried hard to make sense of what he was saying. She shook her head.

"Death does away with the form," he said. "Unfortunately, the matter is often indestructible."

"The matter?"

"Let us say"—he stopped and grinned—"the matter of Nilus Dollsky."

"I don't know what you're talking about, General."

"I think you do. I think you know exactly what I'm talking about."
She shook her head.

"You know about Dollsky. Your husband told you about Dollsky, and you told Valentin Buikov. *La ronde*, as they say."
She began to shake again.

He smiled at her. "Before you jump to conclusions—before you misinterpret my motives for coming here this evening—let me tell you something. Your late husband discovered things about Nilus Dollsky—things that, for one reason or another, we do not want revealed."

"Three little girls have been murdered," she heard herself say.

"Your way of looking at things and mine are bound to be irreconcilable," he said in a tone of practiced patience. "You want explanations. Sometimes there are no explanations. Why did Zorin kill himself, for example?" He hesitated, letting the question sink in. "Perhaps we'll never know. Perhaps no explanation is the best explanation. Your husband's death could cause tremors beyond Department Twelve, beyond the Center. How he died, why he died, is of no consequence to me compared with the knowledge that he carried to the grave. If that knowledge ever got out, there could be no doubting the harm."

"General Khor, you're talking in riddles to me. Say what it is you want from me." Anna was surprised how strong her voice sounded this time.

"Did your husband leave any material evidence—documents, statements, tapes, anything at all?"

"His office would—"

"*Here.* Here with you?"

"No."

"Are you sure?"

"I'm sure."

"But he did discuss Dollsky with you. You admit that?"

"You know he did."

"At length?"

She tried to steady her thoughts. "He needed to discuss it with someone. But just the broad outlines, that was all. We talked about the problems it could cause—how it could affect him personally—that's all."

"He was irresolute," Khor said as if it saddened him. "You cannot be irresolute and ambitious."

"It was on his mind all the time."

"What did he decide?"

"He just hoped the problem would go away."

"But it wouldn't go away, and so he shot himself. Is that what you want me to believe?"

"I don't know what I think."

"You must have some opinion. You think he shot himself because he was unable to resolve this dilemma? It preyed on him so much, you think?"

"I don't know why he did it."

"And you're sure he never found out about you and Buikov?"

"I told you. Not unless—"

"No, no, no, I assure you: you have my word on that."

"Then he never knew."

"You went out to have your hair made pretty, and when you came home he was dead on the floor? You had no idea that he planned to take his own life?"

"None."

"He left no note? No farewell—"

"There was nothing."

Khor shook his head and changed his tone. "It could look bad for you."

"General?"

"If I refuse to see it your way. The suicide theory."

"Theory?"

"You could have shot your husband. If he found out about you and your lover—"

"I did not shoot him," Anna said quietly.

"I want you to understand the situation you are in," Khor said. "The vulnerability of someone like you, someone with your background, your particular—history." He had the look of a man who had waited for this moment for a long time. "I'm told that Jews have a deep thirst for revenge, long memories. Is that true, Anna Slepak?"

"I loved my husband."

"I could arrest you right now for the murder of Colonel Anastas Zorin. I could throw you in the Lubyanka and lose the key. I could have you committed to the Serbsky, no questions asked. There are many possibilities."

"I am not going to plead with you, General."

"I never imagined that you would." A smile came and went on his shiny face like a spasm of cruel humor. "No, those options are too obvious."

He walked around the room, making soft reflective noises with his mouth like a child sucking a boiled sweet. He walked behind the ottoman on which Anna sat. She did not turn; she would not give him that satisfaction. Finally he stopped in a shadowy place to her left, like something unpleasant waiting just outside the edge of light, making soft sounds to let her know that he was there.

"I want you to forget everything Zorin told you about Dollsky and the dead girls. I want—"

"You're going to let him get away with it? Is that what this is all about?"

"There are overriding interests."

"Another cover-up," she said in a calm voice.

Khor said, "I look after my own people, Anna. May I call you Anna? I'm like a pelican; I'll feed my people with my own blood if I have to, Anna. Just remember that some things are best forgotten. We should each of us be prepared to forget some things. What do you say, Anna Zorin?"

"That's a terrible myth about pelicans."

He laughed good-naturedly. "Your integrity is commendable, but it could do grave harm to another's reputation."

She did not react; her eyes were lifeless. He did not know whether she understood or not. He tried a more direct tack: "Think of the consequences if you force me to charge you. Dirty linen. Buikov would have to be involved. He would not thank you for that. No, we can settle this between ourselves now, in this room."

She looked at him with the blankness of shock.

"Your husband is dead. You can't help him now. Buikov is alive; you are alive."

He helped himself to a vodka and asked whether she had changed her mind. "Whisky and soda," she told him in a dull voice.

"How did you know that was my brother?" she asked quietly when he handed her the drink. "The boy in the picture?"

"I knew."

"Zorin told you, didn't he?"

Khor simply stared at her.

"You were here earlier in this apartment," she said calmly. "You killed my husband."

Rufus answered the telephone. "*Pronto.*"

"And in so Italian an accent, my dear," Pandora teased him.

He listened gravely for a moment and said, "Yes, of course." He looked at his watch, said, "In about fifteen minutes?" and replaced the receiver with a thoughtful air.

"What happens in fifteen minutes?"

"Ninotchka," he said quietly. "I think Boy Wonder is ready."

"Christ," Pandora said softly in a genuinely awestruck voice this time. "Christ, Ru, you've done it this time."

He grinned.

She sat on the edge of the bathtub while he shaved and brushed his teeth. "You really do mean it, don't you?" she said.

He nodded and said through a mouthful of toothpaste, "Looks like a good bet to me." Pandora began to laugh. He rinsed his mouth. "What's so funny?"

"I was thinking—if the palace knew what they were staking."

"I've lucked into something this time, though, haven't I?"

"I hope so, Ru. God, I hope so." She followed him into the bedroom and watched him dress. "Take care, Ru," she said when he left.

Sonya Petrovich wore a cream-colored silk robe over a white chemise. "I could not sleep." She handed him a coffee.

"Neither could I," he said. "I shouldn't have let you go."

"Will you help him?" was all she said after a long pause.

"Yes."

Without makeup she looked younger; her complexion was a sort of Degas pink. He preferred her without makeup. She walked to the window and stared down at the water. She was good to look at: her limbs, flat belly and a shadow of pubic hair were visible beneath the silk. His eyes moved around the large bedroom: to the half-open valise on the low trestle stand at the foot of the bed, to the black evening dress neatly folded across a velvet armchair, to the large unmade double bed.

"I don't want him to be hurt," she said. "If it went wrong, the consequences—"

"Nothing will go wrong."

"May I ask you a personal question?"

He nodded.

"This business, it will be expensive. He will come out with nothing, you know that?"

"I can take care of it."

"As long as you know how it is."

He went over to her and took her head between his hands. "I know what I'm doing," he told her quietly. "Do you know what *you* are doing?"

"As long as you tell me nothing, no harm can come to me."

"You wouldn't consider—"

"My home is in Russia," she said. "I don't have his needs or pressures."

He kissed her on the lips. After a moment he felt her tongue. "You don't object to unmade bed?" she said, finally stepping away from him.

"I don't object."

She slipped off her chemise and faced him. She stood still, demure in her camisole, her hands covering herself between her legs as if she were about to surrender herself for the first time.

"Turn around."

She did, slowly.

"You have a beautiful bottom. You have the bottom of a young boy."

"I hope it is not true what they say about Englishmen."

And later she whimpered, "Oh, it isn't, it isn't," over and over while they made love. "You do it to me good."

Afterwards they talked about the usual things most people talk about after the first time together: the surprise, how fine it was, how much they had wanted it, a few lies, the polite endearments.

"Good morning to you." Dollsky stood up when Pandora came out to the terrace. "Where is your friend this morning?"

"I might ask the same question," she said, accepting his waved invitation to sit at his table.

"You have breakfast?"

She ordered orange juice and coffee.

"You sleep well?"

"Not particularly, no."

"I sleep very well. Why you not sleep well?"

"I have no idea."

"You sleep with your friend?"

"To hell with all this polite chitchat, let's get to the point," she said. He grinned.

"I enjoyed last night very much," she said.

"You should sleep with Dollsky."

"God, you're an egotistical bastard," she said pleasantly.

The waiter brought her order. When he had gone, Dollsky said, "Tell me about your friend. You know him long time?"

"All my life."

"That is as long as anything can ever be. You marry him one day?"

"*Toujours amoureux, jamais marié.*" She tried for a light tone and got it just right.

"Good friends, is what you say?"

"English ladies choose their friends with far more care than they choose their lovers."

"Not just English ladies."

"I can only speak for my crowd."

"And Rufus Gunn is best friend?"

"The best there is. I know I can always go to him when my life begins to wobble a bit. He gave me security when I had none. I know enough about him to hang him ten times over, but he's the only man in the world I'd do anything for, go anywhere for. If he called me from Timbuktu in the middle of the night and asked me for help, I'd drop everything and go."

"He is lucky man."

"I'm a lucky girl."

She filled their cups. "I bet you're impossible on the set."

"A Tartar."

"One day you should come and work in the West."

"Why you say?"

"It's not unreasonable for the West to want to meet the genius whose movies—"

"You joke with me," he interrupted in a hurt voice.

"*I'd* like you to come to London," she said reassuringly. "Is that better? I'd *love* you to direct *Daisy Jordan*—I told you that last night."

"Don't talk about things that can't happen," he said.

"That makes me sad," Pandora said, suddenly aware of what it really meant to be a Russian like Dollsky, to have so much fame and so little freedom.

"Why?" he said. "You don't want egotistical bastard make picture with you?"

"I could make allowances."

"You scared about picture?"

"A bit."

"Don't be. First film always easy for actress. You don't know enough to worry. Panic starts third, fourth picture. When you learn things, then fear comes. One day I would like to make picture with you. What you want to be? Big movie star or good actress?"

"Both."

"Not possible." He pushed his thumbs together in a straight line beneath her chin, the palms of his upright hands toward her, and studied her through the three-sided frame. "Stardom," he said, "is here, in face, in eyes, not in heart. Stardom is about big, fat, *fake* emotions—glycerin tears, not real tears, not real emotions. Stardom not about *anything* real."

"I can see I'm moving into a world for which nothing has prepared me."

Sonya Petrovich woke first, her face pressed against the hardness of his back. His skin felt silky, not like a man's skin at all. She ran her finger down his spine.

"What's the time?"

She reached for her watch. "Just after eleven."

"In the morning?"

"We fell asleep a little while."

Rufus opened and closed his mouth several times, making sucking sounds. "I could do with a drink."

"You deserve drink."

"You have screwed me to the point of utter immobility."

"Champagne for the victor," she said. She picked up the telephone, asked for room service and ordered champagne as if she had been doing it all her life.

"And something to pick at," Rufus hissed.

"And something to pick at," she said into the phone.

She went into the bathroom and came out still wet, wrapped in a white terry-cloth robe just as champagne and canapés arrived. She looked almost childlike. Rufus felt a wave of affection for her—always a good sign after you've just made love to a woman you barely know. She sat on the bed beside him, watching the waiter open the wine. He filled two chilled tulip-shaped glasses, put the glasses on a silver tray, brought them over to the bed, then bowed and left the room.

"He didn't say a word!"

"The best servants never do." He touched her glass with his.

After a pause, he said, "Will you talk to Dollsky?"

"I think no need. It will be best if I stay out of it."

"I can hardly go up and put a proposition like that cold!"

"I think yes. I think that is the way. He likes you. He will trust. I know the way he thinks."

Rufus realized that it had already been discussed and settled between them. He did not blame her for not wanting to talk about it, so he said only, "As long as he understands the risks."

"The risks will be part of the appeal."

"When are you due to leave?"

"Saturday."

"I probably won't ever see you again."

"Look after Dollsky for me."

"Who is going to look after you?"

"I can look after me. But you can do one more favor for me." She put her glass of champagne on the bedside table and fell back onto the pillows. "Come," she said, holding out her arms.

41

Toward five o'clock they passed under the last bridge and came out of Venice into the lagoon. It had been a fine warm day, and there was a promise of sunset in the sky. The gondola moved across the water beyond the Fondamenta Nuove. Smoke hung in the air above the glass factories of Murano. Dollsky sat opposite Pandora. Dressed in the pink mandarin-collared shirt and khaki pants he had worn the first morning she had seen him, his face now had a pale golden color. A small wind ruffled his soft, long dark hair. Pandora thought he looked criminally sexy.

"Look." He pointed.

In the distance a gondola with a black pennant and a coffin on a cata-falque in the bows led a small procession of other gondolas.

"They're going to San Michele," she told him after a moment or two, shading her eyes. "The cemetery island."

"Death always breaks in when we don't expect," he said. "It makes me laugh."

"Why is it so funny?"

As he looked at her, she could see the humor in his eyes. He said, "Burying them or getting them into bed, there is not so much differ-ence—same pretty speeches, same white lies."

"You have a weird mind, Dollsky."

"You know ticking sound of deathwatch beetle is mating call? You see how close it is—death and sex and farce."

"I cry buckets at funerals."

"When you make love first time, you cry also?"

"Gosh, yes."

There was a kind of force behind his smile.

"When I was very small, I spent a lot of time working out my feelings. Now I try not to analyze them at all," she said.

Murano had a feeling of great age without the insolence of Venice. The tiny island seemed to be withered by antiquity. Cluttered with small glass factories, there was little evidence left of the sylvan retreat that was said to have been once the earthly paradise of demigods and nymphs, its meadows swathed with scarlet lilies. Dollsky listened with amusement to the island's history that Pandora read to him from her guidebook in an exaggerated English accent of awed solemnity as they walked through the narrow, sag-ging streets.

"Don't you like history?" she asked.

"People exhaust themselves looking back."

He was fascinated by the factories. He talked to the craftsmen, asking questions about their tools and different kinds of furnaces; he wanted to know about their lives, their families, how they lived. Pandora liked the way he could talk to these men without patronizing them.

Afterwards they had a drink in a bar with a sloping floor and small wooden tables. Its dark was poor-man's dark, made behind faded shutters enclosing the aged fragrance of privation. The customers were fishermen and factory people, men with impassive faces baked by sun and furnaces. Without Dollsky, Pandora knew that she would have been a trespasser, but he made it all right. He's at home with these people, she thought. He ordered two beers. She lit a cigarette. In her simple white tunic dress, her dark-gold hair lightened by the sun, she seemed luminescent in the gloom.

"Will you come back to the West again?" she asked when the drinks came.

"I don't know."

"You'd like to?"

"Lady Pandora, the idea of staying here with you, right now, is the most exciting of all ideas to me." He said it so softly, so simply, so tonelessly, that it took a moment for it to sink in.

She put her beer down and looked at him in the gloom. "Dollsky, do it. *Come.*"

"A nightingale does not live on songs alone."

"They'd be falling all over each other to get you in London and Hollywood."

"It is true," he said looking at her but somehow through her, as if his mind was on something else. "Many people urge me to work in West." He changed the focus of his eyes and smiled at her. "It has been on my mind very much."

In the silence that followed there was something crucial, a turning point so delicate and so final that Pandora felt that her whole future depended on it. She waited, not moving, concentrating on the darkness reflected in the old mirror and bottles lined up behind the bar, hoping he would not sense the tension in her.

"I think I get stale, always in Russia."

"The remedy is simple."

"Not simple, I think. You hear glass men, what they say?"

"What they say?" she asked solemnly in his accent.

"When they move furnace from Murano to Venice, even when they use same fuel, same firing, same sand, they cannot make crystal as beautiful as Murano crystal. They say it is because in hundreds of years air made pure by furnaces. Maybe there is something in Russian soil, in the air of my own country, that make Dollsky good. In West . . ." He shrugged.

"Legend," Pandora said, taking the guidebook and dropping it on the table between them. "Like the nymphs and demigods, that's just legend."

He liked the cadence of optimism in her young voice. He took a deep breath. "I am out. At this moment I *am* out." He spoke softly, his lips barely moving. "Let us go to London," he said.

Pandora felt dazed. Everything Rufus had predicted was happening.

"Can your friend help me? I have no money."

"Don't worry, Dollsky. Don't worry."

PART THREE

42

Walking the five blocks from the city library to the station house, Fyodor Gertsen had the glowering look he always got when his ulcer was about to trouble him again. In his office he unlocked his desk, took out a bottle and poured a drink. Rain had smeared the address written in red ink on the brown wrapping paper of the package on his desk. It looks just like a bloodstain, he thought, an old wound that's been reopened.

Stepan Kamenny arrived a few minutes later, sweating profusely. His linen suit, the same color as the Y-shaped vein that stood out on his high forehead, hung loosely on him. Gertsen pushed a glass and the bottle toward him, and Kamenny poured a small one. "What's this all about?" he asked.

Gertsen waved his glass over the parcel and told him to open it. It had been opened before and retied carelessly with the original string. Kamenny noticed the Moscow postmark. Removing the string, he wound it around his hand in a neat loop, removed the loop and placed it on the desk, removed the wrapping paper and folded it neatly. He looks like a man who would always save string and wrapping paper, Gertsen thought as he watched the unhurried performance.

"Files?" Kamenny asked.

"The green one. Open it."

Kamenny did as he was told and began to read. When he had finished, Gertsen said, "Now the red one."

There were five files. Kamenny read them all while Gertsen smoked a thin brown cigarette and waited. After a while he switched on the neon light and lit a second cigarette. Except for the turning of pages, the only sound in the room was the ticking of the clock on the wall. When he had finished, Kamenny unfolded the wrapping paper and rewrapped the files, unwound the string and retied the package with a perfect little constrictor knot, then stretched his mouth sideways and stared at Gertsen reflectively. "When did they arrive?"

"This morning."

"Nothing else? No note? No explanation?"

Gertsen took out his wallet, extracted a sheet of notepaper and handed it to Kamenny.

The doctor read slowly, looked again at the address on the package, then again at the note: the handwriting was the same. "You're sure it's from him?"

"Why do you ask that?" Gertsen asked sharply.

"It doesn't look like a man's handwriting to me—and red ink! I don't know . . ."

Gertsen nodded appreciatively. "You'd make a good detective."

Kamenny studied the note again. "A woman's writing," he said slowly. "It could be a woman's hand."

"It certainly isn't Zorin's, I can tell you that. I checked with the Astoria register. It's nothing like his handwriting—*nothing*."

"It could have come from an aide, somebody he—"

"Zorin's dead. Dead and buried. I talked to Moscow this morning."

Kamenny stretched his mouth again. When he spoke, he sounded skeptical and uncertain. "But *Nilus Dollsky!* Fyodor, he's not a man you should even accuse of *spitting* without a lot of thought."

"Doctor, my old friend, you don't read your newspapers closely enough."

"I don't read them at all if I can help it."

"Dollsky has skipped." Gertsen opened his wallet again and fished out a cutting from *Pravda.* Kamenny lifted his eyebrows, then read slowly aloud: "Large sums of American and French currency were found in his apartment, together with anti-Soviet propaganda."

"He didn't return from a film festival in Italy," Gertsen said. He waved several letters of vilification against Dollsky that had appeared in *Izvestia* and the *Literary Gazette* since the first report.

Kamenny read these too, then turned his attention back to the files. "So this lot is official—authentic?"

"I'd say so, wouldn't you?"

Kamenny took his time answering. He examined the paper and the embossed letterhead, *Committee for State Security,* printed across the top of each sheet. "I don't have a lot of correspondence from these people, but it looks real enough to me," he said eventually. "But if Zorin's dead and this isn't his handwriting—it doesn't make sense. Why should the KGB send it to you? And why use Zorin's name?"

Gertsen held out his hand. "Give me that green file again."

Kamenny untied the package in the same unhurried fashion and gave it to him. The policeman found what he wanted and started reading in his official voice: "It is an exceptional passion that yields exceptional notions. When emotion overflows in such a personality, the creative energies often become ungovernable, generating within the psychic organism sometimes genius—" He looked up at Kamenny and then continued slowly: "It can also cause psychopathic conditions—depravity, insanity—"

"Yes." Kamenny nodded agreement. "Genius and loss of reason are often—"

"Doctor," Gertsen interrupted, "don't you recognize that statement?

They are *your* words. That's what *you* told Zorin and me that morning we found the kid from the Kirov. *Nobody else was in that room.*" He stood up and walked around the desk. "When Zorin last came to Leningrad, the last time I saw him, it was after the Mikhailovna murder. I told him all about that stuff—Friedenthal and the Italian what's-his-name."

"Gamba. And he wanted all those tests on the makeup," Kamenny said ruefully. "I remember."

"I asked him then whether there was anything he could tell me. He said that his interest was—of a peripheral nature, that's what he said. But he made me a promise: he said that if he did come across anything that would help me, he would pass it on."

"And you think that"— he looked at the parcel from Moscow —"he's kept his promise posthumously?"

"Something like that."

"But why the mystery? Why didn't the KGB give you the material openly, tell you that Zorin was dead and—"

"Even the KGB must sometimes use its power with caution," Gertsen said. "They want to destroy Dollsky's reputation, and it will sound a lot less political, less motivated, coming from an ordinary policeman."

"You might be right," Kamenny said, uncertainty in his voice.

Gertsen picked up the cuttings and began quoting extracts as if they were reviews of a bad play: " 'Renegade . . . enemy of the people . . . traitor . . .' *The Literary Gazette* wants the Supreme Soviet to strip him of his citizenship!"

"You might be right," Kamenny said again, but again without conviction.

"I can't see it any other way. Just more nails for the bastard's coffin."

"As long as it's not your own box you're nailing down."

"How could it be? They want to bury Dollsky, not me."

"Take my advice. Think about it very carefully before you do anything," Kamenny said. "I hate funerals, especially those of my friends."

Buikov adjusted the new blinds in his office. The thin autumn sunshine sliced through the slats and made shadows like prison bars across the new gray carpet. It was nine-forty on the first Monday of October. Dollsky was in the West, ticking like a time bomb; Zorin was dead; Sonya Petrovich had returned to the Clinic of Nervous Diseases in East Berlin.

Lieutenant Vlakus came into the room with some papers. Buikov did not notice him; he was thinking of Anna as he stared through the slats into Dzerzhinsky Square.

After Zorin's death she had written that one brief good-bye note, with a promise never to trouble him again. But one phrase haunted him: "Valentin, you have no way of knowing how many kinds of dying there are, how many kinds of extinction we carry deep within ourselves." He had called her several times, but there had been no answer. A week ago he had driven out to the apartment in the Lenin Hills. He had sat in his car across the street and waited a long time, but she hadn't come out.

Vlakus coughed discreetly.

Buikov turned. "Yes, Lieutenant?"

"You have General Khor this morning, sir. Do you want to look at the lists?"

Khor was on time and they went through the agenda quickly. Surprisingly, neither man mentioned Dollsky; it was a conversation between two men with different styles and strengths.

"So you've finally got Rip Van Winkle to the top of the Labour bunch in England," Khor said. Winkle was the sleeper's code name. "I'm told he could be bigger than the Englishman."

"I don't think he has quite his expertise."

"You've had him long?"

"Rip Van Winkle slept for twenty years."

"Sleepers are a fucking long shot. Wildcat drilling," Khor said. "You either come up with oil or piss vinegar."

"It's not like buying oil at the pump," Buikov said mildly. He tried to imagine Khor at home, in his private world, solitary and unobserved. What did he do? Did he read novels? Listen to music? Did he sing in the bath? How did he unwind?

Khor looked at the suede and leather chairs, the steel-and-blackwood desk. "You like your new furniture?"

"It's comfortable," Buikov said, but now he regretted losing his old pieces.

"It's what you wanted?" Khor asked.

Buikov moved his mouth; it might have been a smile, but there was no pleasure in it.

"You seem not happy, my friend," Khor said. "Is something worrying you?"

"I'm fine."

"Good. Because I have something to tell you that would not help an unhappy man. It concerns Anna Zorin."

Buikov's eyes met Khor's unflinchingly.

"She has become a liability." Khor opened his briefcase. "You should have had more control over her, you know," he said in a quiet admonishing tone. "She almost bungled the Dollsky business."

"Explain to me."

"She took it into her head to send the late Colonel Zorin's case notes to a policeman in Leningrad, a detective called Gertsen. Fortunately, he had the good sense to check back with Center." He handed a file to Buikov.

Buikov left it on the desk between them, separating them from each other like a boundary. For a moment he was unable to speak. The idiot, he thought; how could she have been so stupid? She must have known the police would check with Center. Did she *want* to be caught? He said, "Where is she now?"

"Necessity, the force of circumstances, I had no choice."

"Where is she, Khor?"

"The Serbsky, under psychiatric observation."

"We had a *deal.*"

Khor looked at him with astonishment. "But she forced my hand. What alternative was there?"

"Why didn't you come to me first?"

"Your loyalties are different from mine. You were too involved emotionally."

"We can have different loyalties and still share the same objective."

"I appreciate your concern for your little Jewess." Khor spoke slowly; he seemed to be choosing his words. "I will see that she is handled properly. We will treat her with discretion. Nothing of what she has done need ever come out. What purpose would it serve?"

"You know, you really are"—Buikov smiled almost apologetically—"a shit, General."

"We always knew, we both knew, that Dollsky's defection—the side effects— there were high risks." Khor smiled and went on in a friendlier tone. "This business must not come between us, we must not be forced into polarized positions over this woman. If I had not intervened—"

"Intervention or revenge, Khor?"

Khor looked disappointed. He said, "You have not been betrayed by *me*, my friend."

"How long will she be kept in the Serbsky?"

Khor shrugged his heavy shoulders. "What she did was not the act of a rational person."

"She has many friends. Her disappearance will not escape attention."

"Many things are noticed and many things are never talked about."

Buikov felt despair. He knew that there was little he could do to save Anna without compromising his own position. He said, "I would like to visit her."

"The treatment she is having does not permit visitors. The doctors will tell us when it is possible," Khor said in a reasonable tone, as if his perfunctoriness could hide the horror of her incarceration.

Buikov studied him for a long moment, then said almost sadly: "Very well." At that moment he knew *exactly* how to fix Mulder Khor. "Very well," he said again in the same mild, submissive tone.

"I am glad that is settled," Khor said affably. "So, how long will it be before Dollsky is up to his tricks again, do you think? Or perhaps he's lost the habit."

"A tendency to repeat a familiar action at specific times—"

"You sound like a Serbsky quack," Khor said.

Buikov smiled; he was quoting Sonya Petrovich. He said, "It's just that the mind acquires an attachment to whatever has been familiar. Like the instinct to sleep at the approach of dark."

"And you think—"

"It will soon be dark, Khor. It will soon be very dark."

"Uh-ho, Batman, there's a job for us to do. Time to get out of bed and start rolling, Batman." Pandora switched off the alarm before the ring started. "Go chase yourself, Robin."

Her voice was perhaps an octave lower. Her hair had been darkened a shade to emphasize the paleness of her skin. The five pounds she had lost showed in the hollows of her cheeks and seemed to exaggerate her mouth. Falling back on the pillow, she stretched with a small purring sound. In three days' time she would start filming *Daisy Jordan* at Pinewood. Eleven weeks of makeup tests, fittings, dance classes, exercise classes, script readings and rehearsals had gone by since Venice. It had also been a rigorous preparation for the endurance and patience that moviemaking demanded. Now she felt ready, the way an athlete must be ready, for the main event.

Recognizing her determination as well as the underlying anxieties, Lyall Heflin had switched the shooting schedule to capture this quality on film. The first scene they would now shoot, No. 32, read:

INTERIOR, LIMOUSINE. DAY. MEDIUM SHOT. DAISY COMING FROM FA-
THER'S FUNERAL. LOOKS STRAIGHT AHEAD WITH PURPOSEFUL EX-
PRESSION. SHE HAS MADE FINAL COMMITMENT TO LIVE HER OWN
LIFE.

Dollsky had worked on the script, and something new had emerged
which Pandora could not identify but which she knew was exciting and
right for her. The news that Dollsky was going to direct the picture had
been announced a week ago, a month after the deal had been signed. He
had come out of hiding for a press conference with Pandora at the Savoy.
The headlines had been predictable: RUNAWAY RED AND THE BEAUTIFUL
BLUEBLOOD (London *Mirror*); THE LADY AND THE DEFECTOR—$20 MIL-
LION ROMANCE (New York *Post*); NILUS TO DIRECT PANDORA CHILD IN
HIS FIRST MOTION PICTURE OUTSIDE THE SOVIET UNION (*Wall Street Jour-
nal*); DOLLSKY AND CHILD (London *Mail*).

Pandora did not read the stories. She knew that there would be the
usual speculation about her father and their relationship, the familiar lines
about his betrayal and her beauty, the same old mixture of lies and guess-
work. "Who needs it?" she had said when Heflin expressed surprise at her
incuriosity. "I'd read about a girl who is only vaguely familiar to me,
whose past is somewhat similar to mine. I have no intention of sorting out
my life from press cuttings."

She slid out from between the sheets and glanced at her naked body in
the mirror with a satisfied smile. She ran a bath and, sinking beneath the
warm water, closed her eyes and tried to think of matters that had nothing
to do with film studios, script conferences, rehearsal halls, still sessions and
newspaper headlines.

At eleven o'clock she had a hair appointment with Philip Kingsley on
Green Street. She walked from there to the White Elephant.

"In the West everybody has an angle. Always remember that and you've
got wisdom," Rufus said to Dollsky when Rinaldo had taken their orders.

"The world is ruled by angles," Dollsky said.

In a dark-blue business suit, Rufus was sober but looked as if he needed
a drink; Dollsky looked as if he might be too young to drink at all. Pandora
had seen surprisingly little of Dollsky socially since Venice. Both caught
up in the intense activity of preproduction, their meetings had always been
with others: costume designers, makeup and lighting people, publicists
and the front-office executives that Heflin called "the suits" and treated
respectfully. She could not remember the last time she had seen Dollsky
alone.

"Three days to the shoot," Rufus said, holding up his glass.

"Pandora—and Daisy," Dollsky said.

They sipped their drinks.

"How are the nerves holding up?" Rufus asked her.

"They come and go."

"Always before picture," Dollsky said, "inside I get butterfly as big as sparrow."

"Do you take anything to calm yourself?"

Dollsky shrugged. "Nerves is good. Nerves is salutary to creative persons."

"I think it betrays guilt," Pandora said.

"I *am* guilty. I am villain. You see on set. I am different person."

Rufus did not smile. He said, "Well, I hope you're going to compromise a little with—"

"In West, compromise is good word, yes?"

Pandora glanced at Rufus and saw him hesitate.

"Give a little, take a little," he said. "Compromise is the civilized way of carrying on."

"In my country compromise is weakness."

"There is always the middle ground," Rufus said calmly. Things had gone remarkably well so far, and he did not want Dollsky getting a difficult reputation on his first picture in the West. He said, "You're happy, aren't you? The script—"

"Script good."

"And you like it, P.?" Rufus turned his attention to Pandora with a brusque look.

"It's marvelous." This was a side of Rufus that she had not seen before, and she rather liked it. He was incisive and disciplined in a way he had never been before.

He turned back to Dollsky. "I need hardly tell you that a lot of people will be praying that you fall flat on your Commie arse, Dollsky."

"Why?" He sounded surprised. "Everybody love me. Everybody want to meet Dollsky. Everybody want to give me party."

"The movie business is strange, Dollsky." He had fallen into the fashionable habit of calling the Russian by his last name. "People kiss and hug each other without affection. They pursue you today because you're the new face in town. They will just as easily destroy you tomorrow without even thinking. It's not even malice; it's just the way it is in the movie business."

Dollsky laughed and slapped the table. "Don't worry, old boy," he said in an improbable English accent. "Everything be fine as dandy."

"Good."

"As long as they do it Dollsky way."

There was a momentary silence around the table. "A lot depends on this picture," Rufus said finally.

Dollsky patted his hand. "I won't fall on arse," he said gravely. "I promise you, Mr. Agent. Don't worry."

Nobody wanted wine. Lunch was over by two-fifteen. Rufus had an appointment, signed the check and left before coffee.

"You lose weight, I think," Dollsky said.

"Five pounds."

He touched her cheek. "Is good."

Then he talked to her about her love scene in the movie. He had already discussed the lighting with the cameraman and the way he wanted it cut with the editor, he said. "As you move with boy—his hands, your arms, his fingers, your mouth, the lace, skin, hair, everything merge in caress, sort of mirage. We think we see more than we do. No music, no sound until Daisy— What is it, the word, please?"

"Orgasms? Comes?"

He nodded. "When you comes, no more silence."

"When *Daisy* comes. I am not a screamer."

"We see," he said with his boyish grin. He touched her face again. "Is good. But more lipstick, I think more gloss."

She glanced at her reflection in the mirror. "Isn't it sad that vanity never lets us love anything without wanting to change it?"

"I am alchemist. I will make you into goddess."

"I just want to be me."

"You think I change you too much?"

"Perhaps, without knowing it. It's hard for a woman not to be marked by some man."

"Your father teach you that?"

"He taught me how to find my way around a menu, how to order servants about, and then he left me for Mother Russia."

"Perhaps he was making judgment."

"Of what?"

"English hypocrisy? Western values?"

"Like everybody else, he had his fallible moments."

"Why he go to Moscow, you think?"

"I really don't know—all kinds of reasons. I don't like this conversation, Dollsky."

"You don't know why he went to Moscow?"

"He must have had a death wish."

"All death wishes are granted sooner or later."

"Rather sooner in Russia, one fancies."

She sat very straight, her back pressed against the red velvet banquette; beside her, Dollsky looked small.

"You think he was wrong? What you think?"

"The only bit of Marxist dogma in which I see any practical value is to always travel with your chauffeur."

He tugged his forelock, and they both smiled. "We go. I want you take me to good cosmetic shop."

"*Why?*" she asked, giving him a beady look.

"I buy you lipstick. I know shade."

"Dollsky, you are incorrigible."

Buikov dialed the number and, when a man answered, said quietly, "A country's true colors are in its parks." He waited for a moment, then asked, "Remember?"

"I remember." The voice sounded peevish, but wary too. "What is it you want?"

"I must see you."

"I'm feeling rather under the weather. Is it something that—"

"It's important."

After a long pause the voice said in a deliberate tone, "There is a park in Minsk I'm told I should see before I die. I've reached that station in life when I'm obsessed with morbid thoughts like that, I'm afraid."

"It will be cold tonight," Buikov answered in a kindly voice. "Wrap up well, comrade."

The Englishman replaced the receiver with a thoughtful look. He wore a brown woolen dressing gown like a greatcoat over dark-blue pajamas. He had not been outside his apartment for nine days, and had not dressed or seen anybody in that time. Until Buikov's call, the phone had not rung once. He had told his department that he had a chill; it was a bad sign that they had accepted his absence so casually. He had been lonely before, but never had he experienced such a terrible solitariness as he felt now. He turned on the electric fire. It had been a great mistake accepting the chairmanship of the Joint Coordinating Control Committee, he thought, regretting the complaisancy he had allowed to creep into his attitude. He should have been more careful, knowing how they operated, their relish for figureheads, sacrificial stooges, to fend off a more general responsibility. How could he have let himself fall into that old trap? Foolhardiness? A kind of masochism? Some deep scorn of the consequences? But what was there to fear? His faith in their unwillingness to discredit him now was infinite. He found the matches and lit the gas under the kettle. Staring into the flames, he lost his place in time.

He was in the London Library again in St. James's Square, that February afternoon nine years ago, and Sergeevich Stadnyuk, who he thought had gone out of his life forever, was telling him the whole story as calmly as if he were discussing the storm outside. "Nature's most precious secret is within our grasp"—that was how he had begun, a secret so full of promise and consequence that fewer than a dozen people outside the Politburo could be told. Already its physical and chemical properties were almost indistinguishable from the real thing. A year from now—five at the most—they would be able to synthesize it perfectly, like bars of soap, Stadnyuk had said. But why me? he had asked, shaken by the revelation and frightened by the demand that followed it. Because, Stadnyuk had answered, you are the best. But he had not worked for them for ten years, not since his Treasury days; it was all over now, it was all behind him, the passion had gone. It is never over, Stadnyuk had replied with the admonitory little sigh he had used so often in the days when he was his control. This was his chance to affect the course of history; think of it as a challenge, Stadnyuk had told him, a chance to serve humanity, an act of the highest principle. We are so clumsy, he had apologized in his intrusively humble tone, we could bring the whole capitalist edifice tumbling down around our ears, and that would be a tragedy for everybody. Teach us to be kind to the goose that will lay our golden eggs, Stadnyuk had said. Lenin once boasted that one day you would build lavatories of gold in the streets, he had reminded the Russian. But until then we must live with the capitalist world, Stadnyuk had said and completed the quotation: "When you live among wolves, you must howl like a wolf."

The shrill whistle of the boiling kettle brought him back. I had no choice, he thought. The moment Stadnyuk started talking, telling me everything, I had no choice. If I had refused, I would have died, probably right there on the iron-trellis floor of the History Room of the London Library. And now I'm being turned out to grass, he thought. Like all defectors, he knew that his usefulness diminished a little more each day. But he had done what he had to do; the foundations had been laid, the strategy for the next twenty years fixed. Dishonor in the West was the heritage of his sacrifice, but he had known the consequences from the start and would not complain now about his lot. A defector, like a novelist or a recluse, must invent and inhabit his own world, redefine his own reality: he survives only by his understanding and mastery of that private world. He had no sense of dislocation, and he was proud of that. Dislocation as much as drink had destroyed Guy Burgess. He accepted without resentment the Western world's estimate of himself. No, he had no regrets; he hoped he would not be a deathbed penitent; he hoped he would feel the way he felt now when he was called to account.

He made tea, wondering what Valentin Buikov wanted, why he had called from a pay phone, and why he had been so very nervous. He hoped he had understood where they were to meet.

The Englishman shivered a little with the cold as he paid the taxi driver. Winter had set in quickly. The first snows will soon fall, he thought marching through the Byelorusskaya terminal building, his left hand dug deep in his overcoat pocket. In his other hand he carried a walking stick. He wore no hat, but his collar was turned up, covering his ears. He moved in a straight line, as if absorbed by an idea, unaware of the crowds around him.

The dark-blue Moscow–Minsk express was standing at platform 5, smoke starting to rise from the thin scalloped funnels along the clerestory roof as attendants began firing the samovars. Russians still made long train journeys an occasion. Because of the sealed windows, nobody boarded until the last possible moment. The scene of clamoring confusion and lingering emotional farewells was a perfect place for a meet.

Buikov wore faintly tinted glasses and stood beyond a pool of yellowish light twenty feet from the seventh third-class coach. The Englishman passed within a yard of him. Buikov watched him continue along the wide windswept platform behind the crowds and heaps of luggage until he was out of sight, engulfed in darkness. A few minutes later he returned and stopped a tactful distance from where the Russian stood. "You're clean," Buikov told him softly.

"I'm pleased you got it."

"That's what my job is all about." They walked together along the platform in the gloom, behind the piled baggage trolleys and crowds, like two people backstage in a theater.

"I want to talk about Khor," Buikov said.

"Anything concerning Khor is always interesting."

"You know I am in hock to him."

The Englishman collected his thoughts. "The woman, I remember, the wife. Lazar Slepak's daughter. I thought that business was settled now that Dollsky's flown the coop. Wasn't that the arrangement?"

"Khor has gone back on his word. She is in Serbsky."

The Englishman hesitated and tapped the ground with his walking stick. "A change of policy, you suppose, or merely a temporary shift of tactics?"

Buikov smiled plaintively. "The strategy of the trip wire," he said.

They resumed walking. Nobody appeared to be taking the least notice of them. The Englishman said nothing; the silence irritated Buikov. He said, "I am bound in my own interest to abide by his terms, but it offers no peace of mind, no prospect of long-term stability."

"One is occasionally obliged to accept unscrupulous terms," the Englishman answered, "when the cost of opposing them might be too great."

The wind had dropped, and the smoke from the samovar chimneys went straight up into the girders high above. The Englishman glanced obliquely at Buikov. "Do you need some new leverage on him?"

Buikov gave a small affirmative smile.

"My dear chap, I know this must be very unpleasant for you, but what can I possibly do?" He was about Buikov's height, with the same slim build. "When I first offered advice, I had no desire to involve myself in some private quarrel. Khor's unorthodoxies really are none of my business."

"Are you afraid of him?"

"Why should I be afraid of him?"

"You seem to have less taste for intrigue than you used to."

"One grows a little older, one grows—"

"Do you listen," Buikov interrupted, "to the BBC?"

The Englishman said he did not. "It's astonishing how prodigiously boring I now find the news from London."

"Dollsky is to make a film with your daughter. You did not know this? It was on the BBC."

The Englishman smiled. "What an immensely small world it is" was all he said, his detachment confirming Buikov's hunch that he had no idea about Dollsky.

They came to the end of the platform and looked down the track into the grape-colored darkness, tasting the cold in their mouths. Three vertical signal lights with fishtail ends changed from red to yellow as a mournful night sound of shunting started up in the marshaling yard somewhere in the distance.

"Are you and Khor still lovers?" Buikov asked quietly.

"You have no right to ask such a question, no right at all, and I'm damned if I'm going to answer it," the Englishman said furiously, his face pink with anger.

"What I can do for you, what you can do for me, will depend on the answer to that question," Buikov said in the same steady undertone.

The Englishman hesitated; then his whole manner changed. "I think you had better explain," he said as if resigning himself to the worst.

Buikov told him about Dollsky and the Leningrad murders. He spoke in a plain matter-of-fact tone, with no drama or attempt at suspense. He told him about Zorin's investigation up to the moment of his "suicide," and of Anna's attempt to expose Dollsky through the Leningrad police department. The simple narrative gave the story a dispassionate force.

When he had finished, the Englishman felt a spasm within himself, a terrible frisson. Outwardly he appeared calm, his lips a thin line; it was a pose of accustomed self-discipline, practiced self-effacement. He drew in a deep breath and stared into the darkness. After nearly a minute he exhaled slowly. "It's of my own making," he said. "That day in Gorky Park . . . " He did not finish the sentence.

Buikov was pleased that he was not a father. He said, "May I ask one question? If you had no idea, why did you provoke the watch on him in the first place?"

The Englishman shrugged; a resigned smile came into his eyes. "Khor wanted Zorin quiet. Zorin made him nervous. I'd heard the stories of Dollsky's lapses. We all had, hadn't we? His drug habits and so on. It seemed a bit of harmless mischief, and it gave Khor something to chew on."

"That was all?"

"Like Hampden, I was blessed with a head to contrive, a tongue to persuade, and a hand to execute any mischief."

Buikov shook his head in amazement. "You had *no* idea?" he asked again, thinking that perhaps he was too shocked to be capable of remembering what he had heard.

"I was bored. The idea amused me, I suppose. How could I have known he was such a dangerous character?"

A diesel shed door slowly rolled open, silhouetting signal boxes and gantries. They could hear men shouting to each other. Then the door closed and it was dark again.

"How did Zorin really die?"

"Suddenly," said Buikov.

They turned and walked slowly back along the platform.

"I'm prepared to remove Dollsky before he does any more harm," Buikov said. "Are you prepared to discuss a trade?"

"Trade? I don't see what I possibly have to offer in a trade."

"You're close to Khor."

"Short of"—the penny dropped, and he finished the sentence on a lower note—"killing him myself."

"Our time is very short," Buikov said softly.

"I'm not in the killing game."

"We all are. When the last cat is hung, we all are."

"But you could arrange that sort of thing so much better."

"It's a good offer."

"I must think this through," the Englishman said querulously. "It's very difficult."

"I never said I thought it would be easy." Buikov smiled. "And you never answered my question, by the way. I presume the answer is yes."

"We see each other from time to time."

"In private places? Secretly?"

"Yes, sometimes."

"Then do it," Buikov said. "*Do it.*"

They had walked back through the station and out into the street. The sky had a whitish light and there was a smell of snow in the air. It was late and cold, the streets almost empty, and they hastened their steps. They turned left and walked for five minutes, then turned left again. The Englishman asked questions but nothing of importance. He seemed preoccupied, with an air that might have been a kind of panic. The more he thought about Buikov's offer, the more cunning the Russian's handling of the situation seemed to be. Europe was Buikov's territory; he could act with impunity there. Killing Khor in Moscow was the most dangerous thing.

"The girls in Leningrad," the Englishman said after a silence. "They were all in the theatrical profession, you said, all young."

"The oldest was nineteen."

"Pandora is nineteen."

"You must love her very much. Let me express your love—in the most practical way I can."

They were back at the station after a harrowed silence. Buikov said, "You must trust me, just as I must trust you. We must work on the old principle—my enemy's enemy is my friend."

"Will you take care of it yourself?"

"I will go to London tomorrow if you say the word."

"Go to London," the Englishman said. It was beginning to snow.

46

Traveling on a Hungarian passport as Jano Kaczmarek, a Riesling wine exporter from Budapest, Buikov caught the evening British Airways flight from Paris to Manchester. He went through immigration control with the minimum of delay: passport, visa, a letter of credit from the Hungarian International Bank, a letter of introduction to the chief regional buyer for a Midlands supermarket chain.

"You're in the wine trade, Mr. Kaczmarek?"

"The oldest trade, but not the oldest profession," Buikov said. The official returned his papers with a look of polite but bored amusement. "Have a successful trip, Mr. Kaczmarek."

"Thank you, sir," Buikov said with the deference East Europeans have learned to show to officials.

He collected his bag and went through the customs hall unchallenged. In the lobby he rented an Avis with an American Express card made out to Jacek Kodoly. He drove at a steady forty for a while, getting used to the car and the right-hand drive. The journey took just under four hours. He felt relaxed; he enjoyed night driving. He stopped once for a coffee, and from the motorway cafeteria he telephoned a London hotel to book a single room with a bath. He dropped the car at the rental garage in Belgravia shortly after 1:00 A.M., took a cab to the Rubens Hotel on Buckingham Palace Road and signed in as Dr. Jacek Kadar from New York City. He ordered a wake-up call for eight o'clock, with coffee, fresh orange juice and *The Times* at eight-thirty.

Buikov woke just before the alarm call, thinking of Anna. A light sweat covered his face. It was hot and stuffy in the small room, and he got up and opened the window. He switched on the radio. A show called *A.M.* was pumping out commercials, traffic reports, weather forecasts and news items; a couple of announcers called Bob and Doug were doing their best to make the catalog of traffic delays and train cancellations more bearable with cheerful asides.

Buikov soaked in the bath and listened. An author plugging his new book. A politician defending his mistakes. A banker explaining how the price of oil and gold affected all our lives and why the City was watching with great concern what the Russians were up to in the marketplace. It was strange how American it all sounded; he might have been in New York. *The Times* had an interview with Dollsky, datelined *St. Moritz, Wednesday*. Buikov read it carefully. It was a familiar Dollsky interview, acknowledging his own brilliance: "There are no perimeters to perfection." Buikov smiled. He had now read enough about Dollsky to know that it was a favorite line of his. He dropped the paper on the floor. On the radio an American voice was singing a jingle for Pan Am. As he shaved, he wondered what Anna was doing at that moment. He wondered how long Dollsky had been in Switzerland. He thought about the Englishman. Time is running out, he thought.

He left the hotel at ten-fifteen, walked to Victoria Station and joined a short line of people waiting for taxis.

"Saint John's Wood, the underground railway station, please."

The taxi driver did not look happy. The Edgware Road was jammed, he said; he had just come from there. From Marble Arch the traffic was bumper to bumper. It was no way to make a living, he said. Buikov looked at his watch. It was ten-twenty-five. "I have appointment at eleven. I will tell you where we go after underground station," he said firmly but pleasantly. The driver mumbled something to himself and started his meter running. He would have preferred a shorter fare; he would have preferred to stay in the West End; he would have preferred to be in Israel with his daughter and his grandchildren. He looked back at Buikov with unkind eyes. "You German?"

"*Ja.*"

"I thought so."

They reached St. John's Wood a few minutes before eleven o'clock. Felix Crick was already there, his beak of a nose lifted in the air, unselfconsciously enjoying the pale wintry sunshine. He wore a raglan topcoat over a brown tweed jacket and brown corduroy trousers. His cheeks were flushed from the cold.

Buikov leaned forward and opened the door, then sat back in the far corner of the cab. Crick moved across the pavement with extraordinary agility for a man of his size and age. The taxi moved off as soon as he had closed the door. Crouching on the jump seat, he slid back the glass partition of the front seat and told the driver to go to Lord's. He closed the partition and sat down beside Buikov.

"Lord's?"

"The cricket ground."

There was no exchange of greetings.

"Cricket? At this time of the year?"

"Lord's is wonderfully quiet out of season, and very pleasant to look at. We won't be disturbed there." He smiled. "I have a Memorial Committee meeting there a little later on, so I can kill two birds with one proverbial."

Buikov looked surprised.

"Perfectly safe. An omnium-gatherum of old fossils relentlessly reminiscing. Very good on Kipling and Grace but absolutely no awareness of what's happening today."

At their destination Crick showed his MCC membership card to a uniformed commissionaire. "I'm going to show my guest around before the Memorial meeting, Sergeant."

The commissionaire saluted as they went through the gates.

"I have a preposterous weakness for this place, y'know. The older one gets the more one cherishes those places which help one to remember how very splendid life once was," Crick said as they walked slowly toward the outfield covered in brittle brown leaves.

"I don't understand the game. Both teams in white—how do you recognize whose side a man is on?"

"You want instant recognition—villains and heroes?"

"I like to know who is on my team."

"That's the subtlety of cricket, dear Buikov. Good and evil are so indissolubly tangled, don't you think? C'est bonnet blanc et blanc bonnet."

Buikov smiled. "A very English game," he said.

A flicker of amusement came and went in Crick's pale eyes.

They walked slowly. With each step, wizened leaves scurried about their ankles. Buikov matched his steps with Crick's. Occasionally Crick stopped and tested the turf with the toe of his shoe as they made their way to the Coronation Garden. They sat on the circular seat beneath the weeping ash; its sage-green looked almost gray in the November light.

"It's so quiet in here," Crick said. "I love the silence. A friend of mine once called it a bosky cathedral. I rather like that, don't you, a bosky cathedral? I've often thought it would be a perfect spot in which to die."

Buikov reached into his overcoat, took out a brown envelope and handed it to Crick. "Second installment."

Crick put it away. "What do you plan to do with the letters now?" he asked.

"They've served the purpose. What did you tell palace?"

"That I had persuaded Rufus to destroy them, and that he had done so in my presence."

"They accept that?"

"Why should I lie to them?"

"Why should you lie to them," Buikov repeated slowly. They talked like jaded actors bored with a long-running play.

"I dined with Bunbury a week ago. As far as he is concerned, the matter is closed."

"There should be honor in it for you. Knighthood, perhaps?"

"For arranging a bonfire?"

"Very important bonfire."

Crick smiled.

"You've done excellent job," Buikov said.

Crick tapped his jacket pocket. "Is this the only reason for your visit?"

"No."

"I thought perhaps not. Are you going to tell me now the real reason for your visit?" Crick took out a half-hunter pocket watch and looked at the time. "We ought to get on with it, oughtn't we?"

A deeper silence seemed to fall over the garden. Buikov stood up, made a motion with his hand and began. He talked slowly. It was an edited version of the story he had told the Englishman a few days before but contained all the facts that Felix Crick needed to know. He did not look at Crick as he talked with great care for nearly ten minutes. When he had finished, Crick did not know how to answer. He stood up and walked along the path, his chin down on his chest, his hands clasped behind his back. He walked to the end of the garden, turned and came back to where Buikov stood smoking a cigarette.

"Where is Nilus Dollsky now?"

"According to *Times* this morning, in Switzerland, preparing picture with Pandora Child."

Crick sat down, leaned his elbow on his knee and his hid eyes behind his hand like a man at prayer. After a while, he looked up. "It is all a great deal less tidy than it was," he said bleakly.

Buikov smiled a cold smile, which twisted his mouth.

"Does Henry Child know about any of this?" Crick asked.

"Yes."

"And?"

"He ask me to help protect his daughter."

"He knew about the original plan?"

"Some of it, yes."

"And now he wants it aborted, is that it?"

"You surprised? You sound surprised, Professor. The blood is thicker than the water, don't you say?"

"It's out of character."

"Surely you can forgive him a little bit paternal pragmatism? Does not mean he abandons fundamental beliefs. Saving own flesh and blood is not philosophical relapse."

"He believed terribly in what he did. His devotion to the cause—it was sacred to him—"

"Becoming traitor?" He noticed how Crick nearly always spoke of the Englishman in the past. "Becoming traitor was *sacred*?"

"He was never false to his real allegiance."

Buikov shrugged. "Loyalty, betrayal, blind obedience—he still does not want daughter to die"—he dropped his cigarette on the path and stepped on it with the toe of his shoe— "especially when he has himself helped shut up wolf in sheepfold."

Crick looked at him carefully. "You really believe, do you, that she could die?"

"She is in very much danger."

"What—what are we to do?"

"Tell Rufus Gunn situation."

"Rufus!"

"Put him in picture."

"And what is he supposed to do about it? What can he do?"

"Whatever must be done," Buikov said in that tone of indifference which often precedes an ultimatum. "As you said yourself, I think, he has instinctive approach in these matters."

Crick looked up at the sky. Dark clouds were gathering over the block of flats at the Grove End Road side of the Ground. "What an infernal muddle life is sometimes," he said.

"Especially when everybody wear white."

"How am I to explain my . . ." His voice died away.

"That is now matter for you, Mr. Crick."

"I wish I could wash my hands of it."

"The solution is simple, I think."

"Take him out, you mean?" Crick had a habit of pretending to be slow, as clever people often do to hide their quickness. "Take Dollsky out?"

"Final solution is usually safest."

"I don't trust final solutions. Even if it solves the present difficulty, it usually creates a more beastly one down the line."

"When we cannot get what is perfect, we must get what is practicable."

"The practicable is often the most abhorrent."

It started to rain. Crick stood up. "Come, I will show you the Memorial Gallery," he said mechanically. He led the way, pointing out the various treasures in glass cases: Sir Jack Hobbs's cap and blazer; Victor Trumper's boots and pads; the historic collection of bats. It meant nothing to Buikov, and at that moment it seemed almost to mean nothing to Crick, who talked as if he knew the facts only as part of some job. After the Memorial Gallery, they went to the Long Room. Portraits of whiskered cricketers hung from floor to ceiling on the pale-green walls. At the far end of the room, a bald, very pink man in a dark blazer who looked like a wrinkled baby sat in a leather armchair reading a newspaper with the aid of a small magnifying glass. He was the only other occupant.

Buikov and Crick stood in front of a portrait of an Edwardian player. In his white flannel trousers and white shirt, he was clearly a member of the ruling classes; his pose reflected all the grandeur of England's imperial past, and most of the grief since.

"He has a sort of brusque grace, doesn't he?" Crick said, looking from the painting to Buikov.

"You think he knew?"

"Knew?"

"That he was already part of way of life that could not survive?"

"Probably not," Crick said, looking back at the portrait. "Self-interest usually breeds self-deception, don't you think?"

The old man at the far end of the room rose slowly and left by a small door Buikov had not noticed before.

"You will see to this matter?" Buikov said, ending the silence that had lasted for nearly a minute after the closing of the distant door. His voice was more businesslike. "You will see Rufus gets message?"

"The consequence—the remedy—is likely to be drastic. Is that to be the policy—"

"We do not make policy in KGB, Professor, but sometimes we like to think we can influence it."

Crick smiled, but there was nothing but dismay in his smile and eyes.

"I hate the country," Khor said vehemently again. "Do you have any idea how hard it is for me to get away like this for twenty-four hours? And for what? I don't enjoy it. I hate being boxed up like this, out of touch, counting fucking daisies."

"Let me get you a dram," the Englishman said. It amused him to think how Khor was as much a prisoner of his suppression as those he suppressed. He went over to the English butler's table. "I still have some of that excellent malt." He poured a large drink into a cut-glass tumbler, handed it to the Russian, poured one for himself, just as large, and returned to the cane armchair.

It was Khor's second visit to the dacha on the edge of the fir forest. "You really *like* it out here?"

"It satisfies my disposition for indolence. I don't use it nearly enough," the Englishman answered, crossing his long legs and looking around the room with approval. The largest of the rooms attached to the greenhouse, it was warm in the coldest weather. "It's peaceful."

Khor lit a thin brown cigarette and threw the match into the burning logs. "You don't get bored out here alone?"

"I was up at five this morning."

"What's there to do out here at five o'clock in the morning?"

"I love to see the light of a new day on the forest."

"And freeze your balls off."

"There's always something going on in the country. It has the inestimable gift of always being enigmatic."

"The inestimable shit of a city's enigmatic enough for me. You ever miss England?"

"A few special corners."

Khor finished his drink and held out his glass for more. "Now we talk. You said you had matters to talk about. I'm listening."

The Englishman refused to be hurried. He poured another drink. He was nervous, but it did not show. "I want you to call off the Dollsky operation," he said. He was standing by the window, his arms crossed, his glass pressed against his arm above the elbow. He looked relaxed. "I want you to bring him back. I know about Leningrad and what happened there."

Khor laughed. "And you don't want the son of a bitch playing around with your daughter in London, is that it?"

"He's a maniac, Khor. I want you to do something."

"You know I can't sacrifice a national interest for some private consideration."

"You owe me a favor, Khor. I've earned this one."

"Never put your faith in quid pro quos. Not in our trade."

"One hopes. At least one hopes."

"Englishman, Englishman." Khor sighed theatrically. "I am a Russian. I must be motivated by what's in the best interest of the party."

"My daughter's *life* is at risk."

Khor took a pack of cigarettes from his pocket, found it was empty, screwed it into a ball and tossed it into the flames. He stared at the

Englishman with a new kind of interest. "This information you have about Dollsky comes from Buikov?"

"Why should you think that?"

"Instinct?"

"Instinct can be harmful. Whole species have become extinct because they could not control their instincts."

Khor grinned. "You had a meet with Buikov. You forget so soon? The Byelorusskaya station? Did he tell you also about Anna Zorin? I'm out of cigarettes. You have cigarettes?"

The Englishman picked up a humidor and opened it for the Russian. Khor selected a cigar without comment, bit off the end and spat it into the fire. "Let me see if I can guess. Buikov asked you to persuade me to release the widow Anna, and he, in return, would do something about Dollsky. Was that the deal?"

The Englishman said nothing.

"But you preferred to detour that arrangement. It was too complicated, too involved. You decided to come straight to me and get *me* to protect your daughter. Fuck the Comrade General, to hell with Anna Zorin—why get involved with their problems? Am I right? I think I am right. I know you, Englishman. You are a terrible scalawag, Englishman," Khor said with a smile that was at once admiring, mocking and almost benign.

After a silence in which Khor slowly lit his cigar, the Englishman asked quietly: "Will you help me?"

"You must not make your life more a martyrdom than it already is," Khor said, openly examining the room like a prospective buyer in a buyer's market. Then he swung around and looked at the Englishman sharply. "Remember when I asked who Zorin's admirer was?"

The Englishman stared at him, guessing his harbored resentment, knowing what was coming next.

"You said that if I knew the name of Zorin's admirer, even I would be alarmed. Remember that?"

"I put you on your guard. I could go no further. Now I'm asking you to return the favor," the Englishman said blandly.

"You caused me a lot of aggravation. It cost Zorin his life."

"You're talking in riddles."

"I'm talking about Kosygin."

"Kosygin?"

"He's been dumped. It will be announced next month. It was him, wasn't it, Zorin's connection?" Khor spoke almost in a whisper. "Kosygin was the admirer?"

"If the shoe fits."

"Don't fuck with me. I *know*."

"What does it matter now? Zorin is dead. Kosygin is out, you say."

Khor looked intently at him and began to smile. "If only you had given me that name in the beginning, none of this would have happened. He lost it two years ago, my friend. Kosygin's been nothing for two years, a fucking cauliflower. That cunt couldn't have frightened a canary."

"Are you going to help me, Khor?" the Englishman asked quietly, admitting nothing. "Cancel the Dollsky operation, please."

"I gave you my answer."

It snowed steadily through lunch. Khor did most of the talking. The Englishman listened with polite attention, content to put a word in now and then. They had latkes, which the local woman, who looked after the Englishman and took care of the dacha, had earlier prepared for him to reheat.

After lunch, the Englishman suggested a walk. They had got through two bottles of red Georgian wine as well as the whisky, and Khor would have preferred to sleep it off. "You're a fucking masochist," he said, but agreed to a short walk as far as the woods.

In their fur coats and shaggy fur caps they looked almost like animals. Khor looked at the gray sky, heavy with more snow to come. "I'm not going far," he said resentfully. After five minutes he was breathing hard. It was colder than he'd thought.

"Here we are," the Englishman said, pointing with his heavy walking stick to a trail. "This will lead us back to the house."

Khor went ahead. Almost immediately there was a splintering sound like the breaking of glass beneath his left foot as he stepped across a fallen tree onto the snow-covered tread plate. At first he thought he'd gone through a skin of ice beneath the fresh snow. Then he heard himself screaming as he fell slowly forward.

He kept screaming until he hit the ground. The coil-spring jaws of the gin trap had cleaved clean through his boots and skin, burying steel spikes deep into the bone of his ankle.

The Englishman had not moved.

"For fuck's sake, help me!" Khor turned and tried to prize open the spiked claws. He spoke as calmly as he could. "Get me out of this thing. I'm bleeding like a stuck pig."

"I can't help you, Khor," the Englishman said in a quiet, indifferent voice, not moving a muscle.

As the whisky and wine quickly died out of him, Khor was overwhelmed for the first time in his life by a fear of dying. "Fuck Dollsky. I'll fix Dollsky. Just get me out."

"We must never put our trust in quid pro quos in our trade, my dear chap—you said so yourself."

"Don't let me bleed to death, please, Englishman. Do something." Khor pulled off his gloves with his teeth and began to tug savagely at the serrated teeth embedded in his bone. The trap was attached to a length of chain, which was connected to a steel peg driven into a rock twenty feet or more away.

The Englishman watched, just out of reach. "The best hunts always end the same way," he drawled mockingly. "I recall my father saying how the stag has a splendid innings all in all, and only at the very end does he have a beastly half hour of it."

"Help me, you son of a bitch," the Russian screamed at him.

"You had a splending innings, Khor."

Khor dragged himself onto one knee and unbuttoned his coat, as if trying to free his movements for another assault on the trap. The automatic appeared suddenly from the folds of fur and fired.

The shot went through the side of the Englishman's throat, severing his larynx and silencing his scream as he smashed the walking stick down on Khor's hand. The gun flew into the snow, and Khor hurled himself sideways, grabbed it and fired it twice in quick succession.

Khor was vaguely conscious of a sharp blow somewhere on his body, but the pain in his leg and hand prevented him from placing the new pain exactly.

Choking from the inhalation of blood, the Englishman brought the stick down again with a final reflexive force. Khor's skull split beneath the thick fur cap as the stricken Englishman pitched forward across his lap in a sudden mist of snow. The blood ran out of his gaping throat onto his furs, as if he were a slaughtered animal. He twitched once, as if an electric current had passed through his body.

"Die, you bastard, you fucking son of a bitch, die." But the Englishman was already dead, his pale narrow face fixed with the pain of a last soundless shriek.

It would soon be dark. Khor pushed the Englishman's body off his legs, heaved himself up again onto his free knee and again attacked the trap with his bare hands. Three times the steel jaws gave an inch or two only to spring back even deeper into his flesh when his freezing fingers gave way. After that they seemed hardly to shift at all. He was bleeding badly and was growing weaker all the time.

An hour passed. It was beginning to snow again. Khor had managed to stop much of the bleeding in his leg by pressing a flat stone on the artery and bandaging it with the Englishman's tie, winding it tight with the short barrel of his automatic pushed through the loop of the knot. But the smell of blood frightened him; sooner or later it would attract the wolves.

In the dying light he saw the walking stick half hidden under the Englishman's body. Writhing sideways, he could just reach it. After a while he managed to force the stick perpendicularly into the ground between the teeth of the trap that extended some twelve inches in length beyond his leg. Using the stick as a crowbar, twisting his body, he pressed with all his strength. Inch by inch the teeth came out of his torn flesh and the splintered bone. The veins swelled in his bull-like neck and sweat diluted the trickle of blood that ran down his forehead from the crack in his scalp. He wasn't aware of any of this; he was only afraid that the stick would break, that his courage would let him down, that his capacity to bear pain would give out.

But the stick and his courage held. Slowly the jaws continued to open until he could drag his leg free. He swayed for a moment as if in a trance, then fell back into the snow, shaking with fatigue and relief.

The room was exactly as James Anselm had remembered it. He had thought he might have exaggerated its grandeur when he had described it to his wife, but he hadn't at all.

Sir William Bunbury gestured toward a chair.

"Please, Mr. Anselm, do sit down. I'm sorry to have kept you waiting. It's been one of those days."

"That's perfectly all right, sir." Anselm was a little more relaxed than on his first visit.

"I daresay it's something important," Bunbury said with as much geniality as concern in his voice.

"It is, I'm afraid, sir."

Bunbury ran the palm of his hand from his forehead to the fringe of red hair at the back of his neck. "Okay," he said. "Fire away."

He listened with deep intentness to what the MI5 man had to tell him. Anselm talked in a calm voice, like a chairman trying to put unpleasant facts before his board in the best possible light.

When he had finished, Bunbury drew a deep breath and said, "And your people had no idea, no suspicions at all?"

"None at all, Sir William. But naturally, when you told us you had used him . . ."

Bunbury lifted his hand in a sort of benediction. "You ran a check, yes, of course, I understand. And this Russian fellow Buikov is?"

"General Valentin Buikov, head of their Special Services. He's one of their best people, sir. A sophisticated man with a keen political sense."

"He wouldn't come himself on a minor matter?"

"Hardly, Sir William."

"And yet he has been over twice, you say, he himself, in the last few months?"

"Twice that we know about."

"Since this business began?"

Anselm nodded again. He did not look happy.

"The second occasion was when?"

"He flew into Manchester from Paris Tuesday evening. We picked him up at Ringway, traveling on a Hungarian passport. We followed him to London and—"

"Felix Crick."

"Yes, sir."

"Oh, dear," Bunbury said softly. "Have we been out-generaled?"

"It's been more a question of bad luck, sir."

"It's not possible, I suppose, that Buikov is not actually responding to events as we know them?"

Anselm shook his head. "The timing, Sir William, the people involved, the chain of events—all coalesce into something a good deal more than coincidence, I think."

"Yes, yes, of course," Bunbury said in the same subdued tone. It took him a little while to think of what to say next, for he was genuinely shocked. Finally he said, "And what's your reading of Rufus Gunn? Where does he fit into this mess?"

"Either he parted with the letters because he admires and trusts Crick and assumed they would be returned to the sender—"

"The Russians coughed up *nothing?* They got them *free?*"

"Or else," Anselm went on quietly, "he was paid. He seems to have come into some money recently. It's hard to say . . . He's a gambling man, as you know. Money comes and goes with him all the time."

"He's been an infernal nuisance, but I really can't see him going down the Moscow Road."

"It's possible they hid from him the real source of the money, of course."

Bunbury did not react to this. He said, "So what is the next step in this minuet, Mr. Anselm? What is to be done now?"

"Well, sir, until this morning we were in a bind. It looked as if matters were out of our control entirely."

"And what happened this morning, Mr. Anselm?"

"First of all, before we go any further, sir, are we agreed that the letters were not burned in Felix Crick's presence, as he claimed?"

"I suppose that must be a fairly reasonable assumption."

"That in all probability the letters are with Buikov?"

"Inside Moscow Center."

"That's the point, you see, Sir William. I don't think so."

"No?"

"Buikov has gone out of his way to control Crick *personally*. That is very unusual for an officer of his rank. It's my hunch that he is playing the whole operation entirely on his own."

"Is that possible? Off his own bat?"

"It's unorthodox, it's risky, but it's just possible. Buikov could do it."

"But we don't know for certain that's what he's up to?"

"As a working hypothesis, it—"

"I prefer facts."

"There are very few immutable facts in my business, Sir William."

Bunbury knew this as well as Anselm did, but he said, "It's not the way we like to do things at the palace. We like to be sure of our ground."

"If we delay a decision until we are sure of all our facts, Sir William . . ." Anselm shrugged. "The first thing you learn in this business is to be able to live with conjecture."

Bunbury offered a small, understanding, reminiscent smile: "Scientists *have* to be right," he remembered once lecturing his own intelligence staff. "We have only to be more right than the other side."

"The letters have not surfaced in Moscow?"

"I think we would have heard something by now if they had. A whisper—something."

"Then what is he waiting for?"

"Until he decides how best to use them?"

"His ace in the hole?"

"Yes, sir."

"How does this help us?"

"This is where it gets interesting, sir. This morning we learned that Buikov's mistress, a lady named Anna Zorin, was recently transferred from the Serbsky Institute to the Dnepropetrovsk Psychiatric Hospital under the direct orders of Mulder Khor. General Mulder Khor, sir, head of Department Twelve, Internal Surveillance."

"I don't see what this has to do with our own predicament, Mr. Anselm."

"There is no love lost between Buikov and Khor. We're not sure what's at the bottom of it, but we do know that Anna Zorin is the widow of one of Khor's officers who shot himself a few months back. She was committed to Serbsky about five weeks ago, and then moved to Dnepropetrovsk, where she is being treated with heavy drugs normally used on schizophrenics and paranoids. She is under the personal supervision of a Center psychiatrist."

"One of Khor's people?"

Anselm nodded.

"And I take it that she is neither schizophrenic nor paranoid?"

"Buikov doesn't think so."

Bunbury nodded for Anselm to continue.

"Anna Zorin is the daughter of the late Dr. Slepak."

"I suspect I should know that name?"

"He was quite well known in his day. He helped to set up a fund-raising organization in Moscow, the Anti-Hitlerite Committee, at the beginning of the Second World War, which was aimed at American Jews. Later Stalin denounced it as a Zionist organization, and Slepak was packed off to Siberia."

Bunbury began to walk up and down, running his pudgy hand across his bald, freckled head. He stopped in front of Anselm and looked at him for a long moment. "What makes you think Buikov will be willing to do business with us?"

"If he returned the letters and we got our people to lean on the Campaign for Soviet Jewry and on Amnesty International to take up Anna Zorin's case, get her adopted as a prisoner of conscience perhaps, we could stir up a tremendous fuss."

"Buikov would trade?"

"He knows how these things work, Sir William."

"A straight swap?"

"There would have to be a few refinements, I think."

"Refinements?"

"I fancy he'll want us to leave Crick in place."

Bunbury thought about this with a certain apprehension, but also with admiration. He said, "We don't want to start up another series of embarrassing events, Mr. Anselm."

"But neither will Buikov want another one of his people pulled in, sir. We live by give-and-take."

"Crick gets off scot-free?"

"I think it might appeal to Buikov as a fair exchange."

"And you think you could"—Bunbury cleared his throat—"arrange this?"

"I think it's within our compass, sir."

"Isn't it unwise to anticipate these people?"

"Can we trust Buikov, do you mean? We have a choice, Sir William. It's between almost certain eventual embarrassment on the one hand, and an initiatory gamble now on the other."

Bunbury stared out the window for a while, then said without turning around, "We really must do everything we can to get those blasted letters back, Mr. Anselm."

In spite of the pretended repugnancy in the palace man's tone, James Anselm knew that he was being given the green light. He said, "I will keep you informed, Sir William, every step of the way."

Bunbury turned sharply and lifted his hand. "I don't want to know how you do it, Mr. Anselm. You know the saying: 'People who enjoy *pâté de foie gras* and respect the law should never watch either being made.' "

He went over to the drinks table. "Scotch, isn't it? Straight, no ice."
"You have a very good memory, Sir William. Thank you."
"You'd be astonished, dear Mr. Anselm, how much I also manage to forget."

Free of the trap, Khor felt strangely euphoric. He struggled to his feet, swung the Englishman's body across his shoulders and with the aid of the walking stick started back to the dacha. The Englishman was no real weight, but his wet furs had frozen and Khor knew that if he was forced to put him down for a moment, he might never get started again. He stumbled on until he found the frozen stream, and followed it. The wind beat snowflakes into his face.

The dacha was in darkness; the woman from the village had been told to stay away until summoned. He dropped the body into the back of his car.

At first he drove with great care, almost as if he were showing some sort of respect for the man he had killed, but after an hour he began to feel drowsy. The car, which had been gradually gathering speed, swerved suddenly and caught some paling. Khor swore aloud and kept going. He lowered a side window an inch to let the cold air pour over his face. It woke him up with a start and he closed the window quickly.

His skull was barely bleeding at all now. How long had he been driving? He found it hard to calculate. His mind wandered. It's like being drunk, he thought. He could feel, almost pleasurably, his torn foot warmly soaking inside his boot. He began to sing fragments of songs. Unaware of his state, he pressed ahead on nothing more than impulse, his driving veering erratically from caution to madness. Somewhere along the way he had smashed his left fender and lost a headlight. Once his head fell forward, striking the horn in the center of the steering wheel, but the sudden blare brought him back to his senses. The car swung to the middle of the road. He forced himself to concentrate. His mouth was dry and he was beginning to feel stiff, yet he had no foreboding. Except for the warmth in his boot, and a similar sensation he now was aware of in his belly, he only felt cold. "But not as cold as you, Englishman!" he shouted aloud.

She was waiting at the foot of the steps. She wore a white coat over an apricot-colored wool dress, with white shoes and white stockings.

Khor stood and grinned at her. "Customer," he said thickly and jerked his chin toward the car. He was breathing hard and swaying. He had left the walking stick in the car. In the early-morning light Vera Volk did not notice his wounds. He is drunk, she thought with fond amusement.

"Oven-ready?" she asked with her strange laugh.

He stood where he was, still swaying, looking as if he did not know what to do.

She studied him more carefully. "Are you all right?"

"Some vodka."

"Go through," she said, stepping to one side as he started unsteadily down the steps. "I'll take care of this."

Vera Volk dragged the Englishman out of the car by his feet and lifted him like a bag of old clothes in her arms. Rigor mortis had already started in his neck and jaw, she noticed, but his limbs were still malleable; she reckoned he had been dead about five hours. She carried him to the cremation chamber, where she made no attempt to check his clothes for cash or valuables. She set the hearth to automatic, adjusted the air and gas pressures and synchronized the flame control. A radiant shimmer of hot breath flowed into the darkened room. The Englishman appeared to shudder, then rolled slowly forward into the fire.

In the office, Khor seemed to be sleeping, still bundled up in his furs. The room was in semidarkness, lit only by a light in the vaulted roof.

She began unbuttoning his coat. As she pulled open the furs the blood ran out, covering her hands, spilling onto her white coat. His midriff oozed.

Vera Volk let out a terrible cry and Khor opened his bright dark eyes. His nostrils widened, sucking in air. He grinned savagely, but the effort was too much. He felt a violent pressure of pain at the back of his throat. His lips moved, but no sound came out. His nostrils collapsed and the savagery went out of the grin. The grin stayed on his face, transfixed there, like something molded in gray putty.

Vera Volk stayed with him for a long time, savoring his presence for the last time, aware that their bodies would never be one with the other again. She washed the blood off her hands in the janitor's slop sink, poured herself a whisky and drank it down.

Removing her brother's clothes, she lifted his body onto the steel trolley. She washed away the blood matted in his thick gray hair, shaved his face and bathed his mutilated foot as tenderly as if he were alive. She sprinkled him with oil.

When she had finished she took him to the chamber. He has the body of an emperor, she thought. She wished she had a robe for him to lie in. "Life without you will have no purpose for me," she said softly to his face. Then she pressed the control.

She mopped the blood off the floor with a kind of angry exertion, changed her clothes and cleaned her shoes. When she had finished, she poured herself a large whisky.

"Shit!" she said aloud, banging the glass down on the table at which she sat. "Shit!" She had forgotten to operate the rotating transverse sections that prevent the mixing of remains.

Mulder Khor and the Englishman were blended together for eternity.

"Dear God," Rufus said in a stricken voice. "But how on earth do you know all this, Felix? If the Russians didn't nail him and—"

"I cannot be more explicit, but I am not completely locked in an ivory tower, you know. Now, don't press me, dear chap; I'm getting into choppy water as it is, telling you as much as I have."

Rufus was not surprised by the evasiveness. He had suspected Crick's connections with British intelligence since his intervention to retrieve the letters.

"But a murderer! I mean to say, Felix, it's *incredible!* And I'm his bloody *agent!*"

"I think you should do something, don't you?"

"Do something? Like what, Felix? What do I do?"

"Warn Pandora in some way, I suppose."

"What do I say? 'Oh, by the way, Pandora, I think you ought to know that your director's a raving lunatic who kills young girls. Better watch your step, old bean.' "

Crick smiled a trifle vaguely; he disliked questions capable of no unqualified answers. "It's a disagreeable business," he murmured, glancing around Rufus's drawing room.

Rufus Gunn looked like a man trying to calculate his own stress factor. "It's not possible, is it, Felix," he asked after a long pause, "that all this is some kind of trick?"

"Trick?"

"Hoax?"

"To what purpose?"

"I don't know. To discredit Dollsky? Devalue his defection?"

Crick appeared to think about this for a moment. "My friends seem to be pretty sure of their facts," he answered slowly. "It is exceedingly unlike them to make mistakes in these matters at this level. I am sure they would have weighed the evidence in a scrupulous fashion before . . ." He did not continue.

"*Before*, Felix?" Rufus prompted him.

"Before it got to me."

"But if our people know for certain that he killed these girls in Leningrad, why don't they do something about it? There must be international laws that—"

"But my dear chap, don't you see the spot they are in? His defection has been quite a feather in their caps. The welcome we gave him, the fuss, all the brouhaha. They'd look awfully foolish now if— You must see it from their point of view. They're not moralists, not policemen. They—"

"Just want to stop the rot, do they?"

"Discreetly."

"So they came to you, Felix?"

Crick smiled again a little wistfully. "I'm like an old maid coming to the end of her shelf life. They can still find a use for me occasionally."

Rufus made a small gesture of despair. His whole world seemed to be falling apart. He was very pale.

Crick said in a consoling tone, "We live in erring times, Rufus. There is a certain incorrigible logic to the fact that it is impossible to defend democracy democratically."

It was almost eleven o'clock when Felix left. He would not let Rufus call him a taxi. He preferred to walk back to his flat across the river. "I'm a walking gentleman," he said.

Rufus had started to pour himself another brandy when he remembered the letter. It had arrived that morning, a Saturday, and he had left it on the mantelpiece to read later. It had a Swiss stamp, postmarked Zurich. He opened it anxiously and read:

Darlingest Ru, just finished (early) our last day in Gnome City. I stared moodily into the camera in one shot, walked out of the Florhof (divine little hotel tucked away in a very old building in the old part of town) in another, got into a cab in a third. A piece of cake— no dialogue! So far I have only had to look intense and sad. The continuity girl said I looked tragic and thought I must have been think ing sad and beautiful thoughts. Didn't tell her that I was only think-ing about going to Ferragamo's to buy some of those vampy low-cut shoes you love so much!

Your flowers were lovely, but I thought the 'Love R' was a mite cool. Preferred message you put on bunch you sent the day I signed the contract. Remember? *No* is the answer to that one. You wrote, 'Seems silly to be so formal, but thought I'd be nice and Tory. Thank you for being you.'

Just started to snow again. Methinks I'll get myself a whisky and soda. Your genius client I'm growing to like not quite as much, but still find interesting. He's given to saying things like, 'You are certain to be divided in yourself because you are talented actress, but woman first!' and things like that. He has changed since Venice. I can't explain how exactly, except that now the picture has started he has a sort of seething disregard of the world outside. (But I still think he is mainlining his press clippings; I think he shoots up about ninety pounds every morning!) He's abandoned his public charm and seems oblivious of everything but Daisy J. I am pleased I have not (yet!!!) been to bed with him, although I still do find him hugely sexy. Hey ho! Will you be angry or jealous or both when I tell you the deed is done? On the weekend we go up to Val d'Isère, which will be our location hq. in the Alps. I have my first real acting scene (see p. 29 Int. Daisy's Bedroom, Evening!) on Tuesday. Still pretty apprehensive about it. From the start I knew it was the scene I had to lick if ever I'm going places in this business. (And I *do* want terribly to be good, Ru.) D knows how I feel about this scene. He discusses it calmly, very matter-of-factly. ("Girls of eighteen masturbate very much. Is nothing.") He wants to work on the scene with me Monday (crew's rest day). As you will astutely note from my progressively palsied writing, the w @ s is attacking my brain bone and writing skills. I wish you were here to light my way to bed. Farewell, Agnes, but not forever. Lovingly, P

Rufus read the letter twice, then picked up the telephone, rang Swissair and booked a seat on the first flight to Geneva the next morning.

At eleven o'clock on that same Monday morning at the Charles de Gaulle Airport in Paris, James Anselm, the deputy director of MI5, and Major General Valentin Buikov, head of Special Services of the First Chief Directorate of the KGB, met for the first time.

They were almost the same height and about the same age. As they talked in a quiet corner of the concourse bar, they looked like two international businessmen. Buikov might have been a little higher up the executive ladder than Anselm; his suit and haircut looked more expensive, and he smelled of Eau Sauvage aftershave.

Anselm outlined his proposal and stated his terms: within seventy-two hours of the letters being returned to the British ambassador in Moscow, Amnesty International and the Campaign for Soviet Jewry would begin a major operation to have Anna Zorin released from the Dnepropetrovsk psychiatric hospital. He did not explain how he knew so much about Anna Zorin, and Buikov did not ask; nor did he show surprise.

"And Felix Crick?" The Russian continued to look thoughtfully into his glass of Perrier. "What will you do about Mr. Crick?"

"I see no point in involving him in any of this."

"No embarrassing disclosures?"

"It would only muddy the waters."

Buikov nodded his understanding. It was a conversation between two men with sharp, quick, disciplined minds and a respect for each other's professionalism.

"It is acceptable," Buikov said after asking Anselm to clarify some points. "We proceed."

"There is one small matter," Anselm said as if it were an afterthought. "You controlled Crick yourself on this one, didn't you?"

It was not really a question, and Buikov saw no point in denying it.

"Wasn't that unusual?" Anselm asked in the same casual tone.

"It has been unusual situation," Buikov said warily. "Why you ask this question?"

"I think you are the only person in Moscow Center who knows about those letters, General."

"Is interesting theory."

"Felix Crick delivered them to you. I think that's as far as they ever got."

"But you don't know that, Mr. Anselm. You can't be sure."

"You could not have agreed to my offer if it were otherwise, General."

"You are guessing, Mr. Anselm."

"If I were only guessing, General, we would have no deal."

They smiled at each other; it would be absurd to be angry at each other's wiliness. Anselm offered a cigarette; Buikov shook his head. The MI5 man took one himself and lit it slowly with a Dunhill.

"Does it matter?" Buikov asked quizzically watching him.

"It would be naïve and gullible to imagine that the idea of photocopying these documents had not crossed your mind. Do you agree?"

"How is this to be prevented?" Buikov asked pleasantly.

Anselm answered quietly. "If you should attempt to use the letters against us in any way, at any future date, we shall disclose the full extent of our arrangement."

"Your second-strike capability, Mr. Anselm?"

"Serving yourself before the cause," Anselm went on with a small apologetic smile. "If that were to come out, I imagine it would be embarrassing for you in Moscow, General."

Buikov smiled ruefully.

"We don't want to ruffle a lot of feathers if we can help it," Anselm said.

"We understand each other. What is expression? I know the side the bread is buttered on?"

"Exactly."

They shook hands with an ironic tolerance of the distrust and trickery of their trade. They rather liked each other, but it was unlikely that they would ever meet again.

"Inform your ambassador to expect to receive a sealed package for your eyes only within thirty-six hours. There will be no photostats. You have my word."

The whole conversation had taken less than thirty minutes.

At thirteen-forty Buikov was on Aeroflot flight SU252 to Moscow. It's extraordinary, he reflected, how the pieces are falling into place. He closed his eyes and put his mind to the new situation. He calculated how much Dollsky's defection had cost so far: two installments totaling $40,000. It would not be too difficult to write off such a sum against more profitable exercises. If Crick had done his stuff, that account would soon be closed. He smiled. Had the Englishman also closed Khor's account? he wondered. It is strange the way events have a habit of resolving themselves just when they seem most intractable, he thought.

He slept for a while, and awoke thinking of Sonya Petrovich. She had done a brilliant job. It was a pity it had been for nothing. He looked forward to using her again. He admired professionals, and Dr. Sonya Petrovich was a very professional lady.

52

Rufus called Pandora's room from the lobby. There was no answer, so he asked for Heflin. "Mr. Heflin's out," the operator told him in perfect English. "He will be back at five o'clock."

Rufus had his case sent up to his room and told the clerk to tell Heflin he was in the bar as soon as he returned.

The bar was dark, smelled of ski wax and something like hot buttered rum. It was empty except for two girls. One looked French and spoke English with a slight American accent. "Jean-Claude, I said, we can't go on hiding our inward emptiness with screwing and skiing . . ." Rufus ordered a glass of mulled wine and waited.

Heflin arrived ten minutes later looking like a chic lumberjack in a wool shirt and a pair of tweed knickers tucked into four-ply socks. A brown cashmere sweater was tied around his shoulders. He greeted Rufus warmly with a resonant intonation that he always overdid when he was anxious. He hated agents turning up on location unannounced; it usually meant that somebody was going to try to stiff him over money. He signaled the barman, ordered an Irish coffee and another mulled wine for Rufus.

"Why do prices go through the roof whenever a movie company's in town," he grumbled, signing the check. "I was here three months ago, and I swear to God everything was half the price it is now."

"Everybody's looking for the dollar."

"Isn't that the truth," Heflin said. He sipped his drink. "Dollsky didn't say anything about you coming over," he said.

"He didn't know. I'm here to see Pandora."

"She's not here, Rufus. She's up at the chalet."

"With Dollsky?"

"Yes, with Dollsky," Heflin said defensively. He had never understood the curious relationship between Rufus and Pandora; he knew they were lovers, but they were like brother and sister too. "They went up Saturday morning to go over some scenes together. Then the weather came down like a blanket Saturday night."

"Just the two of them up there?"

Heflin nodded. "They're stuck up there till it lifts, Rufus."

"You have the number?"

"The phone's out, but I talked to them yesterday before the lines came down. They're fine. They've got heat up there, and plenty of food and booze. They're quite happy to sit it out till—"

"I've got to get up there, Lyall," Rufus interrupted quietly. "It's very important I get up there right now."

"Rufus, it's impossible—hopeless to even think about it in this weather."

"Where is the chalet, exactly?"

"Rufus, the road is out. The choppers are grounded. Even the birds are having to walk. The weather's changing minute to minute. Crewdson says the turbulence—"

"Where is it, Lyall?"

The persistence alarmed Heflin. "Do you mind telling me what this is all about?"

"It may be nothing."

"Is Pandora in some kind of trouble? Mary mother of God, Rufus, I have a twenty-million-dollar movie on the line here. If she's in any kind of trouble, I want to know about it."

"Lyall, calm down. Let me sort it out, all right?"

Heflin looked at him steadily for several long seconds, then stood up and without another word led the way to the fifth floor, where a suite had been converted into a production office. Filing cabinets, desks, telephones, typewriters and a duplicating machine were crammed into a room that still contained a bed and a dressing table. A map of the mountain and aerial photographs covered one wall; on the opposite one a poster of Pandora bore the legend: "Pandora Child *is* Daisy Jordan." At the window a telescope on a tripod pointed to the peak.

"We're here," Heflin said, jabbing the map with his forefinger. "Mont Blanc's to the north, the Haute-Savoie valleys here—Chamonix, Megève, Argentière. Our chalet's just below this ridge." He turned to one of the aerial photographs. "This gives you a better idea. It's the most sensational location—"

"You said there was a road?"

"A track that normally just about takes a Range Rover. We were able to get our gear to this point here, and Crewdson's helicopters lifted it from there to the chalet." He pointed to two red pins on the map. "But ice falls have taken it out here and here, and the rock just above it in this area is rotten. It could go at any time, according to Viridet."

"What about the other side?"

Heflin shook his head. "Maybe you could get as far as the westerly lower peak, but that would be about it, I reckon . . . You'd be no better off."

Rufus went across to the telescope and stared at the mountain for a long time. "Can you get someone up here who really knows this bastard?"

Heflin picked up a telephone and spoke quietly while Rufus continued to sweep the mountain with the telescope, searching for breaks in the swirling mist and clouds.

A short, hard-looking man in his early forties came into the room. He had a tanned intelligent face.

"Rufus, this is Gunter Viridet," Heflin said. "Gunter's the head of the area rescue team, and is advising us on the picture."

The two men shook hands.

"I want to get up to the chalet," Rufus told him. "The northwest ridge looks like my best line of ascent."

"On safe snow, in tolerable weather, that is correct."

"I'm talking about now."

"Are you a climber?"

"I ski better."

Viridet turned to Heflin. "I don't advise. You pay me to advise. I don't advise. Step-cutting up an ice slope is simple exercise on a fine day. On a fine day this mountain is no problem—a girl can climb it. But when the cloud is on top of you, when this wind is cutting you up like glass . . ." He shrugged. "Even if this man was an expert, fit enough, and knew this mountain, I would not advise."

There was a heavy silence in the room. Finally Heflin spoke. "He's determined, Gunter. With or without your help, I think he means to have a go."

"He is a brave man." The Frenchman spoke in a level voice. "But brave men must also have the courage to turn back in bad conditions."

"But first they must start out," Rufus said.

"If it was a matter of life and death, even then the risk—"

"It is a matter of very great importance to me," Rufus said calmly.

The two men stared at each other and saw the strength in the other.

Finally Viridet shrugged, turned to the map and spoke in a low, serious voice: "The route up lies either by the northeast or northwest ridge, the hogback. If the wind has not dropped, take the northeast ridge; it is less exposed. You must get onto the ridge at as high a level as you can."

Viridet talked for nearly forty minutes. He made Rufus study the photographs, check the map, identify landmarks and their position in relation to others. "Rocks look different from each angle, and close to they look different again. Here the snow will be crisp; you will almost be able to jog up it and will not need crampons. The trouble begins here, on this slope. Here you must follow a diagonal traverse . . . Look through the telescope, it is in shadow now and has a shiny blue-gray color, yes? *Ice.* And what looks like bare rock, that will be ice-glazed also. The snow in this area, beyond this crevasse, is old. It is easy to spot; it has less air and will have an almost gray look." He stopped and stared at Rufus for the first time. "If you have not made too many mistakes, you should have reached here by four o'clock. Eleven hours. You will feel every second and every step of it in your body. But now you begin the drop down. See the hollow to the right here? That should give you a passable descent practically onto the terrace itself."

"Thank you," Rufus said quietly when he had finished. By now it was dark, and the ice glinted in the snowfields on the mountain.

"I hope you have a slow pulse and low blood pressure, my mad friend."

Rufus turned to Heflin. "Can you ask your wardrobe people to get me whatever Gunter thinks I'll need? Climbing suit, boots, ice ax—I don't know—crampons, a rucksack."

The Frenchman shook Rufus's hand. "I will take you up to the Theodule hut after dinner. Sleep there tonight. Start early, no later than five. It will be dark, but the early snow will be firm and not so difficult."

"I think I need a drink," Rufus said.

53

"You had a nightmare. It was just a bad dream." Pandora wiped Dollsky's forehead with a cold cloth she had brought from the bathroom.

It was five o'clock in the morning. Dollsky was sitting up in bed, his eyes still frightened. He looked like a dazed child. His dark hair, freshly washed, shone in the light of the bedside lamp.

"What was it?" She sat on the end of the bed. She wore nothing beneath the white peignoir she had hurriedly put on to come to his room.

"I don't know." His hands trembled.

"You screamed out. Christ, you scared me. You were being hunted, being watched . . . people were hunting you."

"What else?"

"The rest was in Russian. I think you were calling out a girl's name."

"What name?" He sounded belligerent, as if he were being accused of something.

"Lily? Lilya? It sounded like Lilya," Pandora said after reflection, ignoring his tone. "You called it out several times. It's what woke me up."

"You heard in your room?"

"I should think they heard you all the way down in Val d'Isère." She straightened the bedclothes in a maternal reassuring gesture. "You put the fear of God into me, waking me up like that."

"There is no sound in dreams," he said. "Conversations, screams, they come always from silent lips."

"*You* weren't very silent."

"Do you believe in the dead appearing to the living?"

"I don't know," Pandora said, collecting her thoughts. "When we were children, Rufus and I made a pact. Whoever died first would come back and explain what was up ahead."

"Lilya Kuzonev," he said as if he had not heard her. "Lilya Kuzonev."

"That's the girl you dreamed about?"

"She was dancer with Kirov. She was murdered."

Pandora shivered. "Did you know her well?"

"Not so well."

"But well enough to dream about her?"

"We dream about strangers sometimes."

"That's true."

Dollsky pulled back the sheets, slid his feet onto the floor and sat on the side of the bed. A small figure, his head surrounded by that wild mane of dark hair like a poet's, he wore only the trousers of his brown silk pajamas. His penis bulged beneath the thin silk. Hair, thick and tightly curled, much lighter than the hair on his head, showed through the silk. Down there, Pandora noticed, he was almost blond. His nakedness aroused an excitement inside her that was sexual and somehow shocking.

"What?" Dollsky's grave sharp eyes searched her face. He kissed her ear slowly.

"I think it would be a bad mistake. To start something at this stage."

"You think you will regret?"

"I know I will regret and be glad at the same time."

"There will always be conflict between prudence and what we want."

"I'm just afraid," she said, "of starting something that might get in the way."

"Of what?"

"Our professional relationship," she said more firmly. "I don't want anything to spoil that. *Daisy Jordan* is much too important."

"Some things we can't stop happening. We are powerless. They happen against will. I did not want to dream about Lilya Kuzonev. I could not help dreaming about having dead girl in my bed with me."

"Please don't say things like that, Dollsky. It's horrid when you say those things."

He knelt on the bed in front of her.

"You are an incredible man, Dollsky, but you frighten me sometimes."

Smiling, he took her neck between his hands and kissed her on the mouth.

Rufus Gunn had been climbing for three hours. Below was a valley of ice, extraordinarily blue at the top but fading into a mist of fathomless menace. The cold was piercing. Nothing moved in his pale face except his eyes. In less than an hour the temperature had fallen fifteen degrees. His nose had started to bleed badly. He slumped down and waited for the bleeding to stop. The muscles of his thighs twitched with fatigue, his neck ached terribly and he could go no more than fifty paces without pausing for breath.

He took out the raisins and plums that Gunter Viridet had given him for breakfast with instructions to suck them slowly with snow. The thin air would make him very dry, Viridet had warned, and the mixture of snow and fruit would slake his thirst.

The solitude and stillness was like nothing he had ever known. Once, the silence was broken by the sound of a distant avalanche, like a crack of thunder, somewhere to his left. Instinctively he felt for the electronic bleeper that Viridet had made him carry in his rucksack, "to help us find your body if anything goes wrong."

After twenty minutes he resumed the climb. Forty yards further on, the ledge ran into a wall of ice like a petrified waterfall. He turned back and found the alternate ledge at the base of the neck of ice he had passed before breakfast. He stopped for a while and tried to place his position on the map. He couldn't afford to make such mistakes. He decided he was just above a sharp cliff that, seen through the telescope at the hotel, had resembled a wedge of ice propped like a buttress against an almost vertical precipice of the glacier. Somewhere along the new ledge he should come to the long slope, the diagonal traverse.

Viridet was right: everything looked different on the mountain. The ledge ended before he reached the expected long slope. Reluctantly he moved back onto the face, working his way with hammer and pitons, feeling for holds in the baleful rock. It was a tortuous, frightening business. It took him more than two hours to find another ledge. He prayed it was the right one this time.

It wasn't until he was within six feet of it that he saw the crevasse. It was only about five feet wide, but of unknown depth. The opposite side was higher, sloping backward toward the edge, making the jump more difficult than all the others he had crossed that morning. He cut a small foothold in the hard snow and tossed his rucksack to the other side. It slithered back toward him on the ice and rested where he would have to land. "Shit," he said under his breath. He took two careful steps and hurled his body across the gulf.

His left foot hit the rucksack and sent it skittering over the edge, buckling his ankle, and then he felt himself in space, falling. He thought, The bleeper's in the rucksack. They'll never find me now.

When he came to he was lying on his back. Pandora was kneeling on a small ridge of ice, looking calmly at him. "It's all right," she said. "It's perfectly fine." Then she was gone.

He had fallen about eighteen feet. He could see the opening above him. It won't be too difficult to climb out, he thought. Then the shock of Pandora's apparition hit him. He remembered their childhood promise to each other and panicked badly. Trying to stand up too quickly, he realized how much his body hurt and fell back onto his knees. Take it easy, he said to himself aloud; calm down. His ankle ached, but nothing seemed to be broken. He breathed deeply until he felt his control coming back. Fortunately, he still had the hammer and ice pick roped to his belt with a steel claw and the shoulder bag of pitons.

"It's beautiful, isn't it?" Pandora said, watching the snowflakes swirling outside, eclipsing the landscape. "Like bewildered white butterflies."

"From in here it is beautiful," Dollsky said, standing by her side. He wore black velvet jeans and a black sweater. In his bare feet he was several inches smaller than Pandora. "Out there it is— What is good English word for lousy?"

"Beastly."

"Beastly."

"It doesn't excite you?"

He shrugged.

"What excites you, Dollsky?"

"Money."

"*Quel monstre!* No wonder you were a rotten Communist!" She turned from the window. It was a magnificent house, which Frank Lloyd Wright had designed for Barbara Hutton in 1938, when she was the Countess Haugwitz-Reventlow. Cantilevered into the side of the mountain, it seemed to float hauntingly in time and space. Pandora loved the white carpets, the Dexel posters and Breuer chairs, the white baby-grand piano that looked as if it would play only wistful tunes of the thirties. Until the present owner had blasted out a helicopter pad on the south side of the building, the only way up the last five hundred feet had been by funicular railway—unless you fancied the hard way, over the north ridge and a hundred-foot climb down almost to the back door.

"It's like being trapped on top of the world. Do you know what Heflin once said to me? He said that stardom was like climbing Everest." She slipped into Heflin's voice. " 'One's senses get dulled by the altitude.' "

"He says many stupid things."

She picked up the telephone and listened for a moment. "Still dead," she said, replacing the receiver.

There was the rumble of an avalanche. Pandora moved around the room as if she had too much energy to settle in any one place.

"You love many men?"

"A few," she said easily.

"But you don't keep?"

"A lady may make lots of conquests, but only a harpy hangs on to them."

Dollsky put his hands on top of his head. "We are close in many ways, you and me."

"In our evasions." She smiled.

"What you think about when you are alone?"

"Only God should know such things."

"I don't believe in God."

"It must be horrid to be so brilliant and not believe in God."

"When you are alone, how you feel?"

She hesitated. "I don't know. To be alone—how can you explain something like that?" It was too early for a drink. "Want some coffee?"

Dollsky shook his head. He looked interrogatively at her. "Do you fantasize?"

"Of course."

"About?" he said. "Tell me about."

"Ever since I was about six years old I've fantasized about being a movie star," she said with vague facetiousness. The tone hid her anxiety and shyness. She knew they had come up to the chalet to have this conversation, to prepare *that* scene. It's not going to be easy, she thought. There's never going to be a right time to start this conversation, so it might just as well be now. "I'm going to make myself a coffee," she said, going to the kitchen to collect her thoughts and steel herself.

"Sexual fantasies?" he asked calmly, almost clinically, when she returned. "Erotic fantasies?"

"Oh, girls get very good at that. Girls can do that very well. I never felt it was wrong."

"Dirty fantasies?" He spoke in a less serious tone; there was a hint of humor in his eyes, which reassured her. That and the cognac in her coffee. "You never feel guilty?"

"Girls have a special flair for romanticizing their shameless desires," she said, determined to be as professional as she knew how.

"The masturbation scene," he said quietly.

And so it began. They talked for a long time, at first on a purely technical level about the importance of the scene, its place in the structure of the story and in the development of Daisy Jordan. He wanted her to understand its implications as well as its impact. It is the most important scene in the picture, he said. It had to be beautiful and it had to be convincing. He wanted to hear her thoughts about it.

"It should be a *still* scene," she told him. "A *quiet* scene. Girls learn to do it secretly, in the dark. The closer she comes to the moment, the more afraid to move she should become. Perhaps we should see only her face, just her eyes." *What do we see in her eyes?* "Panic almost as much as pleasure. She is young, she is afraid of being discovered." He did not make notes. *Afterwards? How does she feel afterwards?* "Lonely. She does it because she is lonely, but afterwards she is still lonely."

He smiled. "Do you tell always the truth?"

"How do you know I am telling the truth?"

"Girl who has not acted before is best. Like virgin."

"De Sica said the same thing. He said working with a woman on her first film made him feel that he was seducing her."

"It is sort of seduction—if you have sense of sin. I have no sense of sin."

After lunch he said, "Do you remember the first time we met?"

"In Venice. You were standing on the terrace of the Gritti Palace with— I've forgotten her name."

"Sonya Petrovich."

"You wore a pink shirt with a mandarin collar."

"I make good impression."

She poured more coffee. They didn't move from the table.

"Tell me about my agent. When you first meet?"

She smiled. "My memory doesn't go back that far. We've known each other since we were children. It's very boring. Didn't we go through all this in Venice? I'm sure we did."

"I don't remember."

"Rufus and I have been stuck with each other ever since I could walk."

"Why stuck?"

"Our indiscretions keep us together. We know far too much about each other."

"You try apart?"

"We've been our different ways a few times, but somehow we always seem to drift back together again."

"He would make husband for you?"

"We *have* had this conversation before."

"He is first lover?"

"In a long line," she said mockingly. "Who was your first lover, Dollsky?"

"I don't remember."

"Nonsense. Everybody remembers that."

"First sex feeling?"

"You remember that?"

"In war when I was child. I find tomb in graveyard open. Its side is blown open with shells, I think. I climb in."

"You climbed into a *grave?*"

"For dare, I think. I remember the other boys push cart against where I climb in. For many hours I am in grave. I am scared, but it make me hard also." His eyes flickered with remembrance.

"*Hard?*" she said. "You got an *erection* in a grave? Dollsky, that's obscene!"

"Why?"

"That really gives me the willies, Dollsky."

"You hear of Yukio Mishima, Japanese writer? He got same thing looking at painting of saint with arrows in body."

"Saint Sebastian."

"You know painting?"

"I don't understand that sort of thing at all. It's sick. Can we change the subject, Dollsky? This is horrid. I don't know how we got on to it. We were talking about Rufus."

Dollsky stood up quickly. "I want you try something with makeup for me," he said in a different voice. "The way you must be in scene we talk." He looked at her. "Smile."

"I can't smile," she said stubbornly.

"I show you." He smiled, and went on smiling until she laughed. "You're mad," she said.

"I know. You do makeup for me?" He led her toward the bedroom.

"You are mad," she said. "Quite, quite mad."

It had taken Rufus almost two hours to get out of the crevasse. The effort had drained him, and he was moving more slowly. What kept him going was the vision he'd had of Pandora. He knew time was running out.

The light was fading, but if he had got it right he was on the final descent. Another ten minutes, he told himself; in another ten minutes I'll be there. He craned his head forward and looked down. There was no sign of the chalet.

There was a sudden sharp crack of falling rock above. He heard his frightened intake of breath and felt the pain in his chest as he threw himself hard against the face, closed his eyes and prayed.

"I don't like it, Dollsky." Pandora stared at her reflection in the mirror. "Daisy wouldn't put this stuff on. She looks like a whore, for God's sake."

"Two faces," he said, standing behind her. "Two faces."

She looked closely at his reflection. "Either I had too much wine at lunch," she said, "or you smoked too much dope."

"Two paintings on same canvas. She is still there, underneath. When it is done properly with makeup man you see."

"See *what?*"

"The child wearing face of woman, embracing, anticipating her own destiny, her own decay . . ."

Pandora felt a chill down her spine. "It's still a whore's face and I hate it."

"We see her as she thinks in her head. She *wants* to feel like whore."

"*No,*" Pandora said sharply. She picked up a tissue and blotted the lipstick on her mouth. "It's all wrong. You're putting a label on her that is totally false."

"All women need to feel like whore sometime."

"That's *your* fantasy, Dollsky. Why should Daisy want to feel like a whore?"

"To prove to herself she is woman."

"Oh, balls! Sometimes you do talk the most utter rot. I'm sorry, Dollsky, but you do."

"She wants to prove she is desired not because she has money—"

"Utter balls!"

"To arouse and be taken roughly sometimes is more wished for than love."

Pandora began to laugh.

"Why you laugh?"

"Nothing. Something Rufus said, that's all."

"Tell me. I want to know. Why you laugh?"

"He said that the best passion is lust. He reckons that if you yield to lust with good grace it's mistaken for love." Remembering Rufus's cynical joke put her in a calmer mood. "Anyway, Pandora Child *is* Daisy Jordan, right? That's what the posters say." She looked at him defiantly. "I think *I* should know how she feels."

He looked back at her blank-faced. Was it anger, resentment or confusion? she wondered.

He said solemnly, "You are both victim of your class."

"You know what I think, Dollsky? I think you're trying to settle some personal score. And I won't let you use Daisy to settle some private account of your own. Let her invent her own fantasies. If she really has this sense of sexual deprivation that you seem to think she has, let her satisfy it in her own way, in the terms of her *own* experience, not yours."

Their separate silences were like forces pitted against each other. He continued to stand behind her, watching her painted face in the mirror, and she looked back, determined not to give way. She was very good at the staring game, and it was Dollsky who finally looked away. Taking her head like a chalice between his hands, he kissed the top of her head. Her hair, jaw length, cut in a style that would soon be fashionable, felt like silk.

"Thank you," she said, ending the silence. She lifted her face, and he kissed her forehead, the tip of her nose, her closed eyes, his hands stroking the side of her face. He whispered something tender she did not catch, and she asked him to say it again.

"Whore," he murmured.

"Beast," she said affectionately.

He spoke softly in his own language.

"What are you saying?"

"I have acid."

"We don't need acid."

Without a word they went to the bed as if they had been wound up and set in motion by the will of their flesh. He was more powerful than he looked. He continued to talk to her in Russian. It was strange how the foreign language excited her. It was like an incantation.

"Your buckle is hurting me," she said after a little while.

He raised himself to look at her, smiling askance. "You like that? You want to be hurt?"

"I want you to make love to me gently."

"You are not afraid of me?"

"Should I be?"

They smiled at each other. He took an ampule from his pocket and broke the top with his thumb. "Try. Make it good for us."

"It is already good," she said, but not resisting.

A slow throbbing sensation started in her belly and loins. She gasped. She had never felt anything like it before. It demanded no fulfillment, and she wanted it to last forever. She could feel herself drifting farther and farther away, the bedroom dissolving into a strange hallucinatory transparency. She began to tremble as the feeling gathered and spread through her body, finding unrealized nerve fibers in the most secret places.

"Good?"

"You're not even inside me," she answered like someone confiding a secret. He still wore his jeans. She loved the pressure of hardness against velvet.

He spoke to her softly in his mesmeric undiscoverable language.

"What are you saying, Dollsky? Talk to me in English."

"Whore." He repeated it softly and slowly, like a chant. "Whore, whore, whore."

"No, please no." She rolled her head from side to side, moving weakly. "Stop saying that. Stop it, don't spoil it."

"Whore, whore, whore."

He kneeled above her with a look of exultation, his eyes bright and dilated as if there was a fever in them, then lifted his head and drew in his breath in a sort of sob.

At first, as the pressure began, it seemed part of Pandora's dream, a sensual, almost ecstatic terror, bursting her lungs. Only it was not a dream. She was being strangled.

The shock dissolved into a kind of euphoria. She felt no fear or pain; she understood what was happening to her. With a sort of detached curiosity she wondered what time it was. *Now and at the hour of our death*, she thought as she felt herself beginning to die, *pray for us sinners*.

The first blow caught Dollsky on his left shoulder and spun him around. The second got him below the heart. But Rufus was too exhausted to punch his weight.

Dollsky recovered quickly and smashed his knee into Rufus's groin. As Rufus staggered forward Dollsky kicked him hard in the ribs. Rufus doubled over, then fell backward through the terrace doorway with a whimpering sound. A second kick caught him above his left eye. Rolling to the edge of the terrace, blinded by blood, he climbed to his feet and propped himself against the rail and listened for the sound of breathing, which was the only way he had of knowing where Dollsky was.

Dollsky took his time, circling to the left, maneuvering Rufus toward the opposite side of the terrace, above the sheerest drop. Trying to stay out of reach, Rufus edged sideways like a badly hurt fighter caught on the ropes, instinctively covering up, until he reached the spot where Dollsky wanted him.

The Russian had started to move in when he saw the ice pick and the steel claw that had fallen from Rufus's belt. Picking up the claw, he carefully measured the distance and swung at Rufus's head.

Through the blood, Rufus sensed the movement, and stuck out both his arms like a blind man. It was a pathetic gesture, but enough to deflect the claw. Carried by the desperate impetus of the swing, surprised by Rufus's reaction, slipping on the blood and ice, for a split second Dollsky was off balance. Rufus collected all his strength and caught him with a hammering hook to the side of his head.

What happened next seemed to be in slow motion. Dollsky reeled drunkenly across the terrace. He didn't look hurt or angry or surprised the way men are supposed to look when they are hit so hard. All human expression had already gone from his face when he hit the rail with the small of his back, balanced across it for a moment, and then disappeared. There was no sound, no cry, no protest.

In the chalet the telephone started to ring. Rufus stood listening to it, dazed and bleeding, unable to move. Then the ringing stopped and he heard Pandora talking.

"There's been an accident up at the chalet," Heflin was telling Walter Greenspan on the telephone. The shock had altered his voice; he talked in a dull monotone. "Dollsky's dead."

He gave the details as far as he knew them, then listened to the lawyer's reaction in London. Gunter Viridet stood at the window, looking at the mountain, drinking beer from a can.

"No, she's okay," Heflin said eventually. "Shaken up, but okay. Rufus is with her. He finally got up there about an hour ago. The phone's back on, thank God, and the weather's clearing. We probably can get a chopper up there tomorrow early. I'd like you to be here, Walter. The press will have to be handled, you know. It's going to be delicate. What were the pair of them doing up there alone, and all that kind of crap. I want to be sure we have the right answers first crack."

Heflin looked worried, and whatever the lawyer was saying was not making him feel any easier. After a pause he said slowly, "Gunn wasn't there. He got up there about twenty minutes after it happened. The way I understand it is she was sleeping. Dollsky must have gone out onto the terrace . . . Anyway, she didn't see anything."

He held up his empty glass to Viridet. The guide poured him another stiff drink and handed it to him. "She's pretty rattled, and who can wonder? I don't know how much use Rufus is after that climb. He fell a couple of times, once quite badly. He's cut up a bit, black-and-blue and stiff as a board, he says, but no bones broken. Viridet's amazed that he made it at all."

The guide nodded his head slowly, affirming his wonder.

"At least it's not political," Heflin went on. "Nobody's going to be able to blame anybody, you know what I mean? If ever anything was an accident, this was it. Let's be thankful for that."

After he put down the phone, Heflin turned to Viridet. "Who else do we have to talk to, Gunter?"

"All done," Viridet told him. "It's all taken care of."

Heflin didn't look convinced. He said, "What exactly happens in a business like this? You know what I mean—the law, the cops, what's the form exactly?"

Viridet shrugged. "He fell, he fell. There was a similar accident up there in '62. They say that's why the Hutton woman got rid of the place."

"Somebody else fell from that same terrace?"

Viridet nodded. "A moment's carelessness, that's all it takes. You're walking on ice up there."

"That's a real jinxed house, isn't it?"

"People should respect mountains more," the Frenchman said. He crushed the empty beer can with one hand and dropped it into the waste basket. "People don't respect mountains enough."

His hairline beaded with sweat, Heflin sat quietly behind his desk. After a pause, he said, "Gunter, there is one thing. A little problem—perhaps it's nothing at all, but I'd like to see if we can avoid it if possible." A flicker of anxiety in his eyes belied his casual tone. "Dollsky wasn't much of a drinker, but he was fond of— He was into other things, you know what I mean?"

"Dope?" Viridet said easily.

"Dope, yes, dope," Heflin said. "And the fact of it is—well, he may have been a little jagged, bending and bowing a bit up there when—when this all happened."

"That was his pigeon. What he did is not my concern."

Heflin nodded. "But the thing is . . . well, the poor bastard's dead and it doesn't matter a tuppenny damn to him now. Only it could look real bad for the girl. You know what the papers would make of something like that? How they'd blow it all up—drugs, a love nest, a death fall. It could get very messy and do her a lot of harm if anything got out."

"How will it get out? Who will tell?"

Heflin looked surprised; Viridet's naïveté made him nervous. He spoke carefully: "Gunter, a guy was killed up there. There's going to be an inquest, right? If at the autopsy they were to find that—"

"Wait a minute." Viridet held up his hands. "What autopsy?"

"*Dollsky's.* Dollsky's autopsy."

"Without a body?"

"They're not going to just leave him up there?"

"We still haven't recovered the one in '62. Unless Dollsky carried a bleeper when he slipped . . ." He smiled a very French smile, polite and pitiless. "All we've got is an empty body bag."

"But there will be an inquest of some sort?"

"A formality. This is a nice town, a nice resort, with nice people. Why should anyone want to talk about drugs or encourage talk of scandals?"

"That's very sensible, very civilized," Heflin said with relief and something like bewilderment in his voice. He wiped his brow. "What a terrible sadness it all is, though," he said in his old voice.

"The mountains spell God," Gunter Viridet said, opening another can of beer.

"How are you feeling?"

"Very invalidish," Pandora said. Her voice was hoarse, her face white beneath the grotesque mask of makeup. "My throat hurts."

"Don't talk."

"It hurts when I swallow."

"You won't be able to spit for a week."

She didn't smile. "I don't understand, Ru. Why did you come up here, anyway? If you hadn't arrived when you did . . ." She began to cry.

He seemed embarrassed. "I came about the position of guardian angel," he said, stroking her hair. Her neck was red and beginning to show bruise marks. "I saw your ad in *The Times*."

She wiped her eyes and smiled again. "Good help is so hard to find these days."

"I'm so good."

"You are."

"One tries."

"Do you ever do anything commonplace?"

"Certainly not."

"You look a frightful mess."

"I shall change for dinner."

"I should think so."

"I'll even wear my medals."

"You deserve a hundred medals. How are *you* feeling?"

"A bit achy. I've had a pretty tiring day, what with one thing and another."

"You're not bleeding now."

"No, I seem to have run dry."

"That's probably the most expensive tourniquet in the history of medicine."

He looked at the scarf bandaging his arm. "Christian Dior," she said.

"I like a girl who puts Christian Doctrine before her Christian Dior."

"Don't start with the puns. I don't think I could stand that on top of everything else."

"I thought it was a very nice pun."

They talked agreeable nonsense for nearly an hour, avoiding the terrible subject.

The weather had improved. The helicopter would come as soon as it was light. She went to the bathroom, washed away her painted-up face and covered the welts on her neck with a fine layer of pancake. Even with it she could still see the marks made by Dollsky's nails, so she put on a highneck sweater.

"They'll be here soon," she said.

"Yes."

"What are we going to do?"

"You said you talked to Heflin?"

"We both did."

"I don't remember," he said. "What did we say?"

"I said that he went outside and must have slipped. You arrived later."

"That's it, then," he said. "That's the story we stick with."

"It was an accident," she repeated. "A terrible accident."

Then it was light and every sound in the house seemed to stop.

"Listen," he said.

It was the faint throb of the helicopter coming to fetch them.

Three weeks after *Daisy Jordan* opened in London and New York to fine reviews, Lady Pandora Child was married to the Hon. Rufus Gunn at a quiet wedding in the village church in Blewbury. Felix Crick gave the bride away.

After the service, Pandora changed in the bedroom where long ago she had lost her virginity to Rufus. For a moment, before she went downstairs, she stood with her back against the door. The house was full of ghosts and long-forgotten dreams—nice ghosts, mostly, and satisfied dreams, mostly. It was where she had hidden from the world when her father went away. She remembered the wine, the happy days and sadnesses and secrets she had shared with Rufus under this roof. Long before today, she realized now, Rufus had taken possession of her in this house.

"Here's our star," Lyall Heflin said as she came down the stairs.

"You look beautiful, my dear," Felix Crick told her. "When you were ten years old we had lunch together at Claridge's. Do you remember? You and your father and I. I looked at you then and asked myself, What on earth can be more beautiful? Now I know: Pandora on her wedding day."

"I hoped to hear from Moscow today," she said.

"If you haven't, my dear, there must be a very good reason."

Felix was the first guest to leave. He kissed her cheek shyly, holding both her hands in his. Standing at the door with Rufus, watching Felix's car move slowly down the narrow Berkshire lane, she said, "Why do I feel so sad for him?"

"Sad? For Felix? Why on earth should you feel sad for him?"

"There was something in his face. The way he looked when he said good-bye."

On the first Sunday in October, Felix Crick was knocked down by a hit-and-run Cortina in St. George's Road in Kennington, South London. He was taken to St. Thomas's Hospital, where he died sixteen days later without recovering consciousness. *The Times* said that he was one of the all-time finest spinners of a leg-break ever to play for England, the last of an extinct breed of Englishman. James Anselm conveyed the particulars to Valentin Buikov, along with his congratulations on Anna Zorin's release from Dnepropetrovsk.

59

Events during the past twenty-four hours had moved quickly. What was happening in Texas and Minnesota could still be isolated incidents and containable. The Treasury people had already left for Washington on the 11:45 Concorde and would be touching down at Dulles International probably before he left the palace. He had never known Treasury mandarins to move so fast—and they still did not know the half of it. Nobody did, except James Anselm.

"This was found on him when he was killed, was it?"

"After the accident, yes sir." Anselm had thought about it throughout a sleepless night before deciding to go directly to Bunbury. He had developed a great respect, as well as a certain fondness, for the old SIS fox. He knew exactly what Bunbury would ask next, and Bunbury did not disappoint him: "Why have you brought this particular matter to me?"

"I thought that with your feeling for the wider political realities, Sir William, you would appreciate the implications . . ."

Bunbury looked at him strangely. "And he left this letter with Crick to deliver to Lady Pandora in the event of his death, is that what you think?"

"It's not dated, so that's my guess, yes, sir. The other one is our copy of the letter he wrote to her after he defected—the Vienna letter. I thought you should see it."

"This quotation—'Stop thine ear against the singer'?"

"Walter Scott, Sir William, *The Bride of Lammermoor.* Rufus Gunn's been trying to pin it down for her—not very successfully," Anselm said offhandedly, hoping that Bunbury would not go further down that road just yet, not just yet.

Bunbury looked puzzled but nodded for him to continue.

"We knew that Lady Pandora's brokers, Gilbodys, were speculating heavily in gold since her father's defection. They got their instructions through Goldmex in Geneva. Goldmex were clearly getting their instructions from Child in Moscow. He knew the gold market inside out, of course. The European gold pool in '61 was his brainchild: he led the committee of inquiry into the dollar-gold crisis of '68 that closed the London exchange for a day; he was a former chairman of the Organisation for Co-operation and Development—he was simply the best in his field. He knew more about our long-term objectives, our reserves and fiscal policies, than any man alive. He was the consummate capitalist, the supreme wire-puller—Washington, Bonn, Tokyo, London, Paris—he knew everything and everybody." Anselm cleared his throat. "About nine months after his defection, the Russians announced their massive gold find in western Uzbekistan, a place called Muruntau, and almost overnight they increased their gold output by forty-six percent."

"I fail to see where this is leading us, Mr. Anselm."

"There is a point, Sir William, if you will just bear with me. Before we sent the sweepers in after Crick's accident, I took a look over his flat in Lambeth. It was as clean as a whistle, of course—except for one interesting thing. He had an envelope full of newspaper cuttings about the Foxbat—"

"Foxbat?"

"NATO code name for the Mig-25, Sir William."

"He kept clippings about a Russian fighter aircraft?"

"Only about the one that hightailed it to Japan. He had ordered the reports from a clipping service in High Holborn. The bill was still in the envelope."

"Another little job for his Moscow masters?"

Anselm shook his head. "I don't think so, sir. According to his diary, Crick visited Geneva a few weeks after the Mig business in Japan. I went back over the dates, and according to a SIS traffic report, Henry Child left the Soviet Union for four days at precisely the same time. Like Philby, he is reported to have been in a lot of places at different times—Damascus one minute, Beirut the next, Prague, Zagreb. Most of it is plain nonsense, of course—newspaper speculation or simple Soviet disinformation."

"But you think that Crick might have kept an appointment with his old chum, do you?" Bunbury asked in a musing tone. "In Geneva?"

"It's possible, Sir William. It's possible that Child had an urgent and compelling problem he wanted to—"

"What the dickens has any of this got to do with Foxbat or the gold in Uzbekistan or with Pandora Child's investments?"

"Shortly after the meeting in Geneva—"

"The *possible* meeting in Geneva, Mr. Anselm."

The MI5 man nodded acceptance. There was still so much more to explain, to disclose, he did not want to get sidetracked in semantics. "Two things happened after Geneva. Pandora Child's brokers abandoned their activity in the gold market completely. They got rid of every gold stock in her investment portfolio. And Crick developed this sudden curiosity in Foxbat."

"Are you saying there is some connection between these events?"

"It's my hunch that Child told Felix Crick something in Geneva, something about that Mig, something very, very important. So important that Child had to come back himself, had to assure himself that the message was delivered and understood."

"Be explicit, Mr. Anselm." Just for a moment, Bunbury's irritation showed in his sharp tone.

"When Foxbat turned up in Japan," Anselm went on as though he had noticed nothing, "the Americans gave it a good going-over, as you can imagine. They discovered a great deal. They discovered that a great many claims about its performance were pure eyewash. But one thing puzzled them—it was a small matter, and as far as I can discover, it was never pursued, perhaps because their time was running out. It concerned the chemical compound of the windscreen. I don't know if you know this, Sir William, but the windscreen of a modern jet aircraft is layered with gold. It's only something like five-millionths of a millimeter thick, but it prevents frosting, cuts down glare and protects the pilot from the sun's radiation at high altitudes."

Bunbury studied Anselm thoughtfully. "And the Foxbat windscreen—"

"There was a small, apparently insignificant inconsistency in the diffraction patterns. I gather that by firing quantized electron orbits into a mixture of ordinary ore particles, it's possible to compute the properties—"

"You've obviously done your homework, Mr. Anselm, but just tell me simply what it is you conclude from all this gobbledygook."

Anselm hesitated, then, very quickly, like a man taking a plunge into icy water, he said, "I think the Russians might have discovered a way of making—manufacturing—gold, Sir William."

"Alchemy, Mr. Anselm?" Bunbury sounded amused by the word. "Alchemy?"

"Maybe a technological kind of alchemy, Sir William, yes." Annoyed by Bunbury's frank amusement, Anselm fidgeted uncomfortably. "It does seem fantastic, but when you look at all the pieces, a picture begins to emerge— I don't think I'm misinterpreting anything—"

"Are there any more *pieces* that you want to tell me about?" Bunbury asked simply and with no amusement in his voice at all.

Anselm's glance moved from Bunbury to the gold Vulliamy clock; the Concorde will be in Washington now, he thought. He said slowly, "Muruntau is a closed area, one of the most highly restricted areas in the Soviet Union. For some time now we've been getting reports that some remarkable people have been going in and out of there—physicists, quantum mechanic theorists, inorganic chemists, people you would not ordinarily associate with mining."

"And what did MI6, the CIA, think they were up to, Mr. Anselm? They must have been curious?"

"We concluded they were VIPs getting the grand tour, that it was a public relations exercise," Anselm answered. "Presumably the CIA reached the same conclusion."

"I see."

"But I think the Americans were almost on to it with that Mig. I think that windscreen was—I don't know—an experimental module? Almost perfect—but with traces, flecks, something not quite right. I think that's what Henry Child told Crick. He was worried, worried stiff, he panicked. He didn't know how much the Americans had found out, how big a mess it was going to be."

Bunbury stared at him hard. "But this is all conjecture, of course?"

Anselm admitted that it was. Ignoring Bunbury's negative snort, he went on: "What is incontestable is that Crick visited Geneva when his chum Child could have been there; that immediately after that visit, Crick developed a curious interest in Foxbat; and that Pandora's brokers got out of gold in a big hurry—and never went back."

"Is that it?" Bunbury asked. "All the pieces?"

Anselm shook his head thoughtfully. "Ten days ago the CIA's M and S Directorate released a priority interagency signal connecting the collapse of two federally chartered American banks—one in Amarillo, Texas, the other in Duluth in Minnesota—with a possible KGB operation."

"KGB!"

"It was a priority blue signal, Sir William—*the agency has cause to suspect.*"

"Go on," Bunbury said, his head tilting alertly upwards as he thought how little the jargon had changed since he was head of SIS.

"The two banks concerned were relatively small beer. The Federal Deposit Insurance Corporation had them well covered. Since then, however, another similar bank has gone under in Salt Lake City, and four more examined by the Office of the Comptroller of the Currency—a watchdog agency inside the U.S. Treasury Department—are reported to be seriously threatened, a category-five rating, a sort of red alert situation."

"How many federally chartered banks are there in the States?"

"About forty-five hundred, sir."

"The failure of three, four more in a parlous state— Has the CIA raised a blue on all of them?"

"This morning, sir. The bells have really gone off this morning. The Treasury brass are on their way to Washington now."

"Has the CIA been more forthcoming?"

"Not yet, sir. Just the same blue *cause to suspect.*"

"It seems very odd, doesn't it? Small-fry outfits in Duluth, Salt Lake City and, where, *Amarillo?* What would the KGB be up to—what would they *want* in such places?"

"I don't begin to understand the deeper complexities of banking, Sir William—I'm not what you would call a detail man in high finance—but as I understand it, Chase, the National Bank and Trust Company of Chicago, the Michigan National, a lot of the upstream boys, have burnt their fingers buying loans from these smaller outfits. According to our people, if just one more bank crashes under the Federal Deposit Insurance Corporation's umbrella, the payouts could reach crisis proportions, they could make the sort of history that—"

"But I fail to see what any of this has to do with Crick, with Henry Child—Duluth and Amarillo seem a very long way from Foxbat, and alchemy, Mr. Anselm," Bunbury suddenly interrupted irritably.

Anselm had been expecting the interruption, the irritability. But he had now established the necessary background without which what he was about to suggest would sound totally inconceivable, even perhaps hysterical.

"Well, Sir William," he began slowly after an expressive silence, not looking at Bunbury. "We start with the OPEC surpluses. Hundreds of billions—heaven only knows how many billions—are washing around in Western banks: deposits much too massive to be protected by the usual compensation arrangements. It's no secret that a lot of banks have been skating on some pretty thin ice lately, running down their liquidity ratios, so when small banks in America suddenly start going under, involving bigger banks, it could have an impact out of all proportion—"

"The Russians are stirring up a panic?" said Bunbury, frowning. "A flight from paper money, is that what you're suggesting?"

"The price of gold has risen forty-seven dollars an ounce since the bank in Amarillo went bust."

"Do we have any idea how they've done it?"

"The kind of banks we're talking about, Sir William, I'm assured it wouldn't be difficult, given the necessary resources, the know-how, some sophisticated shenanigans. Bankers like to impress us with their responsibility, their air of solid respectability, but they're still sharks at heart. If all of us asked for our money back tomorrow, most of us would be burned to the bone. It's got something to do with solvency not being the same thing as liquidity."

Bunbury looked at him thoughtfully. The more he saw of Anselm, the more he respected him. He knew from experience the effort it takes to grasp the rudiments of another profession so quickly and so well. He said, "Why at this particular moment—do we have any idea?"

"They need every penny they can get right now. Last year they shelled out over eight billion dollars on grain imports alone. They've been feeling the pinch one way and another, and the strange thing is that international tensions that usually boost gold prices have barely caused a ripple recently."

"So they've decided to start a small stampede in the international banking system?"

"A sort of *controlled* explosion, yes sir. Picking off a series of small American banks until the gold price is right. It wouldn't suit their book to bring the whole Western economy down."

Bunbury shook his head slowly. "And Henry Child—"

"The whole operation—so finely tuned, just doing enough to inflate the gold market without shaking us to pieces—I'd say it was his creation."

"And if they continue pulling these sort of strokes without him—"

"Without Child—if their wilder philosophers of economic subversion move into the vacuum, that's when I think the balloon could go up, Sir William."

Bunbury went to the window and stood for a moment gazing at the lake. "How exactly did Henry Child die?" he asked, not looking around. "Do we know?"

"There's a difference of opinion about it, Sir William. The Americans don't believe he is dead. The Russians say he died of a heart attack during a vacation on the Black Sea Riviera. Officially that's the version we go along with, although there have been the usual rumors—he's dying and confined to his dacha, he's a prisoner in Butyrskaya, he's been seen in CLC 36, a corrective labor camp in the Perm area usually reserved for dangerous recidivists, he's enjoying a comfortable retirement by Lake Baikal—there's no shortage of options."

"And your own opinion, Mr. Anselm?" Bunbury asked, turning around sharply. "What do you think?"

"I think he knew too much."

Bunbury nodded with a sort of grim satisfaction. "These—*pieces.* Talked about them to anyone else, have you? MI6? Your company chums?"

Anselm said he hadn't spoken to anyone. "If I'm right—and I must tell you, I think I am, Sir William—it'll make the '31 crash look like heaven in a hand basket. I think we're talking about the financial equivalent of nuclear war."

"It would cause a God Almighty bang all right, Mr. Anselm, but let me ask you this: do you think it is possible that Henry Child himself knew from the first delivery what was happening inside Muruntau?"

Anselm looked at him steadily. The significance of the question was not lost on him, it went straight to the heart of what had been troubling him from the start.

Bunbury went on: "He would have appreciated better than anyone the horrendous consequences if something like this was not properly contained, not properly disciplined. He would have been almost duty-bound to go. He practically wrote his own credentials, you might say."

"That's what's been puzzling me, Sir William. Wouldn't we have known? *Somebody* here would have known. He would have—"

"Told us? That would have defeated his whole purpose, don't you think? No, if he did know, whether he was recruited, coerced, blackmailed, brainwashed, shot through with dope, he *had* to keep the secret—or become very dead very fast," Bunbury said dryly, picking up the Englishman's last letter to his daughter. " 'Stop thine ear against the singer'," he read. "Scott, you say?"

" 'Stop thine ear against the singer/From the red gold keep thy finger,' " Anselm completed the couplet. "I'm what the Americans call a Walter Scott buff," he said. "I think the line about her old Scots nanny is interesting."

"Ah," Bunbury said slowly and, smiling, returned his attention to the letter from Vienna. Anselm waited silently while he read it through twice, then a third time. " *'If I should die before you are twenty-one'* . . . *'Stop thine ear against the singer,'* " Bunbury repeated the lines in his musing tone. "This the key to it, you think? Trying to warn her that once he was dead, once his instructions stopped coming, she must never touch gold again, was he?"

"It would be just about as far as he possibly dare go without utterly upsetting the applecart," Anselm said.

"Spilling all those Golden Russets," Bunbury said without smiling at his pun.

Anselm said nothing and waited for him to continue.

"It would most certainly prove that he knew about Muruntau before he defected, wouldn't it? Puts a fascinating new light on the whole episode—if any of it was true, of course," he said suddenly folding the letter and handing it back to Anselm. When he spoke again, his voice had a firmer but regretful tone that was clearly meant to close the subject forever. "Our business can be so muddling sometimes, can't it?"

"I was hoping, Sir William," Anselm said anxiously, suddenly aware that Bunbury was slipping the leash. "I was hoping that you would . . . If you were in my shoes—"

" 'Stop thine ear against the singer', Mr. Anselm," Bunbury said quietly, like a man repeating an impassioned prayer, " 'From the red gold keep thy finger.' "

ABOUT THE AUTHOR

PETER EVANS, former foreign correspondent and award-winning journalist, has lived in many parts of the world. *The Englishman's Daughter* is his second novel. At present he lives in London with his wife and two children.